THE MAGNIFICENT NOVEL THAT DOES FOR CHINA WHAT *SHOGUN* DID FOR JAPAN!

China—A once great land writhing under the heel of the powerful Khan and his Mongol borde.

Endurance—The name of the one man strong enough to stand up to this grim tyranny and defeat the conqueror . . . but only by mastering the ruthless trade of war and besting traitors at their own game of intrigue.

Peony—The woman whose courage and conviction made her his perfect mate . . . and whose passionate love joined with his to bring the birth of a new dynasty.

Weaving together fascinating history and powerful human drama, this passionate and exotic epic brings fourteenth-century China—and the dawning of the great Ming dynasty—to magnificent life.

RIVER OF LANTERNS

RIVER OF LANTERNS

BY

Ching Yun Bezine

A SIGNET BOOK

SIGNET
Published by the Penguin Group
Penguin Books USA Inc., 375 Hudson Street,
New York, New York 10014, U.S.A.
Penguin Books Ltd, 27 Wrights Lane,
London W8 5TZ, England
Penguin Books Australia Ltd, Ringwood,
Victoria, Australia
Penguin Books Canada Ltd, 10 Alcorn Avenue,
Toronto, Ontario, Canada M4V 3B2
Penguin Books (N.Z.) Ltd, 182–190 Wairau Road,
Auckland 10, New Zealand

Penguin Books Ltd, Registered Offices:
Harmondsworth, Middlesex, England

First published by Signet, an imprint of New American Library,
a division of Penguin Books USA Inc.

First Printing, April, 1993
10 9 8 7 6 5 4 3 2 1

Copyright © Ching Yun Bezine, 1993
All rights reserved

 REGISTERED TRADEMARK—MARCA REGISTRADA

To my eternal treasure—Crystal:
With you as my guiding lantern,
Life is never a dark river.

To my husband Frank Bezine:
If Giacomo Puccini had known us,
He would have created a different Butterfly.

To my editor Audrey LaFehr:
I need you and my eyeglasses;
Both of you enhance my vision.

To my agent Richard Curtis:
You took me from a starting post,
To an elevated pedestat—please don't stop!

To my other editor John Paine:
I've never met you,
But your help is in my books from line to line.

Author's Note

The following story took place in the fourteenth century. The names of many cities have changed in the past six hundred years. For example, Da-du is now Beijing, and Yin-tin is now Nanjing.

All the Chinese characters have been given English names to make pronunciation easier. Endurance Chu was Shu Yuanchang, Vanguard Kuo was Kuo Tzu-hsing, and Prince Eastwind was Timur Tohan.

This is a historical novel; the portrait of a peach tree that actually rooted in China. But the branches have been curved like a beautiful bonsai, and the petals of the blossoms brightened by an artist's brush.

Prologue

A.D. *1227*

IT WAS ONLY the middle of the eighth moon, but already the Mongolian plains had become sere. A chilly north wind swept over the grassland, forced all the desert plants to bow in submission, caught the soft clouds and sent them flying.

Suddenly the wind was overpowered by a thunderous roar. The thick grass was parted by a procession of horsemen.

Their brass armor sparkled in the noonday sun. The scarlet tassels on their pointed hats sailed behind them. Each of them had a long sword, a bow slung across his back, and a quiver of arrows hanging at his side. A brass shield, embellished with sacred designs and adorned with glittering stones, was strapped to every forearm. They were a group of ten: six in front and four on horses that pulled a hide-covered wagon.

A thin man rode on a gray stallion, guarding the wagon closely. The wind tossed aside his silver hair and long white beard, revealing a dark and deeply lined bony face. He was dressed in armor tipped with white fur. Exquisite jewels sparkled from the handle of his long sword. A design used only by noble Mongols was carved on his shield.

"Be careful," he ordered the last four warriors in a deep voice filled with sorrow and despair. "Our great khan cannot stand any more jiggling!"

"Yes, Adviser Zephyr Tamu," the four young warriors answered in the voice of one. The horses were slowed until they cantered so smoothly that the wagon seemed to glide over a calm sea.

The procession gradually crossed the blazing desert, heading for Lake Baikal. When the day neared its end, they reached the Onon River.

"Set up the tent," Zephyr Tamu ordered, pointing at the murmuring stream that reflected the fast-departing rays of a dying sun.

The warriors unpacked their bundles and immediately set to work. Zephyr Tamu dismounted and walked to the wagon. He lifted the fleece and looked in. "How do you feel, Temujin?" he asked softly, calling Genghis Khan by his childhood name.

The large figure lying under soft pelts did not stir. But the dark eyes on his blood-drained face opened; they were burning with pain. A low moan escaped his tightly clenched teeth. With immense effort he muttered through his dry lips, "Zephyr, my friend, I am dying."

"No!" Zephyr Tamu shook his head vigorously, holding onto the wagon tightly. "Temujin! You are only sixty-five! Your grandfather and father lived to be ninety! You'll recover as soon as we reach home. There we have the best medicine man!"

A thin smile appeared on Genghis Khan's distinguished face, but it faded quickly as he winced in pain. "Even the best medicine man won't be able to help me this time. That Chinese bastard stabbed me too well." He raised a hand to feel his heavily bandaged chest. His fingers touched the damp stickiness of the multilayered cloth. A shadow fell over his colorless face and turned it ashen. "Avenge this for me, my friend. Conquer China, and make the Chinese suffer."

Shaking his head, Zephyr raised his voice and forced himself to sound confident. "Temujin, you'll regain your health and conquer China yourself!"

Before Genghis Khan could gather enough strength to speak again, a warrior came to the khan's adviser and reported that the tent was ready.

Under a darkening sky Genghis Khan was carried from the wagon to a willow-latticed, felt-covered tent. Beneath a full moon the warriors built a fire with the dry branches of a desert pine fallen beside the water. Under a sparkling canopy of stars, they set off with their bows and arrows and soon returned with a wild goat. The meat was roasted over a crackling flame, gradually filling the surrounding desert with a mouth-watering aroma.

One of the warriors brought a leg of the goat to the tent, together with a jug of water fetched from the Onon River. "Go away!" Zephyr Tamu shouted from behind the thick entry flap.

The men ate silently, listening to the night wind. They were worried about their fellow warriors who had been left at the frontier. The Chinese fighters of West Hsia dynasty had been stronger than the Mongols had expected. When Genghis Khan was wounded by a Chinese general, the khan's adviser had chosen the best ten warriors to load the injured khan into a wagon and retreated toward the Mongols' northern home near Lake Baikal.

The wind increased in ferocity as the night wore on. The soldiers slept wearing their armor, covering their faces with their shields, trying to protect themselves from the freezing night air and blistering grains of sand. Their mounts were tethered nearby, their backs turned against the wind.

The men were awakened in the middle of the night by a sharp lament coming from the tent. They jumped up, looked at one another in the moonlight, knowing instantly what had happened.

The hideous wail became a heartbreaking moan, then ebbed away. A cold moon shone on the tent's entrance as Zephyr Tamu lifted the flap with a shaking hand. Tears glistened in his weary eyes and then streamed down the chiseled lines of his high-boned cheeks. "Our great khan is dead," he said, his voice a trembling whisper. "We must bury him immediately."

The warriors left their shields on the ground, used their swords to dig in the sand. By the time the moon completely faded, a large deep hole had been made near the riverbank.

As the warriors lowered Genghis Khan's body into the grave, Zephyr Tamu spoke in a hoarse but firm voice, "I shall carry out your last wishes, my lord. China will fall to us again and the Chinese will be made to suffer. The best Mongol princes will rule, and they will forever be advised by my sons and grandsons."

In the golden rays of the rising sun, the men began to cover the grave and Zephyr continued his promise. "Good-bye, Temujin, my dearest friend. I shall join you soon, and our spirits will play as happy children again . . ."

The aged voice described bygone days shared by two boys born only a few days apart. Genghis had received his name from the songs of a desert bird, and Zephyr had been named after the Gobi storm. They grew up side by side, created a code of laws and enforced it on the herdsmen and shepherds they had united to form the Mongol empire. Genghis became a vigorous fighter, Zephyr an ingenious thinker. When Genghis started to conquer the world, Zephyr followed him every step of the way.

Zephyr Tamu came out of his reverie when the grave was covered. Telling the warriors to wait, he returned to the tent, then reappeared with a jug of wine.

"Let's drink to the great khan's spirit," he said, glancing at the warriors who stood in a circle, then gave the jug to the nearest man.

The man drank deeply, then passed the jug to his neighbor. The young warriors were thirsty. Saluting the departed ones with strong wine was their ancient custom. They gulped down the liquor, paying no attention to its unusual taste or Zephyr Tamu's refusing the jug.

When the jug was empty, the warriors were unsteady on their feet.

Zephyr reached for his sword, drew it from its sheath. He raised it high, turned to the nearest man, then stroked quickly, aiming for the front of his neck—the only unprotected part of a Mongol warrior's body.

The sharp blade cut across the warrior's throat, severed his windpipe, sending a geyser of blood from the gaping wound.

The man raised both hands to his neck, then stumbled forward, croaking as blood bubbled from his mouth. His innocent eyes stared at Zephyr Tamu, mutely asking why.

"I'm sorry," Zephyr said, his voice filled with regret. "But one of the many things I promised our khan was that his burial place would be a secret to the world."

The warrior raised his hands toward Zephyr. Blood dripped from his fingers and poured out of his throat, seeping into the sand, glistening in the glaring sunlight.

Zephyr used the point of his sword to push the young man. The warrior fell backward, unable to

get up but still trying to hold onto life. His grop-
ing hands encountered the nearby weeds, clutched
them, and pulled them out of the sand. He
kicked his feet wildly until life mercifully deserted him. He died staring at the high blue sky
with unseeing eyes.

The expression in those youthful eyes pained
Zephyr Tamu. He debated if it was necessary to
execute the rest of the warriors. The poison in
the wine had already dulled their reflexes and
numbed their limbs and would kill them in time.
Zephyr Tamu shook his head. No, he could not
chance it. These warriors were the strongest
among a hardy race. If they made their way to
the Onon River and drank enough water, a few
might survive.

Zephyr moved toward the next man. The man
tried to run, but he was too sluggish. Zephyr
raised his sword, and another young man fell beside the first. One after another, the warriors
were slain by the adviser. Their blood soon created a red lagoon on the yellow sand, and filled
the desert with its odor of death.

"Temujin, no one will ever know your burial
ground, not even your sons or mine!" Zephyr
said, lifting his eyes to heaven.

He went to the men's horses and freed them.
He cracked his whip. Neighing in fear, the
horses ran in different directions, kicking up
clouds of sand that obscured the sun in a yellow-
ish gloom. Zephyr waited for the high-flying
sand to settle, then took a fire starter out of his
inner garment. He set fire to both the tent and
wagon, and watched them burn. Leaving the
smoldering heaps and the carnage of flesh and
blood behind him, he mounted his horse and
rode away with his back straight and head high.

The north wind continued to gust, scooping
up the fine sand and covering the ten bodies,

sculpting a large lumpy grave for them. The Onon River flowed on, weeping softly for the spirits of innocent men buried in an unmarked dune of sand.

Far from the Onon River, in the Mongolian capitol of Da-du, a magnificent mausoleum rose in a year's time. The roof was blue and gold, the walls bright yellow. Behind the many dazzling red doors were numerous altars and gigantic statues of Buddha. People from all over the world came to admire Genghis Khan's shrine, to pay respect to a man who had almost taken the entire globe in his mighty hands.

PART I

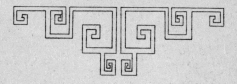

1

Spring, 1344

"I HATE MY CLOTHES! Why do I have to wear so many layers on such a warm day?" Peony Ma complained, raising an arm to wipe her sweating brow.

Over a long-sleeved blouse, she wore a loose vest to camouflage the curve of a rising bosom. A pair of long pants were worn under an ankle-length skirt to hide the shape of her legs. Her hair was braided and entwined with colorful ribbons, then twisted and pinned into a crown. There was no paint on her tanned face, nor did she have bound feet. She was not the daughter of a rich man. Her father was a miner who searched for precious jade buried in the high mountains that surrounded Emerald Valley.

Peony frowned at her blouse. At one time it had been red with bright yellow flowers, but now the red had faded and the yellow was merely spots of gray. She hated the gloomy-colored skirt as much as she did the brown vest. The outer garments of the poor were always hued in murky shades so that the dirt was better hidden and less washing was needed. "I wish I could wear just one thin robe in pink, then float on this cooling water!" Peony yelled.

"Peony Ma is talking crazy again," a barley farmer's daughter said. "Wearing one pink thin robe and floating on the water?" She shook her head. "The pink would become transparent, and you'll appear to be naked." She covered her mouth at the indecent word, then continued in a whisper, "Peony, if you can't wait to show your naked body ..." She giggled. "Well, be patient. When the autumn moon is full again, you'll be married."

The peaceful brook rippled with the laughter of young girls. More than twenty of them were wading in a branch of the Yellow River, collecting floating flowers. Ancient apple trees lined the shores, and their branches arched over the water and formed a canopy of blossoms. The wind was blowing, and petals were falling everywhere. The river was dotted with pink and white, drifting fragrantly. None of the girls dared to pluck a blossom from the trees. They believed that for every flower taken, a pimple would appear on the face.

The girls stopped laughing when Peony Ma suddenly dropped the rattan basket she carried.

Peony was only sixteen but very tall. She had long arms and legs, a narrow waist, wide hips and a full bosom that couldn't be concealed by her loose vest. Her face was oval, eyes round and large. Her lips were full and mouth wide. She was so angry now that her cheeks were red and her nostrils flared. Her flower basket was floating away, but she did not care. She stepped toward the one who had teased her, yanked the girl by the front of her blouse, then gave the frightened girl a powerful push.

"I don't like your nasty words! Can't wait to show my naked body?" She waved an arm around. "Why are you all here?"

The girls lowered their eyes and blushed deeply. They were already in their teens and would be married before reaching eighteen. On the wedding night, a bride would lay with her eyes tightly closed, her head resting on a bridal

pillow that was filled with dried flowers gathered from the many springs of her maidenhood.
Her trembling hands would clutch the corners
of the fragrant pillow as she waited for her
groom to turn her from a blossoming flower into
a fruit-bearing tree.

The silence was broken by a scream from afar.
The girls straightened slowly, listening. Between
the river and the village was a large meadow.
They craned their necks to look, but the grassland was higher than the riverbank. As they
stared at the tall grass, more cries rose from the
village. The laments echoed on and on among the
mountains that encircled Emerald Valley.

"The Mongols have come again!" Peony Ma
said, kicking aside a flower basket. She picked
up a large stone in one hand, gathered her skirt
in the other, and began to run. "Let's go!"

The other girls were shaking, unable to move.
They had been born under Mongol rule, and the
only life they knew was the life of a lamb in a
fenced pasture. The master's hands came often,
each time either slaughtering their loved ones or
snatching them away. They always froze at the
face of horror, then thawed when the slaying
force was gone. Happiness, such as the joy of
gathering flowers for their bridal pillows, was to
be enjoyed only during the interludes between
the raids.

Peony turned to look at her paralyzed friends
and yelled angrily, "You stupid fools! What are
you waiting for? Grab all the sticks and stones
you can find, and follow me quickly!"

She was running toward the meadow when a
scrawny figure in an orange robe appeared in the
high grass, charging toward the riverbank. Peony
bumped full force into the man and was almost
knocked down.

Staggering back, she screamed, "Mongol *guei-*

tze!" She raised the stone to hit the little man
on the face.

Despite his fragile appearance, the man was
very strong. As soon as Peony tried to attack
him, he grabbed her wrist. His fingers closed in
such an iron grip that Peony winced in pain and
dropped the stone.

They recognized each other at the same time.
"Peony! How dare you call a holy man a
devil?" The man smiled and loosened his hold.
His name was Merciful Heart, a Buddhist monk
in his fifties who was in charge of the Heavenly
Temple.

"I'm sorry, my honorable *shih-fu.*" Peony bowed
in apology as she rubbed her burning wrist. "It's
just that we heard our people screaming and
thought the Mongols were back—"

The monk didn't let her finish. "They are
back," he spoke quickly. "And they are massa-
cring the entire village." He hastened toward the
other girls. "I knew it was flower-gathering time,
and I hoped to find you here." He smiled at the
petrified girls reassuringly, then gave firm orders. "We are lucky that the Yellow River is extremely low at this point. You can ford the
stream by holding onto the apple trees. Don't
slip, don't look back, and don't make any noise."

As he talked, Merciful Heart gathered the long
fringe of his robe, rolled up his wide sleeves,
then removed his pointed shoes. Leading the
way to the water, he looked over his shoulder to
urge the girls on.

When the others were still fumbling with
trembling fingers to take off their shoes, rolling
up their pants, and gathering their skirts, Peony
was already splashing into the river with her
shoes on. She didn't need to hold onto the trees
because she had walked on the slippery riverbed
many times just for fun. Waiting in midstream,

she used her free hands to sustain two terrified girls. Her skirt and pants were pulled by the current, and she soon lost one shoe. The deepest part of the river came to Peony's shoulders. All the other girls were shorter and had to seize the apple branches for support. Flowers fell like heavy rain, and they were joined by the girls' tears.

When they reached the other side of the river, their many layers of clothes were sopping wet, and the girls all looked naked. Hunching forward and crossing their arms over their chests, they bowed their heads and followed the old monk into a forest of spruce and pine. Kicking off her remaining shoe, Peony walked barefoot to the monk's side. "What caused this massacre?" she whispered.

Merciful Heart answered in a low voice, "A wine maker trusted only copper coins, and refused to sell his barley wine to a Mongol for paper money."

"Is that all?" Peony asked.

"That's plenty," the monk answered.

She looked up at the noonday sun filtering through the forest's thick foliage. "My mother should be in the jade mine, watching my father eat the lunch she brought him. The miners know many secret caves. They must be hiding in safety."

The monk didn't correct Peony, for he had been to the jade mine before coming to the river. He had seen Peony's parents lying dead at the entrance of the mine, still holding each other. If he told Peony about her parents' death, she would scream. Then the other girls would ask about their parents, and his answer would make most of them shriek as well because more than half of the villagers had already been slain. He remained silent. He would not let his poor little lambs be heard by their pursuing butchers.

The ground began to rise. Merciful Heart and Peony helped the other girls to climb the mountain. A narrow clearing appeared when they were halfway to the top, leading to a path circling the waist of the mountain.

Following the trail, they soon reached a cliff shielded by many tall pines. Hiding among the trees, they looked down at the foot of the mountain, where a rope bridge crossed the Yellow River, which had become wide and tumultuous with spring floods. Mongol soldiers guarded the bridge, preventing anyone from going to the mountain via the normal route.

The girls saw people running from the village, heading for the bridge, but stopped at the sight of the soldiers; they quickly turned back, only to run into the waiting swords of their pursuers.

Peony stamped her foot and rooted for those not yet killed. "Hurry! Run through the meadow for the narrowest part of the river! Wade through it and climb up the mountain the back way! You fools! You—"

A hand covered her mouth. Merciful Heart shook his head at Peony. "Hush. At least some of us must reach the Heavenly Temple safely."

2

THE MOON SHONE BRIGHTLY. Its silver beams cloaked the Yellow River, bleached the pink dots of the white apple blossoms. The girls gathered under the trees wore matching white. Their young eyes were darkened with sorrow, their innocent faces aged with pain. Their pale lips parted to utter words of farewell, as they lighted the lanterns held in their trembling hands.

"Give me the fire starter!" Peony called to a girl at the other end of the riverbank.

In an open wooden box a cord of loosely twisted cotton was soaked in a bowl of oil, its tip hanging over the edge. The box was carefully passed to Peony from one girl to another. Peony took from her skirt pocket a long cord of braided cotton, brought its end to the fire starter, then used the burning coil to light her two white paper lanterns.

Placing one of them on the water, she said to her father, "Baba, with this lantern your journey to the world of the dead will be illuminated, and you'll be able to find the land of eternal happiness."

She set the second lantern beside the first one. "Mama, this lantern carries not only a sparkle of light, but also my love. I give you this lantern, together with a part of myself."

A thin piece of wood held each lantern to keep it afloat. A breeze whispered softly. The ripples carried the lanterns away. Peony gazed at the twin lanterns and stood up. "Baba, Mama, I will join you when it's my turn . . . Oh, no!" she cried when she lost sight of her lanterns.

As far as the eye could see, the Yellow River was a river of lanterns. Thousands of shining dots bobbed in the dark, each an unidentified raindrop in the pouring rain.

"But, Baba and Mama! You are special! Your lanterns should stand out among all others! You can't just disappear like this!" Peony picked up the hem of her white skirt and ran alongside the riverbank. "I must find you, my Baba and Mama!"

She tripped over a rock and fell. She had twisted her ankle, and she writhed in pain. She struggled up and hopped on one foot, trying to catch up with the moving lanterns.

The wind became stronger, and the lanterns from Emerald Valley hurled past Peony and disappeared downstream. But as soon as the last lantern was gone, a new train of lanterns appeared from upstream, sent by people in other villages beyond Emerald Valley.

Peony gave up her pursuit. She would never find her parents' lanterns in this endless river of lights. She watched the bright river whirl, until the night was deep and all the other mourners left for home.

The pain in her ankle eased as she walked in the moonlight, making her way through the meadow to her village. She returned to the two-room cottage that used to be her home, stood outside its closed door, and listened for the laughter that had once filled it. She heard nothing but silence. The house's new owners, a couple and their grown daughter, must be asleep.

When the Mongols had raided the Emerald Valley, this fortunate family had been in another village selling their earthen wares. They had returned to find their home completely destroyed, and they needed a roof over their heads. Peony had sold the place to them since Merciful Heart had offered her sanctuary in the temple.

Tears burned in her eyes. She turned abruptly and walked away. She squared her shoulders, held her head high and back straight. Without looking back, she stated firmly, "Baba and Mama, I'll never forget how you looked when I found you lying at the entrance of the jade mine, covered with blood but holding each other tightly." She raised her voice and said each word slowly, "I will avenge your death!"

She crossed the rope bridge, climbed the moonlit mountain. The blue tiles on the pointed temple roof glistened in the moonlight. All of the villagers who had survived the Mongol raid would be allowed to live under Merciful Heart's protection for as long as they were willing to hide behind the temple doors.

Gazing at the moon, Peony asked in a voice of great doubt, "Will I be content living among the nuns?"

The moon was silent, but Peony found the answer in her heart. She smiled and her voice became strong. "I can put up with the nuns for a while. Because Endurance Chu, my future husband, will come looking for me soon."

3

WHEN DAWN BROKE over Pinetree Village, Endurance Chu was already deep in a high mountain forest, carrying an ax in his right hand and a looped hempen rope over his left shoulder.

Through a break in the trees he looked down at the peaceful town. Nearby, the Yellow River dropped abruptly in a crystal curtain rushing over protruding rocks. The waterfall reflected the sun and blinded Endurance's eyes. He looked at the farmland, found the farmers as many small dots in the field, but couldn't locate his parents and three brothers.

Endurance Chu was sixteen and very tall. His large frame was covered in rock-hard muscle. The faded blue garment, with one lapel overlapping the other, couldn't conceal his broad shoulders and massive chest. The brown cotton sash that was supposed to wrap around his midriff and hang with a double-knotted bow barely met around his thick waist. He had rolled up his sleeves and pants legs as high as they would go, exposing arms and legs like tree trunks. His hands, like the feet protruding from rope sandals, were large and thick with calluses.

Endurance's hair had been left to grow since he was born, following the centuries-old tradition. It was pulled back tightly and braided into a long queue. A strong cotton thread, several yards long, was knotted at the beginning of the queue, then spiraled to its end, covering every bit of the hair. Another knot was tied at the end to keep the queue from becoming loose. During the day it was pinned to Endurance's head with a wooden skewer; at bedtime the skewer was removed. Except on special occasions when Endurance had to be thoroughly groomed, his queue was kept covered by the spiraling thread even when bathing and washing his hair.

Endurance had a large head and a bulky neck to match. His skin was dark and coarse. His eyebrows were black and straight, his nose wide. His eyes were piercing, his lips thick. What set him apart from the other Chinese boys was the short stiff stalks of black hair that covered the lower part of his face. Chinese males under twenty seldom needed to shave, but Endurance had to use a sharp bamboo knife to scrape his face every day.

He was a little afraid to be by himself in a dark woods inhabited by wild beasts. Until two years ago, he and his three older brothers had always worked together to cut wood and hunt.

Endurance swung his ax at a small tree and cut off its top. "I wish you were the Mongol who proclaimed that stupid law!" he said to the headless tree.

Two years ago, a Mongol general had arrived at Pinetree Village with his many soldiers to announce, "These are the orders of our great khan's adviser Shadow Tamu: no Chinese is allowed to learn military skills or keep a weapon in his house. Every ten families can share a cleaver, and every twenty homes an ax. You Chinese are no longer allowed to hunt, and when your woodsmen cut firewood, each man must work alone."

Endurance raised his ax high and swung it down fiercely. This time he looked at the tree as a Mongol who had raided a lovely southern town named Phoenix Place many years ago. His father had repeated the same story often enough for Endurance to know it by heart:

"We Chinese have never stopped defying the Mongols. Even in Phoenix Place the gentle people formed secret groups, including your baba and uncles, who were but simple farmers. Three years before you were born, we killed more than half of the Mongols in our town. In reprisal, the barbarian khan in Da-du sent over a large army of soldiers and put the whole town to the sword."

Endurance's parents had escaped with their three boys and traveled north. Endurance had been born a year later and grew up in Pinetree Village. The Chu couple had settled beside the Yellow River, not daring to return to the River Yangtze except in their dreams.

"I hate the Mongols for making my baba and mama so unhappy!" Endurance mumbled as he continued to chop down trees. He put all his anger into woodcutting. Before the sun became noon high, he had already gathered enough firewood for the twenty families that shared his ax.

He used the long hempen rope to tie the logs together. Finding he couldn't lift the heavy bundle, he lowered himself to the ground, and crawled underneath it until the pile was on his back. He stood up shakily, keeping his knees bent until he regained his balance.

He had only taken a few steps when he heard a commotion in the distance. He stood stock still for a moment, listened to the people screaming and wailing, horses galloping and neighing. The sound was muffled by the waterfall, and he wasn't sure what to think.

He dropped the wood and his ax when he heard the Mongols shouting. He realized he was not imagining things. He raced to a ledge.

The peaceful picture of the farmland had changed. The small dots of farmers were now dashing flecks. Mongol soldiers in bright red uniforms were all over the village, riding horseback and roping the villagers.

The descendants of herdsmen had superb skills with their lassos. Running for their lives, the Chinese were startled when suddenly caught and pulled to the ground with their arms pinned to their sides. They heard the Mongols laugh, then found themselves being dragged by the cantering horses and hauled over tree stumps, rocks, and sand.

Endurance panicked when he realized that his family was somewhere down there among these suffering people. "I'm coming to save you!" he yelled and turned to run.

He froze.

A tiger in a tawny coat with transverse black stripes appeared before him, hissing and baring its teeth. Endurance felt a chill rush down his back and sweat beaded on his palms. "Get out of my way!" he shouted.

The tiger hissed once again, kept an eye on Endurance while pacing to its right first, then its left. Its glaring eyes told Endurance it was hungry and ready for a meal just about Endurance's size.

The boy stared at it and lowered himself slowly. He didn't dare to look for the ax he had dropped, but felt for it blindly. His fingers had just touched the handle when the tiger drew its powerful limbs close to its body.

The beast sprang forward, and at the same moment Endurance threw out his ax.

The blade met the tiger's forehead and stayed buried there, but this didn't stop the powerful animal from reaching for its prey. It continued to sail through the air, then landed on Endurance with a wild roar.

Endurance was knocked onto his back, pinned to the ground. The tiger's head was less than a foot above his, and warm blood dripped on Endurance's face. The tiger opened its mouth wide, its sharp teeth ready to sink into Endurance's throat.

Summoning all the strength, Endurance wrenched his right arm from underneath the tiger's weight. Grabbing the ax handle, he yanked it out of the tiger's skull. The twist of pain delayed the tiger for a precious second. As it hesitated, Endurance swung the ax and drove its blade into the tiger's left shoulder.

Even so, the mighty animal kept its talons sunk into its prey. When Endurance managed to climb from under it, it continued to hold onto its game. The man and the tiger changed positions: Endurance was on top now. He tried to free himself and flee from the battleground, but as soon as he made the attempt, the tiger sprang again. Again and again the two rolled over each other, spattering the ground with each other's blood.

At last the tiger bellowed an earthshaking cry, then died clutching onto Endurance. The boy stood up breathing hard, aching and bleeding from a multitude of cuts, bites, and scratches. He took his ax from the tiger's shoulder and wiped it on his shredded clothes. He began to walk away from the dead tiger, then stopped after only a few steps.

He returned to the massive animal and squatted beside it. "Do you know how difficult it was for me to kill you? But I saw the killing lust in your eyes. Well, I'm sorry. When two warriors fight, one must die," he said as he closed the tiger's empty, gawking eyes. "You have my highest respect."

His legs were weak, but he ran down the mountain as fast as he could. When he passed a lower knoll, he quickly glanced down at the village. What he saw made him bellow much as the tiger had only minutes ago.

4

"YOU SHOULD BE PROUD of your family, my son." A tall man in a yellow robe stood over Endurance, who was squatting by the water in the moonlight. "Your entire family, including your mother, died bravely." He put a hand on Endurance's shoulder. "Some of my young monks were in the village when it happened. They were not harmed by the Buddha-fearing Mongols. They peeked from behind the trees and saw your family fight with their last breath."

Endurance looked up at the man in a yellow robe. Earthly Dragon was a Taoist monk in charge of the Temple of All Kings. Unlike Buddhist monks who had shaved heads, Earthly Dragon's white hair hang straight to his thin shoulders.

Endurance respected the old monk highly, but couldn't help raising his voice in anger. "What's there to be proud of? Death is the ultimate defeat in life. My family lost and the Mongols won. If only I wasn't delayed by that tiger ... !" He had told Earthly Dragon of the battle between him and the beast.

The old monk squeezed Endurance's shoulder with his strong fingers. "My son, the tiger was sent to you by the great Buddha for the purpose of detaining you. Otherwise you would have been killed with your family."

Endurance lowered his head, looked at the five

unlit lanterns in a row. If there were indeed a
Buddha, did He save him merely for the sake of
lighting these stupid lanterns? His parents and
brothers had perfect eyes. They could see in the
world of the dead without any lantern. Buddha
must have saved him for a better reason, he
thought. One corner of his lips curled up, and a
trace of joy appeared on his wretched face.

Endurance mumbled, "Peony! That must be
it. The tiger died so I can live for my future
wife."

The old monk didn't think much of women,
but didn't want to hurt Endurance's feelings at
this moment. "Maybe," he said, then walked
away toward the many others lighting their lanterns on the riverbank. He soon returned with
the fire starter in his hands. "Look at this," he
said, tapping Endurance on the back.

When the boy turned, the monk pointed at the
well-protected flame. "It's only a tiny sparkle.
But as long as it doesn't die, it is capable of burning down an entire city. The flames of your family were blown out by the winds of fate. Since
you alone are left burning, fate must have something great in store for you."

The monk reached into the pocket of his robe
and took out a wick. He lighted it, then handed
it to Endurance. "My son, light the lanterns,
then go home to pack. You'll come and stay with
me in the temple after that."

Endurance watched the lanterns float away,
joining a river of lanterns of death. The river
began to curve, and the lanterns were about to
drift out of his sight when he clenched his fists
and raised them high. "Baba! Mama! My brothers!" he shouted as he waved his trembling fists
at the moonlit sky. "I'll avenge your death!"

Earthly Dragon put an arm around Endurance,
patted him, and soothed him until he stopped

shaking. The monk then guided the young man away from the river. In the village, five new graves stood in a row, behind the small house that used to be the Chu family home. The house of their nearest neighbor was a good distance away, and there had been eight in that family. They had all been killed, and an aged relative was busy covering the last grave in the moonlight. The tired old man, unable to see clearly at night, had stretched the graves too far apart and mistakenly buried the eighth body in the Chus' land.

"I'm sorry," the man apologized to Endurance. "For making it look like you have six graves instead of five."

Endurance shook his head and told the man not to worry. He then went into the house, spread a large kerchief on the table and gathered the few usable things left by the Mongols. He tied the four corners together and put a stick through the knot, then carried the bundle over his shoulder.

"Wait for me here, my honorable *shih-fu*," he said to Earthly Dragon outside the door, then left the bundle on the ground.

He ran back to the house, picked up his mother's cooking oil, and emptied the jug on everything in the two rooms that were made of wood. The fire starter was kept beside the earth stove, and he brought it to the oil-soaked pile of firewood. He left the house without looking back.

When he and Earthly Dragon were far from the village, the smell of smoke caused them to turn.

"My son! What have you done?" the old monk cried, gasping at the lone structure with fire blazing through its sod roof.

"Nothing, my honorable *shih-fu*," Endurance answered calmly. He turned his back to the village and added, "Except to destroy what I no longer want and do not wish others to have."

"But it's destructive!" The monk shivered as he looked from the burning house to the hulking youth, whose childlike face was aged with wrath. "I cannot allow destructive people to stay in my temple."

Endurance answered without hesitation, "I don't intend to stay in your temple for long. I'll rest a few days to regain my strength, then go to my Peony."

5

"READY ... GO!" the commander ordered, and the soldiers burst in.

Twenty-two Chinese scholars were trapped in the building.

"According to the new law proclaimed by the great khan's adviser Shadow Tamu, no Chinese is allowed to hold political meetings. We were informed of your gathering, and have heard enough from outside your windows to prove that you've violated the law," the commander bellowed. He then gave the order for immediate execution.

Before the South Gate of Yin-tin City was a plateau covered by finely grained pebbles with rainbow-like hues: it was known as the Dais of Rain Flowers. More than seven hundred years ago a monk had begged the great Buddha to grant the world of chaos with a touch of beauty. His prayer was answered when the sky opened and flowers fell like rain. When the scholars were beheaded on the dais, their blood added another hue to the multicolored stones.

To the west of Yin-tin City, the Yangtze River murmured softly under the spring moon. Above its gentle whisper rose the sound of wailing, and its velvety surface was wrinkled by the touch of many white paper lanterns. Suddenly the lantern lighters stopped praying, and their hands froze in midair. All heads turned toward the end of a paved path, where a red-tiled gazebo was shadowed by many peach blossoms and weeping willows.

The gazebo was brightened by a procession of men and women in servants' uniform, each carrying a red paper lantern. Behind them were two sedan chairs, each carried by four men. Thick brocade draperies hung from the artfully carved wooden frames; the heavy panels were embroidered with threads of silver and gold. The stitched pictures were those of flowers, birds, lucky signs and two different family crests.

Among the people gathered on the riverbank, several could read. Peering at the sedans in the lantern light, they recognized the names on the crests. "The Lu family and the family of Lin!" they hissed.

Over a hundred years ago, one of the Lu ancestors had designed a covered bridge for one of the Sung emperors. The ruler had granted the architect tons of gold and thousands of acres of land. Around the same time, one of the Lin forebears had led an army and conquered a powerful group of rebels from the western region. The emperor had rewarded him equally well. From then on the descendants of both families had become landlords and moneylenders and lived in grand style.

The sedan carriers stopped at the gazebo, and lowered the chairs to the ground with great care. Rushing into the gazebo, the servants placed their red lanterns in every dark corner, dusted the stone chairs and tables, then covered them with cushions and a tablecloth. In well-practiced speed they began to set up the food and drinks they had carried in lacquered containers.

Two servants, a man and a woman, returned to the two sedan chairs. The male servant reached the first sedan, bearing the family crest of Lu, and lifted the front panel. A young lord in a pale blue silk robe stepped out.

Wisdom Lu was known as the most handsome bachelor in Yin-tin City. He was fragile like a green willow shoot in the spring, and just as soft and graceful. His thin neck was protected by the high collar of an undergarment made of satin as white as snow. His pale hands were half covered by long sleeves in dark blue that belonged to another shirt beneath his outer robe. The legs of his gray silk pants were long and wide. As he moved, his white socks and black shoes were revealed, both spotlessly clean as if they had never touched the ground before.

Wisdom Lu was eighteen, and his lengthy queue was wrapped in many yards of spiraling thread in the lucky color of red, then pinned into a topknot with several jade hairpins. Jade of various colors also adorned his lean fingers and slender wrists. Good-luck charms of jade hung from the long blue sash tied around his narrow waist.

A soft smile appeared on his pale round face as he advanced toward the other sedan. His eyes were small, his nose flat. His eyebrows looked as though they had been painted by a thrifty artist using diluted thin black ink, but while painting his mouth the artist had been very generous with pink.

Wisdom stood beside the other sedan chair and waited patiently until the woman servant lifted the curtain ornamented with the family crest of Lin. A southern gentleman, Wisdom knew that he must not touch either Lady Lin or the portiere on her sedan chair.

"Lotus," Wisdom called tenderly, leaning toward the sedan, "we are at the riverside now." He dared to call her by her first name because their mothers were distantly related and at one time they had played together like brother and sister.

Two feet in pink satin shoes appeared first, feeling the ground hesitantly. Butterflies were embroidered on all sides of the shoes. The pointed toes were sewn with seed pearls. Each shoe was only two and a half inches in length, although the standard allowed them to be three. Lotus Lin had the smallest feet in the city of Yin-tin, and therefore was known as the most beautiful girl.

Lotus had been unable to walk on her own since she was six and her feet were bound. Taking her maid's hand, she stepped out of the sedan leaning against the strong woman. An inch of her peach-colored long pants showed. Her maid gasped and quickly reached over to cover it with the young lady's long pink skirt. Lotus also wore an apple green blouse over a cream-colored undergarment that had a high collar to cover her neck and the lower part of her chin. Over all these clothes was a heavily embroidered yellow tunic that reached her knees. A multicolored sash adorned with pearls were tied around her tiny waist, then draped to her feet.

Her feet moved carefully, trying to keep the ends of the sash from fluttering noticeably. Being a southern lady, she knew how to behave properly. If a sash danced wildly on a girl, then she was fit to be only a gentleman's concubine, never his wife.

Another maid appeared on the other side of Lotus, offering her sturdy body to the young lady as a much needed crutch. Lotus was half carried by the two servants into the gazebo, where Wisdom stood waiting patiently.

Two red lanterns were placed on the table. Wisdom looked at Lotus's fair face in the light, and his eyes glowed with love. Her black hair was divided into two parts, the front piled high and embellished with pins of rubies and sapphires, the back gathered by a carved coral comb and then hung to her waist. Her white face was heart-shaped and small. Her eyes were shaped like two black almonds slanting upward. Her faintly visible brows reminded him of the far-away mountains in the fog. Her features were so soft that her entire face was like a dream except for her mouth—vivid and red, like a ripe cherry ready to be plucked.

Wisdom Lu blushed. Lotus was only fifteen. They were engaged to be married, but he couldn't pluck this beautiful young cherry he loved dearly for at least another year.

"Did you have trouble leaving your home for the lantern lighting?" Wisdom asked as they sat on the cushioned stone chairs.

Lotus did not answer immediately. She sensed that the women servants outside were keeping a watchful eye on the young lord and lady. She also heard in the distance the men servants chasing the peasants away from the riverbank.

Lotus finally replied with a sigh, "At first Baba wouldn't let me come to the river. He said it's foolish to light a lantern for my cousin who was executed for being a rebel." She bowed her head, toyed with the pearls on her sash. "I think Baba is afraid that the Mongols will learn that we are related to one of the rebels. He treasures his royal title, and wants to be called not only a lord but also more—"

She stopped when she remembered another rule for southern ladies: she should listen more than talk, and while talking to a man, a girl should comfort him with pleasantries instead of upset him with depressing thoughts.

Smiling deeply, she lifted a cup of hot tea and offered it to Wisdom respectfully with both hands. "Mama helped me to persuade Baba. He finally gave me permission, though he insisted that I don't wear white for mourning. He ordered me to bring many big red lanterns but only one small white one. He doesn't want the color of death to bring us bad luck."

"Your father is very different from mine. My father urged me to light a big white lantern for my cousin. He asked me not to wear white or bring more than one white lantern for a different reason. He said that we must not let the Mongol governor know how we really feel," Wisdom said as he accepted the tea with both hands in a gesture of great respect. A man did not have to accord this to a woman, but he respected Lotus highly. He still remembered that, as children, Lotus used to beat both him and their cousin in intellectual games, and before her feet had been bound, she used to be as good as they in all the physical games they played.

Wisdom pushed a dish of sweets toward Lotus. He watched her nibbling on a date and admired her beauty. How he missed being with her. When boys and girls reached their teens, they had to be separated. Even with the help of their understanding mothers, who were distant cousins, they saw each other only on rare occasions such as offering prayers in the temple or lighting lanterns for the dead.

"My mother asks me to give your mother her best regards," Wisdom said. He couldn't take his eyes from her.

"And my mother gives yours her warmest thoughts," Lotus answered, blushing under his gaze. She bowed her head like a soft willow in the wind.

As she did, Wisdom noticed the coral comb on her hair and that made him remember the gifts he had brought. He clapped his hands, and his

maid entered immediately. "Give me the boxes,"
he ordered.

In moments the woman had placed two lacquer boxes on the table, one large and one small.
When she left, Wisdom opened the large box first
and took out two kites. Each was made with a
large handkerchief and two chopsticks.

Lotus's eyes misted with tears. In their childhood days Wisdom had made her many beautiful
kites like these.

"Remember I used to undo my queue, then use
the silk threads to fly our kites?" He handed
them to her with a loving smile. "We can't play
together anymore, but our kites are still free to
roam beyond our garden walls. Our homes are
but three lanes apart. When we miss each other,
we can talk to each other through our kites." He
pointed at them. "I made you a red one and a
blue one. When you are happy, send up the red
kite. When you are sad, fly the one that's blue. I
have two in the same colors as yours. Through
them I'll be able to tell you how I feel."

"Thank you, Wisdom," Lotus whispered, holding the kites to her bosom. She wanted to hug
Wisdom as well, but it would be impossible. If
she so much as reached for his hand, the servants would talk and her reputation would be
ruined.

Wisdom opened the smaller box and took out
a jade comb. He lowered his voice so that the
maids couldn't hear them. "I also made this for
you. I worked on it for over two months. Please
look carefully at the two teeth in the middle of
the comb."

Lotus inspected the comb close up and saw on
one tooth the etched figure of a man, on the next
a woman. The man was wearing a lord's robe,
the woman the robe of a lady. The comb was
three inches wide, each tooth no more than an

inch long. But their faces were clear—the lord looked like Wisdom, the lady Lotus.

"You made it?" Lotus looked at Wisdom in surprise. When he nodded, she said, "You are a great sculptor!" She tried to keep her voice low, but couldn't conceal her excitement. "You couldn't do things like this before. Who taught you?"

"An artist in distress . . ." Wisdom hurriedly related how a sculptor had lost his position in the Mongol court and ended up carving window frames in the Lu house. Wisdom was amazed by the delicate flowers that appeared at the touch of the artist's carving knife, and complimented the man.

"He taught me to carve. I've been practicing for over a year now, and I'll keep learning since he is now one of the staff artists living at our house. I hope I'll become better, for when compared to him, I am no good at all. You should see this carving of a boat on a peach stone. There are a group of people on a boat, some holding up scrolls. He can even carve pictures and words on those scrolls . . ."

He halted as a manservant entered the gazebo. "The riverbank is clear now," he announced.

Lotus gave the kites to her maid, but added the new comb to her hair. As she and Wisdom walked toward the river, he went first, and she followed with the support of two women servants.

The poor were always chased from the riverbank when the rich and powerful arrived. The gazebo had been built decades ago by Chinese mandarins as a place to rest and eat and drink. Most of the time the peasants accepted their fate. But on this day, they were angered by this unfair treatment. Standing at a distance, they begun to call out nastily at Wisdom and Lotus:

"Only shameless people use their filthy money to buy court positions from the Mongols!"

"Your fathers are collaborators, and the great Buddha will punish them!"

Wisdom wished he could shield Lotus's delicate ears from those harsh words, but he couldn't disobey tradition. When the crowd began to pick up rocks from the ground and throw them, however, Wisdom could not remain a southern gentleman any longer. He retreated behind Lotus and protected her shivering body with his own. His chest touched her back, and their young hearts drummed.

The maids exchanged disapproving glances, debating if they should report their young master's improper behavior to their elders. The maids breathed with relief when the male servants raised their long staffs on the commoners and drove them out of sight. Wisdom walked away from Lotus, though their innocent hearts continued to pound as they reached the river.

With the riverbank peaceful again, Wisdom sat on a carefully laid quilt and took his lighted lantern from a servant. Lotus kneeled on a pillow placed on the riverbank by her maid, then accepted her lantern. They placed the two on the water. The moon was high, the night wind vigorous, and soon the lanterns had disappeared from sight. The servants urged their young lord and lady to go home, and at last they complied.

The city of Yin-tin was asleep. The procession of servants brightened the dark streets with their red lanterns, caused homeless beggars to stir and dogs to bark.

The sedan chairs were carried from the Yangtze River toward the east, gradually nearing the Purple Gold Mountain. The Mongol governor's mansion rose like a grim fortress on the top. At the foot of the mountain, the Whispering Lake glistened in the moonlight like a silver plate. On the foothills that overlooked the lake, mansions of the rich Chinese stood unlit under the moon. Only two remained brightly lit.

Both Lotus and Wisdom looked up from a distance, found their homes.

"It's strange," Lotus thought, peeking from behind the curtains and seeing her house at a distance. "Why are there candles shining in every window?"

Simultaneously Wisdom looked up from his sedan and asked himself, "That's odd. Why are there lamps glowing in my home?"

The procession reached the shore of Whispering Lake and began to climb the hill. The Lin and Lu houses were three lanes apart, and soon the two sedan chairs had to part. The servants divided into two groups, one to guard Lotus Lin's sedan, the other Wisdom Lu's.

Lotus took her new jade comb from her hair and held it tightly. In the other sedan, Wisdom clutched the memory of his latest meeting with Lotus dearly in his heart. Far behind them the Yangtze River rushed on, an unending river of lanterns. Each speck of flame burned brilliantly with promise and blessing, love and sorrow, longing and pain.

6

THE GRAND HALL was empty but for Merciful Heart and Peony, walking slowly, one in front of the other.

A dozen wooden statues of Buddha lined one side of the wall, and small oil lamps burned at their feet, revealing each one's distinct expression. Peony glanced at the severe image of the judging Buddha, empowered to interrogate the newly dead. She avoided the scolding frown of the punishing chief, then whispered to the smiling face of the rewarding lord. "My parents are with you, I am sure."

Merciful Heart stopped at the Buddha of happiness and twisted one of His long earlobes. Two of the curved panels on the fat belly sprang up, disclosing a deep, dark cavity. "Come over," the old monk ordered Peony.

Peony looked into the hiding place. The lamplight couldn't shine in, but something down there was glowing. She leaned closer and saw light coming from within a large piece of rock.

Rolling up his sleeves, Merciful Heart reached in, put his thin arms around the heavy rock, then lifted it effortlessly. He placed it at the happy Buddha's feet.

Peony gasped. Being a jade miner's daughter, she had seen plenty of raw jade, but never in this size and quality. Once positioned before the shining lamps, the radiance of the rock dimmed. But a touch of soft green continued to beam, as if a green firefly was trapped inside, dancing with its eternal flare.

"This was discovered by your father about a year ago," Merciful Heart said, pointing at the rock. "He asked me to keep it for him."

The monk went on to tell Peony that the Mongols had claimed every inch of the Chinese soil, including all the crops and fish and minerals. The jade miners were not allowed to keep or sell the jade they found, nor were the fishermen and farmers entitled to their catch and produce.

Merciful Heart said, "Your father chiseled this rock from the cave wall, then left it under a pile of twigs until he had a chance to sneak it to me in the middle of the night. He asked me to keep it for him." The monk put a hand on Peony's head. "He said that other than you and your mother, this was his only treasure."

Peony bit her lip to hold back her tears and listened as the old man continued, "Your father wanted his jade to be as protected, as you and your mother. He knew that under the Mongol rule, a man's life is as temporary as a tiny flame in the storm. So he entrusted all that was valuable to him in my care."

He went on to tell Peony that it would take many years' work for a trained craftsman to bring the hidden jade out of the rock, and many more years of polishing before the exposed jade could be used for sculpting. "I'll keep the rock concealed in the happy Buddha until a skillful hand can be found." He put a finger under Peony's chin, lifting her face and looking into her eyes. "And I'll keep you hidden in a nun's habit, not only from the Mongols but also from the endless sufferings in life."

Shocked, Peony gazed at the old monk. He smiled, certain that she would be pleased once she knew what he had in mind. "Let's put away the rock and join the others," he said.

The other refugees were already in the open court when Merciful Heart and Peony emerged. Their tattered mourning clothes had been replaced by shabby garments stripped from the dead and cleaned by the nuns. The filth on their faces had been cleaned, but the sorrow and pain couldn't be washed away. Standing on the platform, Merciful Heart told them to sit on the brick pavement.

"As villagers, you can hide in the temple only temporarily. As monks and nuns, you'll be permanently safe even under the Mongol rule. An initiation will take place tomorrow morning, and I must explain Buddhism to you tonight."

Most of the villagers smiled. It was an honor to become Buddha's sons and daughters. But Peony wanted to get up and run. She raised a hand to touch her hair: she had no intention to have her head shaved. She shivered at the memory of an initiation she had witnessed. The old monk had used incense to burn holes on the shaved heads of the novices. It was not supposed to hurt, but the tears on the novices' faces had proved otherwise. A full-pledged monk or nun would wear eighteen scars on the head, burned into the scalp one at a time as one was promoted through the years.

Merciful Heart began, "Life on earth is but an endless round of suffering, and I'm sure you have no argument about that." The monk looked over the crowd. The glowing moon enhanced the lines of agony on their faces, and the soft wind brought to his ears their sighs of agreement.

He continued, "We are all but spirits. Our true

home is heaven. All spirits are equal, including pigs and cows, who could be our relatives in another life."

Murmurs filled the court, as everyone was struck by the unpleasant thought of having eaten the bodies of their equals. Peony swallowed the saliva that had suddenly filled her mouth at the mention of pigs. She was so hungry that she wouldn't mind a large piece of pork, even if it had been a relative at one time.

Merciful Heart said, "After we die, those who have behaved poorly will be taken by the chief of punishment, those who toiled well will go to the rewarding lord."

The villagers looked at one another, couldn't hide their flinches in the light of the moon. Peony made a face. Regardless of her unruly behavior, her parents had never laid a hand on her. She had always been able to either argue her way out of punishment, or outrun her father and mother. Anyone wanting to give her the taste of the rod better be big, strong, and fast, Buddha or no Buddha.

Merciful Heart was a well-read man and had learned that in all religions, fear was always a strong rope that tied a believer to the sacred stake. He continued to frighten the villagers with the afterworld, saying that in order to avoid punishment, a person must fulfill earthly obligations.

Peony smiled inwardly. Her obligation on earth was avenging the death of her parents, marrying Endurance, then raising a houseful of children. After that she and he would die in old age and ascend to heaven. They would stay among the soft clouds and enjoy everything they had enjoyed in their living days, including the utmost joy shared by a wife and her husband—a joy she had not yet experienced but had imagined each time she heard the sounds of pleasure her parents made at night.

Merciful Heart said, "With perfect behavior, your spirit will achieve Nirvana, where there is no pain or hunger, longing or desire. You won't laugh or cry, love or hate—not ever again."

"That's it!" The words escaped Peony's mouth and turned many heads. Even Merciful Heart heard her. The old monk scowled, and she stood up quickly.

She made her way through the staring crowd and entered the temple, searching for the kitchen. When she found it, she forced the old nun there to give her some leftover barley gruel. She was emptying the last drop into her mouth when Merciful Heart appeared.

"You behaved badly," he said, then sent the old nun away. Once alone, he told her that when she became a member of the Heavenly Temple, her disorderly behavior would be punished severely. "You'll be taken to the head nun, made to kneel with your clothes stripped to your waist. You'll be whipped until your back bleeds. You are the daughter of my good friend, but I must keep order in the temple."

Peony laughed. "The order of your temple is safe, my honorable *shih-fu*," she said, meeting the old monk's eyes unwaveringly. "I have no intention of becoming a nun. Nirvana is not for me. I'd be so bored there that I'd scream and drive all Buddhas crazy."

Merciful Heart shook his head at her hopelessly. "The world outside the temple is filled with danger. I promised your father to take care of you—"

Peony interrupted, "I'll take care of myself until I am together with Endurance Chu, and then he'll take care of me like he did when we were children." When he nodded uncertainly, she told him the story of how the Ma and Chu families had met.

Ten years ago, the many Mongol princes had started to divide China among themselves. They rode from the Yellow River to the River Yangtze, each followed by many soldiers. "Baba told me that a prince would throw a spear on the ground to mark his starting point, then ride away at high speed. When he returned to his spear, the land within the circle marked by his horse hoofs would become his territory and those living in the circle his slaves. People began to revolt, and the men in all villages of Honan Province fought as a unit. During a battle, my Baba met Farmer Chu from Pinetree Village. They became good friends."

The next summer, Farmer Chu arrived in the Emerald Valley with his wife and four sons. The two families gathered on the riverbank and gazed up at the luminous band of stars in the night sky.

Peony said, "Mama came up with the idea that the Ma and Chu families should meet at least once a year, when the summer days were warm and the stars bright."

A shy smile softened Peony's face as she continued. "Endurance and I were seven at the time. We played together alongside the riverbank. Oh, we caught many fireflies. The next year we met in Pinetree Village, and some other children teased us for playing together. We fought them as a team, sent them all running home crying. When we were nine, we met in Emerald Valley again, and this time we both cried when we had to say good-bye. The next years the parting became even harder, and our parents started to plan for our future."

For the first time Merciful Heart saw Peony lowering her head and blushing. She now talked in the voice of a bashful girl. "When we were twelve, our parents gave us a simple ceremony for our engagement. The adults shared a jug of barley wine under the summer stars, Endurance and I a rice cake. We didn't cry this time when the stars faded and we had to part. We knew then that when we reached sixteen, we'd be married under a full autumn moon."

Peony looked at the old monk with tender warmth. "Now, my honorable *shih-fu,* do you understand why I can't become a nun and strive for Nirvana?"

Merciful Heart nodded with a deep sigh.

Peony went on, "I was going to wait for him until he and his family came in the summer. But now I've changed my mind. I can't wait that long. I'm leaving in the morning, *shih-fu.* I'll go to him, and his mother will take me in once I told them that I am now all alone."

Merciful Heart sighed once more. "My daughter, now I understand. Go to the nuns and ask them to give you some dark clothes. Your mourning white is too noticeable for traveling through Mongol-occupied land."

When Peony passed through the open court, the others were gone. The night wind had become stronger, tossing the thick clouds around, spilling them over the moon. Without moonlight the stars became brighter. Peony looked up and smiled. It was only a two-day walk between her village and his. "Endurance," she called softly.

Under the star-filled sky, the open court in the Temple of All Kings was brightly lit. More than twenty young men had survived the Mongol raid and, needing to hide behind the temple doors, were now becoming novice monks in a Taoist ritual.

Holding a candle, each candidate stood with his queue undone and his hair hanging to its full length. They lifted their eyes to the platform where Earthly Dragon stood wearing a yellow robe embroidered with red and gold, with matching headdress and shoes with curling pointed toes.

"To be a Taoist monk, you must accept the truth of life: it never stops changing, nor does the universe." Earthly Dragon spoke loudly with the hope that Endurance, who stood apart from all others at the far end of the court, would hear him and be moved by the ancient belief.

Endurance, though, was shifting his weight from one foot to the other, watching the ceremony impatiently. After the old monk's lecture on burning his home, he had changed his mind about staying in the temple to recover from the wounds he received from the tiger. He couldn't even wait for morning: he must leave tonight. His bundled belongings already hung from a short stick over his shoulder.

Earthly Dragon eyed Endurance with a frown. There was no moon, but the man would be able to see by the stars. He studied Endurance carefully but found no change in the young man's stern features. The old monk shivered and raised his voice: "The sun and moon alternate their appearances, each representing one of the two opposite forces—the day and the night, the yin and the yang, the kind and the cruel. A good man must have the willpower to tolerate life's turns and wait for the evil forces to leave him, without ever changing himself to fight the malevolent world . . ."

Endurance raised his hand to the old monk and waved a silent good-bye. Turning his back on the villagers, he walked away from the temple with long strides. He heard the ritual coming to a conclusion, and the novice monks beginning to chant. He kept walking and then looked up at the stars. All the hardness disappeared from his face as he whispered just one word, "Peony."

7

YIN-TIN CITY slept under a moonless sky, with the Yangtze River swirling on one side and the Purple Gold Mountain towering on the other. Among the darkened mansions in the foothills, two were brightly lit at this late hour.

"Is everything all right? No one is sick, I hope," Wisdom Lu wondered as he walked through the marble-tiled receiving hall, heading for the patriarch's court.

The servants, in gray uniforms, standing along the long hall bowed deeply to their young master but answered only vaguely, "The lord and lady have great news for our young lord."

Wisdom was led to his parents in the grand room used for special occasions. Silk-shaded lamps hung from a high ceiling adorned with hand-painted tiles. Candles glowed on tall brass sticks shaped like long-stemmed flowers.

Lord Lu was a pale, delicate scholar in his late thirties, wearing layers of garments in silver and dark blue. Lady Lu was a fragile woman two years younger, heavily jeweled and fully dressed in red and gold. The Lu family had been a small household since Wisdom's grandparents had died the year before.

Confused, Wisdom bowed to his parents. He didn't know why they were not already in bed, but it was not a son's place to question his honorable parents. He glanced at a low table carved

out of teak and inlaid with mother-of-pearl. Beside a bright lamp, a parchment scroll bearing a
red seal of the Mongol court lay unrolled.

Instantly Wisdom understood the reason for
his parents' being awake and formally dressed
now. When a royal message was delivered, its
receiver must accept it in a ritual similar to wel-
coming a Mongol prince. He looked at the scroll
suspiciously, wondering what news could make
his parents so happy.

Lord Lu said to Wisdom, "Pick it up."

Wisdom obeyed, read, then gasped. "Baba!
You are appointed the mayor of Yin-tin!"

"Aren't you pleased?" As the lord smiled, his
son's face had turned from pale to bloodless
white.

Remembering his manners, Wisdom bowed
deeply and said, "Congratulations, Baba." He
then looked up and hesitated, "But, Baba, in the
past sixty-five years, only three Chinese have
ever received such high positions. How did
you—" He stopped abruptly, noticing that the
servants were present.

Lord Lu ordered them to leave and waited
until they had gone. In a lowered voice he said,
"Since the last mayor of Yin-tin died, the Mongol governor of Kiangsu Province has received
bribes from many Chinese mandarins. My son, I
was one of them."

The father related that he had gone to the governor's mansion and offered not only gold and
silver, but also precious stones and rare jewelry.
These last pleased the governor's wife, and she
persuaded her husband to give Lord Lu the
position.

Wisdom's mother chuckled as she said, "Unlike the Chinese, the Mongols respect their
women, and a Mongol governor can be influenced

by his wife. I wish I had such power over your father."

The lord and lady laughed, but not their son. Wisdom bowed his head, not wanting his parents to see the disapproval in his eyes.

"Wisdom," his mother said softly, reaching over and taking his hand, "your father didn't do this for personal gain." She motioned for him to sit beside them, and explained in a carefully lowered voice that her husband had spent a fortune on the bribery for very complicated reasons. "One of them is that the people of Yin-tin will have a mayor who is on their side. And the others are . . ." She looked at her husband.

Lord Lu's voice was merely a whisper. "I was determined to seize the mayor's position because of a law proclaimed by Shadow Tamu.

"In the past sixty-five years, except for the great khan and the royal families who lived with their warriors in Da-du, the majority of the Mongols still preferred living in nomadic tents in open pastures in the northern and western parts of China. But because the Chinese along the River Yangtze revolted often, Shadow Tamu had become worried."

Lord Lu said, "The khan's adviser is afraid that we may organize a widespread rebellion without their knowing it. As a result, he decided that the Mongols should observe the southern Chinese closely. He ordered us to open our homes to the Mongols."

Wisdom clenched his fists. He had never hit anyone with those dainty fists in his life, but would like to strike at the Mongols right now. The home was sacred to the Chinese no matter how humble their dwellings, just as wives were men's personal belongings regardless of the fact that women were worthless. When a man was forced to open his home to strangers, he was insulted as severely as if he had been ordered to share his wife with others.

Mayor Lu said, "Twenty-five thousand Mongol military men will be arriving in the Yangtze area within the next year. Most of them will come to Kiangsu Province, and at least three thousand will be living in Yin-tin City. Since we have about thirty thousand homes, every ten homes will house a Mongol soldier. You can imagine if these soldiers are not treated like kings what will happen to their poor hosts."

"Baba, by becoming the mayor of Yin-tin, can you keep the Mongol soldiers out of Chinese homes?" Wisdom asked.

Lord Lu shook his head. "No, I cannot. But forcing their soldiers into our homes is only one of the poisoning hornets sent by the Mongols to sting us Chinese. We need to destroy their nest. It'll be a time-consuming task, and attaining success will cost many Chinese lives."

The father looked at the son deeply and put a hand on his shoulder. "Wisdom, I have many plans, and I'll need your help to carry them out. You and I must risk our lives to save our people."

Wisdom bowed obediently, remembering what had happened a while ago on the riverside. He could still picture the commoners of Yin-tin throwing sharp stones and spiteful words at him and Lotus. But it didn't matter. Like his father, he would do all he could to help his fellow countrymen even if he never received their gratitude in return.

Wisdom and his parents talked in hushed voices until the day began to break. While walking away from his parents' court, Wisdom looked out the moon-shaped window at the dawning sky and whispered softly, "Lotus, you won't know

what my father and I are about to do, but I'm
sure you'll soon hear that I am now the mayor's
son."

"So he is now the mayor's son! It doesn't make
any difference! I'll never allow Lotus to see
him!" Lord Lin roared.

He was in his early forties, with a short, fleshy
body and a delicately featured face that was usually pale but now red with anger. He couldn't sit
still in his brocade chair. He jumped up and
paced from one end of the elaborately furnished
room to another, kicking the gold border on his
maroon robe, sending the scarlet sash around his
thick waist flying.

"But . . ." Lady Lin uttered only one word,
then started to sob. Eight years younger than her
husband, her face was beautiful and her body
frail. Her feet were tiny and she couldn't walk.
She had on layers of lavender garments and a
purple sash. She wore splendid jewelry and ex-
travagant ornaments for her hair, but she was
crying helplessly.

Being a wealthy lord's wife, she was deeply
respected by the servants and her husband's
many concubines. But her place was lower than
that of her honorable husband and many in-laws
who also lived in the same mansion. She loved
her only child, although Lotus was only a girl.
She didn't know how to convince her husband
and in-laws that Lotus was just as precious as
the three sons given to Lord Lin by his concubines. Her husband's order would make Lotus
very sad, and Lady Lin wished she could do
something to change it.

Lotus heard her father shouting and mother
crying as soon as she entered the receiving hall.
On both sides were doors leading to various

courts. Lotus looked in through the open doors and saw chaos in every brightly lit room.

In a few steps she reached the sitting room. Several teak chairs were broken. Porcelain vases were shattered and lying on the handwoven rugs in pieces. A tray containing a tea set had been swept off the table. Her mother's favorite pink silk chair was stained and covered with wet tea leaves.

Two maids were on their knees, picking up things and cleaning the room. One of them came to Lotus and whispered into her ear, "My lady shouldn't go near the grand room right now. The lord is very upset. He kicked at the furniture, threw all things against the walls. Everyone else is hiding from him except our poor lady, who couldn't get away."

"Why is my father angry?" Lotus asked, hesitating in the hall, not knowing if she should go comfort her mother or go to her chamber and hide. She and her mother were very close, and she felt disloyal letting her mother face such a difficult situation alone, but she was also very afraid of her father.

The maid muttered, "The lord's informer came from the governor's mansion, and told the lord that based on the governor's suggestion, the court had appointed a new mayor. Our lord didn't get the position."

Lotus began to understand. Her father had tried his best to bribe the governor for the second highest position in Kiangsu Province. Yintin was the capital city, and its mayor had great powers. Once selected, her father could raise the interest rate on moneylending and rent on land. Lord Lin had waited a long time for the nomination. At times he was so certain of it that he had even rehearsed an inauguration speech.

"Baba must be very disappointed," Lotus sighed, feeling sorry for her father. She then thought about what she had heard and was puzzled. "But why is he talking about the new mayor's son? Who is he and why would I want to see him anyway?"

The maid looked at Lotus with sympathy. "The new mayor is Lord Lu, the father of my lady's future husband."

A low scream escaped Lotus's lips. Her legs became weak. The two maids on either side put their arms around her trembling body to keep her from falling.

The other maid repeated her warning, "I advise my lady to avoid the lord right now. He is yelling at everyone."

Lotus nodded feebly. "Help me to my room."

Moving slowly, Lotus could still hear her father hollering and her mother whimpering in a distance.

"There will be a party in the Lu house a few days from now. Mongol officials, noble foreigners with their interpreters, and Chinese elites will all be invited. The stupid governor will be there, too!" Lord Lin shouted. "I must go, but you and Lotus will stay home. Being a man, I need to show my face in that damn house and keep up a good appearance. But I forbid you to ever see Lady Lu again. And I'll never allow our daughter to have anything to do with that Lu bastard's boy!"

"But Lady Lu is my cousin, and Lotus is engaged to Wisdom," Lady Lin said in between sobs. For a brief moment her voice had a faint tone of determination, but then the lady broke into sobs again.

"Forget your cousin, you foolish woman!" Lord Lin's yelling was followed by the crashing of another vase thrown against the wall. "And disregard the engagement of our daughter! Lotus is a beautiful girl and I have greater plans for her!"

Lotus halted in mid-step at this statement, then fainted dead away.

8

WISDOM LU STOOD at the window in his bed-chamber, watching a night sky brightened by fireworks.

"My lord, please hurry. Everyone is already at the Whispering Lake!" a servant said from the door. "The mayor, the guests, and the people of Yin-tin!"

Wisdom reached the lake just in time to watch the servants shooting off the last series of arrows. Fireballs flew high, exploding and forming color-ful designs. A green-gold dragon waved its claws and reached for the moon. A blue-silver phoenix spread its wings and danced across the Star River. A bouquet of yellow chrysanthemums bloomed on a bed of clouds. A forest of red cherry trees blossomed over the mountaintop. None of the enchanting visions lasted long. They became multicolored falling stars that twinkled into smoke before reaching the ground.

Suddenly, gongs were sounded on the far side of the Whispering Lake. Glancing downward, Wisdom saw a painted silk lion over fifty feet long. Twenty young men in black pants, naked from their waists up, held up the willow-framed tunnel and danced in rehearsed steps. The lion's head was supported by an old man who had led the dance for several decades. He controlled the lion's eyes and mouth, made the animated beast blink and flirt, smile and pout.

As the lion skipped and jumped in lively steps around the lake, Wisdom Lu looked around. He saw many peasants standing near him, men and women relishing the rare treat. He spied his father, but his mother and the female guests were nowhere to be seen. Except for the curious foreigners, all the other male guests had seen the lion dance often enough to be blasé about it. They instead kept an eye on the road that led to the Lu mansion. Finally a manservant appeared running and holding a heavy iron pot wrapped in layers of rags.

Wisdom Lu frowned. The pot was filled with heated copper coins and many pairs of iron chopsticks with wooden handles.

"What's all this for?" Wisdom heard a foreigner ask.

"Just watch and see," an interpreter answered. "The rich in China know many ways to entertain themselves."

The pot was placed on the ground. The guests raced toward it, used the chopsticks to pick up the scalding coins, then tossed them toward the lion. The foreigners watched for a while, then followed the rich men's example.

The lion was made of silk, adorned with threads of silver and gold, decorated with beads of glass and semiprecious stones. The costume was the lion dancers' livelihood, and they couldn't afford to have it burned. Because of this, they tried to shield the lion with their own bodies—exactly what the guests wanted.

The rich men's aim was dead-on, and the foreigners soon caught on as well. The white-hot coins landed on the dancers' naked upper bodies, burned the flesh, created hissing sounds and a strange odor. The dancers screamed and writhed in pain. The lion began rolling and staggering as if it had become drunk. The rich Chinese laughed.

The foreigners were amused. Most of the peasants were angry, but some enjoyed the game since it was not their skin being burned.

"That's enough!" Wisdom shouted when he could not stand it any longer. He waved his hand at the servant who had brought out the pot. "Bring the hot coins away!"

The honorable guests turned to Mayor Lu in surprise, waiting for him to reprimand his son.

The mayor ignored them and nodded at the servant. "Do as your young lord says. From now on, when there is a lion dance sponsored by us, don't ever bring out hot coins again."

The lion stopped dancing momentarily. The dancers were stunned, not sure whether to thank the new mayor and his son or complain. Although this edict freed them from further torture, it also deprived them of the coins, which they picked up when cool.

Mayor Lu's voice was heard by all the people along the lakeshore. "Give the whole pot of coins to the lion dancers. They can divide them when the coins are no longer burning hot."

The foreigners were disappointed that the game was over, and the Chinese strongly voiced their disapproval. "Mayor Lu has just violated a thousand-year-old tradition! The lion dancers have always been tipped with red-hot coins!"

For their part, the peasants expressed amazement. "Mayor Lu and his son are different from what we thought. At least two rich men are not totally heartless!"

The multicourse dinner was served in separate dining rooms. Waited on by their maids, the women were free to eat heartily and discuss womanly affairs. The men ate in the company of singsong girls: enjoying the pretty young things sitting on their laps and feeding them food and drink.

They were served hummingbirds' tongues and monkeys' brains, sharks' fins and bears' paws. When everyone finished eating, porcelain bowls of warm water were brought to the tables, each filled with floating flower petals. The guests washed their hands in the perfumed water, dried their fingers on soft kerchiefs brought to them by the servants, then went to the grand room.

Mayor Lu and his lady sat side by side, receiving gifts from the long line of guests. The Mongol governor led the procession, put a present on a large table, then walked away. Each Chinese walked up to the new mayor and his primary wife, bowed and presented a package. Without glancing at any given present, the Lu couple gestured for two servants to take it and put it on the table, which was soon piled high.

The foreigners were puzzled by this seeming indifference to the gifts. "They don't even look at the things!" one of them commented.

"We Chinese are not supposed to show that we like gifts," an interpreter explained patiently. "Confucius taught us that looking forward to receiving is greed, which is a terrible sin. A cultured person always avoids looking at a present until the giver is gone." Without dropping the perpetual smile that had become etched into his facial features, the interpreter mumbled in Chinese, "You barbarians know nothing about true civility!"

Once the gift-receiving ceremony was over, the guests left for the music room, where they were entertained by a band of string instruments until after midnight.

After seeing the last guest out of the door,

Lady Lu retired. Mayor Lu and Wisdom, on the other hand, went to their study and waited.

After leaving the Lu mansion, some of the sedan chairs circled the Whispering Lake and returned to the foot of the Purple Gold Mountain. The chair owners ordered their servants to blow out the lanterns, then returned to the Lu mansion in the dark. They were admitted immediately by two old servants trusted by the Lu family.

Together with their invitations, these particular guests had also received a box of sweet cakes. Each of them had found in his cake box one cake marked with a red dot. When the recipient broke the cake, he had found a note on a strip of paper. Taking the paper to their private chambers, they had read the secret message, "Return discreetly when the party is over, for the sharing of a delicious dessert."

Over thirty men, old and young, gathered in the new mayor's study behind closed doors. Their loyal servants waited nearby in the servants' quarters. Like the Lu servants, they would guard their masters' secret with their lives.

Mayor Lu stood up and cleared his throat. "I thank you for returning. You are risking your lives to do so." He looked at Wisdom and moved aside for his son to take over. "Wisdom was the one who thought of sending you the secret notes in the sweet cakes. He'll reveal what he and I have in mind."

Wisdom bowed deeply, then began. "You chosen ones are scholars and followers of Confucius. We have always behaved like gentlemen and never fought in battle. As Confucius said, true scholars are not supposed to be physically strong enough to kill a chicken, or emotionally sturdy enough to watch it bleed."

Wisdom smiled with a sparkle of stubbornness in his eyes. "Baba and I will always remain gentlemen scholars. But we have decided to form a group of men just like us to save China in our own peaceful and unobtrusive way."

Wisdom examined the faces of his audience carefully, worried that he might have invited a few traitors. Everyone in this room had been persecuted by the Mongols one way or another; each had enough reason to risk his life for the cause. He recognized two scholars whose brothers had been executed on the Dais of Rain Flowers not long ago. The sisters of several other young lords had been taken by the Mongols while praying in the temples and raped and killed. There were aged lords in the room who had been forced to give their daughters to the Mongol khans, and once rich men who had had most of their wealth drained away by the Mongol princes.

Wisdom continued, "There are noble warriors all over China, battling the Mongols with their bare hands and marching on foot. Their swords, knives, and means of transportation have repeatedly been taken away. They need weapons made secretly by patriotic craftsmen, and food, wagons, oxen, mules, plus hundreds of other supplies. All of these have to be bought, and I propose we provide them with the money they lack."

Sorrow darkened Wisdom's young face as he went on. "Besides the brave revolutionaries, the poor are also in need of our help. We are a blessed few. While our stomachs are full, our fellow countrymen are dying of hunger. Among the starving, many are scholars like ourselves but less fortunate."

Mayor Lu and the other older men nodded in consent as the younger ones responded with enthusiastic cries. When Wisdom had finished, the scholars began to take out their gold and silver coins, then piled their jewelry on the table.

Wisdom was elected as the leader in charge of keeping and then distributing the monies among the resisting forces and the poor. He would call for further meetings by using the same note-carrying sweet cakes, and the location would always be the same since the Mongols would not search the mayor's home. In the notes, when signatures were needed, Wisdom would call himself the lord of Whispering Lake. There were many whispering lakes in China, so this alias should be safe.

The group realized that the organization also needed a name. After some discussion they agreed on the title Silent League.

Raising their teacups, the new League members swore to guard their association and carry out their mission for their remaining days.

Mayor Lu concluded the meeting with a simple warning: "We must remember that outwardly we still have to bow to the governor and do our best to please the Mongols."

"Please the Mongols . . . how can I best please the Mongols?" Lord Lin asked himself repeatedly in his sedan chair.

During the party he had overheard the Mongol governor thanking Mayor Lu for the presents that pleased his wife. Lin had cursed silently. "That's how the bastard got his position!" He had then asked himself, "How can I please the Mongol governor better and take the position from the Lu bastard?"

He had suffered through the fireworks, feeling that the bright sparkles represented Mayor Lu and the crumbled ashes himself. He had felt the pain of the lion dancers, thinking that the suc-

cess of Mayor Lu was like the many red-hot
coins burning into his pride. He had chewed
each bite of the food vigorously, treating the
meat as the flesh of his opponent. He had
watched the piled gifts with envy, wishing that
they were his to take home.

"Home," he sighed deeply as the sedan neared
his mansion. "I have nothing at home except my
aging parents, three stupid sons borne by my
concubines, lazy relatives, a weak wife, and an
useless daughter ..." He stopped short and
opened his eyes wide. He had just the right
present.

By the time the sedan had stopped at this
mansion, Lord Lin had made up his mind. He
entered the double doors guarded by two marble
lions, walked through the arched doorway with
a broad smile. "Wake my lady and Lady Lotus,
then bring them to my study!" he ordered.

Awakened from sleep, Lotus quickly dressed
with the help of her maids, then went to her
mother. With the support of four maids, the two
of them moved in tiny steps to the man they
both feared. Neither could guess what was the
cause of their being summoned at this hour.

"Maybe he has finally decided to take my title
away, and give it to one of his concubines who
has borne him a son," Lady Lin quivered.

"Maybe Baba has discovered that I was flying
kites everyday, and wants to punish me for be-
having like a child," Lotus shivered.

They were surprised to see Lord Lin smiling
at them from his chair, whose legs and arms had
ends shaped like claws of a dragon. "Sit," said
the lord, pointing at two other similar chairs.
Lotus and her mother breathed with relief. Both
assumed that he had called them to tell them
about the party.

"My lord," Lady Lin asked, "what did the mayor's wife wear?" She glanced at her daughter and added, "Was the mayor's son there to receive the guests? And—"

Waving his hand, Lin yelled. "Shut up, you stupid woman!"

Lady Lin's pale face turned gray. She stared at her husband as he ordered, "You'll take Lotus to her room, help her pack her clothes and jewelry."

He then looked at his daughter and continued, "Lotus, is there any of your mother's jewelry that you would like to take with you?"

"Mama's jewelry? Take with me? Where am I going, my honorable Baba?" Lotus asked, trembling.

"To your future home," Lin answered. With a happy glint in his eyes, he examined Lotus carefully. It seemed the last time he looked at her, she had still been only a child. When had she become such a beautiful woman? His smile deepened as he eyed her up and down once more. "To capture a man's heart, my daughter."

At first Lotus was elated. Her father wanted to advance the wedding date and make her marry Wisdom immediately. A ruby hue rose from her neck, turning her ears vermilion and her face scarlet. She lowered her eyes and bowed her head, but couldn't conceal the smile that curled up her lips. "Yes, Baba," she answered softly. "I'll obey your order."

"Why hasten a marriage that is not supposed to take place until a year from now?" Lady Lin asked. There was laughter in her voice: she was happy for her daughter.

"Lotus is not marrying the Lu bastard's son. She is going to the Mongol governor's house to become one of his concubines!" Lord Lin yelled.

Lotus felt her world collapse. Suddenly dizzy,

she clutched the arms of the chair tightly, until the carved dragon claws dug into her palms. A few days ago, when her father had said that he might have greater plans for her, both mother and daughter had considered it an empty threat spoken in anger. Now with her eyes lowered Lotus noticed the embroidered butterflies on her tiny shoes. I'm just like them, she realized. I am another butterfly who cannot fly away from fate.

Her ears ringing, Lotus heard her mother's voice as from far away. "I can't let you do this to my Lotus! If you want to give her to a Mongol, you'll have to kill me first. And don't forget that my family is not without wealth and power. If you dare to hurt me in any way, they won't let you go free!" Lady Lin didn't raise her voice, but each syllable was as sharp as the blade of a knife.

Lotus had never heard her mother talk back to her father. She didn't even know that her mother was capable of disobeying. She lifted her eyes and saw her mother standing without the maids' support.

Lady Lin pointed a shaking finger at her husband. "Lotus was promised to the Lu family in an engagement of pointing the womb. Even an unscrupulous man like you must honor that sacred engagement!"

Lotus stared at her mother. It was not ladylike to mention the word *womb*, although her mother was merely reminding her father of the facts. When Wisdom Lu had been three, his mother had brought him to visit the Lin house, for Lady Lin had been with child at the time. Lady Lu had wished her a boy, but also pointed at her swollen abdomen and said, "If the baby should be a girl, then I want her to be my Wisdom's wife." Lady Lin had consulted her husband and then accepted the proposal. The formal engagement had taken place later on the same day Lotus was born.

Lady Lin continued in an unyielding voice, "Such an engagement has been honored since the days of Confucius, and will always be honored as long as Chinese civilization lives."

She went on to remind her husband that even if one of the children should die before the marriage, it would still take place—the deceased would be represented by a wooden plaque that bore a name. When a groom became a widower on his wedding day he was expected to remarry, but when a bride received such a fate she must remain a widow for her livelong days.

Lord Lin was shocked by his wife's stand. Taking a step forward, he raised a hand to strike her. His hand stopped in midair, though, when she didn't flinch or duck. Then he considered what she had said about her family. He couldn't afford to offend her father and many uncles, who were rich and highly respected in Yin-tin. He lowered his hand and stared at her. She wouldn't blink. He was the one who finally looked away.

"I will not waste my breath arguing with a woman," he said to save face in front of the servants. Before leaving the room, he issued one last threat: "But Lotus will become the Mongol governor's concubine before tomorrow is over!"

At dawn, most of the servants in the Lin mansion stirred sleepily in their beds, reluctant to rise for another long day of toil.

Three figures, though, were already carefully tiptoeing toward the back gate. The woman in the middle had large feet and towered over the other two. Supporting them with her arms, she whispered, "Hurry!"

Jasmine, the strong maid, had no surname. She had been sold by her parents to a slave trader, who had soon forgotten what she was called, and her name derived from the fact that Lady Lin's parents had been having jasmine tea when the trader presented them the girl. Now thirty-three, Jasmine had never married. She had been Lady Lin's maid since they were both little girls, and when the decision was made that Lotus must run away, Lady Lin had immediately decided that Jasmine should escort her daughter in the escape.

"You better walk faster if you don't want to become the Mongol's concubine," Jasmine said to Lotus, who was scooting along as fast as she could. "And you, my lady, how can you go back to your chamber without my help?" Jasmine asked.

"I'll manage," Lady Lin said. "I can lean against the walls and grab hold of the trees." She tried to laugh. "If I can summon up the courage to defy my lord and master, I certainly can find my way back to my own bedchamber." Her voice quavered as she looked past Jasmine at her daughter. "My child, you must manage to live happily without your mama. Be a good wife to Wisdom and obey your in-laws. Comply with your lord's every wish when he is right, but if he should push you too far, then you must follow your mama's example and challenge him. Remember my words, my precious baby, for I doubt if we'll ever see each other again."

Lady Lin had no doubt that the Lu family would take Lotus in, nor that the marriage would take place as soon as possible. Since Mayor Lu was now second only to the Mongol governor, Lord Lin would not dare to prevent the wedding once Lotus was safely out of reach. All he could do was torment his wife.

"Mama, come with me," Lotus pleaded, in tears. "You can live in the Lu house, too."

"Silly child." Lady Lin shook her head. "You'll be the young lord's first lady in the Lu house. What would I be? Your dowry?"

Lotus wiped at the tears streaming down her face. Her mother was right. There would be no place for Lady Lin in the Lu house, regardless of the two mothers' friendship. One of the reasons that sons were valuable and daughters were worthless was that the parents had the right to live with their sons but never with their daughters.

Trying to make the parting easier, Lady Lin pointed at Jasmine and said with a forced cheerfulness, "I hope the Lu family will not reject you for bringing them no dowry but Jasmine."

"Don't worry, my lady," the maid said to Lady Lin. "I'll take good care of Lady Lotus, the same as I've always taken good care of you."

When they reached the gate, Lotus turned to her mother and pleaded once more, "Mama, please come with me. No matter what tradition says, the Lu family will let you stay with me."

Her mother smiled sadly. "I married your father when I was about your age. I knew no other man in my life. Every girl has love in her heart and needs to give it to someone. I gave my love to your father. I fear him and dislike him, but I can never stop loving him." Lady Lin shook her head firmly. "I will never leave his house as long as he allows me to stay by his side."

9

ALONG THE YELLOW RIVER, the apple trees were no longer in bloom. The pink-centered white blossoms had turned into tiny green dots of fruit. Making her way beneath them, Peony was traveling the route she and her parents used to take to Pinetree Village. By this time she had finished the food given to her by Merciful Heart, and she was very hungry.

Reaching a village, she saw a tofu peddler and followed him. The man had a pushcart loaded with cakes of soybean curds. He walked from one farmhouse to another, tapping on a bamboo stick to advertise his wares, either selling or trading his tofu for eggs and grain.

Peony watched him bargaining with an old woman, weighing her grain on a portable scale made with a stick, a hook, a small plate, and different weights. When they were haggling vigorously, Peony snatched a large cake of tofu and ran.

The peddler chased her for a while, then gave up his pursuit, worried that the villagers could empty his whole cart. Peony stopped at the riverbank and sat down to eat the tasteless tofu. As she did, she watched more paper lanterns float past.

Mongol persecution was widespread, and everywhere people were mourning their loved ones. Among the other lantern-lighters' cries, she heard a daughter calling her father and mother, telling them that she wanted to drown herself so that the entire family could be together. A lump rose to Peony's throat. Hastily she left the river and resumed her journey.

All too soon her stomach began to growl again. Not only that, but the sky was turning dark. In previous trips she and her parents had always stayed in the house of a friend of her father's who lived in the next village. Remembering this, she rushed on.

When she reached the place, she found the mud-walled, sod-roofed house gone. In its place was a row of brick structures and a stable. Squinting, she saw in the light of the spring moon a sign that bore the picture of a jug of wine and a pot of food.

She moved closer to it, hid behind a tall pine. She heard laughter from inside the open windows. She smelled meat being cooked. The aroma brought her out of hiding. She went to the window and peeked in.

She saw six Mongols sitting around a table drinking. A whole lamb was being roasted on an open fire at the other end of the room. The lamb skin was already golden brown. The juice dripped on the burning logs, causing the flames to shoot up and sizzle.

Peony swallowed deeply as she watched two Chinese servants bringing the lamb to the table. The Mongols reached with their bare hands and dug into the meat despite its heat. They tore the meat off the lamb, held the large chunks in their hands, and took big bites, then sucked their burned fingers. One of them, sitting with his back to the window, was so close to Peony that he kept waving his lamb right in front of her eyes.

A stable man appeared to ask whether they wanted to continue their trip the next day with their own horses or the horses provided by the lodging post. The Mongol near the window leaned back to think. As he rested his elbow on the windowsill, the lamb leg almost touched Peony's nose.

Not thinking, she grabbed the meat. She didn't know the Mongol had such a tight grip on his food. She had to jerk it out of his grasp.

The Mongol was astonished by the invisible snatching hand. He screamed and turned as Peony ran swiftly into the darkness.

Behind her, the Mongols yelled for the Chinese to look around the lodging post. But the Chinese only searched halfheartedly. Peony could hear them telling the Mongols that there was nobody outside.

Finding the Yellow River by moonlight, Peony sat on its bank and ate. It seemed the most delicious food she ever tasted in her life, and the rippling water seemed to be saying that she would be with her Endurance soon. She stretched out on the grass. Her final image that night was of the sky glowing with millions of stars and a beautiful moon.

She rose at sunrise and headed on, stirred with the energy from the lamb. By mid-afternoon she began climbing the mountain overlooking Pinetree Village, remembering the stories about woodsmen being attacked by tigers in this place. She ran through a deep forest, and when a gap opened, she caught a glimpse of Pinetree Village. She frowned at the reduced number of farm workers in the paddy. Where had all the young men gone? Even from a distance she could tell that most of them were women and old people, guiding their water buffalo to level and till a flooded field.

Her worries were lightened when she spied some children wading across a shallow pond that reflected the blue sky and fluffy white clouds. The view was lovely, and her life would be even lovelier once she found Endurance. Standing up, smiling, Peony used her sleeves to clean her face as best she could.

The village was different from what she remembered. Less people were about, so the place looked bigger. She recognized the twin oaks that rose between the Chu house and the house of their neighbor. Then she noticed that the branches of the trees were charred on the Chu side. Where the house had once stood was a pile of burned debris.

Peony ran toward an old man squatting between the trees. Pointing at the blackened heap, she shouted, "What happened? Where are they?"

The old man didn't even look up. He didn't see her pointing either. He had come to visit the eight new mounds of his relatives, and his feeble mind was preoccupied with their deaths.

"Dead . . ." he mumbled, waving a shaking arm at the many new graves stretching behind him. "Mongols . . . horses . . . ropes around their necks . . . bows and arrows . . . all dead . . . every one of them."

"No!" Peony screamed and ran from the old man. She counted the graves on the Chu property. There were six. Two for the parents and four for all the sons.

"No! No! No!" She continued to scream as she ran from Pinetree Village without stopping.

Her Endurance was dead. The old man's broken words drew such a horrible picture. Her heart was filled with sorrow and anger. If she asked anyone the details of Endurance's death, she would bawl. She was too proud to let anyone see or hear her cry, so she kept running without turning back.

Endurance was weary by the time he reached the Yellow River, and he rested at the riverbank. He had finished the food given to him by Earthly Dragon a long time ago. He was very hungry and felt weak.

At last he forced himself to stand up and walked on until he saw the lodging post in the distance. He hid behind a tall pine when he saw a group of Mongols mounting their horses and heading his way. He shifted to the other side of the wide trunk when they passed him by. After ruling China for so many decades, all the Mongols had learned to speak Chinese, and the six of them were conversing in their adopted tongue. Endurance could hear them clearly, but was puzzled by what they said.

One of them was telling the others that there were indeed ghosts. When a Chinese died of hunger, his ghost came back to haunt the Mongols responsible for his death. The haunting was carried out in many strange ways, and one of them was making food disappear from a Mongol's hand.

When they were out of sight, Endurance came out of hiding and went to the garbage piled outside the post. He found many lamb bones with plenty of meat left on them. He gathered them up and walked away eating. He hummed a merry tune as he chewed, throwing away each bone as he finished. He blocked out the death of his family momentarily. Without the old monk nagging him, and knowing that he was on his way to his Peony, he was rather happy at this moment.

When night arrived, he rested at the edge of a pine forest beneath the open sky. He used old, soft pine needles as his bed, his folded arms his pillow. He looked over the treetops at the moonlit heaven, until his eyelids became too heavy.

The next morning, a wild rabbit jumped over Endurance and woke him. He wiped his face with his sleeve and picked up his bundle. Soon he entered the final village before Peony's and found himself walking behind a tofu peddler. He wanted to hit the man when he kept turning and eyeing him suspiciously, as if he would steal any of the tasteless soybean curd.

Walking through the village, he spotted among all the sod houses one beautified by a row of bright red azaleas. Right then he decided that when Peony and he were married, they would have a home like this, with azaleas planted all around.

He also noticed that almost every house had two cracked doors decorated with matching strips of faded red paper bearing last New Year's good-luck couplets written by the town's scholar. When he and Peony were married, he decided, he would want a couplet stating that their house would be the home of many children. At this thought Endurance laughed, and he entered Emerald Valley in high spirits.

His heart quickly sank, however, when he saw the destroyed village. Grabbing an old woman by her bony shoulders, he asked, "What happened?"

The woman stared in fright at him, then said that in the past few days the village had been attacked twice. The first assault had been caused by a peddler refusing to accept paper money from the Mongols, the second by a jade miner trying to sell a piece of jade on his own. The

last massacre had taken place only the morning
before. Besides the killing, the Mongols had
burned down every house in the village except
the Heavenly Temple.

Endurance asked the old woman about miner
Ma's family. The woman shook her white-haired
head and said, "Ma is such a common name.
There are more than twenty miner families by
that name. Now, let me go!"

Endurance released his hold on the old woman's shoulders, and she staggered away from the
village with the few things she had gathered in
her stick-like arms. She headed for the rope
bridge that would lead her first to the other side
of the Yellow River, then the mountain and the
sanctuary of the temple.

Endurance watched her go, then looked around.
She had to be the last person to leave. Except
for some people at the faraway riverbank, he was
standing alone among numerous piles of debris.
From each pile, fine threads of smoke rose and
danced like black ribbons in the wind. In that
moment Endurance thought of the red ribbons
entwined in Peony's hair. Trembling, he walked
toward the Ma house, feeling his heart beating
in his throat.

The three bodies he found were charred beyond recognition, but Endurance could still tell
that they were of a grown man, a grown woman,
and a young girl. No, he couldn't accept the fact
that they were the Ma couple and Peony. He
looked toward the temple half hidden in the
mountain, thinking to go and confirm the Ma
family's fate with the monks and nuns. But then
he thought of Earthly Dragon. All holy people
were the same. They would be just as nagging
as that old foolish monk.

He kept staring at the scorched limbs and
skulls until he was convinced that they were

Peony and her parents. In his imagination he heard them telling him how cruel it was to leave them lying like this.

He kneeled beside the bodies and broke down in sobs. In another few seconds, though, he caught himself and felt both ashamed and angry. He wiped his eyes with the back of his hand, then stood to his full massive height. He waved his fists at heaven and screamed. Again and again he shrieked, like a mighty beast in deadly pain.

When he became hoarse and tasted blood in his throat, he stopped screaming and sagged wearily, all hope gone from him. Finally he went to look for a hoe.

By Mongol dictate, ten families shared a hoe. He had to search many piles of burned things before finding one, though most of its handle was consumed by the flame. He buried the three bodies by the Ma house, then put the broken hoe in his pouch and bowed good-bye to the new graves.

He took a few steps, then stopped and turned to face the graves again. He lifted his face to the sky and shouted once more, "Peony! Your murder will not go unavenged! Do you hear me? I will avenge your death!"

His broken voice echoed throughout the valley, turning the heads of the people gathered on the riverbank. Their homemade lanterns glowed in a distance, reminding Endurance of his unfulfilled obligation to the Ma family. In a towering rage he charged toward the river.

He didn't have any money to buy the needed lanterns, and he certainly didn't feel like begging from strangers. He snatched three lanterns from the woman nearest to him, together with her fire starter, then fled. He kept running until he was far away. He squatted beside the water, lighted the slightly torn lanterns, and placed them on the river. With a broken heart he watched them drift away.

10

LOTUS LIN SAT before an oval-shaped mirror that was a sheet of well-polished brass in a gilded frame. Her face was painted red and white, her hair oiled, perfumed, and piled high. She was wearing many layers of a bridal gown, but still had many more articles of clothing to put on.

Looking up at the roomful of maids, she said, "You may leave now. Jasmine can help me with the rest."

When the other maids had gone, Jasmine helped her to dress. Her outermost red skirt contained exactly one hundred folds. Ten seed pearls adorned each fold to represent the bride's thousand virtues. Her topmost red garment was embroidered with one hundred golden chrysanthemums, each garnished with a small ruby in its center; they would bring her happiness for the next hundred years.

Her tiara was two feet high, embellished with manmade flowers using rubies and corals as petals and jade as leaves. Long strands of pearls hung from the front of the crown to form a veil. They were pinned to the sides now, but would be loosened later to cover the bride's face.

Nine rhymed with everlasting. Nine loops of solid gold chains hung from her neck. Nine butterflies were embroidered on each of her red

shoes. Nine rubies enhanced each of her ear-
rings, dangling to her shoulders.

"My great Buddha!" Jasmine sighed. "These
clothes weigh more than you do. How do they
expect you to move? I might as well carry you
on my back, my poor lady ..." Jasmine stopped,
noticing the tears in the eyes of a bride. "Thinking about your mother again?" she asked softly.

Lotus nodded silently, forced the tears away.

Mayor Lu had invited Lord and Lady Lin to
their daughter's wedding, but Lord Lin had declined the invitation and forbidden his wife to
attend.

A gong reverberated in the courtyard, soon followed by firecrackers. It was time for the wedding. Lotus looked at the moonless sky once
again. "Mama, I love you and miss you, and wish
you were here to share the most important day
in my life," she whispered.

Jasmine clapped her hands for the other maids
to enter. Supported by four of them, the bride
moved inch by inch toward the grand room.
When she lifted her head a little under the
weight of the tiara and peeked through the veil
of pearls, she saw a river of people in ceremonial
clothes of bright colors. There were many foreigners, and everyone was talking and laughing
and staring at her. She lowered her head and
walked on, looking at only her shoes.

The journey to the grand room seemed to be a
hundred miles long. The band of string instruments played on and on. Lotus was exhausted
when she finally stopped and saw a pair of men's
shoes beside her own.

The ceremony had been created during the
days of Confucius, and for over eighteen hundred years the same ritual had been carried out
faithfully. The man marrying the couple was a
gentleman scholar. He started by reminding the

groom and bride that in order to bring order to
the universe, one must begin with bringing order
to oneself.

Lotus heard an old voice, "Order can only be
maintained through obedience. One must obey
one's family and society, carry out one's everyday responsibilities and higher duties. Disobeying
one's superior is an unforgivable sin. A wife
should remember at all times that her husband
is superior to her ..."

Lotus's thoughts drifted to the day she had
left her mother, and she smiled. Wisdom would
never push her into disobeying him. He would
always be gentle and kind and loving, and she
would forever respect her lord. Her thumbs
roamed over the jade rings on her fingers. Wisdom had carved these rings for her since she had
moved into the Lu house. Lotus knew she was
marrying a scholar, a gentleman, a patriot, and
also a man of refinement.

After kowtowing to heaven, earth, the spirits
of their ancestors, and their relatives and guests,
Wisdom and Lotus were married. They were escorted to a newly decorated court that contained
many rooms and a walled garden, where they
would have dinner in their wedding chamber.
From tomorrow on, they would live under the
older lord and lady's supervision, but with plenty
of privacy. When their children were old enough
to run around, the young voices would not disturb the peace in the patriarch's court.

In the patriarch's court, the men and women
separated for dinner.

The guests included Chinese and Mongols,
overseas merchants and envoys, foreign mission-
aries and scholars. The courses were many, and
each had a special meaning: longevity, good luck,

prosperity, and happiness for the newlyweds
and everyone else.

While served by the singsong girls, the men
were also entertained by a program specially designed for this occasion. Monks entered the room
in two lines, one wearing orange robes, the other
yellow. They marched slowly with their heads
bowed. Their palms were pressed together and
their fingertips touched their chins. They formed
a circle in the center of the room, every yellow-
robed Taoist monk alternating with an orange-
robed Buddhist one. They turned their backs
toward the center of the circle, faced their
guests, and bowed deeply.

"Who are they?" an Englishman asked his
interpreter.

"Monks of Yin-tin," the interpreter answered.
"If you've been to the Purple Gold Mountain,
you must have noticed deep in the woods, far
from the Mongol governor's mansion, two ancient temples. The Buddhist one is called Peaceful Stars; the Taoist one, Silent Echo. Mayor Lu
is a generous patron to both temples. The monks
are here to show their appreciation—" He stopped
at a sudden movement of the monks.

They removed their robes at the same time
and placed their garments in the middle of the
circle in a neat pile. Underneath, they wore only
black pants and soft shoes. Their exposed upper
bodies caused the guests to gasp.

"I didn't know you southern Chinese were so
muscular!" A Mongol guest bolted upright with
feet together and fists on his hips. His outrage
changed to fear, though, as the peaceful looks
disappeared from the monks' faces. Their soft
features became hard. All the monks moved as
one. Each took a side step with his left foot as
his left fist opened and made a horizontal circle.
His right fist thrust forward, and the back of

his right hand faced upward. He looked straight ahead; his eyes sparkled with inner strength. The next moment his right leg kicked up and his left fist thrust forward, and he punched an invisible enemy with a deadly force.

Fast as the wind, every monk used his right foot to take a step forward and push off the ground for a high leap. When he was in midair, he rose his left knee and swung both arms forward and upward, making a loud threatening sound by hitting his left palm with the back of his right hand.

Still in flight, each monk kicked up his right foot vigorously with his toes pointed. He landed on his left foot soundlessly, and his right leg was still extended high above the ground. His eyes looked directly at the guests, challenging anyone to come forward to try their luck.

As the performance went on, the audience completely forgot the food on their plates.

The members of the Silent League exchanged understanding glances. They were patrons of the kung fu monks, and knew that the monks all over China had invented a way to defend their country. They alone noticed the fury in the monks' eyes: the fighting spirit of the Chinese could never be exterminated merely by taking their weapons away.

In the women's dining room, the ladies were entertained by a musical play called *Love in the Moonlit Chamber*, written by one of the many destitute scholars dismissed from the Mongol court and forced to make a living by writing for the general public.

"The leading lady is a great beauty!" a Turkish lady said.

Her interpreter said, "The leading lady is a man, and merely a slave in the Lu household."

She went on to explain that a rich family owned
many slaves who were purchased when they
were children. The better-looking boys were
taught to sing, dance, and act by an aged actor
who was also a part of the household; the homely
boys became servants. The slave girls were also
divided by their looks. The pretty ones became
concubines to the many lords, the plain ones
maids until old enough to marry male servants.

The play consisted of lyrical dialogue, beautiful songs, and graceful dances. All the ladies enjoyed it while eating—except one.

At age thirty-one, Sesame was like a flower
still in blossom that needs water to save it from
wilting. She needed happiness to enhance her
remaining beauty and stop her from withering.
Her green garment was better than the gray uniform of the maids, and she was eating instead of
waiting on tables. But she sat at a remote corner
unlit by the lamps, together with three other
women who were just as sad-looking but much
older. The older ones were the forgotten concubines of Mayor Lu, and Sesame had been the first
woman in Wisdom Lu's life.

She had been sold by her parents when she
was six. When Wisdom was born, she was thirteen, and she had helped the nanny to take care
of the baby. Since she was intelligent and pretty,
the lord and lady had made her Wisdom's concubine when he was two. Her new position had
guaranteed her a status higher than that of the
maids, and at the same time reassured the lord
and lady that she would devote her life to protecting and pleasing their son.

The young lords had to learn the art of pillowing, which was also called the melting of
clouds and creating of rain. Parents preferred
that their sons learn it from chosen concubines
who were healthy and uncontaminated. When

Wisdom reached fourteen, Mayor Lu told his aged concubine to teach the art to Sesame, who then taught it to the inexperienced young lord.

The tradition would continue, and the noble brides would always have well-practiced grooms. The concubine who had enlightened a young man's life, however, would languish into the background. And on his wedding day, she would have to hide her tears behind forced smiles.

Sesame picked at her dinner, picturing Wisdom in his wedding chamber, teaching the art he had learned from her to his virgin bride.

All the rituals had been performed, all the traditions obeyed. The attending maids had closed the doors behind them, and the bride and groom were finally alone.

Lotus's tiara and many layers of formal garments had been removed. She sat in a pink robe and faced the brass mirror, watching the reflection of Wisdom in a scarlet dressing gown. Her heart drummed in her ears. She had heard of the melting of clouds and creating of rain, but couldn't imagine what it was and why the strange name. In the mirror she saw her groom coming toward her, and her face burned. When she felt his hand on her shoulder, her entire body shook.

"I have a present for you," Wisdom said softly.

She looked up and saw in the mirror, he was holding a scroll. His expression was very calm. She turned slowly to face him.

As Wisdom unrolled the scroll, a drawing of two people appeared on rice paper. The lord resembled him; the lady, Lotus.

"You are a great artist," she said, starting to regain her composure. She turned to her jewel box, found the jade comb, stood up, and compared it with the drawing. "The drawing is even better than the etching on this comb," she said. "You really need to express your talent on a grander scale."

Already she was less frightened and shy. When Wisdom placed the scroll on the dresser and took her hand, her hand rested in his contentedly.

He said, "Someday I'll find a large piece of jade, and carve a pair of jade lovers." He led her toward the bed. "Like the etching and the drawing, the beautiful lady will be in your image, and the lord captured by her beauty will resemble me."

He pulled her gently to sit beside him on the bed, then began to remove her robe. Noticing that she had begun trembling again, he continued to talk about things unrelated to their wedding night. He said tenderly, "Jade is a precious stone that will never lose either its divine color or exquisite glow. The jade lovers will represent our eternal love."

He took her in his arms and softly kissed her cheeks, then her lips. He brought her down to rest her head on a pillow and shrugged his silk gown off at the same time. He removed her undergarments with his sensitive fingers but never touched her shoes. He had learned that a woman's feet were to be seen only when they were in bondage and neatly shod.

He leaned toward the pillow to kiss her again. His kisses became more passionate, and his stirring hands kindled the long-hidden lust in her young body.

Two individual clouds sailed across the sky. An invisible hand pulled them together. The man cloud moved carefully, wrapping himself around the woman cloud. With great patience he eventually merged with her.

The two became one, rolling across heaven.

The wind roared, the stars fell. The sun and
moon exchanged places, but the joined clouds
kept swirling high.

Thunder jolted them, and they trembled at the
same time. Lightning radiated around them, and
the earth vibrated underneath them until they
became still. At long last the combined clouds
began to dissolve, and gradually they turned into
warm raindrops that showered their wedding
bed.

PART II

11

A.D. *1345*

A MIDDLE-AGED MONGOL galloped on a tall
black stallion, followed by a long procession of
guards.

The wind parted Shadow Tamu's purple cape
lined with white fur, revealing a scarlet robe.
Around his waist was a wide belt and a large
shining buckle adorned with rubies and emer-
alds. Unlike the other dark Mongols, Shadow
Tamu's thin face was white, and so were his
heavily jeweled bony hands holding the reins.
His narrow lips were brown like dried blood, his
eyes deep and cold like bottomless holes filled
with dark ice. His eyebrows were black and gathered into one straight line as he looked at the far
end of the road.

"It's good to be back to Da-du!" Shadow said
to the nearest guard, kicked his horse, and raced
forward.

From a distance Shadow and his men could
see the sun reflecting from the gleaming roofs of
numerous buildings used for the worshiping of
the various gods: the round crowns of Moslem
mosques, the pointed peaks of Buddhist temples,
the curved crests of Taoist shrines, and the
crosses on top of the Roman Catholic chapels.
The Mongol khans were afraid of all gods, and
welcomed various religions to build their churches
in China.

Shadow Tamu and his guards reached the out-

ermost ring of Da-du's three sets of walls. These
four walls enclosing the city were each eight
miles long and contained two gates that were
guarded by Mongol soldiers at all times and
closed at nightfall.

Inside the gate was the section of town occupied by Mongol commoners and Chinese, filled
with shops, theaters, and eating places. Foreigners from Japan, Korea, Turkey, and many Euro-
pean countries roamed the streets, which were
wide and straight like lines on a chessboard. The
sound of many languages and the smells of various food filled the air.

Shadow and his guards hurried to the second
ring of walls, embracing the domain of the Mongol officers. In the middle of each of these four
walls stood an exquisite fortress, and at each of
the four corners was another fortress. In every
castle lived a Mongol general and his family plus
his soldiers and their families. There was ample
space left for their food storage, horses, military
supplies, and Chinese slaves.

At the sight of Shadow Tamu, the slaves got
down on their knees. The Mongol officers and
soldiers dropped whatever they were doing and
stiffly bowed with their left hands clasped over
their right fists. Nodding without looking at
them, Shadow Tamu rushed toward the innermost walls, guarding the imperial palace.

He and his men dismounted at the foot of a
high marble staircase and walked up to reach the
glistening double doors that were solid copper
and over thirty feet high. The soldiers inside had
seen Shadow Tamu from the many watchtowers.
Four of them opened the heavy doors and bowed,
waited for their lord and his guards to enter,
then bolted the engraved doors once more.

As Shadow strode rapidly toward the palace,
he looked up at the palace roof and his heart

beat faster. All this glory belonged to the great khan in name but was his in reality. He walked from one prince's court to another, passing many gardens in order to reach his own court, which was second only to the great khan's in size and extravagance. Once there, his escorts on the road were replaced by a new group of waiting men. They accompanied him into a marble-floored room where Shadow Tamu was undressed and bathed by his court ladies. He was massaged, rubbed with oil, and then dressed in fresh clothes. Standing along the walls, the guards watched two women sample the food served on gold plates, waited to be certain that nothing was poisoned. Shadow Tamu then enjoyed a full-course dinner. After resting, he finally left for the palace of the great khan.

The gilded ceiling of the royal court was over fifty feet high. Multicolored desert birds had been brought over from the Gobi Desert, and they were flying over people's heads and letting out wild cries. The marble floor was crowded with young girls dancing, slim young men tumbling, musicians playing different instruments, and singers crooning various songs.

On a red and gold brocade lounge chair stretched Great Khan Sandstorm. He was in his fifties, and his blue robe embroidered with gold and silver couldn't hide his layers of fat. His face was pale and puffy, his eyes bloodshot. It was hard to believe that at one time this man had fought and defeated his many uncles, brothers, and cousins to gain the throne.

"Ah, Shadow," he told his adviser, "I'm glad you have returned. How was your trip to Tsinan?" The khan was holding a golden cup in one hand and had his arm around a beautiful girl. Buddhism emphasized celibacy, but neither the

great khans nor their advisers ever observed this
part of the doctrine.

"My trip was not bad, but the canal is going
slowly," Shadow Tamu said. Straightening from
a brisk bow, he took the lounge chair next to the
khan's. He had gone to Tsinan to observe the
building of the Hui-tung Canal, which had been
started six decades before. The canal would
eventually link with the Yellow River and make
it easier to travel between Da-du and the rest of
China.

Several young girls quickly surrounded Shadow
Tamu. He allowed the two Mongol girls to sit
beside him and gestured for the remaining Chinese to sprawl at his feet. Unmarried, he had
many court ladies. He intended to marry the first
one who bore him a son, but so far he had produced no children. The Mongols respected their
women for having helped them to survive the
hard life in the desert land. As a result, Shadow
Tamu and his men placed Chinese women in a
position higher than that of Chinese men.

"Now that you are back, I need you to give me
some good advice," the khan said. "I am so
bored. Life is so dull, and I need something to
liven it up."

Shadow Tamu looked at the aged khan, whose
desire for lovely young women was endless.
"Like an autumn garden, my great khan's life
can be brightened only by spring flowers. I'll
send out search parties to comb China for maiden
girls, then bring them back and turn them into
court ladies. But if my great khan is tired of the
Chinese girls and interested in meeting the most
beautiful Mongol girl on earth ..." Shadow
Tamu paused to inflame the khan's curiosity.

"Of course I'm interested," he said impatiently. "Who is she? Where is she? When can I
have her?"

Shadow Tamu bowed once again. "Her name is Starlight, and she is still in Mongolia. My great khan can meet her by the next full moon if we send for her right away." The adviser looked at the khan and said slowly, "Starlight is my own baby sister."

His low voice was no longer hard and cold, but softened by devotion, warmed by deep concern. "My mother didn't want to stay in China after my father's death, and she went back to Mongolia, taking her two younger children with her. Starlight is thirteen years younger than I. She was only seven when we parted. I visit my family every few years, and I saw her beauty becoming more vivid each time. Now she is twenty and the most exquisite flower of the Gobi Desert. Since my mother is dead and Starlight has reached marriageable age, I would like to bring her back to China again."

Shadow Tamu didn't mention that he had saved his sister for just the sort of man who could be controlled by a clever, beautiful woman. His power was great already, but he wanted even more. He shrugged carelessly and said, "But of course my great khan is not obligated to keep her. If she should not please you, then I'll find her another husband."

The Khan Sandstorm expressed great enthusiasm at the idea of possessing a Mongolian beauty, then asked casually, "You said that your mother took two of your siblings back to Mongolia. Is the other one also a girl?"

"No," Shadow Tamu answered with another modest bow. "The other is a boy, ten years younger than I. His name is Mighty Sword, and he will escort Starlight to Da-du." He then added nonchalantly, "Mighty Sword can also be of great service to my great khan."

*   *   *

Starlight Tamu was a desert cactus, beautiful with poisonous thorns. She had pillowed her first man when she was fourteen, bedded many more since then. Her skills in the bedchamber matched her breathtaking beauty. With her in his bed, the aged Great Khan Sandstorm felt young. He was soon her slave. Customarily he had kept his court ladies in various palaces and sent for them alternately. Now he placed Starlight in his own court and desired no woman but her.

One evening, the khan entered Starlight's chamber and saw her stretched out on a lounge chair wearing a scarlet robe that barely concealed her seductive figure. Hurrying toward her, he took her in his arms.

She pushed him away. "Don't touch me when I'm unhappy."

He looked at her beautiful pouting face. "I'll kill whoever dared to upset you. And I'll get you anything to make you smile again."

Starlight took a deep breath that raised her full bosom, then gave a long sigh. "I'm homesick for the desert. Last night I dreamed of the pasture again. I was riding horseback, and the wind was blowing on my face. I was so happy in my dream. Then I woke up and realized I am in China—a hatefully crowded country."

She paused and looked at the khan with tearful eyes. "I want to go home—unless you can turn China into a riding field for me. My brother said you are the great khan and can do anything." She stopped with her wet lips parted sensually, waiting for the khan to answer.

Sandstorm put a hand on her breast, squeezed it passionately, and said without hesitation, "Your brother is absolutely right. I am the great khan, and China is mine." He then snapped his fingers.

Half a dozen guards appeared instantly. "Send for my adviser!"

Shadow Tamu had been waiting for the summons, but arrived with a surprised look. He listened to the khan carefully, pretending that he knew nothing of his sister's notion.

The khan's adviser had surveyed China on his many travels and realized that the poor farmers were making money for the wealthy landlords who should be forced into sharing their wealth with the Tamu family.

"Yes, my great khan, it can be done, but . . ." He made believe he was thinking hard. "The Chinese have become rather unruly in the past year. In order to destroy the existing farms and level them into pastures, we need a strong general to carry out such a command. We must find a young warrior who is capable of such an arduous task. Who can he be? Let me see . . ." He tapped his chin with his claw-like fingers, frowning deeply.

Sandstorm named a few warriors, but Shadow Tamu declined them one by one. Finally Starlight grew tired of waiting. "No warrior is as powerful as my brother Mighty Sword." She looked at the khan with her most convincing smile. "Send for him from Mongolia, and the problem is solved. I'll have my open range and stay in China forever."

Mighty Sword soon rode into Da-du, entering the palace walls on a mammoth black stallion. He wore a red cape, brass armor, and high boots. He carried a specially made bow and arrows over his shoulder, and held a heavy saber that had pierced the hearts of many men and animals alike. He was twenty-six and a handsome man, bulky in build and massive in height.

He had waited in the outskirts of Da-du for a long time to make his grand entrance, wanting to share his older brother's power and prosperity. Like Shadow, he was a good actor, and after listening to the great khan, he pretended that he was not eager to accept the offer.

"I'd hate to be kept away from my homeland," he said, uttering the rehearsed words as instructed by his brother. "I'll consider staying in China only if I'm granted the power to rule the entire Royal Army. I'll need a title such as the supreme general."

The Great Khan Sandstorm glanced from the forceful young warrior to the cunning adviser, debating if it was wise to allow the same family to hold so much power. He then looked at Starlight's gorgeous face and ravishing body. Pushing aside his doubts, he smiled at Starlight and sighed, "You are my woman. Your brothers are my brothers-in-law. I will trust the three of you."

The khan pronounced Mighty Sword Tamu the supreme general of the Royal Army. From that day on, China was ruled indirectly by Shadow Tamu, Starlight, and Mighty Sword.

12

AS SPRING REACHED its peak the surface of the Yellow River was once again showered with white and pink apple blossoms. On the outskirts of a farming village in Honan Province, eight weary young men staggered toward the river in the morning sun. Their rugged appearance frightened the young girls gathered underneath the blossoming trees. They grabbed their wash, carried their rattan baskets, and ran away screaming.

"Stupid girls! Why do you run from us? We are your own fellow countrymen, not the Mongols!"

Then the men saw their reflections in the soiled water. Their clothes were shabby, their sandals torn. Their faces were filthy, their hair matted, and their beards long. Most of them had open sores on their faces and bodies. Every one of them had the look of beasts who had grown accustomed to being hunted as prey.

They didn't waste much time looking at themselves. They fell to the ground, cupped their dirty hands to bring the muddy water to their chapped lips, and drank thirstily.

"That's enough," one of them ordered at length. "Drink more and you'll be sick."

To a man, they quickly stood up. They trusted Endurance Chu, who had proven his ability in leading them away from danger and harm.

"The village ahead seems to be a peaceful place. Maybe we'll be able to find food there ... one way or another," Endurance said, looking at the green field and small houses in the distance.

He had grown taller and bigger during the past year, regardless of the fact that he never had enough to eat. His seven starving friends looked like children next to him. They, too, were victims of a merciless fate which had taken away their homes and loved ones. None of them were willing to become monks, but all were determined to survive. Endurance had met the first one soon after he left Emerald Valley. They had walked alongside the Yellow River and shared each other's sorrow and fury. They had soon met the third one, and after that the fourth and fifth.

The eight of them decided to band together for support. Endurance was the biggest and strongest, and also the wisest and most inventive. His wit made him their protector and leader, and his physical power turned his words into law.

In the past year, the group had lived as beggars, thieves, and occasionally laborers when someone would give them work. Their means of filling their stomachs varied, but their progress ever southward was unchanged by the insistence of Endurance, who was determined to reach the Yangtze River. The group had never questioned him about their destination, the Kiangsi Province, which was more than seven hundred miles away.

"We'll find a town called the Phoenix Place, which is my family's original home. My father told me it's the most beautiful place in the whole of China, where the winters are mild and the summers long," Endurance had told them repeatedly throughout their slow journey. "Once there, we'll find steady jobs and settle down. We'll be ordinary citizens on the surface, while absorbing more men like ourselves to increase the size of our group. Someday we'll become strong enough to fight the Mongols and avenge the deaths of our families."

They left the riverbank and headed for the village. Everyone was weary, famished, and in need of some encouragement. Endurance looked up at the blue sky, breathed in the fragrance of the apple blossoms that lingered in the air. He told his friends once again about the south, remembering how his parents had described it.

"In the south, spring stays all year round, and the sky is always blue, the flowers forever in bloom. Do you hear the sparrows singing? In the south, they sing all year long—"

He stopped at the sound of horses tramping and people screaming. He gestured for his seven friends to hide behind large rocks that bordered the farmland.

They peeked out and saw a troop of Mongols arriving in the village on horseback. Their leader was a large man riding on a black stallion, wearing a scarlet cape and shining armor. His strong voice carried easily to where they were hiding. He shouted in Mongolian for his soldiers to work faster.

Countless rows of small houses were torched, numerous acres of neatly tilled farmland wrecked. Water buffalo were killed, men and women slaughtered, old and young slain. While screaming, the villagers fled in every direction but few escaped. The horses were fast in pursuing, and the riders were excellent ropers and archers.

"Hurry! You're as slow as a damn turtle!" En-

durance shouted to a young boy who was nearing
the rocks where he and his men were hiding.

The boy turned to look at his pursuers. Paralyzed with fear, he halted, and an arrow nar-
rowly missed him. Emerging from his hiding
place, Endurance dashed toward the boy, picked
him up, and ran back to the rock.

The terrified boy, thinking he had been captured by a Mongol, struggled and screamed, "Let
me go! You Mongol *guei-tze!*"

Endurance laughed as he put the boy down.
"You're a brave one. Peony used to call the Mongols *guei-tze* ..." He stopped and swallowed
hard. The memory of Peony lived in his heart at
all times. But he didn't like to mention her.
"What's your name?" he asked the boy.

"Longevity Ma," the boy answered, looking at
the eight rugged men, then toward the village.

"You even have her last name!" Endurance exclaimed, developing an instant fondness for the
boy. He put his big hand on the boy's small
frame and forced him to squat behind the rock.
"Don't look. If anyone in your family survives,
you'll see them later."

It was difficult for Endurance to restrain Longevity Ma from running back to his family. It
was even harder to keep himself and his seven
friends from charging into the village to give
their people a helping hand. "We can't waste our
lives uselessly," Endurance kept telling himself
and the others. "There are so many Mongols, and
only eight of us."

"No! Nine! I can fight, too!" Longevity Ma
glared at Endurance angrily. "How dare you forget counting me?"

"You have my Peony's temper, too!" Endurance mussed Longevity's hair, which was long
and hanging loose. "How old are you? Your hair
is not even braided into a queue yet."

"I'll be fourteen soon. I'm almost a man, and Mama promised to braid my hair on my coming birthday ..." Reminded of her, Longevity peered about to look for his mother. In response, Endurance roughly pulled Longevity to the ground.

The nine of them waited from morning until mid-afternoon. At last the Mongols left the village, leaving a cloud of yellow dust. Running through the dust, the nine young men searched for Longevity's family and any survivors.

Bodies of Chinese were everywhere either dead or dying, their blood soaking the earth. It did not take them long to find Longevity's mother, father, then brother and sister.

A dying old man recognized Longevity and struggled to speak. "It's our landlord's fault. The Mongols came a few days ago and demanded silver and gold. The landlord was scared, but too miserly to part with his money. The Mongols will be back with huge rollers pulled by horses. They'll use those stone rollers to flatten our village into a pasture. I heard them talk. You better bury the dead and run, and never to retu—" He abruptly slumped over, dead.

Endurance helped Longevity bury his family by the light of the setting sun, then took the boy as an additional member to his group. Walking beside the lad, he did not tell him that he had found the younger brother he had always wanted.

They had to sleep with their empty stomachs growling throughout the night. The next morning, they were weak from hunger by the time they reached a large town surrounded by many hills and a high mountain. They soon learned that Prosper Mountain was the largest city in the north of Honan Province.

"Look at the traffic," Endurance said, gazing at the many horses, mules, ox-pulled wagons, and people on foot. "We ought to find some food here. I'm so hungry I can barely lift my feet. I'm sure you're all as hungry as I."

At that instant a sedan chair passed them by. The curtain was lifted by a pale hand. A heavily painted face of a middle-aged woman appeared. She looked at the nine of them sharply, then whispered, "If you want food, come to the third house on the first street with a green lamp."

As the sedan chair went on, the men looked at one another.

Longevity said, "A green lamp house? I'd never go near it. Baba would beat me . . ." Then he remembered his father was dead.

"On the other hand," Endurance said, "Prostitutes can be nice people, too. That woman wants to give us food. Why should we refuse her help?" He looked at the alarmed boy and laughed. "You must go with us, and that's an order."

Upon entering the town square, they were fascinated by the bustling activity everywhere. All of them were village boys, and they had never seen so many shops and eating places on one street. Although it was only morning, they saw several houses with brightly lit green lamps. As soon as they reached the third one, the door opened and the woman who had rode in the sedan chair gestured for them to come in.

"Baba will be very upset in heaven," Longevity said, holding onto the door frame.

"If you don't let go of that door, I'll get very upset right here," Endurance said, raising his fist.

The woman led them to a kitchen. "Feed them until they can't eat any more, then give them some food for the road," she told an aged cook, then left.

The cook gave the nine hungry youths each a heaping bowl of noodles cooked in a thick meat sauce. "Our madame is a kindhearted lady," she said as she gathered wheat buns for them, wrapping them in large cabbage leaves. "But there is a sad story behind the reason of her wanting to feed you."

The woman sighed. "Madame's only child, a fine son, was already big and strong at fourteen, when the Mongols combed the town for young men to work on the Hui-tung Canal. They grabbed the boy. He escaped from the canal site in Tsinan, tried to come home. It was a long way, and he begged for food. When no one was willing to give him any, he had to steal. He was caught not far from here just when he was about to reach home. His hands were chopped off, and he died from bleeding. When our madame saw his mutilated arms, she swore to help all the Chinese young men who seemed to be running from the Mongols."

Their stomachs were full and their hearts filled with curiosity when they left the green lamp house at mid-morning, carrying the wheat buns. They wandered from one end of the street to another, looking at everything.

At one point they passed a fortune teller seated behind a small table. On it was a yellow bird in a cage and many paper scrolls piled in a plate, each the size of a needle. A woman stopped and put down a copper coin. The fortune teller released the trained bird and waited for it to pick up one of the scrolls with its beak.

"Very good luck," the fortune teller read after unrolling. "Provided that when the moon is full, you never go toward the south by southwest."

"South by southwest . . ." the woman repeated as she walked on, nodding her head. Her expression was so serious that the nine observers began to giggle like children.

Not far from the fortune teller's stand, a dentist was pulling a man's tooth. As the man screamed in pain, the dentist shouted over the din, "I told you it won't hurt at all! Try to remember that and you won't feel a thing!"

Endurance and his men laughed loudly. It felt so good to be able to laugh again.

"These Chinese are laughing at us!" a Mongol soldier said, appearing from behind the dentist's stand.

"We have to teach these filthy Chinese a lesson!" a second Mongol added.

Laughter froze in Endurance's throat. He looked around and saw over twenty Mongols materializing from all directions. "Run!" he ordered his friends, who were paralyzed by fright.

His powerful voice awoke them. They bolted into the crowd, and with their ragged clothing they immediately blended in with their wretched countrymen. The Mongols chasing after them soon became bewildered. All the Chinese looked the same.

Endurance was left unnoticed beside the dentist's stand. As a leader he was always the last to run. Seeing that his friends were safe, he was ready to take flight.

He felt someone poking his back. He turned and saw Longevity stand firmly behind him, pointing at the other end of the street. "That's the man who gave the order to kill my family!"

A black stallion was galloping their way. The rider's red cape flapped behind him in the wind. Staring at him, Endurance forgot to run. Most Mongols were big men, but this one was a giant.

Endurance observed his shining armor and high boots, weighty sword and enormous bow and arrows. When he looked at the rider's face, he couldn't look away. The man was more than handsome. He was arrogant and haughty. His eyes gleamed like the eyes of a wild beast, but he had the aura of a mighty lord.

Endurance hated him instantaneously, more than he ever hated any other Mongol. Besides being Endurance's enemy, this one also made him feel like a helpless rabbit in the presence of a vicious tiger. The feeling of inferiority burned into Endurance's heart.

Mighty Sword had just emerged from the largest green lamp house in town and was as yet unaware that his soldiers were chasing any Chinese. He would have never noticed these two pathetic figures if they had not been staring so openly at him.

Mighty Sword was not used to insolent Chinese staring at him. He ignored the skinny boy. But when he saw the defiance on Endurance's face, he curbed his horse.

Advancing slowly, Mighty Sword studied the young man whose powerful magnetism couldn't be concealed by his tattered clothes. The supreme general took in the young peasant's tall frame and powerful physique. He examined Endurance's dark face with the wide nose and thick lips. When he looked into those piercing eyes, he brought his horse to a halt.

The intense hatred in the eyes of this Chinese peasant sent a chill down his spine, though he was fully armed. The general felt himself shivering and was greatly irritated. "Who did you think you are? How dare you look at me like that?" he shouted, raising his sword.

The blade reflected the rays of the noonday sun, dazzling Endurance for a moment. Then he came to his senses and began to run, shouting to Longevity, "Come on! Follow me!"

Endurance dashed into the crowd. Like a chameleon, he quickly melted into a crowd of peddlers and shoppers. He was catching his breath when he noticed all the people around him still looking toward the dentist's stall. Looking back himself, he screamed, "Longevity!"

The boy was being held like a grasshopper in the Mongol general's massive hands. Mighty Sword, angered at having lost Endurance, had centered his frustration on Longevity.

His soldiers raced toward their general, waiting for orders. Mighty Sword tossed the child to the nearest man and barked between clenched teeth, "Kill this boy slowly, then cut off his head for public display!"

A spring moon rose slowly, shading an eerie light over the town square. Endurance and his seven friends had found one another and were now crouched low behind a crumbling wall.

One of them whispered, "We must lower his head from the pole, and take his body from under the platform. They need to be buried together. Otherwise poor Longevity will wander through the land of the dead blindly, forever searching for his head."

Endurance did not answer. His teeth were clenched tightly, and so were his fists. His eyes were dry, his tears in his heart. He looked past the people crowding the night street and the shops brightening it by lamplight. He had eyes only for a platform used for ceremonial purposes. The stage was dripping after having been washed recently with many buckets of water.

Endurance bit his lip as his gaze slowly drifted toward a tall bamboo pole at the back of the platform. In the moonlight, the pale pole was darkened near the top with splattered blood.

Endurance closed his eyes and heard once again the boy screaming throughout the afternoon while being tortured. The soldiers had tormented him skillfully. Every time the child neared death, they gave him time to recover to again feel the additional pain. The general had remained next to the platform with his back turned toward Longevity, searching the crowd for the boy's companion.

By that time Endurance had already located several of his friends. It took all their strength to wrestle him to the ground and hold him down while begging him to hush. When Endurance continued to roar, one of them had taken off his robe and gagged Endurance's mouth with the rag. He had pounded the ground with his fists as he heard Longevity screaming on and on.

Endurance looked at his bleeding fists. The Mongols were no longer by the platform, but they could be lingering in town, waiting to capture any fool who dared to touch Longevity's body or take his head down.

He looked at his seven friends and said, "Let's not do anything rash. Longevity is gone. Burying his head with his body won't help him rest in peace. We'll leave town during the night, and head for the south as planned. When we become a powerful group and slay these heartless Mongols, then Longevity will smile in the world of the dead."

The eight of them left Prosper Mountain when the moon was shrouded by a rising fog. Once out of the town square, they turned to look back. They still could see the top of the pole clearly.

Endurance was rooted to the spot. He saw the moonbeams filtering through the fog, embracing Longevity's disfigured face with their silver rays. Tears filled Endurance's eyes. In his blurred vision he saw Longevity smiling. Blood rushed to

Endurance's head. His ears drummed, and he heard a sound that resembled his little friend's innocent voice:

"My mother is here! Can't you see her loving arms holding me?" The words echoed in the passing wind. "All my suffering is over and forgotten. My large friend, please go on."

Endurance turned abruptly and walked away before his tears overwhelmed him.

13

THE SUN ROSE behind a high mountain and brightened the many hills that surrounded Prosper Mountain. A tall girl was marching toward the town square with her back straight and head high. Her tattered clothes were too short for her long legs, her ripped garment tight around her large bony frame. Peony Ma had continued to grow in the past year regardless of a lack of food.

She had stolen and cheated and lied to survive. Her large feet were bare, her shoes lost when fleeing a food peddler who threatened to kill her for stealing a bowl of noodles. She had walked many miles since then, and her once bleeding, aching feet were now calloused and hard.

At the edge of the town square, she stopped to watch some young girls washing clothes in a pond. She smiled, and her wide mouth opened to reveal her white teeth, contrasting with her dark face. She looked around with large round eyes but didn't spot a riverbank. Her smile broadened. It was so good to have finally left behind the miserable Yellow River.

She had traveled alongside its banks since leaving Pinetree Village, heading south. Every morning when she started on her way, she made sure that the sun was rising on her left. Her father had taught her to tell directions, and that knowledge had helped her escape the bloodstained land that held so many painful memories.

"It's more than painful. It's unbearable," she mumbled. "Baba and Mama and Endurance, I must get far, far away from the places where you were murdered."

She squinted as her eye fell on a deserted platform, trying to identify what was being displayed on top of a tall pole. She screamed when she recognized the object as a human head. She covered her mouth with the back of her hand, uncertain if it was her imagination or if the head was really smiling.

She edged forward, studying the disfigured face more closely. It was a child with long hair, whose ashen lips were parted to disclose a row of broken teeth, and whose vacant eyes were opened wide to stare at a shadow moon in the western sky.

A group of monks in orange robes appeared behind Peony, saw the head, and rushed toward the pole. Two of them started to pull the pole out of the ground. Two others spread a large kerchief on the platform, ready to wrap the head in it.

"Stop!" A dozen Mongol soldiers jumped out from nowhere, pointed their long swords at the monks. "Our supreme general has given his order to arrest whoever touches the head!"

All the monks froze. An aged monk with white eyebrows stepped forward. "My name is Peaceful Essence. I am the head monk in the Temple of White Crane." He pointed a hand at the faraway mountaintop, where a curved blue roof glittered above the tall pines. "Take me to your supreme general."

Curious, Peony waited with the other monks. The elderly monk soon returned with a proud smile. "Take the head down and remove the body from underneath the platform. We'll dig a grave for the poor child somewhere behind our temple."

After the monks carried the cadaver and its head back toward the hills, Peony turned her attention back to the new town.

She walked among horses and mules, ox-pulled wagons and people on foot. She stood beside the fortune teller for a while. She was so hungry that the little yellow bird looked very appetizing. When the fortune teller saw her gazing at his livelihood with her tongue hanging out, he shouted for her to go away.

Peony watched the dentist replacing a woman's missing tooth with a good tooth he had purchased from someone in need of money. The dentist looked at Peony, then asked her to open her mouth. She didn't realize what the man had in mind and did as she was told. When the dentist asked if she was interested in selling some of her perfect teeth, she ran away in horror.

Passing several doors hung with green lamps, she remembered how her mother used to warn her: if a girl pillowed with a man without marriage, a green lamp house would be her future home.

Outside the largest brothel was the stand of a hair vendor. Peony stopped to observe a young woman offering her hair. Regardless of her shabby clothes, the peasant's waist-length hair hung like black strands of silk. When the peddler raised his large scissors, the destitute woman closed her eyes. In only a few moments all the hair had been cropped off. Taking a prepared kerchief out of her pocket to cover her unsightly head, the woman sobbed, "Now my babies will not starve to death . . . not for a while, anyway."

Peony touched her own hair. The red ribbon intertwined with her braid had turned into filthy shreds of gray. She pulled off the willow twig that held her braids over her head to form a crown. Her long braid fell to her hips.

Knowing that her hair was her only good feature, she had washed it daily in the river. She hadn't realized until this moment that her looks no longer mattered. Endurance was dead, and she had no intention of pleasing any other man.

"How much would you give me for my hair?" she asked the vendor.

"Five copper coins," he said, trying to hide his delight. Peony's hair shone like the surface of a black pearl. A rich lady with thinning hair would be glad to pay a fortune for a wig made out of such splendid strands.

"That'll buy me enough wheat buns for ten days," Peony said and undid her braid. Just when her hair was hanging loose, though, a group of Mongol soldiers came out of the house with the green lamp.

Half of them had been assigned to watch the platform, the other half to guard their supreme general inside the brothel. These were drunk, and in their state they saw not Peony's dirty face or ragged clothes, but her young body adorned with a gorgeously sparkling mane.

Peony screamed when the first soldier laid a hand on her shoulder. She started to kick and bite when the second one grabbed her breast. Her sharp teeth sank first into the hand on her breast and then the hand on her shoulder.

The two soldiers were sobered by the pain. In turn, the peddler was stunned by the tall girl's bravery. Seeing the large shears in the peddler's shaking hand, Peony seized it before any of the soldiers had a chance to knock her down. She pointed her new weapon at the soldiers and backed away. "If you chase me, I'll poke out your eyes!" She yelled and then suddenly turned and sprinted away.

She was out of breath when she reached the first foothill. Climbing to its top, she rested behind a tall pine until her sides stopped hurting. She climbed the next knoll and then the next, all the time aiming for the blue-tiled roof on the high mountain.

The night wind whistled through the towering pines that encircled the Temple of White Crane. It sounded like someone wailing in Peony's dream. She opened her eyes and sat up quickly, looking at the dark room, listening to a roomful of women breathing in their sleep.

She gradually became fully awake, not feeling the usual pangs when she woke up. The nuns had fed her, and clothed her with a set of peasant clothes that were clean and only slightly torn.

Moonlight sifted through the rice paper on the window, shining on the other twenty-three figures on straw mats. Peony remembered what Peaceful Essence had told her: they all needed shelter as much as she. Peony knew that these women would soon become nuns to avoid facing the outside world. She sighed. At this moment, she too, regardless of all the strict rules imposed on the nuns, was tempted to make this place her permanent home.

In the past year she had taken shelter in temples now and then. Each time when she regained her physical strength, she had returned to the road. "But I am becoming too weary to struggle on my own," she whispered. Sighing again, she lifted her eyes to the window.

At first she thought she saw the shadow of a pine tree. But then she remembered that only a moment ago she had seen no shadow. Pines did not come and go.

As she stared, the shadow began to move. "A crane!" Peony gasped.

The noble creature spread its wings and flapped them slowly in the most graceful motion Peony ever saw. It then turned and began to glide farther from the window and nearer to the moon. As it did, more of its body was revealed.

"The crane has a human's head!" Peony gasped once again and stood up.

By the time she was dressed, the crane was gone. Long did she gaze at the moonlit window before she remembered that on the other side was an open court. She made her way silently through the sleeping women.

A statue of Buddha guarded the courtyard. Standing behind it, Peony looked at the monks scattered from the brick court to the hilly ground beyond. There were so many of them that Peony was certain every monk in the temple was present. Their long robes had been removed. They had on baggy pants, soft shoes, and short garments with wide sleeves.

As she watched, they spread their arms slowly and their weightless sleeves fluttered in the wind. "I found my cranes!" she whispered.

As soon as the words left her mouth, all the monks stiffened.

"Someone's spying on us!" a young monk said.

Peony didn't hear anyone stir, but the next moment she was a prisoner restrained by iron fingers and steel arms. She struggled but couldn't free herself to the slightest degree. She couldn't even scream. A hand, cold and hard, had sealed her lips with its open palm.

She was lifted off the ground, and she felt herself sailing across the courtyard in the hands of several monks. They put her on her feet again when she was face-to-face with Peaceful Essence.

The moon shone on the old monk's white eyebrows, which were bunched together in a frown. He shook his head slowly and said, "I knew you were nothing but trouble when you showed me the scissors you had. I should have known that a girl who dared to threaten the Mongols would roam around my temple in the middle of the night. You give me no choice. I must send you away. When morning comes, you'll leave with a string of coins and a bag of food."

Having been freed, Peony rubbed her arms and muttered, "I was ready to go anyway. To be a nun and follow those silly rules are too much work for a roof over my head and some food in my stomach. By the way, could I have a big meal before I leave? Also, I want those scissors back. I may need it again some time."

She tilted her head, thinking how convenient it would be if she could move as quickly and soundlessly as the monks. She would be able to steal food and clothes and anything else she wanted, then just disappear like the wind.

Peaceful Essence nodded. "You'll get a full meal and your scissors back. But you must promise that you'll never tell anyone what you saw tonight."

Peony looked into the old monk's eyes and caught a glimpse of uneasiness. While traveling, she had learned that a new law had been proclaimed that forbade Chinese fighting techniques in any form. She added up the facts swiftly. She leaned closer to Peaceful Essence, studied his face carefully to confirm her suspicion. Yes, the old man was truly worried.

Peony smiled. She stepped back, squared her shoulders, announced calmly, "My honorable *shih-fu*, I have changed my mind."

"What do you mean?" The old monk scowled deeply. His expression no longer suited his name.

"I want to stay here and learn what you were doing. But I don't want to become a nun, or be shaved and restricted by rules." Peony bowed deeply, then continued with a broad smile, "I don't dare to threaten you, my honorable *shih-fu*. But I do have a big mouth. It's really dangerous for me to leave your temple and tell tales all over Prosper Mountain. I believe the Mongols are still there."

The monks behind her moved closer threateningly. Seeing them out of the corner of her eye, she raised her voice, "Of course, you can shut me up easily and permanently. You can kill me and bury me next to the child's new grave. The Mongols have already killed everyone in my family. I'm only a poor girl who has nothing to live for anyway." Her voice became tearful toward the end. It was easy to do. She didn't really have to pretend.

Peaceful Essence lifted his eyes to the moon, shaking his head and sighing helplessly.

Peony was allowed to participate that very same night, but not with the monks in the courtyard. She was shown to an inner court, where six young monks new in the temple were taking their first lesson.

The instructor, a monk in his thirties, was unhappy to have Peony as a pupil, but accepted his lot like a good monk should. He even repeated the beginning of the lesson for her.

He said, "What you are about to learn is called tai chi fist, the fist of ultimate extreme. It is the softest style among various forms of kung fu, and practically the most powerful. It was created just before the Mongols took over China, as a form of physical exercise for the Shaolin monks. But the Mongols forced us to change and expand the purpose of the fist."

The moonlight betrayed the wrath in the middle-aged monk's eyes. He closed his eyes briefly. When he opened them again, the rage was gone and he looked peaceful once again. He went on, "It is the combination of the mental and the physical. You must concentrate and use your internal force as a source of your movements."

Peony learned to stand erect with both hands at her sides. She was told to relax and breathe evenly. With her heels lightly touching, she bent her knees and separated her feet to shoulder width. She sank gradually until her bottom almost touched the ground, then straightened slowly and smoothly. She lifted her arms gently in front of her to shoulder height, with her palms facing down. She brought her arms back to her sides and repeated the process again and again.

"The next move is called patting a bird's tail," the instructor said and demonstrated the movement. "Reach up with your left hand and see in your mind's eye that you're holding a fragile bird's dainty neck. Then move your right hand gently downward, to smooth the soft feathers on the bird's exquisite long tail. Slowly, very slowly, shift your weight to your left leg."

Peony followed the monk's instruction and soon found herself sweating. She closed her eyes and remembered that many years ago, when the Chu and Ma families met, Endurance had captured a bird and given it to her as a present. She now pretended that she was holding the same bird in her palm again. She stroke the fluffy feathers and savored its downy touch. She opened her eyes and saw her teacher nodding with approval.

To Peony's disappointment, the tai chi fist

could not be learned either easily or quickly. For the next year she stayed in the Temple of White Crane, helping the nuns cook and clean during the day. Every night she joined the six young monks to practice the high form fist that was the basic movements, until she was promoted to the advanced group who practiced the low form fist, which was very demanding and strenuous.

When the spring of 1346 arrived, Peony had mastered thirty out of the hundred different forms. She still couldn't move as fast and silently as the monks, but was considered quite good in her skills. One night, when the advanced class was practicing again under the spring moon, she finally did the White Crane steps correctly. She was so thrilled that she threw her arms around the nearest monk and shouted, "I'm so happy!"

All the monks halted in mid-step. No one made a sound. The monk embraced by Peony blushed like he was on fire. Peaceful Essence ended the practice and ordered Peony to her room.

Before she could say a word, the monk was already shaking his head firmly. "You can promise never to hug a monk again, and I'm sure you'll remember your promise. But that will not be enough."

The old monk furrowed his white eyebrows, studied Peony's youthful body like a father examining a grown daughter. Peony had been eating regularly and was no longer skinny. Revealed through her many layers of peasent garments, her figure reminded the old monk of a big juicy apple. All monks were but normal men, born to know hunger, thirst, and lust. While looking at such a delicious piece of fruit, the young monks could easily forget their vows.

"You are the only woman in this temple who

is not a nun. You are disturbing the younger brothers, especially during the practice of tai chi fist, when physical contact is unavoidable."

He leaned toward Peony and announced, "If you are still unwilling to become a nun, then you must leave. Please realize that it will be useless to threaten me this time."

Peony stared at the old monk challengingly, but when he did not look away, she smiled and nodded. "I'll make things easy for you and leave immediately." She bowed deeply to the monk whom she had come to respect highly. "Everyone here has been good to me, and I am very grateful. My honorable *shih-fu*, I want you to know that a year ago, even if you had refused to teach me tai chi and forced me to leave, I would have never reported you to the Mongols."

Peaceful Essence nodded calmly. "I knew. And so did the other monks. Otherwise you would have been buried beside that decapitated child." The monk smiled at the surprised girl. "Don't forget to get your last free meal and a string of coins for the road. But I won't give you back that big pair of scissors. With your tai chi, you no longer need a weapon to defend yourself."

14

THE JAIL HOUSE in Prosper Mountain was a brick building that contained only one sizable room for all the male prisoners. The majority of them were caught and sentenced in smaller villages in Honan Province, then transferred here. A Mongol execution team arrived every full moon to hang those sentenced to death and carry out the lesser punishments.

If Jailor Li and his wife had been heartless, their job would have been easy. They never had to worry that their prisoners might have enough strength to rebel or escape. These men had been treated roughly during their transferral. Regardless of the distance, they had walked as their escorts rode on horseback. When they arrived at Prosper Mountain, most were almost dead. But Jailor Li and his wife were far from heartless. Both Chinese, she cooked for the jailed men, and he made sure that no one committed suicide.

That night Jailor Li and his wife had done their day's work and the prisoners were asleep. The couple sat in their resting area, separated from the big room by many thick wooden posts. Glancing out the open window, they saw that the spring moon was a thin wedge: the prisoners had more than ten days before the executioners arrived. They exchanged a sad glance, then looked past the bars toward those sentenced to death.

There were scholars accused of organizing rebel groups and farmers guilty of not paying taxes with crops that they did not have. There were miners caught owning mining tools that could be used as deadly weapons rather than using those tools to be shared by ten miners or more. There were also villagers condemned for walking in the streets at night, and small merchants arrested for owning horses or mules, which Mongols alone were now allowed to own.

"I wish we could make a living by doing something else. Sometimes I have the strongest urge to open the prison door and set all the innocent men free," Jailor Li said.

The jailor's wife nodded, then looked toward the far end of the crowded room. Eight young men lay close to one another, each bearing marks of torture and signs of starvation.

"The big one," she said, pointing at a prisoner sleeping with his bony, well-flogged back toward them. "If our son had lived, he would have looked very much like him. You don't see many young men as extraordinary as him. Those straight black eyebrows. That wide nose. Every time I look into those piercing eyes, I see our son alive again. Whenever he opens his thick lips, I can hear our son calling me Mama." The jailor's wife wiped her eyes at the memory of her boy, killed during a Mongol raid.

Jailor Li sighed. Almost a year ago, the eight young men had been caught stealing steamed buns thirty miles south. On their way to Prosper Mountain, they had passed through one prison after another. The various jailors were all Chinese, but none of them kind. Each had seen the young men as free laborers for themselves and their town, and had kept the eight longer than necessary to work them hard. When they had arrived at Prosper Mountain three days before, tied together with chains around their ankles and a long leather rope around their necks, they had been barely alive.

Jailor Li said to his wife, "Well, don't worry. They are sentenced neither to death nor to have their hands chopped off."

His wife shook her head. "When their sentences are carried out, though, they would rather be dead." She covered her face with her hands. "I know our son would, if he were in their place." She shook her head vigorously and muttered stubbornly, "I don't think I can stand watching it. Not that big one. I'll feel the punished one is not him but our boy!"

At the far end of the jail, Endurance lay fully awake. He was too depressed and furious to sleep. He had overestimated his strength. Mongol soldiers were not like the village youths he used to defeat. For a year, he and his men had lived in hell and not been able to find a way out. They had been eight little ants trying to go south, only to be scooped up by a naughty child named Fate, toyed, tormented, and then tossed back north.

"You won't beat me! I'll triumph yet!" Endurance vowed. But doubt lay heavy on his soul. He had already spent an entire year trying to escape.

Outside the jail, a tall girl leaned against the wall to rest her tired feet. Peony had left the Temple of White Crane immediately as she had promised Peaceful Essence. She had descended the hills and entered Prosper Mountain in the moonlight. She had not forgotten what happened to her the last time in this town.

Peony smiled. A jail house ought to be the best protection for a girl. Even drunken Mongols would not rape a girl right under the eaves of a jail.

She had coins and food in her pouch. Her garments were not torn, and her stomach was full. Besides, she knew tai chi. Although Peaceful Essence had made her promise never to use it unless absolutely necessary, she would certainly defend herself if attacked.

Peony hesitated as she wondered where to go next. After living in the temple for a year, she had grown accustomed to having a roof over her head and three meals a day. She no longer wished to keep drifting from town to town. She decided to find a job. She could cook and clean house. She had learned to sew rather well in the temple.

By staying in Prosper Mountain, she could revisit the temple. That way she could continue her tai chi lessons. As merely a visitor to the temple, she should not bother the young monks too much.

Peony's eyes brightened at a brilliant idea: she could teach tai chi to the nuns and practice with them.

As the crescent moon slowly passed to full, Peony gradually became disheartened. Every day she looked for work, but no place would hire her except one of the green lamp houses. The madame thought that Peony might attract the Mongols, who liked big girls.

"When I join Endurance in the otherworld, I must be able to face him with pride," Peony told the madame. "How can I explain to him that many men have touched me?"

She returned to the jail house every night, to sleep on the ground and be sheltered by the broad overhang of the prison roof. She often heard the prisoners moaning inside. She felt sorry for them, and realized that when compared to them, she was fortunate.

When the moon turned full, Peony's food was all gone and her last coin spent. She was truly worried about her future now. She prayed to the Moon Buddha every night, asking for a steady home in this town.

On the morning after the full moon, an execution team arrived on horseback. There were twenty Mongol soldiers wearing pointed metal hats and high boots with pointed toes: They drank and ate the wine and food offered by Jailor Li and his wife, then started to work.

Six hanging posts stood behind the prison. More than thirty prisoners awaited their turns. People swarmed around the posts. Some were Prosper Mountain people, most had traveled afar. The grief-stricken ones had journeyed to watch their loved ones die and collect the bodies. The nonchalant had come for the entertainment. The prison area was a swarm of noise and movement, and when the first round of six men were hung, it became worse.

All eyes were focused on the kicking feet, the twisting bodies, the flailing arms, the tormented faces. Even the remaining prisoners gathered at the two high windows in the back, trying to look out on tiptoes.

Suddenly Endurance felt someone tugging his arm. Turning, he saw Jailor Li's wife standing behind him. She put a finger over her lips, then pointed at his neck and ankle. After so much numbing torture, he hadn't noticed until now that she had, during the confusion, freed him from the leather rope and metal chain.

She handed him a bundle of old clothes and pointed at a door leading to the jailors' living quarters. Endurance looked at his seven friends

at the back windows and hesitated. The jailor's
wife had given him a chance to defeat fate. He
must grasp the chance. He moved to the door
quietly and quickly, although his heart was
heavy with guilt. Only the knowledge that his
friends were not sentenced to death kept him
from turning back.

The door opened at his touch. Closing it behind him, he quickly began to dress. He was surprised to see that these faded old clothes were
neither too short nor too small, and that the
shoes fit his large feet perfectly.

After the last hanging was completed, the executioners continued with the lesser punishments.

There were a few Mongol prisoners, who had
been brought to the jail house in wagons. None
of them bore the slightest mark of torture. Jailor
Li and his wife had kept them separated from
the Chinese prisoners in a corner where the
ground was covered with straw mats, and served
them better rations.

All the Mongols were guilty of murder. Those
whose victims were Mongols or other non-Chinese,
were fined forty pieces of gold for each killing.
But when their victim was a Chinese, the payment was reduced to either a donkey or its
equivalent.

The executioners collected the fines, patted
the prisoners on their shoulders, then let them
go and wished them better luck the next time.

Then they ordered that the convicted thieves
be brought to the town square.

Among the twenty-nine of them, seven were
puzzled. They kept looking around, as if searching for someone. They exchanged baffled glances,
then shook their heads when none of them could
solve the mystery. Their curiosity was ended by

the executioner's loud voice: "Bring the tattoo artist!"

An old villager appeared among the crowd, carrying a tool box. He bowed to the Mongols, but did not look at the prisoners. His hatred for his job was written clearly on his lined face. Tattooing had been a bodily adornment for the Chinese for five hundred years, but the Mongols had changed the ornamental art into a punishment.

"No! Kill me! Please! I'd rather die!" one of the twenty-nine young men screamed when he was freed from bondage, brought to the platform, and forced to ascend the steps. Two soldiers held his arms, another two his legs. It took four more to steady his shoulders and head. "No! I'd rather die! Please kill me!" the young man continued to scream.

One of the soldiers yelled loudly, "Why do you think we invented this punishment? We know that to you Chinese, face is more important than life!"

The tattoo artist began to work. The young prisoner's screams filled the town, reached the surrounding mountains, reverberated from hill to hill. The word *thief* was tattooed on his face three times, one on his forehead, two on each of his cheeks. After black ink was poured into the wounds, the young man covered his bleeding cheeks and ran. Even when he was only a moving dot disappearing on the horizon, his screams still could be heard.

Three more were tattooed. Afterward one searched for a tree to hang himself, two headed for the nearest bank of the Yellow River.

All the prisoners resisted the tattooing, but none as vigorously as the seven men who had searched for their lost friend. Their friend Endurance had taught them to be proud and brave. They had spent two years with him; the first

year much better than the second. They were
loyal to him enough to keep quiet about his mysterious disappearance. They believed that if he
could have taken any of them with him, he
would. They were happy for his being spared
from a shame harder to bear than death.

"You'll have to kill me before you mark me for
life with that shameful word!" The first of the
seven charged toward the Mongol soldiers when
it was his turn to be tattooed. He kicked and
scratched the soldiers until he was knocked
down.

He gave them no choice. They killed him, cut
off his head, and placed it on a tall pole for
display.

The remaining six looked up at their friend,
then attacked the Mongols at the same time regardless of the fact that they were still tied together. The leather rope around their throats
choked them. They then tripped over the chains
on their ankles. Their stupidity infuriated the
Mongols. One by one they were led to the platform, tattooed first, forced to look into a brass
mirror to see the word *thief* on their foreheads
and cheeks, then beheaded immediately.

Each of them was told just before the execution, "Now you'll know that even in the world of
the dead, you shall lose face and walk in shame!"

Since there was only one pole for head displaying, the six new heads were placed in a row
at the edge of the platform, facing the audience.
No more prisoners dared to resist the tattoo. The
crowd watched in silence.

Jailor Li and his wife nodded at each other:
they had done the right thing by freeing the big
man who resembled their son.

Far from the platform and close to the market,
a big man in peasant clothes stood staring at the

tall pole. His eyes were dry, but his lower lip was bleeding from being bit so fiercely.

"My friends and my brothers, I'll avenge your death, I swear!" Endurance said, then turned and walked into the market. Until this moment the Mongols had not counted their prisoners. But Endurance would not rely on his luck.

The market was usually an ideal place for hiding. However, since most of the people were at the town square, the market was less crowded than Endurance would have liked. He lingered among the peddlers and shoppers, waiting patiently for night to fall. The soldiers should be gone then, and then it would be safe for him to leave Prosper Mountain.

Glancing toward the end of the market, he happened to notice several stables: oxen, horses, mules, and lambs. Attracted by an unusual sight, he craned his neck to look at the stable farthest away, then shook his head in disgust. It was a stable for human beings.

Unlike the other stables, the gate to the human stable was unlocked, and there was no vender. Instead of hay, the ground was covered with straw mats. While other animals were being sold by their owners, humans were selling themselves or their children and babies.

Endurance frowned at the adults standing in the stable and calling out prices for themselves. He was sickened at the parents holding the hands of their children or carrying their babies, begging the rich to buy their young.

Endurance would never sell himself, he had decided long before. He knew that once sold, these people became the equivalent of water buffalo and donkeys on two legs. They had to do whatever they were told just for a roof over their heads and enough food to keep alive. Their owners would have the right to work them hard and beat them mercilessly. Besides being servants, many of them would be used as concubines or male prostitutes. And when a master killed his slave, he was no more guilty than if he had killed an animal. Endurance turned away from the human stable, clenching his fists.

Peony stared at the gate of the human stable for a long while, then put her hand on the hempen loop that tied the gate to a post.

She had left the prison ground before the Mongols arrived. She had no desire to watch either the hanging or the tattooing. She had stayed away from the town square the entire morning.

With her hand on the loop, she looked in. Her heart ached at the sight of parents selling their children. She glanced at the adults selling themselves. In tattered clothes, they knelt with their heads bowed.

"I am for sale. Please buy me, my kind lords and ladies. I'll be your faithful servant. You don't have to pay me. Just give me a place to sleep and enough to eat. I don't eat much either . . ." they begged.

Peony stamped her foot with determination, then lifted the loop and opened the gate. She stepped into the stable and pushed aside the others to give herself a better position. She could not force herself to kneel. She stood proud and tall. She did not feel like bowing her head. She held her head high and looked at every passerby with her large round eyes.

She opened her mouth wide and raised her voice to call out her ware with pride. "It's your lucky day, my lords and ladies. You'll have the strongest maid you ever had in your entire life. But you'll have to pay me enough money, because I need some new clothes . . . what I have on is smelly and torn. I also need new shoes . . .

look at my big feet with their toes sticking out! I'll work hard for you if you'll treat me right, otherwise it's you who will be sorry. And I must warn you—I eat a lot!"

A sedan chair carried by four men stopped abruptly in front of the stable. The silk curtain was pushed aside by a delicate hand. The occupant could not see, but wanted very much to hear the unusual sales speech more clearly.

When Peony stopped speaking, the lady laughed from inside the sedan chair, and then asked her sedan carriers in a kind voice, "Does this girl look like she is strong enough to help a blind woman around?"

Endurance stopped at an old pine east of Prosper Mountain, lifted his face to the spring sun, then breathed in deeply the fragrance of freedom.

"What make you so happy in a world so filled with sorrow?" a hoarse voice asked weakly.

Endurance jumped back, then relaxed when he saw an old man appearing from the other side of the tree trunk. He looked into the man's cloudy eyes and answered, "I am only eighteen. I am still young." He felt his bony left arm with his other hand. "I'll regain my muscle and my strength." He reached his hand to feel the scars on his back. "My wounds will heal, too." His eyes darkened, though, when he thought of all the loved ones he had lost. "I have much to do." A hard and cold glow appeared in his piercing eyes. "And I will do it when I am strong and ready."

The old man nodded but did not understand. He looked at the young man's tall frame and said, "Ah, you must be going to the Chi-chou Canal."

"And what is that?" Endurance asked.

The old man pointed toward the far east and said, "Hush and listen."

Endurance became still, and soon he heard a pounding sound, like hoes digging into the ground. "What is that?"

The old man said, "My four sons. They are tall boys, big, too. The Mongols have run out of captured coolies and begun to hire workers. They hire only hardy men for the canal job. You see, the canal goes north to meet the Yellow River, and south to join the River Yangtze ..."

Endurance interrupted, "You mean, by working on the Chi-chou Canal, your sons are going south?"

The old man nodded again, staring at the horizon with his misty eyes. "When they were not far from here, I visited them. They are fed three times a day, so they can have enough energy to dig fast. They sleep on the ground at night. They are farther south each day ..." The old man stopped, amazed to see the young man running toward the distant sound.

By the time the moon had become full again, Endurance had adjusted to the strenuous toil of digging. These days he could keep bending and straightening his body from morning till night without feeling as if his back was breaking. The blisters on his palms had turned into thick calluses. The muscles on his arms and shoulders no longer ached when he lifted the heavy hoe.

The Mongol foremen noticed Endurance's increasing strength, and when he grabbed more wheat buns and barley gruel than his share, they pretended that they did not see it. The Supreme General Mighty Sword had set a deadline for the canal to reach Yin-tin City, and the foremen needed more workers like Endurance Chu to meet that deadline.

Endurance had caught sight of Mighty Sword right after he was hired for the job. The supreme general had arrived with his guards to inspect the construction site. Endurance had quickly bowed his head and kept it averted until the general had left. He had learned his lesson at the price of Longevity Ma's life. He was certain that the general would recognize him if the two should ever meet again.

Because the deadline was drawing nigh, the coolies were forced to work under the spring moon. Mighty Sword and his soldiers appeared for another unannounced inspection. Endurance clenched his teeth, dug his fingernails deep into the handle of his hoe. He did not raise his head until he heard the horses tramping away.

Mighty Sword's stallion glistened in the moonlight as if carved out of black ebony. The general's red cape flapped behind him in the night wind. In Endurance's eyes the fluttering red was a flowing river of blood: it contained the blood of his Peony and his parents, the boy Longevity and his seven unfortunate friends.

15

1346, Yin-tin City

THE SUN ROSE behind the Purple Gold Mountain, a soft yellow globe for a brief moment that transformed into a fireball. It flared over the Mongol governor's palace-like home, blazed above the Lu mansion, scalding the exposed skin of the peasants who had been standing in line since the moon was still high.

"I still feel guilty for throwing rocks at the mayor's son that time," one of them told another. "I thought then that the mayor was a collaborator. But in the past two years he and his son have kept lowering the rents and interest rates, and saved many of us from the Mongol persecution. And they've risked their lives doing it, as we all know."

"I wish the mayor could hold his position forever. Maybe even become the governor someday. Or, if this rumor about his poor health is true, let's pray that his kind son will take over."

The peasants stopped talking when Wisdom Lu appeared. A pale yellow robe concealed his delicate frame. A dark yellow hat protected his fragile skin. At twenty, Wisdom had the matured look of an older man. Compassion glowed in his sword-shaped slanting eyes as he looked at the poor.

"Bring out tea," he ordered the servants who were transporting buckets of steamed rice and soybean milk. He then took out of his pocket a

143

silk handkerchief to wipe his moistened brow.
"And put up some kind of shade along this
wall."

When the servants had set off on these new
duties, Wisdom rolled up his wide sleeves and
picked up the wooden rice ladle with his dainty
fingers. He ladled out the steaming hot rice, filling the containers held in the hands of the poor.

"The great Buddha will reward you for such
kindness, Lord Lu," a peasant said, bowing as he
received the rice.

Wisdom smiled but could not spare the energy
for conversation. His arm was only used to holding either a pair of chopsticks or an ink brush.
To dig into the solid rice quickly sapped his
strength. The ladle became heavier with each
additional scoop. The hot steam rose from the
rice and burned his hand. He passed the ladle
to his left hand to give his right arm a rest, but
his left was even weaker. He sighed helplessly.

He was exhausted when the servants returned.
Giving the ladle to one of them, he stepped aside
and leaned against a marble lion to rest. Wisdom's valet noticed the young master's flushing
face, dropped the building material he was holding, and came to Wisdom with a fan.

Standing in the shade, being fanned by his
valet, Wisdom watched the servants distributing
the food until another servant came running
from the house with a bright smile.

"My lord, the mayor has good news for you!"

Wisdom instantly forgot his exhaustion and
raced inside.

He was out of breath when he reached the matriarch's court. Mayor Lu and his wife were
kneeling in front of a statue of Buddha, each
lighting many sticks of incense.

His father said, "Get down to your knees, Wisdom. Your wife has just given birth to a healthy son, and I've already named him Ardent."

Tradition demanded that a man stay away from his wife during the last hundred days of her pregnancy, and Wisdom and Lotus had been living in separate chambers since spring. The night before, when her labor had begun, he had been told to leave their living quarters so she could feel free to scream during the delivery. He was not allowed to see either her or the baby until both were neatly clad and the room immaculately clean.

Lotus's personal maid, Jasmine, now married to a servant named Ah Chin and mother of a baby boy herself, bowed to the young lord, then gestured for all the other maids to leave with her.

Wisdom sat on the edge of the bed and smiled at his wife. Lotus was covered up to her delicate neck by a red quilt. Her face seemed paler than usual, and her almond eyes were half-closed. Her cherry-like mouth formed a faint smile when she saw Wisdom. She whispered in a tired voice, "Are you pleased with our son, my husband?"

A bundle of red quilt lay beside Lotus. Only the baby's face showed. His eyes were closed. His face was red and wrinkled, his mouth a tiny wet dot.

"Our son doesn't have any hair or eyebrows!" Wisdom said in surprise.

"He will grow them soon enough," Lotus laughed, then frowned in pain.

Wisdom wanted to hold her but was afraid to hurt her. He reached under the quilt for her hand, held it, and squeezed it gently. "I missed you very much."

Lotus smiled, very happy to hear it. She asked politely, "Did Sesame please you?"

During the last hundred days of a wife's pregnancy, her husband lived in the company of his concubines. Wisdom had only one concubine, and he had no desire for any additional ones.

"Sesame is a nice woman," he answered vaguely. He would never tell his wife that Sesame, though older, could still make the clouds melt and raindrops fall with great passion. "But I couldn't wait to come back here," he said, regarding the empty pillow next to Lotus's.

She blushed. "Only a hundred days more," she murmured. Tradition also stated that a woman's body was unclean after childbirth, and it would bring bad luck if her husband shared her bed within the next hundred days.

Lotus turned her face toward the window to hide her sudden sorrow. She wanted her mother very badly at this moment.

In the past two years, she and her mother had met only once. In was the previous New Year, when the women from both Lin and Lu houses had been offering incense in the Temple of Peaceful Stars. Lotus had just begun to show then, and her mother had cried out of happiness. Angered by this display, her father had forbidden her mother to see any of the messengers sent from the Lu house. Lady Lin had to learn about Lotus from the other ladies in Yin-tin.

Wisdom saw the tears in Lotus's eyes when she turned back. He was angry with his father-in-law for not allowing Mrs. Lin and Lotus to visit each other. "I'll send a servant to your mother. Maybe your father will let her see the man this time," he said and stood up. "By the way, I have a present for you."

He left for his own chamber, and soon returned with Sesame, who held a heavy box in her arms. "Congratulations, my lady," Sesame said, looking at the sleeping baby with love, then placed the box on a bedside table. "In the past hundred days, my lord worked day and night on his present for my lady." She bowed once again and left.

Wisdom took out of the box a pair of statues. They were carved out of teak and resembled a noble couple. He sat on the edge of the bed and put them on his lap. The wood was heavy. "With my carving teacher's help, I used the drawing I gave you on our wedding night as a study for these statues. But these are but another study for the jade lovers I'll carve someday. Teak is not an ideal medium to convey what I want to say."

Lotus felt her eyelids becoming heavy. She forced herself to stay awake, looking at the statues and smiling frailly. Sesame was telling the truth. There was so much work involved in the detailed carvings. The folds on the robes, and the ornaments on the couple's hair. Wisdom couldn't have had much time for Sesame, after all.

Lotus yawned contentedly. Like a mother who feels obligated to ask a child about his toy, she asked softly, "And what is the message you wish to convey through your carvings, my husband?"

Wisdom watched his wife closing her eyes. He lowered his voice to the singsong of a lullaby, "Thousands of years from now, people will look at the jade lovers and realize that China was a beautiful land, filled with not only warlords and rebels, but also poets and artists. China's wealth will be revealed, and also China's magnificence . . ."

He heard Lotus breathing evenly. He left the statues on the table, then stood up and left without waking her.

When Ardent Lu was a hundred days old, there was a grand celebration in Mayor Lu's mansion.

As the sun set, the Chinese guests began to arrive in sedan chairs, the foreigners and Mongols on horses or in wagons. Even in Yin-tin, where a Chinese could become a mayor, the law forbade them to possess horses and mules.

Ardent Lu was bathed and powdered, then dressed in an embroidered red robe. His bald head was covered by a red satin cap adorned with lucky charms of jade and rubies and solid gold. His tiny feet were shod in red satin shoes that resembled the heads of tigers. His face was whitened with powder, his cheeks rouged. In the middle of his forehead, a red dot was painted with lip rouge to ward off evil spirits. He had slept well and was in good spirits, so he smiled at the guests when Jasmine circled the grand room with him in her arms. The guests were pleased because a male baby's smiles would bring them good luck.

Mayor Lu's health had been declining, but when he looked at his grandson, he felt young and strong again. "A part of me will live in this baby." He pointed at Ardent proudly, then looked at the guests. "Let's start the Future-picking ceremony."

Sesame appeared carrying a lacquer tray covered with red silk and loaded with various objects: a gold coin, an ink brush, a miniature sword, a small three-string musical instrument, a candle, and many more.

Mayor Lu took Ardent and placed the baby on his lap. Sesame bent over to hold the tray within Ardent's reach. Lady Lu, Wisdom, and Lotus sat nearby, watching nervously. Everyone held their breath when Ardent reached with his dimpled hands.

"Be careful, my grandson," Mayor Lu warned. "Whatever you pick will determine your future." As if the baby could understand, the

grandfather went on, "Pick the ink brush and
you'll be a scholar. Pick a sword and you'll become a warrior." At that moment the grandfather gave Sesame an accusing look for not placing
the sword out of the child's reach. "Take the
gold coin and you'll be a rich lord. Choose the
musical instrument and you'll create beautiful
songs. Grab the candle, my child, and you'll gift
the world with the light of hope."

The baby could not decide. As Sesame's hands
began to shake at the weight of the tray, the
homemade red candle rolled toward the edge.
Ardent was amused by it and took it in his
plump little hand.

The guests applauded. The parents and grandparents were relieved. Ardent could have picked
the box of rouge, which would make him a lady's
man. The spool of thread meant a tailor, the miniature hoe a farmer, the bamboo pole a fisher-
man, and the toy saw a carpenter.

After a feast and various entertainment, the
guests offered their gifts to the baby. Heavy gold
chains were given so the baby would be chained
to the world of the living. Bracelets and anklets
were presented for the same reason. A table in
the grand room was piled with gifts, but none of
the Lu family members looked at them. Even the
baby was too tired now to show any interest.

When the party was over, a number of the
guests were invited to return, as usual, through
the back door. Going to greet them, Wisdom noticed that the doorstep was piled with gifts for
his son. They had been given by peasants—a cotton cap made of remnants, a pajama robe that
used to be a padded quilt, a wooden cup made
by a carpenter, and a bamboo flute played by
the farm boys when they were riding on water
buffalo. Wisdom was greatly touched.

*   *   *

The Silent League, which had started with only thirty elite members, now had over a hundred and included poor scholars as well. There was no military men among them. Like the name of the League, they were serene intellectuals who could not and would not fight with their fists.

"More fists are waving against the Mongols now, both in the north and the south," Wisdom said, looking around the securely shuttered grand room. Formerly they had held their meetings in the study, but it had become too small. His eyes lingered on the faces of the aged ones, and his heart filled with sadness when he noticed that his father appeared the most feeble of them all.

Wisdom went on, "The new rebel forces are desperately in need of weapons, tents, medicine, wagons, and food. I know I've been asking a lot from you in the past two years, but I must ask for more."

The rich gentry offered their gold and silver, the poor scholars their copper coins. They placed their donations on the table that was still piled with Ardent's gifts.

Wisdom said, "My father and I will contribute all the valuables we received tonight to support the Silent League. Ardent is only a hundred days old, but already is our youngest member. My son will be very happy when he is old enough to know."

The Silent League was now well-known in the shadow world of resistance. The leaders of the uprising forces in need of funding often came to Wisdom through underground connections. Wisdom always used his judgment to decide on either granting or denying the League's patronage.

When the business matters were settled, the older members left and the younger ones began to make ink by grinding ink stones in the ink wells that contained water. They then unrolled their rice paper and started to compose poems.

Some of them used the flooding of the River
Yangtze as a subject. They described how people
suffered during the flood, and why the River
Yangtze was called River of Tears, just like the
Yellow River was known as River of Sorrow.
They aimed at waking up the nation, so the rich
would help the poor.

The others wrote about the building of canals.
The Hui-tung Canal had taken millions of lives,
and the Chi-chou Canal millions more. Now the
Supreme General Mighty Sword was coming to
Yin-tin to supervise the construction, bringing
over three thousand men.

As the scholars composed their patriotic poems,
the night grew deeper. When the moon moved
to the western sky, they were ready to print.

Mirror-imaged characters were carved on the
flat ends of square wooden sticks each four times
the thickness of a chopstick. The scholars picked
the needed characters from a large wooden
crate, then arranged them in correct order.

The sticks were placed in a bamboo-framed
box and tied together. Ink was brushed over its
flat ends, a sheet of rice paper pressed on, a
roller pushed over. The scholars then peeled off
the sheet, passed it from hand to hand, and
smiled. It was a smile shared by writers who
finally saw their hearts' true feelings in print.

The Silent League members printed until dawn.
When one chanced to look out the window, he
saw on the dawning sky a fading crescent moon.
Soon it would be the Star Festival, one of the
many occasions for Chinese to exchange sweet
cakes without causing any suspicion among the
Mongols.

Wisdom entered his and Lotus's bedchamber
and saw the first rays of the morning sun
screened through a rice-paper window, casting a

soft glow on his wife and son. Both of them were
still sleeping soundly. He tiptoed to the bed and
stood admiring the beautiful portrait of tran-
quility.

Suddenly a loud noise erupted outside the garden walls, shattering the peaceful picture. Lotus,
startled out of her dreams, opened her eyes and
sat up straight. The baby jerked his dimpled
arms and began to cry.

"What is it?" she asked.

Wisdom listened for a while, then clenched his
delicate fingers into two pale fists. "I'm afraid
the Chi-chou Canal has reached Yin-tin. It's the
coolies digging!"

16

THE WORKERS RAISED their hoes high. The sound of their digging intertwined with the Yangtze River's lapping waves. The Chi-chou Canal was reaching its last phase of construction. Once the Yangtze and Yellow rivers were connected, these men would become free.

"I'll be free to go home," a young man beside Endurance said. He had been captured by the Mongols and forced into labor two years before. "I can see my white-haired mother waiting for her only son . . . if she is still alive."

"I'll be free to join my wife," another young man said. "She was my bride when I left her a year ago. I hope she did not starve to death the way my parents did." He had been a farmer until his village was leveled into a pasture.

Endurance brought his hoe down with an angry stroke. No loved ones were waiting for him. When he became free, he would have no place to go.

The Chu family's hometown was west of the Kiangsu Province. In order to go there, he would have to cross the province of Kiangsi, then keep going southwest to reach the Phoenix Place. Mongol soldiers were stationed along all the borders between provinces and towns. Traveling south had been easy for Endurance while he worked with the canal team. Once on his own, though, he would have to sneak through the overlord soldiers like a mouse sneaking through the claws of many cats.

"How I hate Mighty Sword!" he said through clenched teeth, his voice drowned out by the sound of digging.

As if to answer his summons, Mighty Sword appeared. Endurance bowed his head, glancing at the supreme general out of the corner of his eye. The general had on a red cape lined with gold. Riding toward the canal site, the cape soared out behind him and fluttered like the rays of sun, turning Mighty Sword into a sun Buddha descending from the heavens.

Endurance compared himself with the supreme general: Mighty Sword owned the world, while he had nothing except a few copper coins.

The coolies were paid no more than their daily meals until the foremen were desperate to meet Mighty Sword's deadline. Those that showed the greatest speed in digging were given one coin per day. Endurance had saved his precious coins while toiling from north to south.

The digging halted at nightfall. While the other coolies fell asleep in tents, Endurance roamed Yin-tin alone.

He moved eastward from the construction site, away from the gushing river and closer to the glowing lanterns. Reaching town, he walked down one well-lit street after another. He had never seen a city so overflowing with people this late at night. Compared to Yin-tin, Prosper Mountain was a hamlet.

Food peddlers were calling out their wares in southern dialect, and Endurance's mouth watered at the sight of noodles. He remembered that he had not celebrated his birthday in the past two years. He stopped at a noodle stand, stared at the large wok.

In the rising steam he saw his mother walking

toward him holding a bowl of noodles. He heard her voice in his memory. "My son, I've made these noodles extra long to bring you a long life. There are red and green vegetables to represent prosperity and good health. You'll find a red turnip hidden there, symbolizing happiness."

"Give me a large bowl of noodles," Endurance told the peddler. "I want plenty of vegetables and a red turnip in it."

The peddler followed Endurance's instructions, but the noodle tasted nothing like he remembered. He emptied the bowl, then walked away unhappily.

A few steps from the noodle stand, a green lamp swung in the night wind, shining on two young girls leaning against the frame of an open door. As Endurance noticed their painted faces, they twisted their slender bodies, giggling and challenging him with their eyes.

He recalled Peony laughing when she had said many years ago, "When wedding night comes, you better know what it is all about . . . I mean this melting clouds and creating rain stuff!"

Endurance stared at the girls. Peony was dead, and so was the most tender part of Endurance's heart. But his young body was still alive.

The girl nearer him smiled at him broadly. Endurance reached into his garment pocket, then opened his palm to show her all the coins he had. "Do I have enough to pillow you?"

She grabbed the coins and ran back to the house. As Endurance followed, she parted two quilted draperies and entered a small room lit with a single candle on a low dresser. The only other piece of furniture was a narrow bed. Endurance watched the girl squat and pull a rattan box from under the bed. She put half of the coins in the bottom of her clothes, then stood up and laid the rest of the coins on the dresser.

Something was wrong. Endurance cocked his head to one side, thought about it, then realized what she was doing. He swept his large palm over the dresser, took every coin and put them back into his pocket.

"Do you think I am a fool? You're overcharging me. You're making me pay both you and the madame." His face was red with anger as he gave the girl a hard push. "Each of my coins is marked with my sweat and blood!"

The girl fell on the bed. Endurance's rage was not extinguished by her look of fear.

"Why don't you save your thieving skills for the Mongols?" he shouted as he took off his pants. He left his upper garment on and heard the coins jiggling safely in his pockets when he climbed over her.

The girl yelled, "Don't tear my clothes, you stupid blockhead! I'll unbutton them! Can't you wait? The mama will beat me if she has to buy me new clothes!"

"Good! A beating will serve you right!" Endurance said, tossing her in all directions, trying to get her out of her clothes, not caring if he tore them.

Once the girl was naked, Endurance let nature be his guide.

His dark, powerful body covered the girl's pale, slight frame like a heavy winter cloud overlapping a spring mist. He penetrated her like a stormy shadow devouring a gentle haze. He yelled out in long pent-up passion. The girl cried under him and shuddered, like mist fading into vapor. His body experienced the melting of clouds and creating of rain, but his heart received no joy.

He got up from the bed, picked up his pants, looked at the girl while getting dressed.

"You bastard!" she glared at him, sobbing in

pain. "I've never had any Chinese as big as you! Actually, never even a Mongol! I won't be able to work for at least the next three days!"

A gust of wind blew through a hole in the paper window, and the candle flame danced. Endurance saw on the soiled sheet and between the girl's spread legs a few spots of blood. He felt sick to his stomach. Turning away from the girl, he emptied his pocket.

"Keep them." He dropped all the coins on the dresser, then ran out of the house.

When he passed the paper lantern hanging outside, he put his fist through it and extinguished the green light.

Heading west toward the construction site, Endurance soon passed a dark alley. Down it he saw two figures stumbling. He could hear them, but couldn't understand a word. From their strange clothing, silhouetted against a faraway lantern, he recognized them as the color-eyed people who used to visit the canal site accompanied by Mighty Sword. He remembered the word Turkey. Yes, that was the name of their homeland.

Both Turks were too drunk to walk straight. As they helped each other along, a heavy leather bag with long straps fell to the ground with a ponderous thump. They did not notice it but staggered onward.

Endurance waited until they were gone, then raced forward. He picked up the leather bag and grinned. It was heavy with coins.

Reversing direction, he returned to the main avenue with the bag concealed underneath his garment. He saw in a distance, a white lantern hanging from a bamboo pole. The character "wine" was written in black ink. An evening breeze rocked the lantern back and forth, tempting Endurance. He had a very strong desire to pour barley wine down his throat, to burn away his loneliness, sorrow, and anger.

The wine house contained only seven round tables. The outer three were occupied by Mongols, so Endurance went to the innermost one, lined with Chinese, since it was customary for strangers to share a table in a crowded place.

He nodded at the other men. They were craftsmen and coolies, each trying to wash away his own misery and uninterested in conversation. Endurance drank silently as time slowly moved on.

"But my honorable sirs, this is a very small wine house and I cannot afford to give credit," the owner, a little old man, pleaded with the two Mongols who were leaving the first table.

"Do you dare to disagree with your masters?" asked one of them. "We Mongols are your masters, you know that!"

"But my honorable sirs—" The owner did not have a chance to finish. The other Mongol punched him on the jaw, sent him stumbling back and crashing against a wall.

The owner's wife, a little old woman, came running from the back room to help him up. The two Mongols roared with laughter on their way to the door.

Looking them over, Endurance recognized them as part of Mighty Sword's guards. They frequently rode behind the supreme general right at the rim of the general's soaring cape. Endurance could taste the bile of hatred rising from his throat. He had emptied two bottles of barley wine, and now knew no fear.

"My old man . . . my poor old man!" the owner's wife wept as Endurance slapped down his payment and started out.

Turning at the sound, she stared at the large handful of coins piled on the counter and gasped.

"You paid us too much!" she said, but Endurance was already gone.

He followed the two Mongols at a safe distance. It was getting late, and the streets were no longer crowded. They passed many broad streets before turning into a narrow alley.

Endurance moved closer to them, then looked at the swords hanging from their waists. His only weapon was the remaining coins in the bag with long straps.

"Stop, you Mongol pigs!" he called and charged forward. In the silent night air, his voice traveled far.

The intoxicated Mongols turned unsteadily. They saw a monstrous form of a man running toward them, twirling a weighted sack over his head.

They screamed in their own language. Before they could draw their swords, the giant was already upon them. The whirling sack slammed one in the temple. A second blow smashed the other in the forehead. Both dropped to the ground like stones.

They retained consciousness only long enough to see the night sky brightened by a crescent moon. In front of that moon the giant raised his weighty weapon with both hands like a coolie lifting his heavy hoe.

For a fleeting instant both Mongols recognized the giant and yelled again in their native tongue. But then Endurance launched more blows about their heads and faces, and the moon for them faded out into eternity, like a lantern caught in a howling storm.

Soon the Mongols resembled cabbages smashed under the hoofs of a water buffalo. Parting with his efforts, Endurance dropped the coin bag, now dripping with blood.

He was debating whether to abandon the coins

with the bag or scoop them into his pocket when he heard a sound from several lanes away. A rider was cantering on a stone-paved street. The unhurried, rhythmical tramping indicated a confident man on his tall horse.

Endurance saw the familiar portrait in his mind's eye, and he sobered up instantly. Fear took control of him. He stayed motionless beside the dead Mongols, hoping that if he stayed still, the rider would not come in this direction.

As he waited, the rider moved closer. When Endurance decided to run, it was too late.

At the other end of the lane, a black stallion appeared in the moonlight; its hide glistened like the water of a lake at night. The horse halted and its rider, already alerted by the dead men's cries, pulled his bowstring and nocked an arrow. Endurance's eyes met those of Mighty Sword. The supreme general lowered his weapon and frowned in puzzlement. The young general had a superb memory, and it did not take him long to remember.

"You! Prosper Mountain!" Mighty Sword shouted as he recognized his old prey.

In a flash he recollected every detail of their last encounter. He smiled wolfishly at the young coolie. This game would bring him much joy.

"You were the one who stared at me so defiantly! It's time that you join your headless little friend!" the supreme general yelled, putting away his bow as he urged the horse closer.

"Your head will make a good display!" Mighty Sword said.

"You'll never get me!" Endurance shouted and darted out of the alley. He heard the general laughing as the hunt began.

Endurance ran, his adrenaline giving his feet wings. But the steady clop-clop of the horse's hoofs followed him effortlessly. He dashed through the abandoned streets, feeling like a helpless rabbit. Soon his lungs felt like they were about to burst, his sides ached. But the hunter continued to come closer and closer, never changing the easy gait of his mount.

When Endurance neared the riverbank, he knew he could not run any farther. Deserted rice fields stretched endlessly to his right. On his left rose an ancient weeping willow. He dashed into its shadow, leaned against the trunk, panting until he saw his pursuer moving in the moonlight.

The supreme general reined in his horse. A chilly smile spread across his face as he took his bow and slowly pulled the shaft back.

"No!" Endurance screamed as he fled from his hiding place and sprinted through the dark.

The moon suddenly disappeared behind a massive cloud. The wind began to blow harder. Endurance heard the whistle of the first arrow just before his left shoulder exploded in pain.

Endurance flew forward, falling to the ground. He heard the general laughing and the horse trotting ever closer. He also heard in his imagination the voice of his little friend Longevity Ma. "Run! My big friend, hurry! Or he'll cut off your head too!"

Gritting his teeth against the pain, Endurance crawled into a fallow rice field, high with weeds. He dragged himself forward on his stomach. He could only move his right arm. His left shoulder, arm, and hand were numb. He touched his left shoulder with his right hand, and found that the arrow had pierced through his shoulder blade. An arrowhead over two inches long was protruding out of his chest just above his heart.

He kept crawling. The weeds that survived the summer sun were high and tough. They hid him, but also cut him like scalpels. He heard a rambling sound coming nearer. It sounded like horse hoofs. He crawled faster.

Lightning exploded in the sky, brightening the path for thunder Buddha. Buddha cracked his whip, and the sound shook heaven and earth. Large drops of rain fell on Endurance, who lay trembling in the wasteland.

The severe pain on his left shoulder spread quickly. His entire upper body soon became numb. He kicked his legs to keep moving. When he was inching forward from underneath a dead tree, a low-hanging branch caught the arrow intended for him. Lurching with a jolt of utter terror, Endurance fell face first to the ground and fainted.

17

MAYOR LU HAD BEEN very sick and unable to attend the Mongol governor's party in honor of the Supreme General Mighty Sword, so Wisdom had to attend in his father's place. By the time the party was over, it was late. The sedan chair moved slowly in the pouring rain, gradually reaching a rice field near the river.

"I hear someone moaning!" Wisdom Lu said, suddenly peering out at the abandoned field. "Stop!" he told the carriers. "Go into the field and see if someone is there."

The carriers had taken only a few steps before they saw, at the foot of a dead tree, a man covered with blood. "A dead man, with an arrow in his shoulder!" they screamed and ran back to their lord.

Wisdom stepped out of the sedan, heedless of the rain. "If he is dead, then we must bury him. If he is not ..." Coming over and examining him, he saw the man's blood-covered chest heaving and he squatted down. Reaching with a trembling hand, he touched the man's neck and felt a strong pulse. "He is alive!"

He turned to the sedan carriers. "Come and lift him up. He has already lost a lot of blood. Just look at that puddle around him! He'll be dead soon if we don't act!"

The carriers hesitated. It was a capital offense

to save any wounded man without notifying the Mongols first.

"Hurry!" Wisdom cried. "Let's put him in the chair and carry him home!"

The carriers were loyal and obedient to Wisdom, but nonetheless they complained while lifting the man. "He is so heavy! Is he made of rock?"

They put him in the sedan chair, dropped the tapestries, then carried him toward the Lu mansion. Wisdom was prepared to walk beside the sedan, struggling in the downpour and mud, when the storm passed.

In moments a silver moon shone through the parting clouds. In the moonlight a rider appeared, moving slowly, searching for something or someone at the rice field.

"Mighty Sword! The Mongol general!" Wisdom Lu whispered and held his breath.

Mighty Sword also recognized Wisdom. "Ah! The son of the mayor of Yin-tin!" he said. "It's good to see you again!" He looked at Wisdom suspiciously. "You are drenched! Why are you walking through the mud instead of riding in your sedan?"

"I ..." Wisdom hated to lie, but he made a quick decision and raised his voice to answer convincingly, "I don't feel well from overeating at the governor's party. I need to walk off the rich food." He then smiled at the general and asked, "Are you not feeling well either? Is that why you are riding so slowly?"

Mighty Sword shook his head. "I am looking for the body of a man I have just killed. But perhaps his remains have already been dragged away by the hungry dogs in the neighborhood."
Mighty Sword took for granted that a Chinese mayor had to be a collaborator and his son a cow-

ard, so he did not doubt Wisdom's words. He kicked his horse and rode away.

Wisdom Lu walked all the way home while the wounded man rode in the sedan. The carriers mumbled unhappily, soon exhausted from carrying a man twice the weight of their delicate lord. But they were patriotic and devoted to their master. They would never betray him.

When they reached the Lu mansion, the carriers headed for the back door. They lifted the wounded man out of the sedan chair, then brought him through the rain-drenched and moonlit garden.

In the inner court, a lady in pink was reading by the lamplight, a woman in gray doing needlework.

"The night is deep. Jasmine, please tell the other servants to go to sleep." Lotus looked up from her poetry book. "You and I can wait for the lord."

Jasmine nodded, then walked to the outer court and related her lady's order. The tired servants were grateful. They had worked a long day and would have to start all over again at dawn. Jasmine was on her way back to her mistress when she heard a commotion at the back door. She raced to the wet garden, spied her master and the sedan carriers. It did not take the men long to tell her what happened.

When Jasmine returned, she had blood on her garment, and Lotus screamed.

"It's not the blood of our lord," Jasmine said quickly. "They've brought a stranger." She then hurried to a spare room that was concealed behind the tall bookcases that lined one side of the walls. She began to prepare the room immediately.

Lotus saw Wisdom and gasped. It was a long way from the rice field to the foothills of Purple

Gold Mountain, and the young lord had never walked such a long distance in his life. His shoes were ruined by mud. The lower part of his garment was splashed with filth. He had lost the gold pins in his hair, and his topknot was now hanging loosely. His face was blotchy but his lips white. He stumbled the last few steps, then fell into a chair.

Lotus knelt beside him and took his trembling hand. The sedan carriers entered with their heavy burden. Lotus caught a glimpse of a huge body clad in blood and closed her eyes. She buried her face against her husband's arm as Jasmine helped the four carriers put the wounded man to bed.

The maid then rushed past Lotus and Wisdom to the kitchen. "I need hot water to clean his wound," she said on her way out.

Wisdom squeezed Lotus's hand to let her know that he was all right. "Go get the medicine man," he mumbled to the sedan carriers. "You know, the one we can trust."

When Endurance opened his eyes, he found himself in the grandest room he had ever seen. The lady tending him was the most beautiful woman he had ever laid his eyes on.

"So I'm dead. So this is heaven," he uttered, then frowned at the divine beauty sitting beside his bed. "Where is my Peony? It's nothing personal. You are lovely, but she is my girl. Will you find her for me? She is about twice your size ..." He stopped at the sight of a tired-looking lord.

He stared at the man and exclaimed, "I must be in the wrong place. Where is the peasants' quarter in heaven? My name is Endurance Chu, and I certainly do not belong here."

The young lord laughed. Coming to stand beside the lady in pink, he introduced himself and his wife. "You are very much alive, Endurance Chu. Even the medicine man was surprised by your strength. He said you'll be able to get up before long. Your shoulder wound was a clean one, and it will heal in time."

Endurance was relieved to know that he was not in heaven, since he had so much left to do on earth. But he was also sad that Peony and he still existed in two different worlds.

Then he remembered Mighty Sword's wolfish smile in the alley.

"The bastard got me!" Trying to rise, he winced in pain. "Will I ever be able to use my left arm again? I need both hands to fight the Mongols! I'd rather die if I'm crippled!" He tried to lift his heavily bandaged left arm, but flinched in agony again.

A woman's voice came from the door. "You watch your language in the presence of my lady!"

Endurance watched a middle-aged woman in gray move toward him holding a big bowl of steaming liquid. "My name is Jasmine," she said, bringing the bowl to his lips.

Endurance eyed the green liquid suspiciously.

"It's the juice of willow twigs. The medicine man prescribed it. It'll ease your pain." The woman put a strong hand behind Endurance's neck and lifted his head. "Drink!" she ordered.

Endurance swallowed the hot juice. It was very bitter, and he grimaced as Jasmine forced the whole potion down his throat. She wiped his chin and left with the empty bowl.

Lotus got up from the bedside chair. She and Jasmine had stayed beside Endurance throughout the night while Wisdom rested. "My husband will watch over you now. Please excuse me." She bowed to Endurance as if he was equal to her in status.

Endurance was taken aback. He had never been treated with such respect by a lady. He tried to bow back to her, but was unable to do so. His entire upper body was numb.

Wisdom helped his wife to the bedchamber, then returned to the hidden room. He pulled a chair closer to the bed and leaned forward.

He asked softly, "You mentioned awhile ago that you need both hands to fight the Mongols. You said those words with such determination. May I ask what exactly you have done to fight them?"

Endurance looked into Wisdom's eyes and saw something much more powerful than the dainty man's frail appearance. He decided to trust Wisdom. "I am heading to Phoenix Place. It's my father's hometown. Two thirds of the people in that town have the same last name Chu. As you know, we Chinese always trust someone who has the same last name as our own, even when he is only a stranger. I believe I can gather enough followers to form a fighting group."

"So you have not been involved in active resistance as of yet?" Wisdom said.

Endurance told him of his frustration and impatience. He had wanted to fight the Mongols for so long. But so far he had not accomplished a thing.

When he finished, Wisdom said, "You need to rest and recover. And then you can start to form a resistance group. When you are ready, let me know."

Wisdom went on to relate his rescue from the deserted rice field. Endurance listened, and besides feeling grateful, he found Wisdom extraordinarily interesting.

Wisdom, in turn, not only respected Endurance's courage, but also was fascinated by Endurance's life story.

They talked until noon, when Lotus returned with Jasmine. It was time for lunch. Wisdom asked to have his meal sent to Endurance's bedside so that they could continue their conversation.

As Jasmine helped Lotus to the dining room, she mumbled, "Yin and yang are opposite forces, but attracted to each other."

Lotus nodded. "Our lord sees in Endurance Chu what his gentlemen friends do not have. And Endurance Chu sees in our lord a world that didn't exist for him until now. They are as different from each other as day and night. But the day advances toward night, and night progresses into day. The two make a complete circle; our lord and Endurance Chu make a perfect team."

In the dining room, Lotus waited until she and her in-laws were alone, then told them about the wounded peasant. Mayor Lu nodded weakly, giving his consent. "Tell Wisdom that I am proud of him for having the courage to save this man. Tell him that his peasant friend can stay in our house as long as he wants."

Two months later, Endurance was introduced to the League members. Unlike Wisdom, they did not find him fascinating, nor he them. They did not bother to look beyond his rugged surface. When he spit on the rug, they frowned. When he wiped his nose with his sleeve, they made faces.

For his part, Endurance was bored soon after the meeting began. He had not even a copper coin to donate for the League fund. He scowled at the shocked looks on their faces when they started to compose poems, and he told them that he could not even write his own name. Since he could not read, he was useless in printing the

pamphlets that were to be placed in the boxes
containing moon cakes for the coming Moon
Festival.

"You can help carrying the boxes," one of the
rich gentry said sarcastically. "Even as an one-
armed man, you can haul more weight than any
servant in the Lu house. The Mongols don't
allow us to own horses or mules. But they cannot
outlaw us from owning you."

"You better work hard, my friend," one of the
poor scholars said sourly as he glanced over Endurance's new garment, purchased by Wisdom.
"You've found yourself a golden rice bowl. Remember to bow humbly to your master, and
you'll never be hungry again."

"I'm not a mule! And Wisdom is not my master!" Endurance responded through clenched
teeth.

The League members stopped working to stare
at him. He searched their faces but could not
find one that was sympathetic. He stormed out
of the grand room.

Wisdom followed him, apologizing on the way
to Endurance's room. "If I had known they
would be so rude, I would have never introduced
them to you. I'm so sorry. Please forgive them
for my sake."

He paused to think, then continued with a
puzzled look, "What made them act like that?
I've never seen such arrogance in them. I thought
they would be grateful to have you as a League
member, since we all have the same goal."

At this innocence Endurance suddenly stopped
fuming and started to laugh. "Am I not lucky to
be a poor man? With your money and status,
you'll never see people's true faces the way I
do."

He stood still and put his large right hand on
Wisdom's slim shoulder. "Don't worry, Wisdom.

You'll always be my friend. You are not like those idiots." The way he glared from beneath his bushy brows, he reminded Wisdom of an angry tiger. "One of these days, I'll make them sorry for mocking me today."

The hidden threat in his chilly voice made Wisdom shiver. But he was glad that Endurance was not angry with him. "My friend," he said pleadingly, "please do not leave because of them."

Endurance nodded. "I will stay until my arm is healed—if you will teach me to read and write." He saw Wisdom's look of disbelief and continued, "Mighty Sword put an arrow in my body, and your scholar friends put an arrow in my pride. I consider both of them my enemies. I want to be as capable as my enemies in every way."

Seeing Wisdom's consternation, he went on, "I want to become a good archer someday. The next time I meet Mighty Sword, I'll be the hunter and he the game. I also want to understand poetry. When I meet your scholar friends again, they will not make fun of me."

Wisdom was greatly touched by his friend's determination. He took Endurance's big hand with both of his and held it tightly. "I'll teach you to read and write. And I know exactly the place where you can practice archery without being discovered by the Mongols."

Wisdom rode in his sedan chair, and Endurance walked beside it. As they climbed higher into the mountain, Wisdom said, "There are two temples hidden in a deep forest on Purple Gold Mountain, and both are far from the governor's mansion. The Buddhist one is Temple of Peaceful Stars. We are going to the Taoist one, the Temple of Silent Echo. I think their head monk,

Calm Fortitude, will let you practice archery on the temple ground."

Ancient willows stood like sentries to the entrance of the temple. As soon as they saw the approaching sedan chair, young Taoist monks high in the branches gave the alarm. They saw the Lu family crest embroidered on its drapery, and carefully studied the big man walking beside the sedan. The old monks were informed, quickly made ready. By the time Wisdom and Endurance arrived, they found Calm Fortitude waiting for them with hot tea and sweet cakes.

The monk had long white hair and a white beard. When he looked at Endurance, the peasant felt as though he were reading every secret in his soul.

"Archery? That's a much lesser form of fighting. It's fit only for barbaric hunters." The old monk shook his head at Endurance. "I'll show you what our monks can do. After watching them, if you still want to practice bow and arrow, you are welcome to use the mountain behind the temple."

Trees surrounded the temple ground and acted like a quilt, cloaking it and absorbing all the sound. The monks were practicing broadswords and spears in an open field. The shouts that came from the throats of the fighters and the loud banging created by the impact of their weapons did not travel beyond the shielding foliage.

"That's why they call this place Silent Echo," Wisdom told Endurance. "This is the only mountain I know where sounds echo silently."

He went on to relate that the broadswords and spears were made by monks themselves, and when intruders were spotted from the observation towers, all weapons disappeared within mo-

ments. Endurance was only half listening, though,
for he was captivated by what he saw.

Over a hundred soft-shoed monks in tight
black pants and long-sleeved jackets were divided into two groups. One group was practicing
broadswords, the other group long spears.

The broadswords were as wide as a man's
open palm and longer than his arm. The spears
were about six feet long. Each monk had tied a
two-foot red scarf on the handle of his sword,
and each spear was adorned with a foot-long
green tassel at the base of the spearhead.

The two groups practiced separately at first.
The broadswords moved so fast that each monk
was but the center of a flashing silver and red
circle. The long spear appeared as numerous
bolts of lightning topped with green flames.

The two groups then practiced together, swords
against spears. Each silver and red flashing circle tried to penetrate a curtain of green-topped
bolts of lightnings. Loud clashes were heard as
the spear fighters fended off the swords success-
fully. Then the two groups traded places. When
a bolt of lightning was jabbed at a sword-holding
monk, the flashing circle increased its whirling
speed and kept the lightning at a safe distance.

"Bring me a bow and some arrows," Calm Fortitude said to a young monk when the practice
came to a pause.

Endurance had barely recovered from the
stunning scene of swords and spears when Calm
Fortitude began to pull the string on a large bow.
The old monk didn't even bother to roll up his
wide sleeves, and effortlessly sent one sharp
arrow after another flying toward the group. The
monks did not move until the arrows were only
inches from them. Then they flicked their swords
and spears, and all the arrows were deflected.

Endurance stood with his mouth open. Calm

Fortitude cast the bow and arrows aside, then smiled at the large peasant. "The monks in both temples also excel in empty-fist fighting technique. They have demonstrated for the mayor's guests once. They can catch flying arrows with their bare hands. Do you still wish to practice archery?"

Endurance had never kowtowed to anyone. When his parents were alive, one of their worst problems was making him kneel in front of the statues of Buddha or the plaques of the Chu family ancestors. But Endurance dropped to his knees willingly and quickly, kowtowed three times to Calm Fortitude.

"My honorable *shih-fu*," he said with his head touching the old monk's feet, "I want to learn all three forms of kung fu: the empty-handed fighting technique, the broadsword, and the long spear. I will not leave Yin-tin City until I've mastered all three."

18

MIGHTY SWORD did not like south China. It was too warm and crowded for a Mongol. He could massacre people and create open range, but not change the weather. He also missed his brother Shadow Tamu and his sister Starlight, who had remained the great khan's favorite. He wanted to return to Da-du so that he could visit them more frequently.

Leaving over two thousand soldiers in Yin-tin City, he took his personal guard corps back to the north. He stopped often in places that interested him, and recruited Mongol warriors along the way. He reached the Yellow River in the winter of 1347, having recruited over five hundred new fighters.

After occupying China for almost seven decades, the Mongols still preferred to live in hide tents. Upon his arrival in Prosper Mountain, he ordered Chinese homes burned to the ground, farmland leveled, and towns destroyed. In their place felt-covered and willow-latticed tents were set up to form a tent city. Once settled, the supreme general and his soldiers began to persecute the Chinese along the river.

The Chinese in this northern region had a savior, and his name was Vanguard Kuo.

"I am so proud to be a maid in this house!" Peony said as she combed Lady Joy Kuo's hair.

The room was richly furnished, but there was no mirror, because Lady Kuo was blind.

"Is the master still standing in the snow?" Joy Kuo asked.

"Yes," Peony said, looking out the window.

Vanguard Kuo, a tall, slender man in his late thirties, was in his walled garden, so deep in thought that he was unaware of the freezing snow that surrounded him.

"Does my lady want me to call the master into the house?" Peony asked.

"No," Joy Kuo sighed. "He needs to sort out his troubled thoughts, and he likes to do that outdoors. He has been that way ever since I married him . . ." She went on to tell Peony that her father had been a wealthy merchant who loved her regardless of the fact that she had been born sightless. Vanguard Kuo had been a poor man, but the only one trusted by her father. Her wise father had been right. Through the years Vanguard had used her dowry to open one store after another and become rich, but still remained a loyal and loving husband.

Joy Kuo said, "Peony, you know our secret. My husband is known as a merchant who owns over twenty stores in different northern towns and villages, but he is actually one of the two most powerful leaders of the resistance movement in Honan Province—"

Joy's story was interrupted by an old woman at the door. It was Meadow, the housekeeper who used to be Joy's nanny. She had a hard face and a cold voice. "The sedan chair is ready for my lady. But I strongly object to the lady's going out in this weather. It's snowing and hailing, but no one cares about my lady's health."

Joy ignored Meadow and said to Peony, "Please go to Scholar Tou for the printed messages."

Knowing that Joy could not see her, Peony

stuck her tongue out at Meadow. When Lady Kuo had brought Peony home from the human stable a year ago, Meadow had insisted that one of the male servants should take Peony back to the market.

"Why, you bawdy street girl!" Meadow raised her hand to strike Peony.

Peony stepped easily out of Meadow's reach, put her thumbs beside her nostrils, flapped her fingers at the old woman, then ran out of the door.

She ran across the courtyard to Scholar Tou's room. The door was open, and the aged scholar was all alone. Standing in front of a large sheet of polished brass, he was using it as a mirror to check the many reversed characters carved on a large block of wood.

"Why don't you do it an easier way?" Peony asked, startling the old scholar. "I can help you carve the most frequently used words on sticks. When you have something to print, all you need is to arrange the words and tie the sticks together, instead of carving them again and again."

Scholar Tou turned from the brass mirror. "I am an old man who likes to do things the old ways. You can help me print," he said simply.

He liked Peony. Soon after she had been purchased by the Kuo house, she had watched the scholar print a message for the master and become fascinated by the many characters, each resembling a picture. She had told him that she would like to learn reading and writing. Scholar Tou had been surprised by the unpolished girl's quick mind. In the past year, Peony had learned enough to help the scholar carve and print.

When he mixed black ink with oil for printing, Peony stood facing the brass mirror and studied herself. At nineteen, she had finally stopped growing. Fine food and a good life had put more meat on her large bones. She had also lost some of her weatherbeaten tan. She had on a jade green garment over dark blue pants, and was once again able to use bright red ribbons to braid and tie her shining black hair. Meadow had insisted that as a maid Peony wear only dark colors, but Lady Kuo had given her the freedom to enhance her limited beauty however she desired.

Peony lifted her eyes to the beamed ceiling. "Endurance, if you are looking down from heaven right now, you'd have to say that I do look prettier than I ever have before," she muttered.

Finally the ink was ready. Scholar Tou brushed it over the wooden block, then pressed a sheet of rice paper over it. He used his hands to smooth the paper, so every part of it would touch the block.

Peony read the message: "The only way to make a good moon cake is to mix the ingredients well. Taoist and Buddhist monks must combine their recipes."

The true meaning behind these words was: "The Taoist and Buddhist monks must join forces to fight the Lamaist monks, and that is the only way to fight the Mongols."

"The monks had better listen to Master Kuo," Scholar Tou said. "Mighty Sword is leveling villages not only for pasturage, but also to create a building site of a Lamaist temple. A large number of Lamaist monks will soon arrive from the desert land. They are not kind, religious men, but cruel and greedy like the Mongol warriors."

When a large stack of messages were printed and dried, Peony brought them to the kitchen, where homemade cakes were waiting on a rack. Peony inserted the messages into the cakes, then boxed them and loaded them onto an ox-pulled wagon.

She was still standing beside the wagon when

a peasant hurried toward the Kuo house. The man recognized Peony and gave her a box. "These are preserved dates from Yangtze River. Master Kuo must taste them personally."

Peony ran to Vanguard Kuo, who was still standing in the garden. She watched him open the box, then she peered over his shoulder to read the words written on a piece of paper. "The lord of Whispering Lake welcomes all date-loving Chinese to contact him. Let us combine all the preserved fruit we have and bake a nice spring cake."

Vanguard Kuo, who trusted Peony as much as his wife did, remarked, "The lord of Whispering Lake. That must be the Wisdom Lu I have heard so much about. He is asking me to go there some-times in the spring, and join force with the other revolutionaries." He looked at Peony and smiled. "This is the message I've been waiting for."

Peony and Lady Kuo left the house in two sedan chairs, since it was not safe for any Chinese woman to walk through the Mongol-filled streets. As soon as the two sedan chairs reached the foothills, though, Peony jumped out of hers. She climbed the mountain on foot, enjoying the fresh air. It had stopped hailing, and snowflakes drifted softly about her. Winter honeysuckle bloomed in the snow, filling the land with a sweet fragrance. The flowering trees were over a hundred years old, and sported blossoms of red, pink, yellow, and white. Peony ran from one tree to another, laughing when the cold petals fell on her and tickled her nose.

Soon she saw a beautiful blooming branch just out of reach. She jumped, disappeared among the snow-covered foliage. The next moment she landed with her arms spread. She dashed to

Lady Kuo's sedan and offered a bouquet of flowers.

"Be careful, my child," her mistress warned lovingly as she smelled the flowers. She knew of Peony's proficiency in tai chi, but it was difficult for a blind lady with bound feet to imagine how a person could do such things and remain unhurt.

In another hour they arrived at the Temple of White Crane. Peaceful Essence greeted Lady Kuo with respect, then smiled at Peony fondly. The old monk had been worried about Peony after ordering her to leave, and he had been relieved when she returned with Lady Kuo a year ago. The Kuo couple were patrons to the temple. From then on each time Lady Kuo came to burn incense, Peony had accompanied her.

During one of her early visits, Peony had gone to the nuns and persuaded them to learn tai chi fist from her. With each visit she had taught them more, and after her visits the nuns had practiced enthusiastically. Some of them had been transferred to other temples in both north and south, and they had brought their knowledge of tai chi with them. Because of this, the fist of ultimate extreme was being learned by nuns all over China.

Once Peaceful Essence had settled Lady Kuo in a chair, she said, "I've come to you to ask a favor for my husband. We have brought many sweet cakes in a wagon. Will your monks distribute them to all the temples along the Yellow River? There is a message in every box, and we must be careful that none of them fall into either the hands of the Mongols or the Lamaist monks. If they should guess the true message, we'll be in dire trouble."

The old monk answered slowly, "I would do anything for you and Master Kuo. But when it means endangering the lives of all of these monks, a meeting is in order. I'll let my lady know in a few days."

As Lady Kuo and Peaceful Essence continued to talk, Peony left them and headed for the nuns' quarter, separated from the monks' living area by a vegetable garden. The nuns could practice tai chi in their tight black pants and jackets, and they did not have to worry that they might disturb the young monks' tranquillity.

As Peony approached, she heard some nuns giggling. It was such a joyful sound. She smiled proudly to herself. It was she who had brought gaiety to their otherwise gloomy life.

As she entered the courtyard, her eyes opened wide in astonishment. The nuns had been practicing tai chi in the snow and hail, covering their shaved heads with bright red turbans. Now that the hailstorm was over, they still wore the scarlet turbans. The vibrant color contrasted to their black clothes and made them seem quite beautiful.

"A rich lady donated us many yards of red silk for making quilts. Of course, red quilts do not belong to a temple, and it seemed a shame to waste such fine silk," a nun explained.

Peony was further surprised by an unusual sight: even the few nuns with bound feet were practicing.

"Tai chi fist eliminated our handicap. We are no longer crippled!" cried one of these nuns, formerly a landlord's daughter. "Now I can avenge the death of my family!" Nuns and monks were not supposed to have thoughts such as vengeance. But Peony had washed that rule out of the nuns' minds.

"Talk about vengeance, I have something to tell all of you." Peony proceeded to tell them of the message being delivered to the Honan temples along the Yellow River. "The monks are asked to join in battle. But not one word is said about us female warriors. This is an insult. We are just as good as the men, if not better. Since they didn't invite us to join their cause, we'll have to fight on our own."

Before continuing, Peony climbed onto a pedestal and stood with her back to the statue of Buddha. In a low voice she told the nuns about the outrages being committed by the five hundred soldiers that arrived with Mighty Sword.

"Our people are being slaughtered every day. We cannot fight openly during the day, but at night you can sneak out of the temple, and I can meet you in Prosper Mountain. We'll use our tai chi technique to comb the streets soundlessly. When we come upon women being harassed by the Mongols, we'll kill the monsters."

Peony saw the frightened looks on some of the faces, and she said accusingly, "You don't have the right to be cowards. Have you forgotten how your families were killed? Can't you still see their heads being displayed on tall poles? Look at the prairie that used to be your homes. The Mongols' horses are tramping ground that's stained with your parents' blood!"

Peony softened her voice when she saw tears in some of their eyes and courage in their uplifted faces. "When you come to the town square of Prosper Mountain tonight, wear your black pants and jackets, and cover your heads with red turbans."

Soon thereafter Peony left the nuns, accompanying Lady Kuo. The lady was amazed when Peony traveled the entire journey in a sedan chair and never uttered a word. In truth, Peony was using the opportunity to nap, because she knew there would be no sleep for her tonight.

In the clear winter sky, a full moon shone over the snow-covered town square.

A tall figure appeared from the street leading to the homes of the rich. The tight pants and jacket revealed the figure of a woman with full bosom, long legs, and large feet. When she tilted back her head, the moon shone on the red turban on her head. Her large round eyes showed disappointment when she saw no one at the platform.

"Peony," a young nun whispered and came out of hiding from behind a tall pole. "We've been waiting for a long time. How come you're so late?"

"That stupid old woman Meadow wouldn't let me leave the kitchen—" Peony stopped when she saw three more nuns crawling out from under the platform, all dressed the same as she. "I am so proud of you! Well, the five of us can make a good start."

Peony led the others to search the night streets of Prosper Mountain. They passed the jail house, then ventured through the green lamp district. The market was deserted. Only a few wine houses were still open.

"Leave my daughter alone!" A man's angry shout pierced through the closed paper windows of a wine house. "Take your filthy hands off her!"

A Mongol cursed in his native tongue, followed by the sound of a man's shrieking cry. A woman screamed, and then came the shrilling plea of a young girl.

Three frightened customers came running out the door. One of them cried as he fled, "The old fool! When a Mongol wants to pillow his daughter, he should leave the room and pretend to be blind and deaf!"

Peony and the four nuns shook their heads at the cowardliness of the three men, then entered the wine house noiselessly.

They saw a father lying on the ground with

his throat cut from ear to ear, a mother sitting on the earth shaking and holding her husband's upper body in her arms, and a half-naked daughter struggling in the hands of a Mongol.

Peony, using her favorite fighting form, a white crane spreads its wings, swept the Mongol across the room by its force. The four nuns used spread your cloud-like hands to carry the mother and daughter away from the wine house. When the Mongol struggled to get up, Peony quickly changed to a set of steps called pluck the flower, and the Mongol screamed in agony when his eyeballs were extracted by Peony's stealthy fingers.

She quickly caught up with the six women. Sternly warning the mother and daughter to silence, she and the four nuns showed then how to lower themselves to the ground and move in a step called fish at the sea bottom. They melted into the darkness, left the town unseen by shouting and running Mongol guards.

Peaceful Essence took the mother and daughter into his shelter. He had to reprimand Peony and the four nuns for fighting without permission, but the old monk's eyes gleamed with pride as he looked at the five women.

The other nuns saw his pride and were ashamed that they had not participated. They treated the four brave nuns like heroines, and decided that the next time they would join in.

Peony returned to the Kuo house before Meadow found her missing. But when morning came, she confessed to her master and mistress what she had done during the night. They both were shocked, and Lady Kuo trembled when she imagined the risk Peony had taken. But when she convinced them that she and the nuns had merely joined the fighting force of the men, the Kuo couple were proud of her.

"Does it mean that tonight I can leave the house openly, without having to sneak behind Meadow's back?" Peony asked her master and mistress.

The Kuo couple could not say no.

Six moons later, the name Red Turbans was known by people from the Yellow River to the River Yangtze.

In whispering voices both the Chinese and Mongols said that the nuns in red turbans could walk on water and float in air, and that their leader was a tall, large girl whose name was unknown but whose feet were as large as those of a male coolie.

19

1348

WHILE THE MONGOL KHAN and his favorite Starlight enjoyed the spring weather in Da-du, a warm breeze danced her way through Yin-tin City, embracing the soft branches of the weeping willows with her invisible arms.

In the garden of the Lu mansion, Wisdom said, "Try to see the breeze as a loving mother, each of the willows her young child. She holds him, whispers in his ears, and tells him that she likes his new robe."

Endurance stared at the willows for a long while, then turned to Wisdom. "Do poets have to be crazy?"

The young lord laughed. Endurance had learned to read and write in the past two years. But when he read, he could not read silently; he shouted out each word. When he wrote, each character was the size of his fist; he filled a sheet large enough for a long verse with only two or three words at the most. As to his poems ... Wisdom shook his head. "Tell me, my friend, what do you see in this beautiful weeping willow tree?"

Endurance frowned and tightened his lips, studied the tree seriously. "I see good material for weaving baskets. And I also see firewood, but that will have to wait until the tree is dead and dry. Otherwise there would be a lot of smoke—"

Wisdom interrupted him. "Let's forget poems.

It's a lovely day. Would you like to visit the temple?"

He was surprised when Endurance shook his head.

"The monks look at kung fu the same way you look at the willow," Endurance said. "The last time I was there, Calm Fortitude wanted me to swear never to use kung fu for personal gain. He also said that during a fight, I must spare a man's life if I don't need to take more than his eyes, and that I should spare his eyes if breaking his arm is punishment enough for his crime."

"Did you swear?" Wisdom asked with concern, stopping at the moon gate. When a person reached a degree of excellence in kung fu, the monks demanded such a commitment. If the person refused, then there would be no more kung fu lessons. Wisdom knew that in the past two years, Endurance's kung fu lessons had been a chain keeping a wild eagle fastened to a tree. Without it, he would soon take flight.

"Of course not!" Endurance answered loudly. He went on to tell Wisdom the argument between him and Calm Fortitude. The old monk wouldn't let him return unless he changed his mind, and he had no intention of doing so. "I've learned plenty. I've captured the main elements in empty fist, broadsword, and long spear. I do need to perfect my kung fu, but that I can do on my own."

Endurance put his large hands on his friend's dainty shoulders and said, "You can never make me a poet. And I can never agree with the monks. My arm is fully recovered, and my learning period is over. I must find work."

The horse was a dappled brown and white, not comely but very strong. Endurance rode on its back, heard the wind in his ears, and felt the sun on his face. When he passed through a town, people parted to make way. When he raced through an open field, the trees ahead of him were left behind at the blink of his eye.

"Now I'm truly alive!" He cheered, gave the horse a kick, and galloped even faster.

The horse carried not only its rider, but also a large bag of mail. Wisdom had used his influence to find Endurance this job. In their yellow uniforms, mailmen were allowed to travel on horseback from one province to another without being stopped at the borders.

Endurance crossed the border to Kiangsi Province on a summer day. When he reached Phoenix Place, the sun was setting, creating the illusion of a dreamland protected by a phoenix's wings. Endurance's heart drummed with emotion. "I'm finally home!"

He delivered a letter to a Mongol officer's mansion, then looked for a place to spend the night. Mail carriers were allowed to have horses, but not to share the lodging posts with the Mongols and foreign travelers. Endurance stopped at a village home, asked for their last name. When the man told him reluctantly that their name was Chu, he was elated.

"My father was right! He told me that most of you will be related to me one way or another. My name is also Chu. I need a meal and a bed. My ancestors were—" Before he could say more, the door was slammed in his face.

As the night grew deeper, Endurance found more homes owned by people named Chu, but they all turned him away. He was deeply hurt and couldn't understand why his own people were so cold to him. Angrily he thought of his little friend Longevity and the other seven young men. He also thought of Wisdom and Lotus, and Jailor Li's wife who saved his life. He finally shrugged and gave up knocking on doors. "There are just as many coldhearted Chinese as there are warmhearted ones," he grumbled and sped away on his horse.

Riding under a summer moon, he soon left the last street behind and reached the graveyard. He remembered the names of his relatives and was glad that he could read the gravestones. Walking in the moonlight, he found the graves of his ancestors.

He kneeled and pleaded, "Forgive me for not coming here any sooner. Fate has forced me to make many detours. But I am ready to take action now. Please help me take China back from the Mongols and avenge the deaths of all my countrymen!"

Endurance found a Buddhist temple not far from the graveyard. The head monk took a quick look at the tired man and exhausted horse, immediately led the horse to a stable and Endurance to a room through an open court.

It was crowded with monks in tight clothes and soft shoes. In the moonlight their faces were wet with sweat and aglow with power. "Your monks are practicing kung fu, too!" Endurance said in surprise.

"Can you find any monks who are not?" the head monk answered calmly. "Even nuns are practicing in their own quarters."

Endurance nodded, having heard of the Red Turban nuns. Oddly enough, he had thought more than once, the description of their leader reminded him of his Peony. Perhaps she was also practicing kung fu in heaven and disturbing poor Buddha's peaceful world. He was suddenly too sad to sleep. He asked, "Is it all right if I watch?"

"Of course. But if you are a spy for the Mongols, then you won't leave the temple with your tongue."

The monk's voice was serene, but Endurance shivered at its force. "I'll never tell anyone what I saw," he promised.

He watched the monks for a while, then couldn't help joining them. Their style was different from that he had learned. He absorbed their technique, added it to his own. When the eastern sky paled into a dawning gray, the monks retired and Endurance went to sleep practicing kung fu in his dreams.

His next destination was Hangchow, the capital city of the last Sung emperor. After delivering his mail, he stopped to visit the famous West Lake and found a Taoist temple nearby. Once again he joined the monks to practice kung fu and assimilated the best of their style.

He traveled many moons, heading ever south. Finally he reached the banks of the Pearl River in the province of Hu-kuang. He could not understand the monks' dialect, but when he stayed in their temples, he grasped their unique kung fu style and felt like a rich man grabbing more gold to add to his treasure, which was already piling high.

"You look different," Wisdom said when he saw Endurance again in the spring of 1349. He studied the peasant's muscular body and glowing face, "You've grown older, bigger, and happier."

"I've learned a lot about people, life, and fighting techniques." He went on to tell Wisdom about his experience with the cold Chus, the kind monks, and the creating of a new kung fu technique that combined the best of all styles. He examined Wisdom's pale face and fragile frame and laughed. "Well, you did not age, nor did you grow any bigger. But at least you did not shrink either. And you look very happy, too."

"I'm not only happy but also proud. Lotus and I now have another son. He was born last winter. My father named him Earnest."

He took Endurance to his study, insisting that he spend the night in his old room. "We have so much to tell each other," Wisdom said.

He told Endurance of the messages he had sent to various resistance leaders. They all wanted his financial support, but none would agree to join forces with any other groups.

"I'm very disappointed," Wisdom said. "Our revolutionary commanders are fighting for themselves instead of China. I heard about a man named Vanguard Kuo, who lives in Honan Province to the north. Rumor has it that he is very different from the others. I've sent him an invitation, but he has not yet answered me."

Finally, Wisdom started to tell Endurance about the Silent League. "We're still doing the same things—"

Endurance interrupted, "I don't care for those snotty creatures, and I don't want to hear about them. I hate all scholars except you!" Without giving Wisdom a chance to reply, Endurance said, "But I do need your help."

He reminded Wisdom of his dream long ago. "I mentioned it to you the first time we met. You told me to let you know when I was ready. I didn't think I would need your help then. I thought the inhabitants of Phoenix Place would follow me because my father was one of them. But I was wrong."

On his next trip to Phoenix Place, Endurance carried in the bottom of his mailbag, coins of silver and gold.

The coldhearted Chinese who were unwilling

to trust a poor mailman changed to some degree at the sight of a silver coin. When shown a gold coin, Endurance's words became very convincing indeed.

Endurance gathered over twenty men in his ancestor's hometown and brought them to the graveyard at night. "Your responsibility is to spy on the Mongols. When I come back, you'll take me into your homes instead of closing your doors. You'll tell me if a small group of Mongols are camping nearby, and lead me to their camp-site. And, of course, you will be handsomely re-warded for your information."

Backed by Wisdom's money, Endurance was able to recruit more people from various villages as spies. But when he stayed at temples and tried to bring the monks under his sway, he found that silver or gold could not change their minds. They were bound by religion to use kung fu merely in defense.

What soon became the core of Endurance's force was a group of a dozen mail carriers. Brave and strong, they did not need to be paid to fight; they were filled with patriotic fervor. By day they rode on horseback from town to town, col-lecting information from the paid spies. At night they attacked isolated groups of Mongols and then ran away to hide in temples. With each new dawn, they rode off in their yellow uniforms, innocuous mailmen again.

Endurance worked with them closely, and soon became as close to them as he had with his initial group of seven young boys.

Endurance arrived back in Yin-tin in time for the Moon Festival. Wisdom sent a personal note to Endurance's superior, asking that he be granted a day's rest, and Endurance shared a feast with the Lu family. When he and Wisdom were sitting alone under the autumn moon, the young lord congratulated him for his success.

"My twelve fighters are like my brothers. Let us drink to their health and success, too," Endurance said, raising his wine cup high.

For the rich in Yin-tin City, no Moon Festival feast was complete without the crabs that lived in the nearby streams of the Yangtze River. When a crab was alive, it resembled a gray chrysanthemum. When the crab was cooked, the chrysanthemum turned bright red. People believed that when the autumn moon was full, the flavor of the crab reached its height.

The chrysanthemum crabs were also brought to Da-du, almost twelve hundred miles away, and presented to the Great Khan Sandstorm's favorite court lady, Starlight. She savored not only the taste of the crabs, but also the sight of them changing color and the sound of them struggling to crawl out of the boiling wok. Due to her command, twelve sacks of live chrysanthemum crabs always left Yin-tin on Moon Festival day and arrived at the palace a few days later.

For the delivery of these crabs, a dozen mail carriers were relieved from their ordinary duty. Instead of mailbags, they carried large sacks filled with live crabs. Endurance's twelve fighters were the fastest riders, and they were chosen for this duty. Endurance would have been chosen also if he had not been invited by the mayor's son to a festival feast.

The twelve men rode more than two hundred miles a day, changed several mounts, and made the twelve hundred miles in five days. They delivered the crabs to the palace, then turned to leave Da-du. They were arrested before going far.

For reasons unknown, all the crabs were dead.

Starlight was furious. The great khan ordered all the delivery men executed.

Endurance was in Phoenix Place when he heard the news. He raced back to Yin-tin, jumped off his horse and charged into the Lu house in broad daylight, found Wisdom in the inner chamber.

"Please tell me it is only a rumor!" he yelled at Wisdom.

"I'm sorry, my friend," Wisdom said, his voice trembling.

Endurance's face was ashen. Lines of blood filled his eyes. He yelled in a broken voice, "Is it true that Starlight wanted to see them torn apart like crabs? I heard that her brother Mighty Sword was there, and he carried out the execution . . ." He did not have the heart to continue.

Each of the mail carriers had been tied to four horses, one limb to a different horse. Mighty Sword cracked his whip, and the horses ran toward four directions. The tied man was torn to pieces, just like a cooked crab when being eaten.

Wisdom nodded, then turned toward the bedchamber. A woman was vomiting. Lotus had heard what Endurance had said.

Jasmine bolted out of the bedchamber and pointed a finger at Endurance. "Get out of here, you inconsiderate peasant! You made my lady sick! How dare you speak of such abomination in a house of peace?"

"Never mind what she says, please sit and—"

Wisdom tried to grab Endurance, but he was already flying out of the house like a storm.

Endurance wandered aimlessly through the streets of Yin-tin, then stomped alongside the Yangtze River in the bright sun. He knew Mighty Sword was in the great capital. But on every face of the Mongols who roamed the riverbank, he saw the general's image.

"You killed my second group of followers! And you killed them in the cruelest way possible, just when they had become my friends and brothers! I hate you! I must destroy you! There is not enough room in the world of living for both of us!" he shouted, unmindful of anyone around him.

Three Mongols nearby heard him and started laughing. "A crazy Chinese!" One of them said, pointing at Endurance. "A big man talking to himself like a stupid baby!"

The trio's laughter ended abruptly when Endurance advanced on them. With lightning quickness he kicked the middle one and punched the other two. "You filthy swine!"

Though dazed, the Mongols rapidly drew their swords. Surrounding Endurance, they pointed their weapons to hem him in. All three raised their swords at the same time, ready to chop him to pieces.

Endurance turned like a whirlwind. The Mongols could not see him clearly, but felt the wind grabbing their swords. They tried to hold onto the handles, but their strength could not compare with the power of the wind. Their swords sailed out of their hands, landed on the riverbank. Then the Chinese giant used a foot to snap one of the swords back up into his hand. The last thing they saw was the peasant grinning at them.

Several Mongols not too far down the river saw Endurance swing the sword and cut off the three Mongols' heads so quickly that it seemed like in one stroke. One of them recognized him and shouted, "That is Endurance Chu, the mailman!"

The cry brought back Endurance's senses.

Glancing around, he dropped the sword and began to run.

In the inner court of the Lu mansion, Lotus gave him a backpack that contained food, clothes, and a pouch of silver and gold coins.

Wisdom said, "You must leave the south immediately, and you cannot return for a long time. You have to walk now, because you are no longer a mailman. Do not worry about me. Even if they remember you were my guest for the Moon Festival, they cannot prove anything. You must hide in the temples. You cannot trust anyone but the monks."

Lotus reminded her husband, "Don't forget the gift you made for our friend."

Wisdom sighed. "I made you something and was saving it for your next birthday. But I have to give it to you now."

From a dresser drawer he took out a small box. Giving it to Endurance, he waited to see his reaction.

On a gold chain hung a jade pendant chiseled into two grasping hands. Endurance brought the pendant closer to his eyes, then smiled. "How do you do such a fine work? One hand is dainty like yours, and the other big and rough like mine!"

Wisdom pointed at the two wooden statues on the dresser. "I am very fond of sculpting. Someday, I will create a pair of jade lovers." Endurance laughed, for he had already heard of this lifetime dream many times.

"I'll always wear this chain, and every time I feel it, I'll think of you. You are my best friend. We will meet again when this chaos is over," Endurance said confidently, trying to fasten the chain around his neck.

Wisdom walked around to help Endurance

from behind. He had to stand on tiptoe to reach Endurance's neck. Wisdom then leaned his face against Endurance's back. His voice was shaking with sorrow and his tears fell. "Why must there be this cruel war? Otherwise you'd be a farmer, and I a sculptor. But now we must each fight in our own way, and our paths may never again cross."

Endurance felt Wisdom's tears wetting the back of his thin garment. He wanted to say something, but his voice was choked in his throat. He raised a hand to touch the pendant, pressing the two clasped hands tightly against his heart.

PART III

20

THE ROYAL CHEFS were preparing a grand feast. It was five days after the Chinese Moon Festival, and as usual, the Mongols in Da-du did not celebrate it then, but enjoyed the Yin-tin crabs now. Starlight was pleased that in the past two years, all the chrysanthemum crabs had arrived alive.

The royal feast was attended by all the princes, princesses, court officials, and their families, and in a prominent place the Great Khan Sandstorm sat between Shadow Tamu and Mighty Sword. Over the years his adviser had made all the decisions for him, and his supreme general carried out the fighting. He had devoted his languorous days to loving Starlight and enjoying her beauty.

"Look at her." The aged great khan pointed at his mistress, who was at the other side of the grand dining room watching the live crabs being cooked. "Laughing like a child, and wearing a child's loveliness."

Mighty Sword and Shadow Tamu looked at each other over Sandstorm's head. Neither of them had any children, and they loved their younger sister as if she were their daughter. As of late, though, they had been worried about Starlight's fading youth, for she was now twenty-nine. Already the fact that she had been Sandstorm's favorite for the past six years was astonishing. Usually, a great khan would stay fascinated by the same woman only for a year or less, and few were captivated by a woman older than twenty-five.

"Our sister is a wonderful woman," Shadow Tamu said, smiling at his brother.

Mighty Sword raised his jeweled golden cup, "To the great khan and our little sister!"

As the feast continued, no one noticed the absence of Prince Tempest, one of Sandstorm's many nephews. A young man, the prince was powerful in build and brilliant in mind. He was also extremely ambitious.

His court was far from the grand dining room. His personal guards stood outside the shut doors, ready to stop anyone who dared to enter.

The strong odor of explosives filled Prince Tempest's court, for the prince stood among six craftsmen chosen for their excellent skills. Various firearms crowded a large table. They were invented more than seven decades ago by the Chinese of the Sung dynasty.

Prince Tempest picked up a soaring serpent. It was a flying rocket made by filling sections of thick bamboo with explosives. When they were shoved out of the short bamboo by a long rod, they could hit a target twenty feet away and set it aflame. "Not good enough!" the prince said and put it down.

He then chose a gliding snake, a clay container shaped like a snake and filled with explosives. When thrown, the container would shatter upon landing, the explosives would make a loud bang, and a flame would rise high. "It's effective for locating enemies in the dark, but not what I want." The prince shook his head and put it down.

"My Royal Highness, I think we've created something to suit your purpose," one of the craftsmen said excitedly.

An iron tube the length of a man's arm, curving slightly toward its end, was filled with a mixture of explosives, crushed stone, and powdered iron. There was a trigger where the curving began, and it was locked in place by a thin wire.

The craftsman explained, "Once the trigger is released, the mixture will fly out with great force, hitting and destroying your target. You can be fifty feet from your enemy and kill him, provided that you aim well."

Prince Tempest took the iron tube in his hands, aimed it at an imaginary target. A smile appeared on his face as he said, "From tomorrow on, the six of you will go with me deep into the forest where no one can see or hear me practice." The prince continued slowly, "What shall we call this thing? Let me think ... It'll be a hand that does the killing for me. Killing Hand! That's it!"

One day in the spring of 1352, the Great Khan Sandstorm was walking through his garden, well protected by many guards as always. Undaunted, Prince Tempest hid behind a large rock on the other side of the garden. Aiming his Killing Hand at the khan, he fired. The explosive mixture punched a hole through the khan's heart.

Although not crowned, Prince Tempest soon gained control of the palace and all the lives in it. "Kill all the childless court ladies who are older than I!" ordered the twenty-one-year-old future khan. "I want my palace filled with young beauties. When an aged court lady has no child to mother, there is no reason for her to take up space."

The future khan's order was carried out immediately. When Shadow Tamu heard the beheading of Starlight, he dropped his gold and screamed. "My poor sister was only thirty and still a beauty!"

The dead khan's adviser was not only saddened by his sister's death, but also offended that the new khan had given an order without consulting him first. Shadow Tamu was a cunning fox, however, and when he buried Starlight beside the dead Khan Sandstorm, his face was expressionless. No one could read his thoughts except Mighty Sword, who had rushed back for the funerals.

"We will avenge the death of our sister," he said when the two brothers were alone.

"Of course we will," Shadow Tamu answered. "We just need to bide our time."

Spring neared its end, and the ground of the palace garden became thick with fallen flowers. Shadow Tamu stepped over the petals to reach the Lamaist temple and pray for the spirit of Starlight. He was facing a statue of Buddha, pleading humbly, when Prince Tempest barged in.

"I need your help," said the future khan. He told his guards to leave the temple and close the doors behind them. He laid his Killing Hand on the altar, then sat beside it. The prince was never seen without carrying his magic weapon. "I'll be crowned tomorrow, and you'll stay on as my adviser. That is, if you can solve a problem for me. Let's see how clever you really are."

Prince Tempest wanted to fill his palace with young beauties for the pleasing of his eyes, but his heart belonged to a married woman whose husband was a general only one rank lower than Mighty Sword. As one of many princes, Tempest had been able to carry on an affair with her discreetly, but as the great khan, his every movement would become a public event.

"I cannot bear to stop seeing her. But I cannot

afford to anger her husband either," the young prince said in distress.

Shadow Tamu's eyes gleamed, for in fact this general was an obstacle to overthrowing the new khan. In a voice revealing no emotion, he remarked, "It is easy for a great khan to kill a general. He doesn't even need a reason. A general's widow can then be brought into the palace to fill one of the many empty courts." He waited for the young prince to take the bait.

"No. I don't want that," Prince Tempest said. "I only want to meet the general's wife in secret. If she lives in the palace, then she will be a barrier between me and the other young beauties." The young prince added hesitantly, "Perhaps I don't love her enough. I'm not sure I know what true love is."

Shadow Tamu concealed his disappointment. Thinking the matter over, he soon devised an ingenious plan. After all, first he had to win the new khan's trust.

Two hundred Chinese were forced into labor, digging a tunnel. One end of it opened into the head monk's room in a Lamaist temple near the general's home, the other end into the palace garden.

The men worked day and night, and were kept in isolation. The secret passage was built within twenty days. All two hundred men were killed as soon as their work was done.

When Shadow Tamu informed the newly crowned great khan of the completion of the tunnel, the khan left his young beauties and followed his adviser to the palace garden.

At the same moment a messenger was on his way to the general's wife. Upon receiving the message, the beautiful woman put on her best garment and left for the neighborhood temple.

She offered her prayers to Buddha, then told her
servants to wait outside the temple while she
continued a discussion with the old head monk
in his private chamber.

The Great Khan Tempest did not see the need
of taking his Killing Hand with him on a tryst,
and he left his magic weapon with the head of
his twenty personal guards. These men stood
back when the great khan reached a set of steps
that led to a statue of Buddha. As the great khan
kneeled at Buddha's feet, he pressed down on
the statue's left big toe.

The guards stared wide-eyed as a piece of the
wood at the edge of the platform started to glide
sideways, revealing an entranceway. The khan
stood up and descended a narrow stairway. From
within came a woman's voice: "I've missed you
so much! I thought you'd forgotten me!"

Shadow Tamu was standing next to his creation, but he felt no pride. His eyes burned in
sheer hatred as he watched the great khan taking
his mistress in his arms and descending the
steps that led to a small but elaborately adorned
room. When the khan turned a gold candlestick
on the bedside table, the board began to glide
back to its rightful place, concealing the entrance.

Both Shadow Tamu and the guards waited patiently until the great khan reappeared with a
satisfied smile on his young face. "Tell my trea-
surer to give you a bag of gold," the khan said
to Shadow Tamu. "You deserve to be rewarded
for your cleverness."

The adviser bowed his thanks, then narrowed
his eyes after the departing khan. Winning over
the young Tempest had been child's play. Now
there was no doubt that his sister's death would
be avenged.

21

A PROCESSION OF TRAVELERS moved under the blistering sun. Two sedan chairs were followed by ten ox-pulled wagons, each accompanied by six men.

Peony, oddly enough, rode in one of the sedan chairs. Vanguard Kuo had been late coming home from a long trip, and Joy Kuo had been worried. As a result, Peony had been sent to investigate. She had met her master two days before at the border of Honan Province. After sending a fast rider home to tell Lady Kuo of his safety, Peony had accompanied him home to Prosper Mountain.

Looking out from inside her sedan, she saw at the outskirts of town, blue tiles on the nearly finished Lamaist temple reflecting the summer sun. Chinese laborers were working on the detailed adornments, and she frowned. Her scowl grew even deeper as they approached a Mongol sentry post. All who entered Prosper Mountain were subject to a search.

"Stop!" A Mongol soldier said, appearing in the middle of the road with his feet parted and sword pointing at the sedan carriers.

The oldest of them answered with a smile on his face but sarcasm in his voice, "Do you not see the family crest on the drapery? But of course I don't suppose you can read. We are Master Kuo's men. He and his maid are returning from a buying trip in the south."

By this time three more soldiers joined the first one. One of them studied the silk drapery, then said, "We've heard of your master's name, but we must search the wagons just the same. How do we know there are no weapons? You Chinese are a thieving lot. Don't think we haven't heard of all the knives and swords you have been making secretly."

The sedans were lowered softly to the ground. The drapery of the first was lifted by a steady hand, and then a tall, slender middle-aged man emerged wearing a brown silk robe.

Vanguard Kuo said calmly to the four soldiers, "You may search my wagons, but you'll find only porcelain. Each of you is welcome to a gift of your choice. All I ask is that you please be careful in handling these delicate artworks."

The soldiers' eyes widened when they saw a girl coming out of the second sedan. Tall and large-boned, she reminded them of their native women. Standing with her feet parted and hands at her hips, she glared at them challengingly.

The soldiers looked away, more interested in the goods in the wagons right now. Two more soldiers joined the first four, and they advanced on the booty.

Vanguard Kuo's sixty men stood watching, showing no expression on their faces but clenching their fists tightly. His army had grown in the past five years to almost a thousand fighters, and these were the elite among them. They also knew that in the last wagon, underneath the porcelain, was something which must not be found by the Mongols.

The six soldiers stopped beside the first six wagons, taking one apiece. They tossed aside the straw and uncovered the porcelain plates and bowls, vases and jewelry boxes. They soon found a suitable prize and did not bother to search the four remaining wagons. They waved their gifts at Vanguard on their way back to their post.

Peony breathed with relief. The Kuo fighters loosened their clenched fists. Vanguard said caustically to the departing soldiers, "I'm glad you like Yin-tin porcelain. It is the best in China."

The procession resumed their journey home, and soon Peony saw in a distance the Kuo house, with long strings of firecrackers hanging from bamboo poles. As they approached the house, the watchman shouted and then the firecrackers went off. "Welcome home, Master Kuo!" the entire household called, bowing their greetings to their admired lord.

Vanguard said to four of the guards, "Bring me the two items I have hidden in the last wagon." He then hurried into the inner court.

Rushing inside after her master, Peony saw her mistress sitting in a satin chair in a pale green robe. Peony made a face at the aged housekeeper Meadow, who stood beside Lady Kuo, then yelled, "My lady, I did exactly what you told me. I made sure that the master ate three meals a day, and went to bed early every night!"

Vanguard Kuo squatted beside his wife and took her delicate hand. Oblivious to the presence of the others, he kissed her hand, then pressed it against his cheek and said, "I've missed you very much."

Joy blushed. It was not proper for a man to kiss a woman's hand in company. Then she frowned, puzzled. Her ears were much sharper than that of the people who could see.

"I hear disappointment in your voice, my honorable husband," she said, trying in vain to free her hand. Instead, she used her other hand to feel her husband's face. Her fingers lingered between his eyebrows and felt the deep lines. "Did something go wrong?"

Vanguard looked in time to see the four guards appear with two large boxes in their hands. "I've brought home some very interesting things," he said as he gestured for the men to put the boxes on a table. "I'm glad the Mongols did not find them."

Meadow was uninterested in whatever was in the boxes. "Wasting my lady's money on useless things," she uttered under her breath as she left with the men.

Peony had no intention of leaving. She watched her master bring the small box to her lady. Opening it, he revealed a bunch of wooden sticks each about eight inches long.

Vanguard took one out of the box and placed it in his wife's hand. "This is a fire stick invented by the clever southerners."

"I smell firecracker," Joy Kuo said, sniffing the red end of the stick.

"You are right," Vanguard said. "The makers dipped these sticks in a mixture of explosives and glue." He let Joy feel one side of the wooden box, which was very rough. "And they also glued fine grains of sand to the box. When they need fire, all they have to do is this . . ." He took the stick from his wife, scratched its red end quickly over the rough side of the box.

"It's burning!" Peony shouted excitedly. "Like magic!" She brought her lady's hand over the flame to feel the heat, then looked at her master pleadingly, like a child asking permission to try a new toy.

"Go ahead," Vanguard said, smiling at his wife's favorite maid.

Peony watched the stick catch on fire and cheered excitedly. "The fire Buddha finally shared his secret with us! We no longer need to rub fire stones together to make the first fire each morning!"

"The fire sticks are easy to make. I already learned, and I'll teach the people of the north," Vanguard Kuo said proudly. "I wouldn't be surprised if someday the whole world knows the secret of fire sticks."

"Fire sticks," Joy Kuo repeated the words. "I like the name." She then asked in puzzlement, "Why must you hide it from the Mongols?"

"I was not hiding the fire sticks as much as I was the other thing," Vanguard pointed at the large box. "Peony, please bring it over here."

The box was over three feet long and heavy. Peony lugged it to her master, watched him take out a flared iron tube, then waited for him to explain what the strange thing was.

Vanguard's voice was low and ominous. "The current khan has six craftsmen who invented this killing hand for him to kill the previous khan. While one of the six men was dying, he gave the design to his number-one son, who went to the south and sold the pattern to our revolutionaries. We Chinese have changed the name to Flaming Snakes. I paid a high price for this one."

Joy ran her hand over the cold iron tube and shivered. Vanguard took her hand in his and lifted it. "I share your fear for this thing."

The Khan Tempest, he went on, did not want anyone else in his court to have a Killing Hand, meaning that the weapon would not be used by the Mongols as long as the current khan was alive. The southern Chinese revolution leaders, for their part, were beginning to make the Flaming Snakes, but they were costly and no one could afford to make many. Among the northern leaders, Vanguard was the only one who had a Flaming Snake.

Vanguard said, "If the khan's private weapon becomes the general weapon of the Mongol soldiers, and if all Chinese rebels use it in return, then the war between us will become ten times more bloody than it already is." Sorrow filled Vanguard's voice as he continued, "When the world beyond China is affected by this invention, there will be endless deaths of men."

Peony liked the feel of this iron tube. She played with it while listening to the conversation between her master and lady.

"You did not tell me the reason for the disappointment in your voice," Joy said with deep concern.

"The main object of my trip was to respond to Wisdom Lu's invitation. I was hoping to unite the southern forces with the northern and set a date for a national revolt . . ."

Vanguard Kuo went on, and Peony listened while slowly putting away the Flaming Snake.

"Every Chinese in Yin-tin City knows where Wisdom Lu's home is. They spoke of the Lu family with great respect as they pointed toward a mansion near the Whispering Lake. There were tears in their eyes when they told me Mayor Lu had died recently and they had lost a fatherlike protector.

"It was raining when I arrived at the Lu mansion. I waited in the rain, but Wisdom Lu refused to see me. Then I learned that the tradition of Hundred Day Mourning is followed much more strictly in the south than north, especially by wealthy intellectuals who can afford to do so."

According to tradition, after the death of his father, a son must mourn for a hundred days. During that period he must stay home and wear black, eat vegetables, and drink cold water, practice celibacy and shun everyone except immediate relations.

Vanguard said, "I waited in the rain wishing he would change his mind, but he never did. I could not stay in Yin-tin for that many days. Being a stranger, I could not find a go-between who is immediately related to him. So I had to leave without meeting Wisdom Lu. I guess I'll have to wait until the end of autumn when Wisdom Lu is out of mourning, then contact him again."

Peony kept Lady Kuo from being lonely as Vanguard Kuo spent the summer of 1352 supervising his men making fire sticks. He distributed them among the people of Prosper Mountain, and the making of fire became much easier.

When autumn began, the Lamaist monks arrived from Mongolia, riding horses and wearing brightly colored robes with matching headdresses. They settled in their new temple, and quickly showed that the Buddhism of Mongolia was wholly different from that of China.

"The new monks came to buy wine from me!" the wine house owner told Peony in disbelief. "And I had to sell it to them."

"They also came to buy pork and beef from me!" the astonished butcher told her. "And then asked if the girls in the green lamp houses would make temple calls!"

The people of Prosper Mountain believed that in this corrupted world, the Confucius scholars and the Buddhist and Taoist monks were the three pillars of morality. Believing that one of these pillars was crumbling, they were enraged. Accordingly, five young men chose a dark night to set fire to the Lamaist temple. The fire was extinguished before any harm was done, though, and the arsonists were arrested and beheaded in the town square. The villagers were infuriated beyond the control of either the nuns and monks or even Vanguard Kuo.

"Master Kuo," Peony said when she told him what she had heard, "the villagers are ready to revolt with or without your approval."

After a long pause, while he thought the matter over, Vanguard sighed. "I guess the north has to declare open rebellion without the south." He then asked Peony, "will you and Joy pay Peaceful Essence a visit to inform him of our plans?"

Peony and Lady Kuo, riding in sedan chairs, ventured to the Temple of White Crane that same afternoon and found Peaceful Essence waiting for them. His usually peaceful countenance had been replaced by one of fury.

"The behavior of the Lamaist monks has sparked the anger in the hearts of all the monks in this temple. And the current khan's open acceptance of Christianity adds fuel to this fire. We were wrong to curb the use of our kung fu. We will not hesitate to go on the offensive from now on," he declared. He went on to say that he had contacted the other monks along the Yellow River as Vanguard had requested. They had all agreed to fight as one should there be war.

Lady Kuo said, "My husband needs your help, and also the help of all the other monks in the temples of the north." As she talked, Peony sneaked away.

She reached the nuns' quarter and called them out to the open court. Jumping up on the pedestal, she stood facing the nuns. "There will be a war," she said. "The northerners will unite in revolt against the Mongols. But my lady and master are recruiting the monks only. No one has thought of us nuns!"

In truth, Peony considered herself a nun. She was twenty-four, old enough to be considered an old maid. Lady Kuo had suggested she marry

some male servant, but she had turned down the
offer. Leading the Red Turban nuns had become
the center of her life. She avenged Endurance's
death every time she punished a Mongol for vic-
timizing a Chinese. She felt accomplishment
every time she heard that because of the Red
Turbans, the Mongols now looked over their
shoulders when they harassed Chinese people.

"Let us Red Turbans show the men what we
can do!" she raised a fist and yelled.

The nuns cheered, waving their fists as well.
Only a few of them had entered the temple because of religious devotion: most of them had
been forced by fate. Each had a sad story, and
for a long time had been accustomed to live the
life of a helpless lamb. Becoming a Red Turban
nun, though, had given them a chance to protect
the weak and punish the mighty. Possessing
such power gave them pride and confidence, and
they were no longer lambs toyed by a cruel wolf.

"We are ready for war whenever you are,
Peony!" they shouted.

"When Master Kuo is ready, I'll inform you.
We'll follow the men to battle, whether they like
it or not," Peony said. Finally she told them that
the Red Turbans would not meet in the town
square for the time being, since a bigger battle
was soon to be fought.

Peony returned to Lady Kuo and heard Peaceful Essence saying, ". . . I'll send a monk to your
house tonight to have a detailed discussion with
Master Kuo."

When Lady Kuo and Peony were gone, Peaceful Essence ordered the young and strong monks
to line up. He told them of the upcoming revolt
of the north. "I need someone for a dangerous
mission. He will go to Master Vanguard Kuo's
house first, and then all the other temples in the

north. Master Kuo will tell him the date our uprising will begin, and he will share that with the
head monks in all temples along the Yellow
River. He must be brave and clever, because
when traveling on foot from one place to another,
his chances of being caught will be very high . . ."
Peaceful Essence stopped when he noticed a
monk he hadn't seen before.

He was very tall, and his shoulders were
square and broad. His neck was massive like a
stump, his waist a barrel. His arms and legs resembled large tree trunks. His face was dark
with a wide nose, thick lips, straight eyebrows,
and piercing eyes.

He had been in the Temple of White Crane
only two days, but already caused a lot of trouble. His irascible temperament brought out the
worst in the monks, and several even-tempered
monks had been forced to fight him.

He fought with a strange kung fu that was a
combination of all fighting techniques but at the
same time violated all rules. He was able to use
a bamboo stick as a spear, a wood board as a
broadsword. He used them so proficiently that
no one could get near him or defend themselves
against his assaults.

The bad-tempered giant had been transferred
to Peaceful Essence by another head monk in a
Buddhist temple north of Prosper Mountain.
Upon arrival, the towering man had looked down
at Peaceful Essence and gave him a note. "Just
to save you the trouble of reading it, I can tell
you what it says." The enormous young monk
smiled, not hiding the fact that he had read the
note, meant for Peaceful Essence alone.

He told the old monk brazenly, "It says that
you have to keep an eye on me. I am wanted in
the south for murder. I've killed many Mongols
in towns and villages alongside the Yangtze

River, especially in Phoenix Place and Yin-tin City. I've never killed a Chinese, but when I killed the Mongols, it was not purely in self-defense or as a punishment for their evil conduct. Sometimes I would kill one Mongol as revenge for the crimes committed by another."

The giant-sized man in a monk's robe grinned as he continued, "And the note also tells you that I am the best fighter but worst monk. In the past three years, I have served as a novice in many temples, but neither the Buddhist nor the Taoist monks could tolerate me. They say I would make a better Lamaist monk, because I hate vegetables and like meat, and also need a little wine at times. Anyway, everything in the note is true."

Who would make the best messenger? Peaceful Essence thought as he eyed the figure towering over the crowd of monks. He turned toward the statue of Buddha and said in his heart, "Forgive me, my great Buddha, for wanting to send him away from my temple. But honestly, he is also the best man for this dangerous job."

22

THE NIGHT SKY of autumn was cloudless, and a new moon was overpowered by many brilliant stars. A hulk of a man in a monk's robe left the Temple of White Crane, closed the door behind him, and moved soundlessly toward a narrow path that led him through a forest of ageless pines.

As Endurance Chu heard the old pine cones crushing under his feet, he remembered the tall pines in his hometown. In the past three years, he had traveled through many small northern towns, but avoided Emerald Valley and Pinetree Village. He would return to those two places someday, but not before he felt he had avenged the deaths of Peony and their two families.

Vengeance was a mighty fire burning in his heart, giving him pain. Sometimes he hated himself for not having accomplished anything at age twenty-four. After hiding behind temple walls and failing to gather a rebel group for what seemed like a lifetime, he now welcomed a chance to fight under a man who was, according to Peaceful Essence, the most powerful revolutionary leader of northern Honan Province.

Descending the mountain, he saw the new Lamaist temple. He heard from behind the closed doors a cacophony of sounds that drew him a picture of monks having fun, drinking, eating, and being entertained by women. "If the Chinese monks were as willing to compromise as the Mongolian monks, perhaps they could have accepted me better," he mumbled under his breath and walked on.

When he reached the road that would take him to the Kuo house, according to his directions, he saw Mongol soldiers camping in tents not far away. A few of them were roasting wild rabbits over the roaring camp fires. The aroma of meat reached his nostrils and made his mouth water. Eyeing the rabbits, he took a step toward the camp fires.

The vegetarian diets of the various temples, had irritated Endurance as much as their strict rules. He had offended many head monks by sneaking out of their temples to either steal or rob food from both Chinese and Mongols. How could anyone blame a big young man for his inability to live on tofu and bean sprouts? After all, he had never vowed to restrict himself from using kung fu for personal gains.

"Stop!" A Mongol soldier appeared in the middle of the road, with his feet parted and his sword leveled.

Endurance grinned: It would be simple to take the man's sword away. Just when he was about to act, however, five more Mongol soldiers emerged from the darkness, forming a circle around Endurance.

He thought quickly and decided it would be impossible to kill all of them without alarming the entire camp. He raised his hands to his heart with his palms together and forced a humble tone into his voice. "May the great Buddha protect you, my good men, and bring you long lives and many bags of gold."

"Why are you out of the monastery at night?" one of the Mongols asked, looking at the big monk suspiciously.

Endurance answered, "One of the old monks is very ill. I must go to the herb man for help. If I don't hurry, the great Buddha will blame me for the old monk's death ... me and whoever delays my trip."

At this threat, the Mongols stepped back immediately. Endurance kept going and soon entered Prosper Mountain. He had not visited here since returning to the north, for he had taken Wisdom's advice and stayed away from large towns. If the head monk of the last temple had not transferred him to White Crane, he would have never revisited this area.

The sights filled him with painful memories. When he reached the town square, he discovered a bamboo pole was still there. He found himself thrown into a dark river of yesteryear, being carried by a powerful current, and then left on the shore of 1345.

He could see a thirteen-year-old boy's head being displayed on top of the pole. He looked at the pole top, which seemed to be touching the radiant stars, and called softly. "Where are you, my little friend? In the loving arms of your mother, I hope?"

He forced himself to look away from the pole, but the cold water of the past washed over him once more. This time the tide deposited him on the beach of 1346.

He stared at the platform and recalled the faces of his seven friends. He heard in his ears their voices screaming, "I would rather die than wear a tattoo!"

He shambled forward and soon reached the jail house. He felt better when he thought of the kind old jailor and his wife. He wanted to thank them for having saved his life. When he knocked on the door, though, a young jailor answered it and looked at Endurance skeptically. "Why are you looking for those two foolish old lawbreakers? Jailor Li and his wife had been turning prisoners loose. The Mongols finally caught them and killed them about two years ago, right over there in the town square."

Endurance ran blindly from the jail until he was out of breath. In the center of town, he stopped. The town had grown. Red and yellow lamps shone over many shops and restaurants, like floating flowers blooming in a night garden. Green lamps outnumbered the red and yellow, like leaves outnumbering petals.

Among them was one larger than the others. Its light illuminated the Mongols standing in front of it, revealing their faces.

"Mighty Sword!" Endurance gasped, stepping hastily into the shadow of a food peddler's stand.

The supreme general was in his early thirties now. He had his pointed metal hat in his hand. The hair on his temples began to show a few strands of silver, but it only enhanced his handsomeness. His high boots with pointed toes were so well polished that the black leather reflected the lantern's green light. He had gained weight. A heavy sword hung from the wide belt around his thick waist. He was accompanied by four armed guards. He said something to them, then entered the green lamp house laughing, his scarlet silk cape sailing behind him.

As his guards followed him, Endurance stayed in the shadow, gazing at the closed door. He then looked himself over. He was wearing a pair of old sandals and a monk's humble cotton robe.

"This is unfair!" he screamed, frightening the food peddler. Endurance dashed out of the shadows, toward the green lamp house.

Rational judgment told him that he had a mission to accomplish, that he could not afford to behave emotionally. But his heart was mad with the desire to destroy an enemy who had killed his friends, demolished two groups of his men together with his youthful dreams. His heart won.

Stealing down the side of the house, he effortlessly gained access to the roof. He moved soundlessly across the tiles, listening carefully for Mighty Sword's voice. When he was certain that he had located his prey, he assessed the location of that room, then leapt to the ground in the courtyard as if his massive body were as weightless as a feather.

He moved around the house with the soft steps of a cat, until he found the window he wanted. Retreating a few steps to give him a running start, he charged forward. The paper window was shattered, and he landed on the floor right beside the bed.

The lamp on the beside table had blown out. Although the window was gone, the light from outside wasn't enough to clarify the faces of the two entwined bodies in bed. Endurance heard the girl scream and the man curse. When his eyes were more adjusted to the dark, he saw something gleaming on the floor, on top of a pile of discarded clothes. He grinned at the sight of a sword.

He picked it up and drew it out of its sheath. Prowling toward the bed, he plunged it into the man. The force of the blow was such that the blade pierced the man's body and nailed him to the bed.

"Now you can rot in hell, Mighty Sword!" Endurance said as he stared at the glistening handle of the sword swinging back and forth in the unlit room.

The sound of Endurance crashing in and the girl screaming had alarmed the entire house. Endurance heard people running toward the room.

He turned to leap out of the window, then noticed a pair of men's shoes on the floor. They were not Mighty Sword's black leather boots. He raced back to the bed and leaned toward the dead man's face. It was not the supreme general.

He glanced at the girl and found her staring at him. She had been in the dark for a long time, he realized, and her eyes were already accustomed to the blackness. She could identify him. He must kill her. Instinctively he put his hands over her throat. The girl closed her eyes and sank her teeth into her lip.

For a brief moment Endurance's hands froze in midair. His heart wouldn't allow him to proceed with the killing. Once again his heart fought with his rational mind, but this time reason won out. As people pounded on the door, his hands closed around the girl's throat and tightened their grip. She opened her eyes and stared at Endurance with deep hatred. Her eyes began to bulge. She opened her mouth and her tongue stuck out.

The pounding turned into hammering. The door was about to be crushed. Endurance was certain that the girl was dead. He dashed out of the window and melted into the night of Prosper Mountain.

In the Kuo house, Vanguard said to his wife, "Dear, you have the ability to tell if a person is sincere by merely listening to his voice. I want you to come and hear this young man. We have to be careful not to fall into the trap of a Mongol spy. Peaceful Essence is old, and he could have been fooled by this young monk he is sending us."

A four-paneled silk screen stood at one corner of the living room, concealing a comfortable chair. Square on her large feet, Peony helped

Lady Kuo walk behind the screen. Peony stayed beside her mistress and waited patiently for the arrival of this monk. She wondered who could he be. In the past six years every time she and Lady Kuo had visited the temple, Peaceful Essence had kept the young monks from them.

Someone banged on the door, and Master Kuo went to meet the visitor. The men did not waste time in pleasantries. When they entered the living room, introductions had already been exchanged, and their conversation had already reached the core issue of this meeting.

"Other than myself, there are at least six major rebel forces in China, each based in a different province," Vanguard Kuo said. "Our goals are to fight the Mongols and to consolidate the Chinese revolutionaries. Both tasks will be difficult ones. You see, each of the rebel leaders wants to become the supreme ruler of China himself, and they probably will refuse to unite as one."

Vanguard went on to tell the visitor that each of the leaders called himself the king of his province. South of Prosper Mountain, a leader named Wan had crowned himself king of Honan.

The women behind the screens could not hear the stranger's voice. He had not said anything yet.

Vanguard went on, "It's the same with the monks. The lust for power and wealth exists in the hearts of many religious men. Peaceful Essence is exceptional in his selflessness, and your job is to persuade all the other monks in north Honan Province into thinking his way. But first of all, I must be assured that you are qualified for such an important mission."

Peony and Lady Kuo heard the stranger answer in a low but powerful voice, "Master Kuo, I can assure you that my reason for fighting the

Mongols is not based on either power or wealth.
I want to avenge the deaths of my loved ones—"

He stopped as a woman suddenly screamed.
He turned quickly toward the screens and saw
beneath them two pairs of shoes, one tiny and
the other very big.

The big feet moved in such large steps that
the screens were nearly knocked over. A tall girl
charged toward the young monk.

"Endurance! Endurance Chu! I thought you
were dead! I saw your grave! How come you are
alive?" Peony cried. She put her hands on Endurance's shoulders to squeeze him hard, to
make sure that he was not a ghost.

"Pe-o-ny! Peony M-ma!" Endurance stuttered.
The blood drained from his face, and his entire
body trembled as he went on, "I saw ... your
body! I buried you and ... your parents! You
were all burned to ash! How ... come you are
standing here, alive and ... taller and bigger
than you ever were?"

"I, burned to ash? You must be out of your
mind!" Peony shouted as she studied Endurance's pale face and shaking frame. Letting go of
his shoulders, walking around him, she started
to laugh.

"You look ridiculous in this silly robe! How
ugly you are with your head shaved! And this is
the first time I have ever seen you clean-shaven.
Your face doesn't go with your outfit at all. A
monk is supposed to be peaceful-looking. You
look like you've just killed someone."

The next moment, she stopped laughing and
started to cry. Facing Endurance, she began to
pound him on his chest with her fists. "Where
have you been hiding the past eight years? Why
didn't you come to me and let me know you are
alive?" She was ready to let him taste one of her
tai chi punches when she saw tears in his eyes.

He had watched Peony laugh and cry, unaware
that he was doing the same thing at the same
time. He put his hands around Peony's waist,
lifting her up high.

"Peony! My Peony!" He shouted as he turned
around and around holding her. "We'll never be
parted again!"

They held onto each other like two incomplete
people who suddenly recaptured their long-lost
selves, and began to fight for a turn to tell the
other what happened in the past years.

Vanguard Kuo went to his wife, brought her
out from behind the screens, and led her to another chair. He sat beside her, took her hand as
they both listened.

Endurance and Peony were still talking when
one of Vanguard Kuo's men entered the room
breathlessly.

The man said, "The Mongols are searching
this area for the killer of a Mongol officer. A
Chinese prostitute witnessed the killing. She was
almost killed by the killer but survived. She gave
Mighty Sword a detailed description of the as-
sailant. A large, tall monk is wanted dead or
alive. The prize for his head is twenty pieces of
gold."

The man went on to say that the killer was
seen heading this way. "The Mongols are searching all the streets, shops, private homes and
boardinghouses, and other possible hiding places,
including the Temple of White Crane!"

23

Autumn, 1352

"WE HAVE NOT SHARED the same pillow for over a hundred days, my Lotus," Wisdom Lu said to his wife in their bedchamber. "My heart mourns my father, but my body yearns for you. Sometimes I don't understand why our tradition so often denies pleasure. When anything happens, it's always a hundred days without what is most enjoyable."

Lotus blushed as she leaned her head against her husband's shoulder and moved slowly toward the bed. "We are in broad daylight. Tradition says it's the wrong time," she said, glancing at a small statue of Buddha on the night table. "We cannot offend the great Buddha."

Wisdom took off his garment and placed it over the statue's head. "For Buddha, it is night."

After being married for eight years and giving birth to three children, the once shy girl was now a mature woman. Lotus glanced at the veiled Buddha and giggled. She did not wait for Wisdom to remove her garment, but unclothed herself.

Wisdom was the man cloud, Lotus the woman cloud. They devoured each other hungrily. Lightning brightened a sky that had remained dark for a hundred nights. Raindrops fell on an earth that had remained thirsty for a hundred days. The

autumn wind turned into a storm, shouting out
its joy of fulfillment.

Outside the bedchamber, the faithful maid,
Jasmine, listened and smiled understandingly.

She guarded the closed door until she heard
her lady calling. Entering the bedchamber, she
saw Wisdom and Lotus fully dressed and sitting
with a table between them. The cyclone had left
a fragrance in the room, and the aftermath of
turbulent weather still lingered in the air. Jasmine opened the paper windows, then went to
smooth the wrinkled bed and disarrayed pillows.
She then helped her lady to rearrange her
smeared makeup and mussed hair.

"I must go to the grand room now," Wisdom
announced, standing behind his wife, looking at
her lovely face in the brass mirror. He did not
want to leave her, but had no choice. "They are
all waiting for me. The Silent League has not
met for the past three moons."

Wisdom faced the pale-faced scholars in their
multilayered long robes. "In the past three moons,
life has been extremely difficult for our people,"
he said, then went on to describe what had been
done.

Mongol soldiers had forced their way into the
homes of the people in Yin-tin, and their hosts
were obligated to satisfy the Mongols' appetite
for meat in every meal. When their money was
gone and they served vegetable meals to the
Mongols, they were killed. In addition, while living in Chinese homes, the Mongol warriors were
easily tempted by the young wives and beautiful
daughters. While defending their women, more
Chinese were murdered.

"During the past hundred days, I could not do
anything for the people. How I have wished that
I were a peasant and didn't have to follow tradi-

tion so strictly!" Wisdom frowned helplessly. "I wanted to come out of mourning, but I couldn't. I almost disobeyed tradition when Vanguard Kuo visited me from the north. It was raining that day, and he waited in the downpour. At one point I was on my way to the door to meet him, but then my mother started to weep and tell me that I would make my father's spirit cry in heaven. How I prayed that Vanguard Kuo would find some of my immediate relatives, and ask them to be our go-between. But then I realized that being a stranger in town, there was no way for him to know them. Well, my relatives would have never trusted a newcomer and a northerner, anyway."

He added, "Perhaps we should send someone to Vanguard Kuo ..." He paused as he thought of Endurance Chu, who would be a perfect messenger.

In the past three years, the two men had communicated only occasionally. Endurance did not like to write because of his large handwriting, and it was difficult for Wisdom to write Endurance, since his address kept changing from one temple to another. In the last letter, Endurance had told Wisdom that he had been trying to gather a group of fighting monks, but for some reason none of them were willing to follow him. "I am straightforward and extremely persuasive, so it can't be my—"

Wisdom's thoughts were interrupted by the voice of a Silent League member. "Money is running low in our league fund. We've been buying explosives for the southern revolutionaries so they can make a few Flaming Snakes. Except for the greedy and miserly gentry like Lord Lin, all the rich have already given all they could. In today's meeting, we must plan carefully our future expenditures."

The League members suggested that they should
stop supporting the lesser northern leaders who
had constantly asked for financial aid since receiving Wisdom's secret message. One of them
said, "We should give our money to the southern
leaders only. We are more learned than the
northerners, and once China is returned to the
hands of a Chinese ruler, we will want him to
be just like us."

The League members reached an agreement:
their money would go to the southerners only,
and they would start searching for a suitable
messenger to contact Vanguard Kuo.

Wisdom walked through the garden, covered
with autumn leaves, and as he neared his chamber, he heard his six-year-old son, Ardent,
reading.

"When a man lives to be a hundred, he has
dreamed a fleeting dream. When a man travels
around the world, he has covered the distance
of a chess board. There are many galaxies, and
we mortals are insignificant specks of dust."

Wisdom smiled at the familiar words. He had
memorized the same ancient poem when he was
Ardent's age.

"Mama, I can read, too!" Wisdom heard Earnest, who was only four, shouting impatiently.
" 'Only fools fight for fame and success, because
both are like smoke that can never be possessed . . .'
But, Mama, what is fame and success?"

Wisdom smiled again. It was another age-old
poem taught to youngsters. He stopped at the
doorway to take in the heartwarming picture.

While the poor no longer could afford to wear
white for the new rash of deaths, the rich continued to be dominated by tradition. Lotus was
wearing gray garments and pearls. Like Wisdom,
she had to shun bright-colored clothes and jew-

els for the rest of the year. Only when a new
year began could they stop wearing mourning.
Sitting on a chair beside the open window, her
black hair contrasted with her pale robe, and her
divine face glowed in the autumn sun. In her arms
was a pink bundle, Peace Blossom. Seeing her
husband, Lotus smiled. The boys, who were sitting on the rugs at a low table, stood up and
bowed to their father. Jasmine, who was doing
needlework beside the boys, also stood and went
to pour tea for her lord.

"Ardent and Earnest, I heard you reading and
I'm very proud of you," Wisdom said to his sons.
Going to his wife, he looked at Peach Blossom's
sleeping face. "Our daughter is as beautiful as
her mother, and just as gentle," he laughed
softly. "She never screams or kicks the way the
boys did."

"Baba! I never scream. I'm a southern gentleman!" Ardent protested.

"Baba! I never kick. I'm a gentleman scholar!"
Earnest argued.

"Your tea, my lord," Jasmine said, putting a
steaming cup in front of Wisdom.

Wisdom noticed the sorrow in the woman's
eyes. "Jasmine, I know how difficult it is for
you to be parted from your husband and children. If you wish to join them, please do so.
I've freed both you and Ah Chin the day he was
wounded. You are not obligated to stay with us
anymore."

While delivering a secret message, Ah Chin
had raised a Mongol soldier's suspicion. An
arrow had pierced through his leg. He had escaped, but had to limp for the rest of his days.
Wisdom had given him his freedom, together
with a generous pension, a house, and a large
farm near Dais of Rain Flowers. Ah Chin and
Jasmine had a six-year-old son and a two-year-

old daughter, and both children were with their father. Jasmine insisted on staying in the Lu house, but became sad every time she watched the Lu family laughing together.

Ardent heard Ah Chin's name and shouted, "I want to go to the farm! It's so much fun there. The last time we visited Ah Chin, he let me ride the water buffalo."

Earnest did not remember Ah Chin, but joined his brother. "Farm! I want to go to the farm!"

"Here goes your gentleman scholars . . ." Lotus said, then stopped at the commotion outside the garden walls.

There was the sound of horses and men, and then someone shouted, "Make way for the court messengers from Da-du!"

Wisdom Lu's face became pale. Lotus trembled in her chair and almost dropped her baby. Jasmine took Peach Blossom in her arms. The boys ran to their father, and each took one of Wisdom's hands.

The same thought went through the three adults' minds: could the court have discovered that Wisdom was the leader of the Silent League?

Wisdom freed his hands from his sons. "Take care of your mother and sister," he said, then gave Lotus one more loving look before leaving the room.

The two women and three children huddled together until Wisdom returned. They breathed with relief when they saw their lord smiling.

"The messengers brought me this." Wisdom showed his family a parchment scroll that bore the seal of the royal court. As he unrolled it he said, "The position of the Yin-tin mayor has been vacant since Father died. Both the Chinese and the Mongols were feuding over it, but I never even gave it a try. However . . ."

He began to read, "Due to the recommendation of the governor of Kiangsu Province, the court has appointed Wisdom Lu the new mayor of Yin-tin."

24

As snowflakes danced over Prosper Mountain, firecrackers announced the New Year. Each exploded into thousands of red speckles, and every speckle became a dance partner for the snow. In Vanguard Kuo's house, a magnificent feast was taking place. His fighters, disguised as merchants and craftsmen, poured in through the front door carrying gifts. Taoist monks arrived in yellow robes, Buddhist monks in orange. Even a few nuns appeared in their humble gray, moving slowly with their eyes lowered and palms together in an unceasing pose.

Being a northerner and more a merchant than a scholar, Vanguard did not believe in separating men from women guests. He headed one dining table, his wife another. Lady Kuo sat in her chair wearing a red garment and a kind smile. Peony stood beside her wearing bright yellow and describing the feast in detail.

She said, "There are ten round tables in this dining room, and ten more in the living room. Round tables are set up everywhere. The study, the entrance hall, and even the servant's quarter."

Joy Kuo nodded. "It sounds like New Year's Day in my father's house. My father always told me this is the day for a well-to-do man to host all his friends and acquaintances, especially the less fortunate ones. Describe our guests, Peony, and then the food."

Peony did. "Meatballs called lion's head are big enough to match their name. There are sweet cakes made with powdered rice and filled with dates . . ." She stopped and sighed.

Joy Kuo read her maid's mind. "Go ahead. Go feed your hungry young man," she said.

Peony thanked her lady and ran to the kitchen. Claiming a large tray and four soup bowls, she filled them with meat balls, chicken soup, roast duck, and lamb chops. There was no room for sweet cakes, she saw, annoyed. "I'll have to come back for them later." She was turning to leave the kitchen when she ran right into Meadow.

The old housekeeper stared at the four bowls and screamed, "Is your young man's stomach connected to the bottomless sea? He will put a hole in the Kuo family vault with his mouth!" The old woman made to seize several of the bowls. "Give me back the roast duck and some of the lamb chops!"

Raising a protective shoulder, Peony moved out of Meadow's reach. If she was not so loyal to Lady Kuo, she would be glad to give the old witch a good kick. She carried the tray through the garden, hurried to the tool shack. "It's me," she called softly as she climbed a ladder half hidden by rakes and hoes. Two big hands appeared from above her and took the tray.

"I'm starved," Endurance said. Sitting on the hay-covered floor cross-legged, he put the tray on his thighs and began to eat immediately. Peony sat beside him. The sod roof was very low, and neither of them could stand up straight. The floor creaked underneath them, for the boards were barely sturdy enough to carry two people's weight. With furniture it might collapse. Endurance had no choice but to sleep and sit on the floor all the time. He had been hiding in this room since the beginning of autumn, and the reward for his head was still in effect.

Vanguard had told him that he must not leave the house until things calmed down. In the beginning Endurance had not minded, since he and Peony had so much to tell each other. But Peony's spending most of her time with Endurance angered Meadow. The woman yelled at Peony for ignoring her household duties, accused her of throwing herself at a man who was not yet her husband, and complained about the amount of food Endurance consumed in each meal.

"How did you manage to bring me such a big meal?" Endurance asked as he swallowed the last bite of meat and looked at all the empty bowls sadly, "Did you kill the old witch?"

"It's tempting," Peony shook her head. "But Lady Kuo needs her." She stood up, stooped, and began to gather the bowls. "I'll bring you sweet cakes later."

"Don't go." Endurance looked up pleadingly as he took her hand and pulled. "Stay with me a little while longer. I'm so lonely all day long. No fresh air, no view. I feel like a caged animal. I don't think I can stay in hiding much longer."

Peony's heart ached. She sat facing him and pressed her cheek against his heart. "I stay with you as much as I can. Right now it's New Year, and I have to help to serve many guests. I know how you feel, Endurance. But please be patient."

Endurance cupped her face, held her away a little to look at her. "Patience is something I do not have, and neither do you."

They both smiled. As children they had been a winning team in every game except hide-and-seek. They simply had been unable to stay hiding for long.

Peony said, "But we must have patience now.

This is not a child's game. We are playing with your life, my Endurance."

The way she said his name made him forget all his misery. The windowless, gloomy room suddenly seemed bright. He looked into her eyes and felt that they were children again, running in the wind along the riverbank. He brought her face close to his, lowered his head. He kissed her gently first, then hungrily. She kissed him back with equal passion, put her arms around him, and held him tightly.

"Peony! Everyone in this household is working their fingers to the bones! How dare you hide with that lazy and useless man?" Meadow's voice came from the bottom of the ladder.

"I'll kill her!" Peony jumped to her feet and bumped her head. "And I don't care if it'll break Lady Kuo's heart!"

Peony left, taking the sun, the wind, and the riverbank with her. Endurance lay on the hay and folded his arms under his head. He stared at the low ceiling. It felt like lying in a coffin. "I'm not a lazy, useless man!" he shouted at the sod roof, abruptly deciding that he would hide no longer.

The following morning he would carry out his mission to unify the northern monks. Vanguard Kuo had not yet decided on the date for the joined resistance. Endurance would deliver that message in his next assignment.

"And I'll take Peony with me this time! By then she and I will be married!"

The night was deep and all was quiet as Peony lay awake, turning her head toward the open window and watching the snow continue to fall.

"Close that window, you crazy girl!" Meadow yelled from the next bed.

"Close it yourself, you old witch!" Peony said.

Restless, she started to get dressed again. She went to the kitchen, used a fire stick to light a candle, and started to pack food. A rattan basket was soon filled with cold meat and wheat buns. They were for later. Right now she wanted to give Endurance something hot to eat, then tell him that they would start traveling tonight.

Peony lit the wood logs, then poured some water into a wok. She placed four chopsticks in the curved bottom of the wok to support a bowl, then put several sweet cakes in the bowl. As she covered the wok and waited for the water to boil, the candlelight flickered. She saw her own shadow dancing on the wall. Her heart also danced with excitement: she and Endurance were about to challenge fate.

Holding the rattan basket with one hand, she used the other to hold the steaming hot bowl, which was wrapped in a rag. When she climbed the ladder in the tool shack, she leaned one side of the bowl against her chest and felt it burning her chest. "Endurance, it's me," she called, then entered the low room.

She saw a candle burning on a thin brick, and Endurance squatting beside it tying knots to make a kerchief into a small bundle. "You're leaving!" she yelled as she dropped the basket and the bowl, squatted beside him. "Are you leaving without me?"

"Only for this trip," he said, then told her his plan.

She shook her head. "I am not Lady Kuo. I will not wait for my man to come home from battle. I will fight beside you, and don't you dare tell me I can't." His sad face had lingered in her mind, she told him, and she had not been able to sleep. Finally she had decided that it was time for her and Endurance to move on.

"We are people of action. I'll leave a note for

Master and Lady Kuo, and go with you tonight. When you eat the hot cakes, I'll go back to my room and throw my clothes into a bag."

"I'm so glad you made this decision!" Endurance said, taking her in his arms. "I hated to leave you, but felt I should not take you with me since we are not yet married." He held her tightly, and she moaned in pain. "Did I hurt you?" He held her away and asked with a frown, "Since when have you become a delicate flower who cannot take a hearty hug?"

"It's my breasts," Peony answered, reaching under her garment. "The bowl containing the sweet cakes is very hot. I think it blistered my skin."

"Let me see," Endurance said, lifting her garment and looking carefully by the candlelight. "You poor thing! It's all red between your breasts, and a blister is just forming!"

When they had been children and one of them was injured, the other had always licked the wound to make it better. With this in mind, Endurance bent toward her and began to lick the burned area with the tip of his tongue. His tongue moved from one breast to the other, until he felt her body trembling in his arms. Thinking he was hurting her, he stopped for a moment. But when he looked at her, he realized that she was shivering in pleasure instead of pain. He smiled: the little girl had become a grown woman.

They gazed at each other for several long moments, then moved their heads closer until their lips met. They took and gave through their kisses the love that they had saved for each other but never thought they would have a chance to share.

While kissing, his hands took his tongue's place to sooth her wound. His fingers moved

gradually away from her blister to her buttons.
He removed her garments one by one, then
started to take off his own.

Meadow could not go back to sleep after closing the window. She twisted and turned in bed,
waiting for Peony to return. When she realized
that Peony had gone farther than the toilet room,
she thought about the food in the kitchen and
became worried. She got out of bed and put on
a robe.

When Meadow saw Peony packing food, she
cocked her head to one side and thought: she is
not just feeding the giant! She is running away
with him! A smile cracked the old woman's face,
until it struck her that Peony might steal more
than food. For this reason, Meadow hid outside
the kitchen door and watched Peony steam the
sweet cakes. She then followed Peony to Endurance's room.

Meadow, very thin and agile, climbed the ladder without making a sound. She stayed on the
upper part of the ladder with her eyes at the level
of the hay-covered floor and watched the young
lovers' every movement.

She was ready to charge into the room while
the lovers were kissing. But then she decided to
wait. Although never married, she knew that
lust was an irresistible part of life. A lady and
a lord would stop at the borderline drawn by the
hand of tradition, but not two peasants like
Peony and Endurance. Meadow narrowed her
aged eyes and thought quickly, then went down
the ladder quietly. She was an old gambler bet-
ting on uninhibited human nature.

Meadow woke up four male servants loyal to
her. She told them to bring torches and gongs.
She calculated the time carefully, and prayed
that the two young lovers would not carry out

the actual act of pillowing either too soon or too late.

"Peony, you told me once that before our wedding night, I better learn the art of melting clouds and creating rains. Well, I learned," Endurance whispered as he climbed over Peony and continued to massage her breasts.

"You did?" Peony opened her eyes wide. "Was she pretty?"

"No!" Endurance answered bitterly. "She was a southern whore and a breakable little stick. And she acted like I was hurting her!"

"Well, you are not hurting me," Peony answered. "It feels so good to have your hands on my breasts. The burning pain is all gone. Touch me all over, Endurance. I won't break, I guarantee . . ."

The two of them jumped when gongs were banged right above their heads. Four men suddenly materialized, two holding burning torches and the other two clanging. From behind them Meadow appeared, dashing to the quilt and sheets and discarded clothes. She gathered all of them in her arms, then ran out of the room. The floor started quivering under the weight of so many people.

"Get the wooden door ready! Bring nails and hammers! A shameless couple have been caught! Come and see the naked sinners!" the old woman went down the ladder screaming.

Peony and Endurance were bold and brave, but unaccustomed to show their nakedness to four men. They were so shocked that they forgot to fight. They searched the room but could not find anything to cover themselves. Endurance stood stooped in front of Peony, used himself as her shield. Peony backed herself to the wall, bent forward with one hand over her breasts and the other between her legs.

Vanguard Kuo appeared at the door. He took one look at the naked young couple and turned his head. According to tradition, when a man and a woman were caught pillowing out of wedlock, they were supposed to be nailed to a wooden door side by side through their hands and feet. The door was thrown into the Yellow River, and as it floated down the stream, people in the villages passed by it would throw rocks at the couple in sin. No one dared to save the suffering sinners. The couple would die slowly, and two skeletons would be seen continuing to float on a half-rotted door.

"You'll break Joy's heart!" Vanguard shook his head at Peony, wondering how the couple could avoid their fate.

Meadow's head appeared at the top of the ladder. "The door is ready," she said, smiling as she nodded at the four men. "Bring the sinners down!"

The men put down their gongs and gave their torches to Meadow. They advanced on Endurance and Peony. Vanguard was helpless in the face of an unbreakable tradition. Peony whispered quickly into Endurance's ear, then murmured, "One, two, three!"

At the count of three, they both bent low and jumped. Their heads banged against the ceiling and the next moment their feet punched through the floor. The impact was so great that the thin boards cracked wide open and the walls began to crumble. Peony and Endurance descended gracefully to the ground, like two snowflakes twirling through the air.

When the four men dropped through the hole after them, they were astounded as they watched the entire room collapsing over their heads. The ladder lost its support and toppled. Meadow fell with it in slow motion, screaming and waving

the torches, plunging into a thick pile of hay.
She moved her arms in frantic motions to keep
the torches from touching the dry hay.

Vanguard managed to jump to safety, though,
and he hurried through the chaos to the tool
shack door. He was just in time to see two naked
figures running through the garden hand in
hand. "There are things hanging on the clothesline!" he shouted, then started to laugh. Soon he
was laughing so hard that he had to bend over
and hold his aching sides.

When he finally caught his breath and straightened himself, he saw Endurance and Peony
climbing the garden wall, each with a garment
in hand. The young couple stopped on top of the
wall and turned to wave at Vanguard.

"Please say good-bye for me to my lady!"
Peony shouted.

"We are on our way to unite the northern
monks!" Endurance yelled.

Peony and Endurance stopped to get dressed,
then continued to run in the falling snow and
under a crescent moon. They had grabbed two
sets of men's clothes from the clothesline, but
had no shoes. The ground was freezing cold.

The town of Prosper Mountain was sleeping
at the dawn of a new year. Even the Mongols
celebrated the most important Chinese festival.
The green lamp houses were packed with customers, most of them Mongol officers wearing
leather boots. Peony and Endurance sneaked into
one of the houses, crawled into two different
rooms, and stole two pairs of leather boots while
the owners snored beside their prostitutes. Both
pairs were old and cracked, but protected the
new owners' feet.

"You look beautiful in men's clothes and high

boots!" Endurance said, admiring Peony by the moonlight. He kissed her quickly on her lips.

"I'll wear nothing but men's clothes and high boots from now on," Peony said, returning his kiss. "As long as I am beautiful in your eyes, who cares what the rest of the world thinks?"

Although the town was asleep, they moved cautiously in the shadows, avoiding brightly lit streets. Whenever they heard people coming their way, they detoured. "I've never been so careful before," Endurance said. "When I thought you were dead, I did not really want to live. But now I'm terrified of dying." He smiled at her in the moonlight. "Can a woman turn a warrior into a coward?"

"No," she said. "She can only turn a foolish boy into a clever man."

They passed the Mongols' campsite and the Lamaist temple, climbed up the foothills, ascended the high mountain. They reached the Temple of White Crane as the snow stopped falling and the moon began to wane. They woke Peaceful Essence and asked him to marry them.

Her brown garment belonged to a man with long arms, and the sleeves reached the bride's fingertips. The blue robe was too tight on the groom. He twisted uncomfortably in it and soon burst the seams around his shoulders. Neither of them had had time to comb their hair. Remnants of Vanguard Kuo's tool shack lingered in the bride's long braid and the groom's newly grown beard. They had not bothered to wash their faces. She had a splotch of mud on her forehead, and he had dirt on his cheeks. But in his eyes she was the most beautiful woman on earth, and in her eyes he was the handsomest man.

Their wedding hall was the ancient temple with the numerous statues of Buddha. Each looked down at them with either a smile or a frown, accented by the glimmering candles and the sparkling incense sticks. Their witnesses were aged monks and old nuns, youthful Red Turban women and kung fu men. ". . . You are now as one," Peaceful Essence finally said.

When Endurance and Peony entered their wedding chamber, they were surprised. The nuns had brightened the small praying room with all the red candles they could find. Kneeling cushions served as wedding pillows and were piled with dates and peanuts. "We'll have many fine sons," Endurance said, pointing at the nuts, and then folded his loving arms around his bride.

When Peony rested her head on the cushions, she heard a crunching sound. She found a real pillow among them that was filled with dried flower petals. Her eyes became misty with tears. Many years ago, when she and her friends had been gathering spring flowers for their marriage pillows, her nightmare had begun. She blinked away the tears and smiled. The bleak years of her past were over. She and her Endurance would never be out of each other's sight again, she thought as she held her husband tightly.

The wind whistled through the ancient pines as the long-parted clouds finally folded into one. Again and again they melted and combined and lost themselves in each other, and with each additional meeting they stayed as one for a longer time. For the first time in its history, the old temple was warmed by the heat of hot raindrops, which kept falling passionately until the morning sun was high.

PART IV

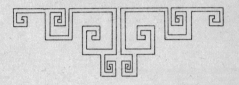

25

Spring, 1353

"WHERE IS MY Killing Hand? Where? Where? Where?"

A young man ran out of the palace, dashed into the garden. His golden robe was unfastened, and he had on only one shoe. The spring breeze parted his robe, revealing his bare chest, which was stained with red rouge and white powder. His long strides exposed his lower body, for he wore no pants.

"Who took my Killing Hand? And where are my guards?" he screamed again as he ran, looking over his shoulder.

He bumped into an apple tree and the petals showered him with pink and white. He stumbled through a bed of roses, and their thorns clawed his legs. Beautiful ladies gasped and covered their faces with their silk fans, peering over them to see the great khan in distress.

Tempest stopped at an immense platform. He climbed the stairs, taking several steps at a time. He threw himself at the feet of a statue of Buddha, which centered the platform. His trembling hand pressed hard on Buddha's left big toe.

One of the wood boards began to shift and uncover a secret entry. The khan cursed the board for not sliding faster and squeezed himself through when the entrance was still half-opened. As he dashed down the steps and bolted through a narrow passageway, he heard his pursuers entering

the garden and shouting at the court ladies for
his whereabouts. He recognized the voices of his
brothers and uncles, cousins and nephews, and
even his soldiers and bodyguards.

Tempest reached a small but splendid room
dominated by a magnificent bed. Immediately he
grabbed a candlestick of solid gold and turned
it. Panting hard, he heard the platform over his
head slide back to conceal the entranceway. He
smiled and fell back on the bed, leaned back
against the satin pillows.

"I made it," he said, catching his breath and
pondering his next move.

He would go through the tunnel to reach the
Lamaist temple near his mistress's home, but
this time, instead of the woman, he would send
for her husband, the most powerful general in
Da-du. The local general would combine his
force with the force of Mighty Sword. Tempest
could visualize himself coming out of hiding
after all the rebel princes were killed by the two
strongest military forces in his kingdom.

"My great khan seems very pleased with the
situation." The low voice came from behind the
gold-framed brass mirror, which was taller than
a man.

"It's you!" The startled khan breathed with
relief. "Am I glad to see you! So you couldn't
stop their betrayal and knew I would come here.
But why didn't you warn me . . . ?" The khan
stopped.

Shadow Tamu reached behind the brass mirror and brought out the Killing Hand. His thin
face was expressionless, his black, cold eyes
sinister.

"You kept it for me!" The young khan, not
noticing the look on Shadow's face, was delighted to see his magic weapon. "I looked for it
everywhere when they burst into my court. I had

to flee without it when they neared my bedchamber. Thanks for bringing it to me. You are truly my loyal adviser . . . what are you doing?"

Shadow Tamu had raised the iron tube slowly and aimed it at the khan. "You stupid bastard! Do you think I'd be loyal to you after you killed my sister?"

"No! Please!" The khan held his hands in front of him, pleading and trembling. "Don't kill me! I'll give you anything! I'll even let you be the khan!"

Shadow Tamu's jaw was set, his lips displaying a cynical grin. Laughter rose from his throat and filled the room with its chilling sound. While laughing, Shadow Tamu squeezed the trigger. The small room rang with an ear-shattering blast, and thick smoke filled the limited space. When the deafening reverberation stopped and the acid cloud thinned away, Shadow Tamu stepped toward the bed.

The khan's body had been knocked back by the force of the Killing Hand, but the satin pillows held his head up. His mouth was open and his eyes staring at his adviser. Blood poured out of the hole in his heart, turning rapidly into a red river flowing across the enchanting bed.

"You fool!" Shadow Tamu spat in the dead khan's face. "All of you who want to be the great khan are but fools! No khan can live long, while the same adviser—who truly rules the kingdom—lives on and on."

Shadow Tamu twisted the gold candlestick. The next moment the entrance was revealed and the passageway filled with princes and their followers. When they entered the room, they saw Shadow Tamu standing beside the dead khan. Bowing humbly to all of them, he said in all sincerity, "I am ready to offer my loyal service to the new great khan!"

*   *   *

There were a total of twenty-seven princes in the court, and twenty-six of them were present in the grand hall. Behind each prince stood his bodyguards, and every guard held a long sword. The khan's Killing Hand was now in the possession of Shadow Tamu. The adviser intended to share the weapon with no one but his brother. Only if the supreme general thought that the Mongol soldiers ought to use it as a weapon would it be produced in larger numbers.

The meeting had started in the morning, and now it was night. Meals had been served, several breaks taken. But still no successor had been chosen.

All the princes were equally powerful, and none of them could kill all others to become the sole ruler. Tired and irritable after so much wrangling, they were happy to see Shadow Tamu finally open his mouth.

"I have a suggestion," the adviser spoke slowly. "Prince Eastwind will make a perfect khan . . ." He closed his mouth again when all the princes began to laugh.

Prince Eastwind was only nineteen, the only prince not involved in the killing of Tempest, and the only one missing from this meeting.

"But he is not even a warrior! He has never killed a man in his life!"

"He doesn't even like to hunt! The last time he saw us skin a deer, tears poured out of his silly eyes!"

"He is not much of a man in all aspects. For example, he stays with only one woman. He and his Sunflower do not live in the real world. They are but two useless dreamers!"

Every prince took his turn to object and criticize Prince Eastwind. Shadow Tamu waited patiently. Only when no one had any more to say, he spoke again.

His voice was low and unhurried, his words few, "Prince Eastwind makes a good puppet. All of you can pull the strings. The puppet can be torn apart, but the puppeteers will remain safe."

In a small court far from the grand hall, a handsome young prince and his beautiful princess entertained several traders from Mecca and a few travelers from Rome.

Prince Eastwind had been studious since he was a child. Foreign languages and unfamiliar cultures fascinated him, and he was engrossed in the study of art, music, and literature of various countries. He was also eager to pursue all forms of aesthetic and scientific inventions.

"I did not know glass was invented more than a thousand years ago. Just imagine, glass artifacts found in the ruins of Pompeii," the young prince said in Italian to a clutch of Roman travelers. He then turned to several Arab traders. "Are you certain that your people brought glass vases and bowls to China four hundred years ago?"

Princess Sunflower, who was a distant cousin to Eastwind and had shared his learning as they grew up together, corrected the prince's mistake. "Glass objects were brought to China by the Romans soon after it was invented. The Arabs merely brought the formula of glassmaking to China." The prince smiled at her knowledge as she went on. "The Chinese admired the glass artifacts and thought they were transparent jade. Because of that, they expected to mine the glass out of the ground but never thought of making it. The formula has remained unused by the Chinese for the past four hundred years."

Prince Eastwind looked at Princess Sunflower

with great respect. Her ability to speak and understand foreign languages exceeded his. He then turned to the Arab traders and asked, "Will you help me make glass? I don't mean glass vases and bowls. I want plate glass for practical uses."

The prince's eyes brightened as he thought aloud. "Just imagine if all lanterns were made of glass—they would no longer be shattered by rain and wind. And picture all windows covered with glass instead of rice paper—we could see through them and have more light in the room."

The traders nodded and one of them said, "We need sand, silica, lime, and soda ash—"

The door was suddenly opened, and Prince Eastwind's handful of guards were pushed aside by the intruders. Shadow Tamu was followed by twenty-six princes and their armed men.

Without trying to hide their disrespect, the princes and their guards bowed to Prince Eastwind slightly as a formality.

Shadow Tamu marched up to the prince, looked down at the young man, and said arrogantly, "Your Royal Highness is now our new great khan. The coronation will take place tomorrow."

Prince Eastwind and Princess Sunflower huddled together in shock and fear. Neither could help shivering as they noticed the princes' mocking smiles and the adviser's chilly grin.

26

Summer, 1353

BESIDE THE SILVER CRESCENT of the seventh moon, a galaxy of stars formed a luminous band, floating across the heavens. The stars touched the horizon and met the Yellow River. On a meadow near the riverbank stood a young couple.

A coarse brown robe was draped over his massive body, tied loosely around his bulky waist with a hempen rope. The open neck revealed his hairy chest, which was half-covered by a long beard. She wore a man's blue garment and high boots. Her hair was braided but not pinned up. The thick queue was tied with a scarlet ribbon and swung at her hips with her every movement.

They had been moving toward the river when she stopped abruptly, yanking him back in mid-stride. She said, "Endurance, can we practice tai chi for a few minutes? I need to calm myself. It angers me when I remember the deaths of our families."

He nodded. Under the crescent moon, unseen by anyone, they began to move slowly and smoothly, advancing from one routine to another, waving their arms and legs rhythmically like two dancers.

Soon after leaving Prosper Mountain, Peony had taught Endurance tai chi fist, and he shared with her his kung fu. The merging of their fighting techniques thrilled them almost as much as

the art of pillowing. As they traveled from one
northern village to another, every deserted hill
and abandoned wood were their practicing ground.
Bamboo sticks were their long spears, wooden
boards their swords. Besides learning from each
other, they also absorbed new skills from the
monks and nuns united by them.

By the time they finished their tai chi routine,
Peony's anger was gone. They moved on, and
soon reached Pinetree Village.

They went to Endurance's old home and found
his family's graves. They kneeled and asked the
spirits to bless their marriage.

Peony looked up at the night sky and talked
to the spirits. "The Chu family used to meet the
Ma family at this time of the year. Endurance
and I are together and happy. Are all of you also
together and having fun in heaven?"

A gust of summer wind whispered through the
surrounding trees. The stars winked. The Yellow River splashed in the distance. Endurance
and Peony listened for the voices of their loved
ones, but could not hear any answers. Finally
they stood up and headed for the Temple of All
Kings.

The tall and forceful Earthly Dragon had aged
but not forgotten Endurance. "You've grown so
much!" he said as he looked him over.

Like the monks and nuns in the other parts of
China, most of the men and women here had
been practicing fighting techniques regardless of
their religious garments. Earthly Dragon sighed
and said, "Have you ever seen a little mouse cornered by a cat? Knowing that the cat will eventually devour it, it'll stand on its hind legs and
fight with its front paws just the same. We
monks and nuns are taught to be peaceful, but
the Mongols have cornered us with their prefer-
ence for Lamaism and Christianity."

Endurance and Peony had no trouble persuading the men and women to join a rebellion. "As soon as we hear the signal, we'll charge out of our temples and chase every Mongol from Pinetree Village!" Earthly Dragon vowed.

Endurance and Peony left Pinetree Village behind, and after another two days' walking, they arrived in Emerald Valley at dawn.

Heavenly Temple had become more crowded than before. The thin but strong Merciful Heart took Peony in his arms and examined her with misty eyes. "I am happy to see you married, my daughter, and to a man who matches you in size."

The old monk listened to the young couple's long story, then shook his head and said, "Don't blame fate for your long parting. All marriages are arranged by the hands of Buddha. The two of you were not meant to marry earlier than you did."

Peony tilted her head to one side and asked in disbelief, "I've seen many bad marriages. Why does Buddha play tricks on people?"

Merciful Heart laughed. "Peony, I can see that marriage has not taught you to mind your big mouth." The monk went on to explain that even bad marriages had their purposes. "When in this life a person does something bad to another, in the next life the bad one will become the good one's wife. The husband will be abusive, and the wife has to take all the abuse."

Endurance threw his head back and roared. "I must have done something bad to my Peony in our previous lives. She abuses me all the time. You should see the bruises on me . . . ouch!"

Peony punched her husband hard on his arm. "So far I've only bruised you when practicing kung fu! But that can be changed if you dare to speak one more word that is untrue!"

Endurance rubbed his arm in exaggerated motions and looked at Merciful Heart with a pretended sad look. "Do you see what I mean, my honorable *shih-fu*? I'm an abused husband who doesn't even dare to fight back like a cornered little mouse!"

Merciful Heart laughed. "I wish all couples were as happily married as you two. You must have been very good to each other in your previous lives."

The monks and nuns in Heavenly Temple were gathered that afternoon to listen to Endurance and Peony. They eagerly agreed to rebel against the Mongols.

Once their mission was accomplished, Endurance and Peony shared an evening meal with Merciful Heart. They were preparing to head on to the next village when Merciful Heart said, "Wait. I have something to show you both."

The three of them went to the grand hall, and Merciful Heart closed the door behind them. They stopped at the statue of happy Buddha, and the monk twisted one of its long earlobes. A secret hiding place was revealed in the Buddha's fat belly. A green glow joined the light of the flickering candles.

The aged monk reached into the dark hole, cupped his hands around a stone, and lifted it out carefully. When he put it on the altar, Peony gasped and said, "It looks like an oval-shaped moon that fell to earth, burning in green flame and wanting to return to its heavenly home!"

"This green moon is your father's jade." Merciful Heart smiled at Peony.

She eyed the radiant gem, wanting to reach for it but afraid to touch it. "It can't be! My father dug out of the mountain a rough piece of rock. It was nothing like this."

Merciful Heart nodded with a deep sigh.

"Since you left Emerald Valley, there had been several massacres in the village. A jade miner crippled by the Mongols came to hide in my temple. I showed him the rock. He had lost his entire family but found a new reason for living in your father's gem. He worked day and night to chip the precious jade out of its rocky shell then polished it with the love and tenderness possessed only by a mother for her child. He died a month ago, holding the polished jade and wearing a serene smile."

The old monk cupped his hands around the jade once again before handing it to Peony. "This is a family heirloom. You can take it with you."

Peony shook her head and backed away. Undaunted, the monk turned to Endurance. "Tradition states that all the valuables owned by a wife become her husband's possession. The jade is yours, Endurance."

He refused to accept it. "Peony and I are in no position to keep any valuables." He paused as he raised a hand to touch the gold chain around his neck. Hanging from the chain, half-hidden by his beard, was a jade pendant shaped like two grasping hands. "But if this precious jade ever reached the hands of my best friend, it would become the most beautiful piece of art in this world."

Endurance's piercing eyes softened as he continued, "He told me once that his life's dream was to carve a pair of jade lovers. His name is Wisdom Lu."

27

Winter, 1354

A FULL MOON shone over River Yangtze, accompanied by a sky filled with glittering stars. But then the temperature plunged suddenly, and thick layers of clouds began to roll across the sky. When the wind subsided, millions of white flakes swept over the river, reaching every corner of Yin-tin City, including the Lu mansion.

Wisdom Lu and the Silent League members talked in hushed voices. As scholars, they had been trained to whisper since they were children; talking loudly was a sign of ill-breeding. When Wisdom listened carefully, he could hear above the soft voices of his friends, Lotus in the inner court playing the flute for the children. He smiled. His home was a melody of peace and harmony regardless of the war.

"The war will soon come to an end, Wisdom," one of the League members said. "How much time do you give the current khan before he surrenders to one of our revolutionary leaders?"

Wisdom replied slowly, "The war will not end as soon as you think, because the leaders of our forces are not united." He sighed and then reminded his friends to look back at the many battles fought between Chinese and Mongols in the past year.

Soon after Vanguard Kuo had begun fighting the Mongols openly, the kung fu monks and Red Turban nuns of northern Honan Province had joined forces with him. They had driven the Mongols out of their villages and towns, broken into the nearby jails, and released all the Chinese prisoners.

Wisdom said, "If only the laymen had been as cooperative. Unlike Vanguard, who was known as Master Kuo, the other six laymen leaders called themselves kings. They are scattered in four regions: northeast, southeast, central, and west. Vanguard Kuo is but one of the two leaders in the northeast."

The other scholars nodded as Mayor Lu continued in a low voice, "Vanguard had sent messages to all the other leaders, asking them to rise on the last Moon Festival night. But when that night arrived, all the six leaders told their men to let Vanguard's men fight alone, hoping that Vanguard's men would be destroyed by the Mongols. Of course, he disappointed them. With the help of the monks and nuns, he has won every battle he fought. The Kuo force has not only driven the Mongols out of Prosper Mountain, but also recaptured many towns and villages alongside the Yellow River. They own all of northern Honan Province now."

One of the scholars suddenly remembered a rumor he had heard. He looked at Wisdom and laughed, "Mayor Lu, is it true that your barbaric friend, Endurance Chu, is now one of the Kuo Fighters? If it's true, then what is his position? A messenger? A foot soldier perhaps?"

Wisdom Lu frowned. None of the League members had forgotten Endurance Chu, and they constantly teased Wisdom about the strange friendship between a scholar mayor and a barbaric mailman. Irritated, Wisdom sat quietly, then decided to reveal what he had known for quite some time.

"As a matter of fact, I'm very proud of Endurance," he said, raising his voice. "I know you don't like him, so I did not tell you this . . ."

Wisdom had sent his retired servant Ah Chin on several trips to the north, since a crippled man occasionally traveling between north and south would not worry the Mongols. Ah Chin had brought back good news from the north that in last winter, Endurance Chu had become the second in command to the Kuo fighters.

Wisdom regarded his scholar friends' shocked faces and continued proudly, "And his wife, Peony, is the founder of the infamous Red Turban nuns. They have a baby boy now, who was born on a battlefield. The mother fought beside her husband until it was time to give birth. And she did not rest long after the birth before she was once again fighting. Now, my friends, aren't you ashamed of yourselves for being so useless compared to such a courageous couple?"

The grand room was a cacophony of murmuring. The scholars did not stop talking until a male servant knocked on the door. Wisdom read the message and gasped. He ended the meeting and rushed toward the inner court.

Lotus had changed from her red garment into a white robe. She asked Wisdom if the three children should also wear the mourning color. "They have never met my father."

When each child had been born, Lotus had sent a messenger to the Lin mansion, asking her father's permission to return with her baby. All her requests had been denied. When each child was a hundred days old, Wisdom had invited his in-laws for the Future-picking ceremony. All his invitations had been turned down.

Wisdom thought, then sighed. "Let them wear white. After all, Lord Lin was their maternal grandfather."

Jasmine began to put mourning robes on the children. They were now eight, six, and three.

"How did my grandfather die?" Ardent asked while putting his hand through the sleeve of a white robe.

"How did he?" Earnest repeated after his brother.

"How?" Peach Blossom uttered only one word.

Wisdom and Lotus looked at each other, but neither knew how to answer.

Lord Lin had not changed his mind about pleasing the Mongol governor with a beautiful Chinese girl. Since his own daughter had refused to cooperate, he had turned his eyes on other lovely young things. In past years he had purchased more than a dozen enchanting beauties as gifts to the governor.

The last gift had been sent to the governor's mansion only three days before. The divine young woman was the most beautiful of them all, but when the governor was ready to pillow her, she pulled a dagger out of her inner garment. The governor had screamed for his guards. The woman had jumped up onto the windowsill, thrown her dagger at the Governor, then leapt from the second story window. Her dagger had barely missed. The guards had chased her through the woods of Purple Gold Mountain, until she disappeared before their eyes like morning dew vaporizing in the sun.

"Only a Red Turban nun can perform such magic," the guards had reported to the governor. They had then continued hesitantly, "We can search the two temples and arrest every monk and nun. With torture, they'll probably give us some information. But the great Buddha will be very upset."

The governor had trembled at the thought of

offending the great Buddha. Instead he had held
Lord Lin responsible for the assassination attempt.

Lotus lowered her eyes. Wisdom answered his
children vaguely, "Your grandfather was killed
for upsetting the Mongol governor."

Jasmine made a face, but Wisdom and Lotus
ignored her.

Eight sedan chairs traveled in the snow, crossing the three streets until they stopped at the
Lin mansion.

"It's Mayor Lu and his family!" A servant ran
toward the inner court, shouting all the way.

The lord's three sons, their mothers, who were
concubines, and the many relatives of the lord
all hid in their private chambers. They knew
that Lord Lin had never concealed his animosity
toward the Lu family. If the mayor had come to
humiliate anyone, they would rather that Lord
Lin's widow receive the insult alone.

Lotus followed Wisdom and leaned against Jasmine, advancing slowly through her childhood
home. Behind her were Ardent, Earnest, and
Peach Blossom plus two more maids. When she
reached the grand room, she saw her mother sitting there in a white robe that matched her hair,
which was now mostly white. Lady Lin was un-
accompanied except by an aged maid.

"Mama!" Lotus cried. The last time she had
seen her mother had been almost nine years ago,
in a temple where they were both lighting incense. Lady Lin's hair had been black then.

Blinking away her tears, Lady Lin examined
her daughter closely and smiled with approval.
Her little girl had grown into a stunning woman.
She found Lotus looking at her white hair, realized that she had aged without her daughter's
comfort. "My child, when riding on the wheels

of sorrow, one reaches the land of the aged fast," she explained.

Jasmine tried to smile at her old mistress, but ended in a sob. "My lady ... !" She couldn't continue.

Wisdom picked up Peach Blossom and gestured the two boys to come forward. Bowing to his mother-in-law, he said, "Please come home with us. My mother is waiting for you. She will upbraid me if I fail to persuade her best friend. She has missed you deeply, and is impatient to exchange all sorts of news with you. We have brought with us two maids to assist you, and an extra sedan chair." Wisdom then put Peach Blossom on Lady Lin's lap.

Ardent and Earnest bowed. "Come with us, Grandmama," they said at the same time.

Lady Lin held her granddaughter tightly, looked from one loving face to another. She thought carefully, then made a decision. Her aged eyes twinkled with happiness when she said, "My children, I am ready to go home."

28

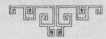

Spring, 1355

"DO I HEAR birds singing? Or is the pain making me imagine things?" Peony asked, lifting her head to listen. She tried to sit up on the straw mat where she had lain for more than a day, but the next moment she screamed and fell back.

There were five people in the tent: Peony, Endurance, and three experienced midwives. Since the beginning of the war, Endurance and Peony had lived on the run. Their tent was dome-shaped, made by laying felt over a framework of boughs, then lashed down with ropes. It could be folded into a lightweight bundle and loaded together with their household furnishing onto the back of a water buffalo.

"You are not imagining. We are in South Honan, where spring arrives early. As soon as the child is born, we can walk along the riverbank and look at the flowering trees," Endurance said softly, drying his wife's sweaty brow, shifting his weight from one knee to another. He had been kneeling beside her ever since her labor pains began, and his legs had gone to sleep.

Peony looked at her husband's suffering face, wanting to send him away, but she knew her effort would be wasted. Regardless of tradition, he had stayed beside her through the birth of their first child, Power. She tried to talk, "After this child, we'll be a family of four, and will need a larger tent . . ." She could not bite back another scream.

Endurance took Peony's hands, leaned forward until his face almost touched hers. "It's all my fault. I gave you all this pain." He announced loudly, regardless of the presence of the women, "No more pillowing for us!"

Peony breathed hard. When her agony was momentarily over, she tried to smile. "Endurance, you are a fool!" She paid no attention to the presence of the women either. "I enjoy pillowing! I'll find myself a male concubine if you don't do it with me again . . ." She screamed as water poured out from between her legs.

The three women, whose faces were red from embarrassment after hearing the conversation, came forward and told Endurance that he really must leave. He ignored them and remained kneeling until Peony nodded her head weakly and said, "Please go . . . I think it's time."

He was greeted by Vanguard Kuo outside the tent.

"How is she?" The first commander asked with deep concern. Endurance had become not only his second commander but also a friend. Besides that, Vanguard had always liked Peony for what the strong girl had done for his fragile wife.

"She is very brave—" Endurance answered, then stopped as Peony screamed again. "I hate Buddha for making things unfair!" Endurance waved a fist at the sky. "Why don't men suffer childbirth? I'd take Peony's place if it was at all possible!"

Vanguard took Endurance's arm and guided him away from the Chu family tent. In their army, twenty tents formed a circle. The officers and their families had private tents, but the soldiers were not allowed to bring their families.

The high-ranked ones shared tents, while the low-ranked men slept on the campground.

In the first commander's tent, Vanguard motioned for Endurance to sit with him on a mat. Beside a straw-stuffed pillow was a framed drawing on silk. Picking up the drawing, Endurance saw Joy Kuo's face, smiling with her eyes closed softly. It had been painted by Scholar Tou, the artist scholar who had taught Peony to read.

"She looks like a beautiful child having a happy dream," Vanguard said, taking the portrait from Endurance and pressing it against his heart. "She encouraged me to come because she knew I must fight this war. But the most difficult combat for me was the struggle to leave her." He kissed the portrait, then returned it to his pillow-side. "Women are stronger than men, my friend, and that's why the great Buddha lets them endure the pain of childbirth. If we men had to go through that kind of torture, most of us would die."

Vanguard clapped his hands for wine. He and Endurance started to drink while birds chirped in the spring sun. They were still drinking when the sun was replaced by the moon and the birds had gone home. Throughout the day Endurance returned to his own tent, but was told each time, "Your wife said you'll have a taste of her tai chi fist if you dare to enter."

As Endurance staggered back to the tent of the first commander, all soldiers kept out of his way. They still remembered that the last time the second commander's wife gave birth, several men that had gotten in his way had found themselves lying flat on their backs.

By the time the crystal moon had crossed to the middle of a deep blue silky sky, a baby's cry filled the campsite. Endurance jumped up and ran toward his tent. Vanguard followed close behind. All the officers and soldiers left their sleeping places and watched as one of the three midwives appeared at the felt-covered door of Endurance's tent. "It's another boy," the woman said. "And the mother is doing fine."

Everyone cheered. Vanguard smiled with relief.

Inside, Endurance kneeled beside Peony and framed her wet face in his large hands. "You look so weak. I've never seen you like this before. It's all my fault—"

Peony interrupted him by lifting a hand to cover his mouth. "Hush. Don't start that again. I'll be as strong as ever in a day or two. I'll challenge you to a duel of tai chi, and you'll know I am right then." She pointed at the bundle beside her. "Our second son is as beautiful as the first one," she said proudly.

Endurance glanced at the red and wrinkled tiny face. He saw no beauty there. He wanted to say that such an ugly thing was not worth his precious Peony's misery, but he did not dare. He uttered, "Mothers have sharper eyes than fathers, I suppose. I can't wait until our sons are big enough to do things with me: hunting, wrestling, killing Mongols, dominating soldiers ... how about naming this one Dominance?"

"Dominance," Peony repeated the word. "I like it." She closed her eyes.

"Please don't sleep yet, Peony." Endurance called tenderly. "You have to tell me what you want as a gift for going through all this pain once again."

Peony opened her eyes a little, answered sleepily, "You were ready to drive the Mongols out of south Honan when I started my labor. You've held back the attack on my behalf. How about giving me a Mongol-free Honan as a gift?" She saw her husband looking at her hesitantly

and added just before she drifted into sleep,
"Don't worry about me. Vanguard will stay at
the base and protect your wife and sons."

As she fell into slumber, Endurance stayed beside her, gazing at her sleeping face. At length
he reached behind his neck and unfastened the
gold chain he wore at all times. He put the chain
beside Peony's pillow, then whispered, "Until I
can give you Honan, the jade pendant from Wisdom is yours."

The Mongols had lived in tents for over three
thousand years, and the nomadic life ran deeply
in their blood. The royal families had learned to
live in the palace buildings in Da-du, but the
average soldiers felt like caged animals once
placed within four confining walls. The great
khan's adviser had forced them to live in the
Chinese homes in the cities, but in rural areas,
the Mongols continued to live in tent cities.

Endurance and his two hundred Kuo Fighters
moved soundlessly as they surrounded a Mongol
campsite that stood in the middle of a bamboo
grove. Once they were in position, he whispered
a terse order, "Be still and wait!"

His words were passed from soldier to soldier
in hushed voices, overpowered by the sound of
bamboo sticks rubbing one another in the wind.

Stillness was the most difficult part of kung fu
to learn. The well-trained Kuo Fighters became a
part of the bamboo grove as the night grew
deeper and the Mongols sleepier. When the last
of the camp fires died down and the soldiers
around it began to nod their heads, Endurance
suddenly yelled, "Attack!"

The Mongols woke up. Startled, they looked
for their weapons. They saw Chinese pouring
out of the bamboo grove. Most were empty-
handed but some waved homemade spears or

broadswords. The Mongols found their knives
and swords, bows and arrows. The skirmish
began.

The Mongols were excellent warriors when
fighting in the open, but the bamboo grove and
the tents confined them. Chinese fighters zig-
zagged through the tall bamboo, ducked behind
tents, jumped to face the Mongols, and then disappeared into the inky shadow. Though the
Mongols were stronger than the Chinese on an
average, their foe was twice as nimble.

Amid the battle one Chinese with a long beard
stood out. He had the strength of a Mongol and
the agility of a Chinese. He fought bare-handed
most of the time, and the Mongols shivered
when they saw him breaking the necks of their
soldiers like a woodsman breaking a twig. When
the Mongols turned their bows on him, he
grabbed either a sword or a spear from the nearest man and waved the weapon to create a flickering shield around him. All the arrows were
deflected with surprising ease. No sword or
knife could touch him.

The most frightening part about him was that
each time he killed one of his enemies, he took
time to cup his massive hands around his mouth
and raised his voice to scream like a wild animal,
"Mighty Sword! I've killed one more of your
men!"

The battle was over in the darkest moment of
night just before dawn. A few Mongols escaped,
but all others were slain. The Mongol campsite,
which had been the largest in south Honan, now
belonged to Vanguard Kuo, Endurance Chu, and
their men.

The Kuo Fighters of the lowest ranks dragged
the bodies of both forces into the bamboo grove,
stripped the dead of their weapons, armor, and
boots, and made what was useful theirs. Beyond

the grove and up on a hill, silhouetted against
the spring moon, hungry wolves were waiting.

The higher-ranked Kuo Fighters examined the
horses and ponies left by the Mongols, and divided the best animals among themselves.

The officers entered the deserted Mongol tents.
In the light of the lanterns, they found fine garments, gold coins, and other valuables, and a few
shivering village girls trying to shield their
naked bodies with fur-lined quilts. Patriotism
for China and vengeance for their loved ones
were momentarily forgotten. The officers shared
the finer things and also the young girls.

"Shall we save that one for our second commander?" One of the officers pointed at a delicate young girl. "She is the most beautiful one.
Maybe she'll bring a smile to Commander Chu's
grouchy face."

The other officers laughed. "No one can make
Commander Chu smile except his wife. And
Commander Chu sees no beauty in the most
beautiful faces, unless that face belongs to his
wife."

While the soldiers and officers enjoyed the triumph, Endurance walked toward the largest
tent alone. Lifting the heavy tapestry, he stood
in the doorway and peered in at the well-lit
interior.

Within the crude exterior was the atmosphere
of a lavish home. Embroidered hangings encased
felt walls. Thick layers of fur blanketed the
straw-matted ground. Brightly colored rugs covered sections of the tent to make them the eating
and sitting areas. The bed was a wide board resting on low legs, softened with tiger skin and the
skin of the snow leopards, and piled with fur
pillows. An iron stove stood in the center of the
room, with a chimney rising up through the tent
roof. On the stove was an iron pan, bubbling

with white liquid. Endurance walked toward it, dipped his fingers into the liquid, and tasted sheep's milk.

"From now on, my Peony will have a tent as good as this," he said, and reminded himself that he would order the low-rank soldiers to bring everything including the tent itself back to the Kuo Fighters' base.

Exhausted, Endurance dropped onto the bed, closed his eyes, and whispered, "Peony, I can't wait to pillow with you on tiger skin and snow leopard fur."

29

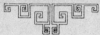

THE SPRING MOON WANED, leaving the morning
star alone on a dawning sky. All the Kuo Fighters
including their Commander Chu slept soundly. Beside Endurance's tent stood a weeping willow,
and its ancient branches embraced the home of
an owl. The wise owl hooted peacefully, then
suddenly opened its eyes wide.

Over a hundred Chinese wearing the same
black uniform appeared from beyond the bamboo
grove. They spread to form a circle, then threaded
themselves in and out of the thicket. They
moved quietly but quickly through the woods
and soon surrounded the campsite. The owl took
a look at the white crests embroidered on the
lapels of their black uniforms, flapped its wings,
and flew toward the moon.

The crest was a skeleton. In its eyes were two
words. The left said Wan, the right said Tin-
check, which meant "heavenly lord." Heavenly
Lord Wan was equal to Vanguard Kuo in power
and called himself king of Honan. His followers
were known for their cruelty. Even the owl was
frightened by their aura of evil.

Tin-check Wan was a little man with big ideas.
His white face stood out in the dark bamboo
grove, like the embroidered white skeleton stood
out from his black garment. His eyes were narrow but beamed with a penetrating cold light.
His lips were concealed by a mustache that hung

like the large wings of a dead bird. Wan studied the campsite carefully. A chilly laughter escaped his throat when he saw that even the guards were asleep. His mouth opened from underneath the droopy wings of the dead bird to give the order, "Attack!"

The Kuo Fighters were assaulted exactly the way they had assaulted the Mongols a while ago. Taken by surprise in their sleep, Endurance and his men stared at the striking Chinese, not believing what was happening.

They had heard that Chinese rebel forces fought among themselves, but this was the first time they had confronted enemies who were their own fellow countrymen. They looked at the skeleton crests on the Wan Fighters' uniforms, blinked to make sure this was not a nightmare.

When Endurance and his men saw their comrades' blood being spilled, though, reality sank in. They started to grope for their weapons, beset by fatigue, drunkenness, and shock.

The Wan Fighters were no better than the Kuo in technique, nor were they better equipped. But King Wan and his men had stalked the Kuo Fighters for a long time. They had stopped on the other side of the bamboo grove, rested, and ate the food in their backpacks while Endurance and his men fought hard with the Mongols.

King Wan had told the soldiers then, "If the Kuo Fighters should kill all the Mongols, it's good. If the Mongols should kill Endurance and every one of his two hundred men, it's not bad either. The winner's men will be reduced to about half of its original number, and it'll make things much easier for us. As usual, the winner will celebrate. We'll wait until they are drunk and soundly asleep, then kill them like stepping on grasshoppers."

As the Wan Fighters continued to kill the Kuo

Fighters in the dawning light, they saw the
agony and fury on the faces of their victims.
Every soldier had been thoroughly brainwashed
by their leader to believe that when King Wan
became the emperor of China, they would receive high posts in the royal court. But as they
looked into the accusing eyes of other Chinese,
some of them faltered.

"Run, you stupid fool!" one told the Kuo
Fighters when King Wan was too far to hear.

Although the Kuo Fighters had their chances
to run, their loyalty to Endurance kept them on
the battlefield. By this time he had been surrounded by King Wan and twenty of the best
Wan Fighters who were excellent in kung fu.
Wounded and bleeding badly, Endurance was
aware that half of his men had already been
slaughtered. He realized that his remaining men
would not leave without his order. While keeping his eyes on his many opponents, he screamed
like a cornered beast, "Run! Don't stop until you
reach Commander Kuo's base!"

The midday sun shone on Endurance, who
was tied to a post with all his clothes stripped
away.

There were stab wounds over much of his
body. The largest two were on his right thigh,
inflicted upon him during the fight. The multi-
ple small wounds were the result of his being
dragged behind a horse all the way to the Wan
base.

"I have a table in my tent set for two." King
Wan smiled at Endurance, pointing toward the
largest tent. "All you have to do is nod, and
you'll be sitting there enjoying a feast."

Endurance glared at him. "To become your
first commander, help you kill all the other Chinese revolutionary leaders, starting with Van-

guard Kuo? Tin-check Wan, you are out of your mind!" He spat in King Wan's face, watching his saliva run down Wan's droopy mustache.

King Wan wiped the saliva off with a steady hand, then laughed softly. "All right. Then let me give you another chance. Tell me where Vanguard Kuo's wife is right now. We found their home in Prosper Mountain. But no one was there except a few servants. We tortured an old housekeeper, but she died without telling us her mistress's whereabouts. We need to find Joy Kuo. We heard that she is a blind woman who means everything to her husband. I want to capture her and force her husband to surrender."

Endurance remembered Meadow. He no longer hated her for wanting to nail him and Peony to a door. So the brave old thing did not go with Joy Kuo to the Temple of White Crane. Endurance closed his eyes and sank his teeth into his lip, refusing to either look at Tin-check Wan or talk to him.

Wan sighed. "You are very foolish. Loyalty is an empty word. Pain is real, and death is irreversible." He moved a hand, and a big man appeared, holding a long leather whip.

Wan ordered the man, "Whip the foolishness and stubbornness out of him! Every time he faints, let me know. For a man his size, he'll faint at least five or six times before he dies!"

As Wan turned to leave, the big man raised his whip.

After the whip landed on Endurance, the experienced man waited for the pain to sink in.

At first Endurance felt only the impact. A moment later the agony began. It was like a river of fire pouring over him, drowning him in its burning flame.

He struggled to float to the surface of the

water, but the man raised his whip again and
again, and the torturing river overpowered him.

Endurance heard himself scream. He wanted
to stop but could not. Then he heard his own
voice decreasing in volume. He sank to the bottom of the river and lost consciousness.

When he opened his eyes he saw Wan standing
there, ordering the big man to throw buckets of
water over him.

Seeing that Endurance had regained his consciousness, Wan grinned. "I hope you have changed
your mind. Honan Province is my territory. I
have no intention of letting anyone else take it.
With or without your help, I'll kill Vanguard
Kuo and all the other Chinese who dare to refuse
my rule."

Endurance, still awash in pain, barely gathered enough strength to mutter, "I . . . have . . .
never killed a Chinese. We Chinese . . . are supposed to . . . kill only the . . . Mongols. I'll never
help you . . . no matter what you do!"

Wan turned and walked away, waving a hand
for the whipping to continue.

The first lash brought to Endurance the memory of the young prostitute in Yin-tin City who
had cheated him of his hard-earned money. With
the second blow, he remembered the Phoenix
Place people who had closed their doors at his
face. In the third, he saw the prostitute in Prosper Mountain who had described him to the
Mongols. With the next flogging, the cold faces
of the Silent League members appeared.

The beating went on. Each additional lash
helped to change Endurance's opinion about his
fellow countrymen. Just before he fainted once
again, his loathing for the Chinese reached the
level of his abhorrence for the Mongols.

Buckets of water were thrown on Endurance

to bring him around. Wan returned to grin at him. "Are you ready to wise up?"

Endurance shook his head. Wan left and the whipping resumed. Endurance shrieked on and on as he felt himself being torn apart by the fire of pain. He could not take it any longer. His body was tied to the post, but his spirit was free to escape.

A strange sensation came over him. He left his body and levitated above the tied man. He watched the poor man being whipped, but the pain was unfelt by him. He saw the helpless man's skin crack and blood seeping out, and realized how foolish of him to think that kung fu could make him unbeatable.

From midair, Endurance shook his head at the dying man. From the tent, King Wan reappeared holding half a chicken and using his teeth to tear the meat off the bones.

"Is he dead?" Wan asked.

The big man laid down his whip, walked to the tied man, and took a handful of his hair. He pulled the motionless man's head up and checked. "Yes," the big man answered.

"How many times did he faint?" Wan asked with his mouth full.

"Six," the big man said.

Floating above the tied man, Endurance tried to remember. He could only recall fainting about two or three times. Was pain this easy to forget? He remembered Peony's smiles after each childbirth. She had screamed in unbearable torment, but then forgot it as soon as it was over.

Peony! Endurance suddenly realized that he could not die. Peony! His spirit called her name, then lowered itself back into the body of the tied man.

Immediately he felt the intolerable pain.

Vanguard's words reappeared in his mind:

women were stronger than men. If men were
given the responsibility of childbirth, they wouldn't
be able to take it.

"I'll take the pain for you! I must live for you,
my Peony!" Endurance's lips moved, but no
sound came out. The slight movement of the
blood-covered lips was unnoticed by either the
executioner or Wan.

King Wan had started his noon meal before all
others. Now it was lunchtime for the entire
camp. The big executioner left in a hurry. There
was no need to untie a dead man from the post.

Soon after the meal, the watchmen sounded
the alarm: A large group of Mongol soldiers had
been seen in the nearby forests, and it was best
for the Wan Fighters to move on.

"What shall we do with the dead man?" someone asked.

"Leave him tied there," King Wan answered.
"Maybe the Mongols can feed him to their
dogs!"

Flexing his muscles, Endurance painstakingly
began to work his wrists free of their bindings.
At long last he finally worked himself loose of
the post. He fell to his knees from the effort.
Forcing himself up, he staggered from the campground. He could hear the Wan Fighters being
attacked by the Mongols. Their screams made
him hurry. A sea of fire surrounded him, continued to burn him with waves of pain.

After a while Endurance could not stay on his
feet any longer. He sank to his hands and knees
and crawled. After crawling for what seemed
like miles, he was unable to take the pain and
exhaustion any more. He lay on the ground panting. Then with an inner determination, helped
by thinking of Peony, he forced himself to go on.

He hid in the forest until day turned into

night. The rest gave him more strength. He looked at the stars and located the direction of Vanguard's campsite. He crawled under the moonlit sky, and his vitality gradually disappeared with the waning of the moon.

As the eastern sky turned gray, he knew he could not crawl one more inch. "I am sorry, Peony," he whispered, then closed his eyes and allowed his spirit to leave his body.

It felt so good to be freed from misery.

He once again felt the intolerable pain return. The sea of fire had caught up with him. He twisted his body and the fire burned with greater intensity.

"Bring more ointment, and hurry!" It was Peony's voice.

Endurance opened his eyes and found himself in his tent, lying on a straw mat and wrapped in ointment-soaked strips of cloth. Vanguard stood at the door looking at him in deep concern. Peony knelt beside him, crying.

"Don't let your salty tears fall on my wounds ... my Peony!" he murmured in a barely audible voice.

"Endurance! My Endurance!" Peony cried out through her tears. She held his hand and sobbed, "They found you near the campsite. They brought you back here, but you never moved. I dressed your wounds, but you never made a sound. Now you talk! Why didn't you talk earlier? You scared me to death!"

While crying and talking, she put the gold chain with the jade pendant beside Endurance's pillow. "You didn't take your lucky charm with you, and that's why this happened. Now it's yours again. And you'll wear it as soon as your skin is healed ..." She wept. "There is not one

inch of skin that is not torn on your entire
body!"

Vanguard Kuo came to Endurance and squatted beside him. "My friend, I'm truly sorry for
what happened. I wish I had gone with you."

He told Endurance that half of the Kuo Fighters had made it safely back to the base. They
had reported how Endurance had ordered them
to leave with no concern for himself.

"We were on our way to rescue you when we
found you lying on the ground." Vanguard paused,
then said, "I have good news for you, and it may
help ease your pain. The Wan Fighters were
caught by the Mongols outside their campground. All of them were slaughtered. Tin-check
Wan's head was displayed on the same post
where you were tied and whipped. The Mongols
then left Honan for Da-du."

He added with a smile, "You did bring the
entire Honan Province home as a gift to your
wife."

The good news did not bring a smile to Endurance's face. He looked from his wife to his
friend, gathered enough energy to speak a few
words more. "I hate the Mongols for killing Wan
. . . I wanted to kill that bastard myself. From
now on, we must . . . kill not only the Mongols,
but . . . also all the unfaithful Chinese. There is
more than one Wan. We need to destroy them
. . . before they can hurt us."

30

Spring, 1356

WISDOM LU STOOD in his study, facing the open window. His garment was deep blue, and at this moment his mind was also a dark blue sea, bottomless with troubled thoughts.

He regarded the low clouds over the top of the mountain, but could not see either the Temple of Peaceful Stars or the Temple of Silent Echo. "Endurance, I cannot see the true meaning of your letter any more than I can those mysterious temples," Wisdom said, lowering his eyes to a note in his hand. He had read it many times, but still could not understand it. He left his study and walked to the inner court.

He was happy to find Lotus alone. In a yellow robe, Lotus was as beautiful as a chrysanthemum in full bloom. She looked up from her poetry book and smiled at her husband.

"Where are the children?" he asked as he walked toward her.

"The two grandmothers took them to the Dais of Rain Flowers," Lotus answered with a smile. "They won't be back until tomorrow afternoon."

Ah Chin had become sick in the past year, and Jasmine had left the Lu house to join her husband and children in the farmhouse near the Dais of Rain Flowers. The Lu children missed Jasmine so much that they often pleaded with their two grandmothers to take them to the farm. Fortunately, both Lady Lu and Lady Lin loved the many trips to the countryside.

Wisdom Lu sighed. "I wouldn't mind going there myself."

Lotus looked into her husband's eyes. "What is troubling you?"

It was so good to have a wife who could read his mind. Wisdom gave the note to Lotus. "Read it and you'll also be troubled."

Lotus laughed in the very beginning. "I can see that Endurance still writes each character in the size comparable to himself."

Her laughter stopped as she read on. Her smooth brows were gathered into a frown when she finished the note. "There has to be some mistake," she said. The note slipped through her trembling fingers and fell to the floor.

Wisdom picked up the note, read it out loudly once again, "We the Kuo Fighters are not only fighting the Mongols, but also the Chinese. We want to destroy the Mongol empire, and at the same time eliminate all other Chinese rebel forces that stand in our way!"

Lotus saw the paper rattling in her husband's shaking hand, and she put her hand over his to stop it. "I can still see our tall friend clearly. He is bold and honest, brave and compassionate. He cannot fight against his own fellow countrymen," she said firmly.

"But the note is in his own writing!" Wisdom said.

Lotus thought, then answered carefully, "Endurance has a bad temper. He could have been angry at a particular Chinese at the time he wrote you this note. Maybe he exaggerated his feelings."

"Endurance's notes are always so short," Wisdom murmured, staring at the few large words.

"If only I could send a messenger to him and ask him to explain things. I also need to tell him that the Silent League financed the southern leaders in their making of Flaming Snakes. If he finds it out without my telling him first, he will be very upset."

Lotus read her husband's mind again. "But you cannot contact Endurance. Ah Chin is too sick to travel. And no one else is dependable. Yin-tin City is still controlled by the Mongols. You are lucky to receive this message from Endurance without getting into trouble with the governor. He has ordered that every mailman's bags be checked."

Wisdom stood up and walked to the window. He still could not find the two temples from behind the thick clouds. "I wish I could pray to the great Buddha. I want my best friend to remain unchanged. I wish Endurance will win all the battles against the Mongols and stay unharmed, but not lay a hand on even one of his own people."

Lotus clapped her hands and two maids appeared. "Prepare the sedan chairs," she ordered. "The mayor and I are going to the temples."

The couple offered their incense and prayers first in the Temple of Peaceful Stars, and then the Temple of Silent Echo. The monks and nuns in both temples were practicing kung fu, ready to join the forces to drive the Mongols out of Yin-tin City.

While returning to the Lu house, the long procession passed the Mongol governor's mansion. It would be rude for the mayor to go by the governor's home without paying him a visit, and Wisdom and Lotus were received immediately. As they sat in the grand room and talked to the governor and his Mongolian wife, they were

shocked by the obvious fear and worry that appeared in the Mongol couple's eyes.

"They must be aware that their days in power
are numbered!" Wisdom whispered to Lotus on
their way out.

PART V

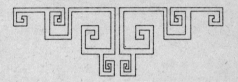

31

IN THE BEGINNING of summer, 1360, a young girl died of illness in a small village on the Yellow River. She was one of many daughters in a poor family and the father, burdened with life's sorrow, did not grieve at her death. Her grave was but a shallow hole. Hungry dogs came, uncovered the hole and ate most of her corpse. What was left of her was exposed in the boiling sun. White maggots and black flies blanketed the cadaver. The flies then flew into people's homes and rested on their rice bowls, carrying the seeds of death.

The plague spread quickly, infecting Chinese and Mongols alike. In Da-du, the latter blamed the deadly ailment on the natives, and no Chinese from outside the city walls were allowed to enter. The Chinese merchants and shopkeepers between the first and second rings of city walls were quarantined. Beyond the second wall where the Mongol officers and soldiers lived, their Chinese slaves received daily inspection. At the first sign of illness, the slave was slain and the body burned.

Because of these precautions, the plague did not spread inside the walls surrounding the royal palace. The great khan's adviser would celebrate his fifty-first birthday in midsummer, and the mood was festive. A celebration would soon take place in the grand room. Every royal prince

and princess was busy looking for a gift for
Shadow Tamu that would outshine all the
others.

"Why give him anything at all? In the past
seven years, besides forcing you into becoming
the khan, he has given you nothing but orders
and humiliation," Queen Sunflower said, and
her beautiful eyes gleamed with anger.

The Great Khan Eastwind sighed. "We have
no choice. Let's not give him anything special,
but something we don't want."

The royal couple began to tour their room.
Eastwind was handsome in his golden robe, and
Sunflower divine in her pale green garment. Neither of them wore much jewelry. They preferred
looking at the finer things to wearing them.

"I certainly won't give him this. This is my
greatest pride," Eastwind said, indicating a marble stand. A lantern hung from the mouth of a
rising dragon made of wood. The lantern had
eight panels, each a sheet of glass. The flowers
of four seasons were painted on the panels, alternating with scenes of spring through winter.
When the young khan lit the candle inside the
lantern, each panel became transparent, and the
flowers and scenes seemed to be floating in
midair.

Queen Sunflower leaned her head on the
khan's shoulder as they watched the lantern
glow. "It's a shame that glass is not being made
throughout the country."

"The country is at war. The Chinese are busy
making weapons to fight us, and we are doing
our best to destroy the rebels. At a time like this,
glass is a useless thing and no one is interested
in my formula of glassmaking," the Khan said
sadly as he moved on, leaving the glass lantern
shimmering behind them.

They stopped at an abacus made with jade

beads and gold sticks. "I won't give this away. I like it," Sunflower said. She picked it up and pushed the beads around. "The court mathematicians said I am the most clever student they ever had," she said proudly.

After putting down the abacus, they looked at a life-size brass man that was hollow and covered with hundreds of tiny pin holes. "And I can't part from my patient," the young khan said. He took a long needle from a nearby box and pushed it into one of the holes. "With practice, I'll become a great acupuncturist someday."

Leaving behind the brass man, they paused at the largest display table in this grand room. On the table was a dragon boat large enough to carry the khan and his queen.

"Remember last spring?" Eastwind put his arm around Sunflower's waist. "We sailed in the Hui-tung Canal . . ." They had used pretty Chinese girls for coolies and dressed them in clothes to match the silk cords that pulled the boat, which resembled a dragon. The dragon could open and close its mouth and eyes while being tugged from the shore.

"The Chinese were very unhappy to see us going down the canal in a dragon boat." The young queen shook her head, trying to shake off the bad memory.

They came to a halt before a large platform centered by the statue of a beautiful girl carved out of pink coral. Dressed in a Mongolian costume, she proudly carried a silver bow over her left shoulder, and her right hand held a gold arrow vertically by its tip. The arrow proceeded to enter a brass container of water placed at her feet. Water was poured into the container once a day, then drained slowly through a small hole and a long pipe. The gold arrow bore twenty-four marks, each adorned with a red ruby. As

the water went lower in the container, more red
marks became visible.

The great khan counted the number of red
marks above the water and said, "Lady Time
says its the eighteenth hour of the day and time
for the feast to begin. We better go to Shadow
Tamu's birthday party."

Queen Sunflower was unwilling to leave. "Lady
Time is the most precious to me, because it was
invented by you. You are a genius, and you
should invent more beautiful things."

Eastwind pulled his queen away from the
statue. "We are late for the feast and have not
yet found Shadow Tamu a gift." He stopped at
the glass lantern. The candle was still burning,
and the glass panels transparent. Since Sunflower did not consider it her favorite, he did
not mind parting from it to please his fearsome
adviser.

Shadow Tamu, his thin face deeply lined, was
wearing a purple garment of the lightest summer
silk. Around his neck several heavy gold chains
hung with pendants of precious stone. He looked
at the empty seats of the Great Khan Eastwind
and Queen Sunflower, and frowned. It was disre-
spectful of them to arrive later than he. His eyes
fell on more empty seats, and he could not believe what he saw. "How dare so many of them
be late?" he asked Mighty Sword, who sat next
to him.

Mighty Sword was forty-one, and like his
brother, he had waited to marry the first woman
capable of bearing him a son. Since none of his
women had turned his seed into a child, he had
remained a bachelor. His scarlet summer robe
looked tight on him. Most of his massive body
was muscle, but a part of it fat. His temples had
turned silver, and lines had appeared between

his brows. The extra weight, the silver hair, and
the lines of age only enhanced his handsomeness,
like time strengthening the taste of wine. He
laughed at his brother's comment and said, "I'm
sure no one dares to be late, not even Eastwind
and his queen. They must be playing with their
silly collection again. As to the other empty
seats . . ." Mighty Sword glanced around to make
sure that no one was listening. "I'm afraid they
will never be filled."

"Do they dare to overlook my invitation?"
Shadow Tamu stared at his brother.

"No one dares to offend you when they are
alive, but they can't help it if they are dead."

"Dead?" Shadow Tamu's pale face turned
ashen. "You mean the plague has arrived in Da-
du?"

"No," Mighty Sword looked around once more,
then lowered his voice. "Many of the empty
seats belong to high-ranked officers in our military forces. In the past four years, many of our
officers and soldiers have been killed. My dear
brother, don't you know that we have lost a large
part of China to the hateful Kuo Fighters?"

"I know," Shadow Tamu nodded confidently.
"I'm not worried. Whatever territories the Chinese took, you'll soon take back."

The supreme general said hesitantly, "I used
to be as confident as you."

"Are you no longer confident?" the khan's adviser snapped.

The supreme general answered slowly, "It's
hard to explain. I'm sure the Kuo fighters will
be defeated, but I'm no longer positive that they
will be defeated by me." He glanced at his puzzled brother, sighed, then continued, "I've confronted the Kuo Fighters many times. At the
beginning of every battle, I thought I could van-

quish them, but at the end I always lost more men and retreated farther back toward Da-du."

Shadow Tamu was impatient with losers, even when that loser was his own brother. He glared at Mighty Sword through knitted brows. "Perhaps you have forgotten the old saying: When killing a snake you must go for its throat, and when destroying an army you must go for its leader."

"I have not forgotten!" The supreme general glared at his brother angrily. "The Kuo Fighters have two leaders. It's difficult to beat Vanguard Kuo, and it's impossible to defeat Endurance Chu!"

Moving closer, Mighty Sword began to whisper of his many battles with Endurance.

What frightened him the most was the peasant's rapid growth. He had witnessed Endurance maturing from a boy to a man, and an unskilled brawler to a trained fighter.

"He and I have such strong mutual hatred that I am thirsty for his blood, and I know he is thirsty for mine—" He stopped at the sudden appearance of Eastwind and Sunflower.

The great khan was breathless and so was his queen. "We are sorry for being late. We were looking for a suitable birthday present for you," the khan said as he ran through the grand room. Reaching his adviser, he placed the glass lantern on the table. "This is one of my most treasured inventions. It is very valuable to me. I hope you like it as much as I. Many years from now, this lantern can still be lighted and its soft beam will shine on people of a future world—"

While the khan was still talking, his adviser spread his arms and knocked the lantern off the table. The candle was extinguished, the delicately carved dragon broken into several sections, the glass panels shattered into hundreds of pieces.

"Ah, how careless of me," Shadow Tamu said in mock regret. "Now the poor lantern will never have a chance to shine on people of the future world, and I must do without a birthday present from you."

"You!" The young khan took a step toward his adviser. "You broke my lantern on purpose!" Suddenly he felt someone pulling his arm. He looked at Sunflower, who had followed him to Shadow Tamu. She was not looking at him, though, but at Mighty Sword.

Eastwind followed his queen's eyes and saw the supreme general had raised a Killing Hand.

Shadow Tamu had taken the Killing Hand from the last khan and shown the weapon to his brother. They had summoned some craftsmen and made a few more, but Mighty Sword had never carried one before.

The long iron tube frightened the young khan. As he stared at the weapon, he heard Sunflower saying to the adviser, "Since the lantern is broken, I'm sure the khan can give you something else for a birthday present." Sunflower pulled the khan's arm vigorously. "How about one hundred gold coins?"

A smile gradually softened Shadow Tamu's hard face. He tilted his head to one side and pretended that he had not heard the queen clearly. "Did my queen say five hundred gold coins?"

Eastwind felt the pull on his arm again. He looked away from Mighty Sword's Killing Hand, saw Sunflower nodding. The young khan said stiffly, "Five hundred gold coins will be fine!" Without wishing the adviser a happy birthday, Eastwind hurried away tight-lipped.

The khan and his queen were seated at the

opposite end of the room, far from the adviser and the supreme general. Eastwind was still fuming when the feast began. Taking a large sip of his wine, he whispered into Sunflower's ear, "I cannot take this anymore! I am a man, not a boy! I've been hiding behind my toys for too long! I've been sitting on the throne, but have never been a khan. I've been a slave to twenty-six princes, a supreme general, and an adviser!"

Sunflower waited patiently as Eastwind vented his fury. She had already waited seven years for her young prince to become a great khan. For this reason she was thankful Shadow Tamu had smashed that glass lantern.

Eastwind went on, "I want to remove Shadow Tamu and appoint a new adviser. And I must eliminate Mighty Sword!"

The queen was very proud of her khan's decision, but she saw that she would have to serve as his faithful adviser before he could replace Shadow Tamu. She said, "Be patient. You are not ready yet. Look around the room, and you'll realize that you have no one but me on your side. From tomorrow on, you must begin to gather a handful of loyal guards. Increase the number of your guards gradually until they become a corps. Enlarge the corps until you have an army."

She smiled at the great khan encouragingly. "Learn from your Lady Time, my khan. Don't move, but wait for time to drip away slowly. One of these days you'll rule."

The khan took his queen's hand and held it tightly. They smiled at each other without exchanging more words.

"How sickening!" Shadow Tamu said, looking at them from across the room. "After all these years, still gazing at each other like moonstruck calves." He turned to Mighty Sword. "Please continue with what you were saying."

The supreme general looked at the Killing Hand and said, "I'm a proud swordsman, and I despise playing tricks. Explosives are but tricks in my eyes. I've never used this iron tube in the past four years. But starting six moons ago, my craftsmen have been making plenty of them. Here is my plan."

He would leave Da-du in the morning and head south. He and his men would stay alongside the Yangtze River and wait for the Kuo fighters to enter Kiangsi Province. Mighty Sword had decided to cast aside his pride in swordsmanship. He and his soldiers would use Killing Hands to fight the Kuo Fighters from now on.

"But if my calculation is right, we may not have to fire our weapons at them at all," he said.

The adviser looked at his brother questioningly. "What do you mean?"

The supreme general explained, "We Mongols are not the Kuo Fighters' only enemies."

In the past four years, the Kuo Fighters had moved from Honan westward, conquered a large part of Shensi Province and the entire province of Szechwan. When the kings of Shensi and Szechwan had met Endurance Chu on the battle-field, they had been defeated and later tortured to death.

"Talk about cruelty!" The Mongol general shook his head. "The Chinese can display the most ruthless brutality. I've heard the details, but I'm not sure I want to repeat it over dinner."

"I couldn't care less how the Chinese kill one another. All I care about is our empire," Shadow Tamu said, flicking his hand impatiently. Neither of them had any children, but both of them desired to rule China forever. "You were saying that we Mongols were not the Kuo Fighters' only enemies."

Dipping a finger into his flagon of red wine,

the supreme general drew a map of China on the tablecloth. "South of the Yangtze River are two Chinese rebel factions, each as strong as the Kuo Fighters. If the king of Kiangsi near Phoenix Place does not defeat them, the King of Kiangsu at the outskirts of Yin-tin most certainly will."

He took a gulp of wine, then continued, "King of Kiangsi is Yu, and king of Kiangsu is Chen. They both have plenty of Killing Hands—by the way, the Chinese call them Flaming Snakes. There is a secret organization in the south that gives the rebels money to make these weapons. We tried to uncover the organization but couldn't. Anyway, in every battle we have fought with the southern Chinese, they have never used their Flaming Snakes. It's obvious that they are saving their precious explosives to use on their own kind. And, according to the information given to me by my spies, the Kuo Fighters do not have Killing Hands."

The supreme general's stratagem comforted his brother. No longer would he have to worry. The two raised their large golden cups adorned with precious stones.

"May the southern Chinese destroy the Kuo Fighters!" Shadow Tamu hollered.

"May the Kuo Fighters slay hordes of southern Chinese!" Mighty Sword bellowed.

"May we kill all the remaining Chinese fighters easily after that, and rule China forever!" the brothers shouted together.

32

Autumn, 1360

THROUGHOUT THE SUMMER, the plague spread from north to south. Alongside the Yangtze River, entire extended families died, leaving no one to bury them. Numerous bodies were thrown into the river. What the fish did not eat was left to rot.

Entering Kiangsi Province, the Kuo Fighters reached the bank of Yangtze and camped beside the river. Endurance and Peony left their children in the care of nannies and walked from their tent to the riverbank.

Brown leaves were falling from weeping willows to the water, and white lanterns bobbed among cadavers. They saw people using the river for bathing, laundering, and emptying toilet buckets. They watched their cooking staff wash vegetables in the river and fetch drinking water from it.

"We better make sure that the vegetables are thoroughly cooked and the water boiled for our children," Peony said. By now she and Endurance had four sons. The older ones, Power and Dominance, were six and five. Bravery was fourteen months old, and Vigorous only two months.

"Don't worry. Like us, our sons have been drinking river water every day of their lives," Endurance said, walking away. He was excited to be back in the south. He had run away as a wanted killer and had now returned as second

commander in one of the strongest rebel armies.
"Let's go to Vanguard's tent. He is waiting for
us to discuss our plans for the morrow."

After camping all these years, the officers and
commanders of the Kuo Fighters now had better-
equipped tents. When Endurance and Peony entered, Vanguard was lying on a quilt-covered cotton
mat with his eyes closed. Seeing them, he sat up
and leaned against a pile of pillows. "Tomorrow
is a crucial day. We'll enter Phoenix Place, King
Yu's territory. His men will be waiting for us
with their Flaming Snakes." He looked at Endurance sadly. "I hate to fight them, especially with
the same lethal weapon. We've already killed far
too many Chinese than I would like to. With the
Flaming Snakes, we'll kill a great deal more."

Though Endurance and Peony disagreed, they
remained silent.

"The monks and nuns agree with me," Vanguard said, reading their minds. "We used to
have many kung fu monks and Red Turban nuns
among us, but they have left us one by one when
we started to kill our own people. The remaining
ones will feel useless once we start to use the
Flaming Snakes."

Vanguard sighed as he remembered how they
had started manufacturing Flaming Snakes. When
Joy had moved to the Temple of White Crane,
she had brought the sample weapon with her.
Vanguard had been reluctant to make such
weapons for the Kuo Fighters until Endurance
convinced him that they must have the Flaming
Snakes to defeat the southern leaders. Endurance's torture by King Wan had helped Vanguard to make the decision to go ahead. He had
sent a monk to Joy Kuo, and the sample had been
brought back to Vanguard together with all the
money Joy could send. Craftsmen had been gathered, and the weapons had been made secretly.

The Kuo Fighters had many Flaming Snakes now, but neither the other revolution leaders nor the Mongols knew.

Endurance and Peony listened politely, straining to remain patient with Vanguard. They each thought of different things. An idea began to take form in Peony's mind. It became more solid as Vanguard said, "Maybe we should send someone to Phoenix Place and talk to King Yu. If he will join forces with us, then we can fight together."

Endurance said, "Phoenix Place is my family's ancestral home. Believe me, I know those people." He related his unpleasant experience in gathering fighters in Phoenix Place. "Money means more than patriotism in that town, as it does in most places. Since King Yu is rich enough to make Flaming Snakes, the Phoenix Place soldiers must be well off. They will try their best to blow us to pieces, Vanguard, whether we are their fellow countrymen or not."

Vanguard said weakly, "Just promise me once again ..." He was too overcome by sorrow to finish his sentence.

Both Endurance and Peony knew what they were supposed to promise. They said at the same time, "We will order our soldiers not to use our Flaming Snakes until they have used theirs first."

While making this promise halfheartedly, Peony's idea became a concrete plan. "Instead of the Flaming Snakes, though, we should use another means to fight the southerners."

Vanguard's murky eyes brightened. "Something less dangerous? Something that will lessen the killing?"

Peony shook her head. "I've watched those craftsmen making the Flaming Snakes, and it seems that enlarging the weapon and increasing its power would be rather simple."

She told the men what she had in mind: if they made iron tubes ten times the original size, they could stuff the tubes with ten times the original amount of explosives.

Endurance patted her on the shoulder. "Great idea! I can just see an iron tube the size of a large tree trunk. We can call it the Firing Dragon. Once fired, the dragon will knock down walls, destroy blockades, and kill ten times more of our enemies than if we had used merely a Flaming Snake."

Then he frowned, thinking. "But we'll need money to make the dragons." He looked at Vanguard. "You and Joy have used all the money on feeding our men and making the Flaming Snakes. We need someone or some group to support us. I wonder who is helping the southern leaders to make their weapons? If only we could persuade this person to support us."

Endurance and Peony looked toward Vanguard. To their surprise, he did not object to their suggestion. His eyes were shut tight, and he seemed to be searching for an answer. Both Endurance and Peony had to restrain themselves as he meditated.

After he had remained silent a long time, Endurance cried impatiently, "Well, do you know who is behind the southern rebel leaders?"

At his touch, Vanguard began to slide off the pillows and he fell soundlessly to the cotton mat.

"He is shivering!" Endurance said after taking him in his arms.

"He is burning with fever!" Peony said after feeling his forehead.

They looked at each other. Panic appeared in their eyes. "No!" they shouted simultaneously.

A medicine man was summoned immediately.

The man confirmed Endurance and Peony's fear: Vanguard had contracted the plague.

Bowls of herbal juice were poured down his throat, but Vanguard only vomited. Teacups were heated, then placed upside down on Vanguard's naked back, but the evil spirits inside refused to be sucked out of his body. The Kuo Fighters stayed at the bank of the Yangtze River for the next ten days. During that time more than twenty of them died of plague.

Due to his high fever, Vanguard remained in a coma. But on the tenth day, just when the sun was setting, his mind became clear again. He opened his eyes and saw Endurance and Peony squatting beside his straw mat. The tapestry over the tent entrance was raised. The radiant sun behind the peasant couple made them look like two faceless figures wearing a giant-size golden crown.

"The crown . . ." Vanguard mumbled. "Do not abuse the crown . . ."

Endurance and Peony looked at each other. Their friend was dying and delirious, and they could not make any sense of his words.

"Don't worry, my friend," Endurance said, taking Vanguard's hand. "Peony and I will take care of Joy for you—"

Vanguard withdrew his hand from Endurance's grasp, opened his eyes wide, and suddenly roared, "How about China? I love China as much as I do Joy!"

Peony was surprised by the dying man's sudden strength. She said, "We will take care of China for you. We'll fight for her—"

"Fighting for her is far from enough! You must be kind to her, too!" Vanguard shouted.

The yelling drained his energy. His eyes moved slowly from Peony to Endurance, and he uttered in a fading voice, "Be kind to China . . . and be

kind to the Chinese . . . Please . . . my friends . . ."
He stopped breathing before they could answer.

Vanguard was buried beside the Yangtze River.
As the monks and nuns stayed at the riverbank
to pray for his spirit, Endurance and Peony
walked away from his grave, stopped to sit on a
large rock protruding out over the water.

A chilly autumn wind blew fiercely, stripping
the willows of their remaining leaves, matting
the water with a thick layer of brown. "Winter
is in the air," Peony said, crossing her arms in
front of her to keep herself warm. "The plague
will go away when cold weather arrives. We
shouldn't lose more men to the horrible curse."
Her eyes became blurred with tears. She remembered how kind Vanguard had been to her ever
since his wife brought her home from the human
stable. She and Endurance had sent a messenger
to Prosper Mountain, and she knew that Vanguard's death had to be unbearable for Joy. If
only old Meadow had not been killed by Wan!

Peony blinked through her tears, trying not
to sob, when suddenly she was struck by a real-
ization. "Endurance!" She put a hand on his
arm. She no longer felt cold as excitement
warmed her body and heart. "Have you realized that you bare now the chief commander of
the Kuo Fighters?"

Endurance stared at her for a few moments,
then suddenly stood up, pulling her with him. "I
am the chief commander," he said thoughtfully.
"You are the chief commander's lady. We will
lead the Kuo Fighters—" He stopped in mid-
sentence and frowned. "We cannot call our men
Kuo Fighters. We need a new name."

They left the protruding rock and headed
down the riverbank. They walked fast, raising
their voices to be heard in the wind. "Chu Fighters is too common a name. The name for our

men must be unique," Peony said. "It has to represent something that will be accepted by all
Chinese, especially the southerners. Your name
is well-known in the north, but in the south you
are nobody."

"But I soon will be," Endurance said. "After
I start my campaigns down here, everyone will
know me!"

They could not find a name they both liked,
though, and in the end they settled on the Chu
Fighters temporarily. As they planned on killing
more people to make themselves famous, they
did not notice that the monks and nuns had
heard their every word.

The Chu Fighters left their base the next day
at dawn. The chief commander and his lady rode
on horses, followed by high-ranked officers on
mules. The soldiers walked on foot, and the
monks and nuns walked with the soldiers because they didn't like to burden any other animal, which they regarded as their equals. Women
and children formed the end of the procession,
riding wagons pulled by mules and water
buffalo.

Advancing through Kiangsi Province, they reached
the outskirts of Phoenix Place at noon. They
stopped and set up tents. They ate, rested, then
waited for night to fall. When the autumn moon
reached the top of the tallest weeping willow,
Peony and Endurance went to the tent where
their four sons were.

"Listen to your nannies and be good. Baba and
Mama will win another battle and come back to
you soon." Peony hugged the two babies, speaking lovingly, whether the boys understood or not.

"Grow up fast!" Endurance said to the two
older ones impatiently. "So you can become

brave warriors and fight beside your baba and
mama!"

The warriors had been trained to walk with
rapid, noiseless kung fu steps, but their animals,
of course, had not. So the chief commander, his
lady, and the officers left their horses and mules
at their campsite. The Chu Fighters moved in
the dark, were soon able to see the city of Phoenix Place in the moonlight. They could tell that
a heavy blockade had been placed at the entrance of the main road.

"I see men behind the blockade," Endurance
said, at the very front of the line. "Are they Chinese or Mongols?"

Peony was right beside her husband, as always
on the battleground. "The men are not wearing
pointed hats, and they do not have armor. And
the moon shines on something white on the lapels of their dark uniforms. I would say they are
definitely Chinese."

Endurance squinted his eyes. Like Peony, he
too, saw dark uniforms and light-colored crests.
The autumn moon cast its magic beams over the
men behind the blockade, turning the crests into
white skeletons with two sockets, one filled with
the word Wan and the other Tin-check.

All of a sudden, Endurance felt a river of
flame burning through him with powerful surges
of pain. He forgot the promise he had made to
Vanguard, and he did not hear the protesting
voices of the monks and nuns.

"Pick up your Flaming Snakes," he whispered.

"Aim," he said.

"Fire!" he shouted.

The explosives burst out of the iron tubes and
a number of men fell, shrieking with pain.

Behind them, King Yu was touched by panic.
"We built the blockade to protect ourselves from
swords and spears, but not explosives. The

northerners are not supposed to have Flaming Snakes!" He stamped his foot on the ground. "I'll kill my informer for misinforming me!"

With their element of surprise, the Chu Fighters rushed the city, overwhelming their foe and capturing King Yu. Endurance, Peony, and their fighters returned to their base under a dawning sky.

Endurance then gave orders to tie King Yu to the post in the middle of the campground.

"Whip him to death, but whip him slowly," he told the executioner. "Every time he faints, pour cold water over him. Make sure that he does not die until he has fainted at least five or six times!" He did not have Tin-check Wan, but this one would do. They were now all the same to him.

From morning to noon, the campground was filled with painful screams. Except for the brave Chu boys, the children covered their ears with their hands. Many of the soldiers and officers lost their appetite. Other than Peony, the women cried. The monks and nuns went to Endurance and protested, but Endurance only grinned at them.

Instead he ordered a feast for his family and himself, specifying a roasted chicken. He walked out of his tent, stood facing the naked man tied to the post, tearing the chicken meat off the bones with his teeth as he watched King Yu's blood dripping to the ground.

"You are but another Wan!" Endurance spat at the dying man. "Except for a handful of decent souls, all Chinese bear the last name Wan in my eyes!"

He did not leave the dead man tied to the post. He ordered the body decapitated, then thrown into the woods to feed the wolves. He did not notice the mutinous looks on the faces of all the monks and nuns, nor did he pay attention to their hushed meeting in a remote corner of the camp.

The Chu Fighters were rewarded with a celebration in mid-afternoon, but no liquor was allowed. They were then divided into two groups. Endurance went to sleep at the same time with the first group, and Peony would sleep later with the second group.

"The Mongols are here!"

Endurance was wakened by Peony as the sun began to set. "A general and his men, all on horseback, are surrounding our campsite!"

Endurance was fully awake the next moment. His men were just as alert as he. They formed a circle around their tents, facing outward, aiming their Flaming Snakes toward the advancing enemies.

Mighty Sword had told his men that this would be an easy victory, for he expected to surprise the Chinese fighters in their sleep. In addition, he had told his men that the northern Chinese rebels did not have Killing Hands. Those explosions they had heard from Phoenix Place had belonged to the Flaming Snakes of the Yu Fighters, he explained.

"Fire!" Endurance ordered, and all the iron tubes blasted.

Some of the Mongols were instantly killed or wounded. The others stopped dead in astonishment. For them, too, the Killing Hands was a new weapon, and under fire they started aiming their guns badly and missing their targets. In a very short time they lost faith in their new weapon, and the attack faltered.

Their hesitation, though, only gave the Chu Fighters time to reload their Flaming Snakes.

"Fire!" Endurance shouted again.

More Mongols fell off their horses, and the

survivors panicked. Regardless of their supreme general's order, they did not bother to reload their Killing Hands. They turned their horses and started to flee.

Mighty Sword was an experienced leader, and he knew that when soldiers were withdrawing on their own, it would be impossible to force them forward unless he was willing to kill them all.

Even the Mongol horses were not used to the sound of explosives. Like all the others, Mighty Sword's black stallion was startled by the explosions. It raised its front legs high both times when the Chinese fired their Flaming Snakes. The second time it nearly threw Mighty Sword off its back.

"Return to the base!" he yelled, trying to steady his frightened horse. Riding among his petrified men, he turned to look over his shoulder. His eyes glanced over the dead and wounded, searched among the living, and met the eyes of Endurance.

The Chu leader stood with his feet parted and his hands resting on his hips, grinning at Mighty Sword.

The eye contact lasted only a moment, but seemed like many moons for both men. Both knew that Endurance had emerged victorious. Mighty Sword then rode on and disappeared quickly in the rising dust.

Endurance knew Peony was standing beside him. He took her hand, stared at the fading dust as a broad smile brightened his features. "Now I'm certain that avenging the deaths of our families and friends is no longer a dream," he said.

The sun was setting, and the sky resembled an emperor's red-gold robe. Peony and Endurance turned to look at a magnificent heaven, then returned to their campsite on wings of glory.

"Baba and Mama are back safely, my babies!" Peony said, rushing to Bravery and Vigorous and taking one in each arm.

"Baba and Mama have taken back the Chu family's ancestral home, my sons!" Endurance said to Power and Dominance. "We must go to the Chu family graveyard tomorrow to give thanks."

33

THE CHU FIGHTERS were weary after fighting
two battles in a row, but did not dare to relax
their guard. They slept in shifts for the rest of
the night. The next day they would pack their
supplies, bring their children and women into
the Phoenix Place to take over the city.

Peony had gone to sleep with the first group
of fighters, and was awakened by a hiss:

"Wake up, Peony!"

Opening her eyes, she saw Endurance kneeling beside her feather-stuffed mat.

"Another battle? Who is attacking us this
time?" she jumped up, rubbing her eyes, wide-
awake and ready to go.

Endurance laughed. "There's no battle, my
poor Peony. The richest fellow in Phoenix Place,
a man named Fong, has come to welcome us. He
has brought sedan chairs for you, the children,
and all the other officers's wives and babies."

Peony giggled. "Sedan chairs? For me and the
children? I have not been in one since I left Joy
Kuo. Well, we can try to act comfortable in those
little square boxes, I suppose. The other officers'
wives? Most of them have never been in a sedan
chair in their entire lives."

By the time they arrived, the people of Phoenix Place were lining the main street to express
their gratitude to the Chu Fighters. Formerly they
had paid taxes to two masters: King Yu and the

Mongols. Now both forces had been driven off.
"We are shivering rabbits. The Chu Fighters
saved us from two hungry wolves. Let's hope
that they are not a tiger in turn," they whispered
as they bowed to Endurance atop his powerful
horse.

Their jaws dropped when they saw Peony in
a curtainless sedan, wearing a man's robe, crossing her booted long legs, and waving at everyone
with a smile so broad that her teeth showed.
Their hearts sank when they saw the other officers' wives in the next sedan chairs. These wom-
en's postures were no more graceful than that of
Peony's.

"We're in trouble," one of them said. "They
are neither gentlemen nor ladies. If they stay
here, then we've jumped from the jaws of two
wolves to the claws of one tiger."

As the soldiers and officers enjoyed everything
Phoenix Place had to offer and the monks and
nuns went visiting the local temple, Endurance
and Peony stayed in Lord Fong's mansion. Peony,
though, soon found Lady Fong unbearably bor-
ing. She left her children to the dull lady and
joined Endurance and the lord.

Lord Fong asked, "How long do the Chu Fighters intend to stay in Phoenix Place?"

Endurance said, "We are moving on tomorrow
morning."

The lord was relieved, but felt he had to be
polite. "The people of Phoenix Place and I would
like to have you with us much longer than that."

Endurance said, "I used to come to Phoenix
Place often, and many times had doors slammed
in my face. I think I tried your door, too, but
your servants kicked me away. I don't intend to
stay in a place that carries such bitter memories."

He saw Lord Fong's frightened expression, and
he smiled in satisfaction. Abruptly he changed

the subject. "King Yu was the most powerful rebel leader in Kiangsi, but there are many lesser ones who may become strong. I cannot rest until I crushed them all. After that I'll move on to Kiangsu Province and head for Yin-tin."

Lord Fong, who was well aware of the fierce reputations of Endurance and his tall wife, couldn't believe that their avenging hands would spare him. While the peasant couple bathed and rested, Lord and Lady Fong had a talk.

Endurance and Peony soaked in a large wooden tub for a long time. The steaming water washed away not only layers of dirt, but also fatigue. They then rested in the largest guest room, pillowed passionately on a silk-covered bed.

When they came out of the room, the lord was waiting with a jade plate filled with glittering jewelry.

"Please accept these as an apology for what my ignorant servant did," the lord said.

Endurance touched the gold chain around his neck. "I don't need anything other than this pendant," he said.

Peony had little fondness for jewelry herself, but a ruby ring caught her eye. She tossed it up, watching it sparkle like a red shooting star. She caught it on its way down, put it on her little finger, where it fit snugly. She then pushed the plate away, continuing to admire the ruby ring.

Pleased, Endurance said to Lord Fong, "Since Phoenix Place no longer has a mayor, I'll give the position to you. If you manage things well, when I have conquered the entire province, I may appoint you the governor."

Lord Fong bowed deeply and answered, "Commander Chu, I'll look forward to your becoming the king of Kiangsi, and I'd be honored to be your governor."

Endurance touched his jade pendant, and his

piercing eyes were softened by a fond memory. "I'd rather become king of Kiangsu, where Yin-tin City is. I have a good friend there, named Wisdom Lu. I can't wait for my wife and sons to meet him and his family." He went on and told the mayor how Wisdom Lu and he had met, and how he had stayed in the Lu house for two years.

"Wisdom Lu! The mayor of Yin-tin! I know him. But I didn't know the two of you are so close!" Lord Fong looked at Endurance with sudden respect. "You must be very proud of your friend. People all over the south regard him highly. When Kiangsu Province is returned to us Chinese, as long as Wisdom Lu supports you as the king of the province, all the other southerners will follow his example."

All softness abruptly disappeared from Endurance's eyes. A wounded look took its place. "I'll need Wisdom Lu's approval to be accepted as the king of Kiangsu?" he said.

Peony noticed her husband's change of mood and said, "My husband and I risk our lives on the battlefield. Wisdom Lu is merely the mayor of Yin-tin City. What great things does he do to make people think so highly of him?"

Without noticing the tightness in her voice, Lord Fong counted all the good deeds performed by Wisdom Lu. He then added, "And I'm sure he gives you money to make the Flaming Snakes just like he does for the others."

Endurance and Peony looked at each other in shock. His injured expression stabbed Peony. She had heard him telling her so much about his best friend. And she knew how deeply he loathed the nameless man who was financing the southern leaders. The beloved friend and despised enemy was now combined into one. It was too much for her poor husband to take.

"He gave money to the others ..." Endurance's voice quavered and faded away.

Peony had never seen her husband so hurt. She asked Lord Fong, "Are you certain about this?"

The lord hesitated momentarily. He saw no reason to keep a secret from a couple who had just driven the Mongols out of his city. He was impressed by Endurance's story of how Wisdom Lu had taken care of him for two long years. The detailed description of the Lu mansion had convinced the lord that Endurance had told the truth. Lord Fong said, "I am certain about this because I am a Silent League member. Whenever I have received a note from Wisdom, I traveled to Yin-tin for the meetings. Wisdom Lu is the leader of this League."

Lord Fong told Endurance the League's decision in helping only the southern leaders but not the northern ones, then said, "Since you are his best friend, of course he helped you without touching the League funds." He then repeated that once Endurance was ready to be the King of Kiangsu, all he needed was Wisdom Lu's approval. "Once he nods his head, all the other southerners will say yes. And so will the two-thirds of the Chinese population who live in the south."

After visiting the Chu family graveyard and giving thanks to the spirits, Endurance and Peony started off from Phoenix Place at sunrise.

"You did not sleep at all the whole night," she said while riding beside her husband. "I heard you cursing and hitting your palm with your fist. You can't win any battles if your body is exhausted and your mind is troubled."

He kept riding in silence for a while, then said, "Peony, do you remember we talked about finding a new name for our fighters?"

Peony did not understand the sudden change of subject, but she nodded and Endurance continued, "Please help me find a name that will reach the hearts of all the southerners. A name that's beautiful and soft, so the intellectuals can identify with it. Our military power is strong, but the civilians of the south don't care for you and me and our fighters. Did you notice how happy the new mayor and his wife and the whole town were when we left Phoenix Place?"

As Peony nodded, Endurance clenched his fists. "I want to be respected and admired the way Wisdom Lu is. I could not sleep last night because I envy him. He is my friend, but not better than I. I resent the fact that I'll need his, or anyone else's approval to achieve my goals. Maybe a new name to our army will cast an aura of magic over us and make us appear differently in people's eyes. You must think of a name that will put us on a pedestal much higher than the one on which Wisdom Lu stands."

Peony waited for her husband to tell her all that was on his mind. When Endurance did not go on, she asked, "Are you troubled only by envy? Or also by anger? Are you angry with Wisdom for giving the southern leaders money, but nothing to you?"

Endurance looked away, studied the autumn leaves sailing in the wind. "That has to be a mistake on Lord Fong's part. Giving money to the other leaders but not me would be a betrayal of our friendship, and Wisdom would never do that. He is more than my friend. He saved my life. He would not help my opponents so they can make weapons to kill me. I simply cannot imagine him helping people like Tin-check Wan."

He flinched at the memory of his agony. He forced a smile on his face as he continued. "By the end of the winter, we should conquer Kiangsi and reach Kiangsu. If nothing goes wrong, we should be in Yin-tin by next spring. I'll ask Wisdom then, and he'll explain. You'll see that Lord Fong is wrong."

Peony leaned closer to her husband, but he continued to avoid her eyes. She sighed. She felt sorry for her husband. The poor man was trying to convince not only her but also himself.

"A name for our fighters ..." she said slowly, then paused. "But we need more than a name. We need something concrete. Something that people can see and touch and worship. Something not only beautiful but also valuable and uncommon and sacred ... I have it!"

She reined her horse to a halt, and Endurance stopped as well. The entire procession came to a standstill in the middle of the road. Peony told her husband what she had in mind, and he smiled for the first time since he had talked to Lord Fong.

Endurance summoned a messenger. For the sake of avoiding Mongol persecution, the job usually went to either a nun or a monk. But this time no monks or nuns could be found. He and Peony were not worried, since the monks and nuns liked to travel apart at times. A young soldier was chosen as a messenger, and Endurance told him to ride to the north.

"Go to Emerald Valley and find the Heavenly Temple. Talk to an old monk called Merciful Heart ..."

Endurance and Peony had visited the monks in their hometown as often as possible. Earthly Dragon had died in Pinetree Village, but Merciful Heart was still healthy and strong the last time they had seen him.

Endurance said, "Bring him back to Yin-tin City. Be careful of the Mongol soldiers and avoid trouble. You and Merciful Heart should arrive in Yin-tin no later than next spring."

He continued confidently, "By that time we should have taken Yin-tin. Just go to Mayor Lu, and he'll tell you where we are."

His eyes darkened once again when the messenger was gone, and his thoughts returned to Wisdom Lu, his best friend.

"Don't you dare say horrible things about my best friend!" Wisdom Lu's voice trembled as he faced the other Silent League members.

"But we have only told you the truth," one of the members said. "In the past fourteen years, he has become a monster. He was only a rude mailman then. But now he is a giant, an inhumanly cruel ogre!"

Wisdom turned his back to his friends. The windows were closed, and the snowflakes plastered on the outside of the oil-coated paper were blocking out the light. The room was warm, with fires burning in several iron stoves, but winter stayed in Wisdom's heart as he thought of the League members' opposition to Endurance Chu.

He turned to face them. "You never liked him. Because he is forthright, you called him a barbarian. And because he is unpretentious, you accused him of being a peasant. Now you are telling me he is cruel only because you've heard some ridiculous rumor."

"This is not a rumor," another League member said. "If the snow wasn't so heavy and the roads so bad, the new mayor of Phoenix Place could tell you so himself. When I visited him and he told me about Endurance Chu, I think he held back some of the worst details because Endurance Chu had told him that you are his best friend. It is absolutely true that King Yu was whipped to death. Many people could tell you

that this is Endurance's favorite way of killing
his Chinese opponents. It is rather strange that
he kills Mongols quickly, but likes to torture the
Chinese slowly."

The man's words rang in Wisdom's ears, then
thundered in his heart. His heart ached and his
stomach turned. There was not enough air in the
room. He could not breathe. He staggered to the
window, pushed it open.

The Lu mansion was situated on a foothill, and
the meeting room window was higher than the
top of the garden walls. Whispering Lake could
be seen at the bottom of the hill. The narrow
path that circled the lake was smooth and un-
touched by footprints. Winter honeysuckles
stood blooming in the falling snow. Snowflakes
sailed into the room on the wings of the north
wind, filling the room with cold air and sweet
fragrance. The other League members shivered
and moved closer to the stoves, but Wisdom was
calmed by the serene picture and felt better.

He breathed in deeply, then said to his friends
without turning away from the lovely scene, "I
don't care what you say, I will listen only to Endurance. I have received a brief note from him."

He paused and frowned. The note had been
shorter than all the other notes he had ever received from Endurance. It was not openly rude,
but anger appeared in each of the bold strokes.
In places the rice paper had been torn from the
greater power applied to the soft brush. It had
simply said, "We'll be in Yin-tin by spring."

Wisdom decided that the League members
were painting a false picture. He squared his
fragile shoulders and continued, "I pray that Endurance will arrive in Yin-tin safely by next
spring. My wife and I are eager to meet his wife
and four sons. When he arrives, I will give them
a magnificent party and invite all of you and

your wives. You will see for yourselves that Endurance Chu is just as kind as you are, only in
a different way. And I'm sure your wives will
admire his wife, who must be quite a brave lady.
You'll feel like fools then, for what you've said—"

Wisdom suddenly stopped. It had to be his
imagination that he saw a group of monks and
nuns running across the path that circled the
Whispering Lake, heading for the foot of the
mountain.

Purple Gold Mountain was serene as fourteen
monks and twelve nuns climbed it, traveled
through the snow-covered forest, and ascended
the high cliffs to reach the Temple of Silent
Echo. They kneeled in front of the head monk,
Calm Fortitude. "Merciful *shih-fu,* please listen
to us."

They were among the numerous kung fu monks
and Red Turban nuns who had fought for Vanguard Kuo. They had traveled with the fighting
force from north to south, helped to drive the
Mongols out of many villages and towns. But the
cruelty of Endurance and Peony had shocked
them, and the changeover to Flaming Snakes
from kung fu had made them feel useless. Because of these factors, the monks and nuns had
deserted the fighting force.

One of the monks said, "We would have left
them a long time ago, but we had vowed to be
loyal and we seldom break our vows."

Another said, "We are disappointed not only
in Endurance and Peony, but also the whole
human race. We want to find an abandoned temple in the high mountains and shun society once
more."

One of the nuns said, "When we left the army
in Phoenix Place, we were ready to head for such
a mountain, but then we realized that at least

some of us should come to Yin-tin City first. Endurance and Peony will be here next spring. We
need your help to convince the citizens of Yin-
tin that Endurance and Peony cannot be trusted
to rule the Kiangsu Province. That's what they
want: to become king and queen of the richest
province in China."

With their message at an end, all the monks
and nuns kowtowed to Calm Fortitude. They
kept their heads on the ground and waited for
the old monk to answer.

Calm Fortitude thought for a long time. When
he spoke, his voice was sad and low. "You've
convinced me. I'll pay Wisdom Lu a visit. No
one can influence the people of Yin-tin more
than he."

34

SNOW KEPT FALLING over a field in Kiangsi Province, covering the dead bodies and bloodstained ground. Two soldiers moved slowly, bending over and pushing the snow aside with their bare hands. Their fingers were numb and their backs aching, but they did not dare to stop. They glanced at the distant tents anxiously, wishing that they were inside and beside a warm fire.

"Why did our chief commander assign us this job?" the first soldier asked while searching. "We are just as tired as the others after the battle."

The second one answered, "I've learned to obey our chief commander without asking questions. You and I were nearest to him when he found his lucky charm was missing." He brought his hands to his mouth, blew some warm air at his frozen fingers. "I wish we could wear gloves. But I guess we won't be able to feel the stupid chain if our fingers are covered."

"Hush. Don't call that chain stupid. Our chief commander said it's from his best friend." The first soldier looked over his shoulder in fear, then continued to sweep the snow. "Our chief commander has been in a bad mood ever since we left Phoenix Place. You want to be whipped to death? My great Buddha! I think I found it!" He picked up a broken gold chain with a jade pendant dangling from it. "This has to be the thing our chief commander lost while fighting the Mighty Sword's men!"

The second soldier looked at the short chain and green pendant, and shook his head. "It doesn't look that valuable to me. I wonder how losing it can upset our chief commander so much that even defeating the Mongols couldn't make him happy."

They brought the chain and pendant to Endurance, expecting at least to be praised.

"You didn't find the whole thing!" the chief commander shouted at them. "Look how short the chain is! A large section of it must be out there under the snow yet! You fools!"

He ordered the trembling soldiers to continue searching, but Peony stopped the departing men. "Wait," she said, then took the broken chain from Endurance. She measured its remaining length and smiled. "The craftsmen are making you a new steel dagger. They asked me if you want to garnish the handle with any precious stones or gold. This chain and pendant will look handsome on the dagger."

The two soldiers breathed with relief when Endurance smiled at his wife's suggestion.

The dagger was made. The gold chain spiraled around the handle, and the jade pendant served as a centerpiece for the cross guard. Endurance carried it in a brass sheath strapped to his waistband.

Throughout the long winter, Endurance used the dagger in one hand and a broadsword in the other to fight both the powerful Mongols and the trivial Chinese rebel forces. Every time he won, he brought the dagger to his mouth and touched the jade with his lips. "Thanks for helping me win another battle!"

Spring of 1361 áppeared on the yellow-green

leaves of weeping willows. Warm sun shone on
the pink-white petals of peach blossoms. The
Chu Fighters conquered the entire Kiangsi Province and crossed into Kiangsu Province. Soon
they reached the outskirts of Yin-tin City.

"Now you must help me break through the
blockade protecting the King of Kiangsu," Endurance said to his lucky dagger.

King Chen, the man who led the strongest
rebel force in the south, was known for his superior fighting techniques and strategies. The Chen
Fighters were brutal and their numbers vast.
After a series of skirmishes, Endurance and
Peony camped at the outskirts of Chen territory
and waited for the right moment to attack. While
waiting, a messenger arrived from Prosper Mountain, carrying the news about Lady Kuo: she had
hung herself in the Temple of White Crane after
hearing of the death of her husband.

"Why did she do such a foolish thing?" Peony
cried. "She should have lived to avenge Vanguard's death!"

Endurance took her in his arms. "A blind
woman can't do much. Besides, Vanguard Kuo
was the only light in her life."

They mourned Joy Kuo's death under the
spring moon, then attacked King Chen's men at
sunrise.

A rice field stretched between a graveyard and
a low hill. At the start of the battle, the Chen
Fighters had the hill, Endurance's men the
graveyard. At the order of their chief commander, the Chu Fighters came out from behind
gravestones, charged across the rice field and up
the hillside.

Holding the higher ground, the Chen Fighters
held a commanding advantage. Picking off Chu
Fighters in a low field was easy, especially when
they had to stand still to aim their weapons at

the hill. The Chen Fighters were not only well trained in using their Flaming Snakes, but they had saved these irreplacable weapons for important battles only. King Chen and his soldiers cheered each time more Chu Fighters fell to the water-soaked field made ready by the farmers to plant rice.

It was difficult for the Chu Fighters to hit the targets hiding behind the many weeping willows on the hill. Endurance and Peony stayed behind the largest two gravestones, watching their men firing without hitting anyone. Angered, Endurance was raising his arm to order more men into the field when Peony pulled it back down.

"The hill cannot be captured this way," she said. "We must employ a different strategy. We need to return to our base. I have an idea."

Once back at the base, Peony took Endurance's dagger and ordered a soldier to give her his shirt. She cut a section of one of his sleeves off, then filled it with explosives. Before tying the ends, she placed a fuse in it. "Pass this around and use it as a sample," she told the soldier. "Tell everyone to make them with his shirt and make them as fast as possible!"

In a short time Peony's order was carried out. The Chu Fighters returned to the graveyard wearing sleeveless shirts.

The men on the hill had seen their opponents withdrawing and were congratulating one another when they spotted Endurance's men emerging from the graveyard again and running through the rice field. This time, however, the Chus did not stop to aim their Flaming Snakes, and it was not easy for the Chen Fighters to hit a moving target. Most of the Chus were able to reach the foot of the hill without being shot. Then they lighted their fuses and swung the small heavy bags in an arc to gather force, and

tossed the bags up the hill. The bags exploded
almost as soon as they touched the ground. The
impacts were strong enough to blast holes in the
enemy line.

The Chu Fighters kept advancing up the hillside, throwing out more bombs, and the hill soon
became a bloodstained mound covered with severed trees and dead men.

"Retreat!" King Chen ordered his men.

"Pursue!" Endurance shouted.

On the other side of the hill was a peach or-
chard in full bloom. The Chu Fighters caught up
with the Chens in the grove. Flowers fell on the
fighters as they battled underneath the branches.
Pink and white petals shrouded the fallen bodies.

Endurance and Peony had trained their men
well, but Chen's men were also excellent warriors. For the first time Endurance and Peony
missed their kung fu monks and Red Turban
nuns.

Gradually, the Chen force retreated and the
Chu force advanced. They were winning, but the
cost of victory was high and the ground won was
extremely little.

At mid-morning, Endurance and King Chen
happened to meet at the edge of the peach grove.
Endurance carried a broadsword, Chen a long
spear. After a few swings Endurance was positive that his opponent had learned his kung fu
from the Temple of Silent Echo. The duel continued like two dancers trained for the same routine. Then Endurance suddenly changed his
technique.

The past flashed through his mind: how he
had learned from monks in various temples and
created a unique kung fu style. He used this new
style to fight, and quickly knocked the spear
from Chen's hands. He backed Chen into one of
the remaining trunks of a dead peach tree.

Endurance did not have time to torture the man. He had to lead his men into Yin-tin. He laid down his sword, pulled his dagger out of its sheath.

He waved the dagger at Chen's face. "Who gave you the money to make those Flaming Snakes?" he asked.

Chen grinned. "You'll never know."

Sunlight shifted through the tall peaches around them, casting dancing shadows on Chen's face. Endurance lowered his dagger slowly, stopped at Chen's lower abdomen.

The scream reverberated through the grove with such a powerful resonance that more petals fell like a rainstorm. Endurance wiped the blood off his dagger then kissed the jade piece on its cross guard.

As the Chu Fighters neared Yin-tin City, Peony slowed the gait of her horse, eyeing the lotus ponds on both sides of the country road.

The large leaves were like jade plates, and each long-stem flower was the size of a baby's head. The fragrance was delicate but strong enough to perfume the air. Young girls in peasant clothes stood in small boats, pushing with long poles, gliding across the lotus ponds.

"The Yin-tin people must be rich. Even the peasants have time to play," Peony said, pointed out the girls.

Riding beside her, Endurance told her that the girls were not playing, but searching for lotus seeds. "The rich believe that eating these seeds will bring them to Lotus Land."

"Where is Lotus Land?"

Endurance pointed a finger at heaven. "Lotus is a symbol of eternal happiness for the southerners. Lotus Land is another name for Nirvana."

Peony shook her head slowly, remembering the

way Endurance killed King Chen. "If there is a Nirvana, you and I will never get there." She inhaled the fragrant air and said, "But if I can live in a place as lovely as this, then I've found my eternal happiness on earth. This is the most beautiful place I've ever seen."

"We will settle in Yin-tin as soon as all our battles are fought." Endurance said, reaching for Peony's hand and squeezing it.

"Lotus Land . . ." Peony nodded, repeating the name. Then she turned to look over her shoulder at the following procession, and an idea began to take form.

It was nearly noon and they were moving parallel to the Yangtze River when they were confronted by Mighty Sword's men.

The Mongols had been waiting alongside the riverbank. The soldiers were divided into two groups, one firing their Killing Hands, the other shooting arrows.

Seeing that they were on horses, the Chu Fighters on foot, Endurance determined that he had to eliminate this disadvantage first of all. He gathered his kung fu fighters, told them what they had to do, and then these men began to snake forward on their bellies.

Each of them held a sword in his mouth and kept his head up as he wormed his way toward the Mongols. A number of them died before reaching their enemy, but by crawling they were a lesser target, and most of them reached enemy lines.

Up they sprang, swinging their swords at the horses' legs. Surprised, the Mongols toppled from their mounts. Their attack wave spent, the kung fu fighters jumped into the Yangtze, intending to swim back to their own lines.

"Fire!" Endurance ordered as soon as his kung fu fighters were out of the line of fire.

While struggling to free themselves from their dying horses, the Mongols were perfect targets for the Flaming Snakes. Endurance's men kept firing until the returning kung fu fighters climbed ashore.

"Forward!" Endurance yelled, spurring his horse.

Peony rode beside her husband, and behind them, their entire force advanced on foot. The archers, swordsmen, and the dripping kung fu fighters screamed at the same time, "Kill! Kill! Kill!"

The battle lasted from noon to sunset. At last Mighty Sword appeared at the rear of his remaining force. The supreme general's handsome face was twisted with anger, for Mongols loved their horses. The divine animals were the extension of the riders' legs. Mighty Sword's black stallion was unharmed, but the sight of so many other horses dying in pain was unbearable.

Mighty Sword glared at Endurance, then shifted his gaze to Peony. Even the Mongols had heard of the tall Chinese woman who fought alongside her husband. The supreme general looked back at Endurance, then grinned chillingly.

"You killed our horses, so I'll kill your woman!" he shouted in his native language, charging toward the Chu couple.

Endurance did not understand what was said, and he galloped forward to meet his opponent, leaving Peony behind. He and Mighty Sword advanced through the battlefield, passing the fighting men, heading for a collision.

Endurance held his broadsword in one hand, dagger in another. This was the duel he had awaited for a long time.

Suddenly, however, Mighty Sword changed

his course. He led his horse out of Endurance's reach and headed for Peony.

"No, you don't! You Mongol bastard!" Endurance shouted as soon as he realized what Mighty Sword was doing. Bringing his horse to a high-kicking halt, he yanked it around. But by this time he saw that Mighty Sword was only a few feet from Peony.

Endurance knew Peony was no match for Mighty Sword. He realized he would not be there in time to save her. He felt a sudden pain in his heart many times greater than the pain once injected into his body by Wan's whip. "No!" he shrieked as he galloped toward them.

Peony, meanwhile, had brought her horse to a standstill to wait for Mighty Sword. Like Endurance, she held a sword in one hand and a dagger in the other. She did not move until Mighty Sword was within range. Keeping her eyes focused on him, she spread her arms gracefully but forcefully, like a crane suddenly spreading its powerful wings. The dagger flew out of her hand and plunged into the supreme general's left arm, while the tip of the sword gashed the supreme general's forehead.

It was not a deep cut, but blood poured out of the wound into the supreme general's eyes. Mighty Sword panicked. He wiped his eyes to clear his view, then saw the dagger in his arm and began to feel the stabbing pain. He turned in circles on his horse until he saw the sun setting to his left. "Retreat!" he shouted, motioning for his men to follow him toward the north.

Exhausted after a second battle in one day, the Chu Fighters did not pursue.

The next morning, the second commander led the Chu Fighters into Yin-tin City, while the chief commander and his lady stayed waiting in their tent.

Peony was reluctant to stay behind. "We have always fought with our men. Are you sure they can take Yin-tin without us?" she asked, looking at the food without appetite.

Endurance poured two cups of wine. "Without Mighty Sword and his men, even a child could take Yin-tin. That Mongol governor has but a handful of soldiers." He gave Peony one cup of wine and picked up the other. "I cannot fight right now, and I cannot allow you to be out of my sight. I was too shaken when I thought the Mongol bastard was going to kill you. I have not recovered yet." He smiled at her proudly. "What you did to Mighty Sword was superb. I could not have done it any better."

Peony smiled. "It was one of the most difficult motions in tai chi fist. It's called white crane spreads its wings. You and I have practiced it together. Remember? When we were first married and traveling alongside the Yellow River?"

Endurance raised his cup high. "To being together. May we never part, either on earth or in heaven." He emptied his cup.

"You skipped hell." Peony drank her wine and laughed. "What makes you think we won't go there?"

Endurance shook his head firmly. "If there is no Buddha at all, then no one cares what we do on earth. If there is a Buddha, then he has to have bright eyes. He should be able to see that we have done nothing wrong."

"Nothing?" Peony poured wine for her husband this time. The red wine reminded her of the blood of their many enemies.

"Nothing!" Endurance drank the wine and said loudly. "We were two poor children who wanted to live a peaceful life. Life forced us into

becoming what we are today. My hatred for the
Chinese and Mongols are forced into me by fate.
If fate had been kind, you and I would have
never killed anyone."

Endurance and Peony ate and drank, then lowered the tapestry over their tent opening. They
pillowed with passion and were asleep in each
other's arms when the second commander returned with the entire force.

"Your every order has been carried out," he
reported. "We captured Yin-tin City. The entire
Kiangsu Province is now freed from Mongol control. The Mongol governor was executed. His relatives were either killed or thrown out of the
mansion. His vault was broken, and everything
in it was loaded onto a wagon."

The second commander pointed at the wagon
outside the tent. "The governor's wealth is
yours, and his mansion is waiting for you to
move into. Mayor Wisdom Lu was getting into
his sedan chair when I told him you were here.
He must be on his way to welcome you, and
should be here at any moment."

35

"WHY ISN'T WISDOM LU here yet?" Peony asked impatiently.

Endurance and Peony had been waiting a long time, but he still had not arrived.

"Let us hide the Mongol governor's money while we're waiting!" Endurance said. Like Peony, he was unable to sit and do nothing.

Silver and gold were unloaded from the wagon and buried under the chief commander's tent. Endurance and Peony dug the deep hole themselves, and the digging made them sweaty and filthy in their carefully selected new garments.

Endurance ordered his men, "During our stay in Yin-tin, you are free to roam the city during the day. But every soldier must return to your tents at night, to guard the campsite and especially my tent." Endurance explained to his men that they needed the money under his tent to feed them and their families, buy explosives for their Flaming Snakes. "But this money is not enough. We need much more for making the Fire Bags and Firing Dragons. I'm counting on receiving help from the mayor of Yin-tin and his rich friends."

"The mayor of Yin-tin is here!" the soldiers announced.

"My friend!" Endurance strode toward Wisdom and gave him a big hug. "It's been a long time!"

"Too long . . ." Wisdom winced in Endurance's embrace. "We need to talk."

"This is my wife and my fighting partner, Peony," Endurance said with pride.

Following her husband's example, Peony also hugged Wisdom. "Thanks for saving Endurance's life fifteen years ago! Somehow, I always pictured you as a much bigger fellow!"

Her hug set Wisdom's face on fire. "It is an honor to meet you, Lady Chu," he uttered, bowing.

Turning toward Endurance, he said, "Can we sit in your tent and talk? There are things I need to ask, and also things I must tell you."

Endurance pushed Wisdom right back into his sedan. "Let's talk on the way to Yin-tin!"

"But . . ." Wisdom glanced at Endurance and Peony. He wanted to tell them that they were not properly dressed to meet the populace, but did not want to offend them.

Weeping willows formed an airy green canopy that stretched from east Yin-tin to the west. People stood under it, waiting to capture a glance of Endurance and Peony. They had heard all sorts of stories about the two, and now they wanted to see them with their own eyes.

Once again, Peony refused to be confined in a sedan chair. The procession entered Yin-tin with Wisdom's undraped sedan in the middle and the Chu couple riding slowly on both sides. Behind them were the Chu boys and their nannies in a wagon, several of Endurance's men and a few of the mayor's servants on foot. The rest of the Chu Fighters and the second commander remained at the campsite.

Endurance and Peony rode proudly. Due to the bad reception they received in Phoenix Place, they had groomed themselves carefully. Endurance had combed his hair and trimmed his

beard, which were the things he seldom had
time for. Despite the warm spring weather, he
wore a garment stripped off a dead Mongol: a
scarlet robe bordered with white fur. The fur
was soiled and the robe bloodstained, but Endurance was certain neither would be noticeable.
All the same, the fur around the collar made his
neck itchy. He pulled the robe down and exposed the thick black hair on his chest.

Peony had on a jade green robe which had belonged to a Mongol officer also. On its back was
a dragon embroidered in gold. It was her favorite, and she wore it for special occasions only.
The legs of her brown pants were tucked into
her best leather boots. She had braided her hair
and used willow twigs to pin it into a crown. On
top of the crown was a red lotus freshly picked
from a pond.

As they neared the city, both Endurance and
Peony expected to hear, "Our hero and her ne
look splendid! What a magnificent pair they
make! They are exactly the king and queen of
the province we have in mind!"

When they entered the city, though, many pale
faces wearing the same expression: astonishment.

For a brief moment Endurance and Peony
thought that they looked grander than people
had expected. But then the spring breeze began
to carry words into their ears.

"Endurance Chu looks every bit a barbarian!
His face is disgusting and his size, frightening!
I can smell filth and blood on him!"

"Peony Chu is the first Chinese woman who
has ever ridden horseback! How dare she expose
her parted legs in a man's pants? Look at those
large feet! And how ridiculous to wear a huge
lotus on top of her head!"

Endurance and Peony looked at their critics
just in time to see them turning their eyes to

Wisdom Lu. The change of expression was obvious, the comments loud and clear.

"Ah, here is our man! Mayor Lu has protected us from the Mongols for so many years, and now he can do more since the Mongols are gone. Maybe he can become our next governor, or the king of Kiangsu!"

There soon rose a chant echoing from street to street, "Governor Lu! King Lu! Governor Lu! King Lu!"

Peony yanked the lotus from her hair and threw it to the ground. Her hair became unpinned and her long braid swung free, sweeping the horse's back. Wisdom Lu's sedan was now leading the procession, Peony and Endurance riding together behind him. This made them feel like they were Wisdom's guards, he their master.

Peony said to her husband, "Your friend should have prepared us for this. He could have told us that the Yin-tin people are bastards with weird tastes."

"It can't be Wisdom's fault," Endurance defended his friend. "He couldn't have known this."

She disagreed. "Well, he knows what's the proper way to dress for these pale-faced bastards. If he wanted us to look good in their eyes, then when he saw how we were dressed, he should have told us to change."

Wisdom Lu turned back and looked out of the sedan. He took one look at the faces of Endurance and Peony and knew how they felt. Wisdom had also heard the public commentary. He was greatly embarrassed by the way the Yin-tin people treated the Chu couple. He wished that he had asked them to change, but there was no way for him to repair the damage now.

As Endurance and Peony rode on, they continued to talk. She insisted that Wisdom wanted them to look bad so he could look good, and her words rooted in Endurance's heart; a seed of doubt about his best friend was born.

When they reached the foothills of Purple Gold Mountain, the Chu men continued on to the mountaintop to prepare the governor's mansion for its new owners. Endurance, Peony, and their children turned off with Wisdom, passing Whispering Lake, and stopped at the Lu house.

"Are you having a party?" Endurance asked, pointing at the many sedan chairs in front of the mansion.

Wisdom smiled. "Yes, the biggest party I have ever given. I invited all the elite of Yin-tin and all the scholars. Their families are here also." He paused, then said sincerely, "Please don't pay any attention to what you heard on the streets. Only unmannerly peasants stand on the streets. You'll be received quite differently by my cultured friends, I guarantee."

Endurance and Peony were heartened by this, and she looked at herself and Endurance. Their garments were soaked with sweat, and their faces were flushed with heat. "Shall we go somewhere else first, bathe and change then come back for the party?" she asked hesitantly.

Wisdom smiled confidently. "My guests are like me. They will see the two of you as what you are, instead of what you wear."

While Peony was still uncertain, Endurance dismounted. Tossing his head back, he answered firmly, "Wisdom is right. We are what we are. Let the people of Yin-tin adjust their taste for us instead of us changing ourselves for them."

"You are absolutely right!" Peony said, also dismounting. Taking her husband's hand, they entered the mansion holding their heads high.

Lotus Lu was waiting in the entrance hall to-

gether with her mother and mother-in-law. They
moved with the support of their maids, then
bowed deeply to their honorable guests. Politely
they looked away from Endurance and Peony's
entwined hands. They had never seen a husband
and wife holding hands in public before.

"Welcome to our humble home," Lotus said,
and the two older ladies repeated after her.

The three ladies and their maids stayed bent
forward, for they were not supposed to straighten
themselves until their guests returned their
bows. Tradition demanded that the guests
should bow deeper than the hosts.

Endurance and Peony, busy looking at the fine
ornaments in the hall, eventually noticed the
bending women and nodded their heads slightly.

Lotus straightened herself. She remembered
how Endurance had been fifteen years before
and was not offended. Though Peony's appearance and manners were shocking, Lotus's up-
bringing helped her conceal her astonishment.

Lady Lu and Lady Lin, on the other hand,
were astounded by what they saw. What's more,
they considered their guests arrogant. They were
insulted, and disliked Endurance and Peony
instantly.

The Chu babies and their nannies were shown
to the nursery. The two older boys were led to
play with children their age. Wisdom escorted
Endurance into the grand room, where the male
guests waited. Lotus took Peony into the inner
chamber and introduced her to the prominent
ladies.

In the inner court, none of the southern ladies
hid their shock as well as Lotus could. They
stared at Peony's garment and high boots, large
feet and rough hands, unpinned hair and powder-
free face.

When Peony picked up the teacup and gulped

down the tea, then smacked her lips, they
gasped. When she sat first with her long legs
crossed, then shifted into a more comfortable position with her knees parted, they widened their
eyes. When she grabbed a sweet bun with her
hand, bit off half of it, and chewed with her
mouth open, they shook their heads.

Because Peony hated to see the sesame seeds
that covered the bun wasted, she wetted the tips
of her fingers with her tongue, then pressed her
fingers over the bottom of the porcelain plate to
pick up the seeds. She propped her feet on a
low table, leaned back, licked her fingers as she
studied the other women.

Their multilayered clothes made them look
like round vases. Their bound feet were the tiny
bases that gave the vases a funny and unbalanced
look. Their faces were powdered so thickly that regardless of their various ages, cracks showed beside their mouths, around their eyes, and on
their foreheads. There were two red circles on
each one's rouged cheeks, and a scarlet dot in
the center of everyone's painted mouths. They
looked funny when compared to the northern ladies, who dressed differently and used very little makeup.

They wrapped silk handkerchiefs around their
teacups and held the cups with both hands, as
if the porcelain cups were weighing them down.
They pursed their lips to blow the tea softly,
then sipped no more than a few drops. After putting down their teacups, they sat with their
knees touching and hands folded on their laps.
They used chopsticks to break the buns to small
pieces and bring only one piece to their mouths
at a time, chewing it for a long time. They did
this with their lips sealed, as if afraid that the
buns might become alive and fly away.

Peony wiped her mouth with the back of her

hand, grabbed another sweet bun, and took a
hearty bite. She glanced at the dainty ladies and
laughed so hard that she spit out crumbs of the
bun. Pieces of wet bun flew, landing on the fine
ladies. Peony looked at their expressions, and
her laughter turned into a roar.

At one end of the grand room, two chairs were
placed side by side. Wisdom stood from his chair
and introduced Endurance to those who had
never met him before.

"My best friend . . . freed us from the Mongols
in five provinces . . ." Wisdom said with strong
emotion in his trembling voice, then went on.

Endurance looked at the roomful of people,
and their expressions told him that they did not
think any more of him than the peasants had.
Like them, too, they all regarded Wisdom with
great admiration. The comparison hurt. Endurance tried to tell himself that their opinions
were just as worthless as those of the peasants,
but the hurt wouldn't go away. Endurance had
trouble believing that Wisdom had not done this
on purpose. Peony had to be right: Wisdom
wanted to make Chief Commander Chu look bad
so that in contrast Mayor Lu would shine.

As Endurance eyed Wisdom's guests, he could
not hide his repulsion. These people had never
worked to earn a single copper coin. Their
wealth was handed down from generation to generation. Most of them were landlords. One of
their ancestors had pleased an emperor at some
point, and had been granted thousands of acres
of land. The descendants continued to live off
the blood and sweat of their tenants. Some of
them were moneylending house owners. The
yearly interest rate was one hundred percent.
When someone borrowed one copper coin from

one of these houses, ten years later he owed the house a thousand and twenty-four coins.

Endurance's attention shifted to the intellec-tuals, and he frowned in distaste. He could visu-alize hard times as a turbulent river, and these dreamers as boatmen in various vessels. They would throw their own lives and the lives of their loved ones overboard, but never their ethi-cal standards. If they had been placed in his and Peony's situation, they would have perished long ago.

Finally he recognized a familiar face, that of Lord Fong, now mayor of Phoenix Place. He also remembered that the members of the Silent League must be assembled in this room. He stood up abruptly, interrupting Wisdom's endless speech.

The commander said loudly, "Lord Fong told me something a year ago. I have a question for you!" He pointed his finger from one man to an-other. "Did you give money to my opponents?"

No one answered. Mayor Fong bowed his head. The others turned from the barbaric guest to the civilized host.

Their averted eyes were oil added to the fire of Endurance's anger. "Are you all deaf? Did you not hear my question?" He clenched his fists and raised his voice.

Everyone continued to remain silent and avoid eye contact with Endurance, and finally Wisdom reached out a hand. "Please, let us discuss it later. I was going to talk to you in your tent—" He stopped when Endurance pushed his hand away.

The commander pointed at Mayor Fong. "It was last autumn when I talked to this man. It bothered me from autumn to winter, and then winter to spring." He turned to face Wisdom Lu. "I am not a patient man. I've waited long enough. You will answer me, not later, but now!" He looked into Wisdom's sad eyes and lowered his voice a little. "Please tell me that you never helped my opponents make their Flaming Snakes."

Wisdom lowered his eyes momentarily, then raised them bravely and met Endurance's steady gaze. "I'm sorry, my friend, but we did."

His voice was merely a whisper, but it had the force of ten Flaming Snakes. Endurance felt as if he had been knocked back to his chair by the fist of an invisible giant. He sat with his elbows on his thighs and his face buried in his hands. He mumbled from behind his palms words that could be heard only by Wisdom, "My best friend on my opponents' side!"

Those words stabbed Wisdom in the heart. He tried again to touch Endurance. "Please. You must let me explain. There was not enough money. The League members voted on the expenditure. I was on your side, but I was overruled. I am so sorry," he said with his hand on Endurance's shoulder.

Endurance dropped his hands and looked up at Wisdom. "Sorry? Are you really?"

"Yes, my friend," Wisdom answered with tears in his eyes. "I . . ." He wanted to explain that if only he had had a way to contact Endurance, he would have helped the Chu Fighters with his own money. But his lips quivered and he lost his voice.

A bitter smile twisted Endurance's mouth, and distrust glowed in his penetrating eyes. He said, "All right, I'll give you a chance if you want to make it up to me, my best friend!" He spit out the last words.

"I'll do anything to make it up to you," Wisdom said.

"This is my proposal . . ." Endurance paused, looking at Wisdom in the eye. "My wife invented

a powerful weapon, and we call it the Fire
Bags." He described them briefly. "We need
money to make more of these bags. Can you give
it to me?"

Wisdom hesitated. He was willing to give Endurance money of his own, but he had no right
to use the League money without the other members' consent. He could only tell Endurance this
when they were alone.

Endurance took his hesitation for unwilling-
ness. Smiling sarcastically, Endurance continued, "I can see how enthusiastic you are in
making up to me. I'm overwhelmed by your gen-
erosity. With the large amount you are about to
give me, I can also make some Firing Dragons,
which should help Peony and me greatly in our
future battles." He described the Firing Dragons
to Wisdom and the League members.

"Endurance," Wisdom whispered pleadingly,
"can we talk about this later? You know—" Before he could say more, a man in the front row
stood up.

"Commander Chu, we would like to know
what will you do with the Fire Bags and Firing
Dragons before we consider helping you make
them."

"Do with them?" Endurance cast a disgusted
look at the man, then tried to be patient as he
explained. "I'll be leaving Yin-tin and the east
coast soon to fight battles in the central and west
parts of China. I'll then go north to the Yellow
River, fight my way up the Hui-tung Canal to
capture Da-du. Do I need to tell you that the
Fire Bags and Firing Dragons can help me win
battles?"

A man stood up from the far end of the room
and looked at Endurance accusingly. "Commander
Chu, the people in central and west China are
also Chinese. How can you expect us to give you

money and help you build the weapons to kill them?"

Enraged by this sophistry, Endurance charged toward the man. "The Flaming Snakes you helped my southern opponents make killed plenty of my men!" he shouted. "What am I and my fighters? Are we Mongols or color-eyed people? Or are we but dogs in your eyes?"

"Endurance," Wisdom chased after him. "Please!"

As Endurance crossed the room, another question came from the crowd. "Commander Chu, did you really whip your Chinese opponents to death?"

Endurance stopped abruptly. Wan's face reappeared in his mind as he answered, "Yes, I did." He hesitated, then decided it would be degrading himself to share his pain with these fools.

His hesitation gave Wisdom time to catch up. "Endurance, I made a mistake by inviting these people here. Please don't ..." His feeble plea was interrupted by a loud kick on the door.

Peony flung the door wide open with her heavy boot, then stormed in waving her hands over her head. "Endurance! Let's get out of here. I can't stand those stupid women! Lotus is like a little mouse who sees me as a big wild cat. She bores me to death! She tries to please me but does not know how. The others are shocked by me, although I do not know why. I put up with them the best I could, but one more moment in that miserable room and I won't be as calm as I am now!"

"You are right. Let's go—" Endurance stopped when he saw his two sons come running.

Power yelled, "Baba and Mama! We looked everywhere for you! Those strange weaklings do not know how to play war! And they're made of straw! We barely touched them and they broke!

They all started crying and bleeding right after the game began!"

Dominance shouted, "They don't like us! They call us barbaric peasants! Even Ardent and Earnest Lu blame us for making their sister cry and giving her a bloody nose! Baba, they say you are a cruel man who used to be a poor monk! And, Mama, they tell us that when a woman has big feet, she is not a lady."

From behind the two boys appeared the Chu family nannies. The two women, wives of the Chu Fighters, held the toddlers, Bravery and Vigorous, in their arms.

"We had a fight with the other nannies," one of them said. "They told us their master is a gentleman, but ours is not!"

The other nanny nodded. "And they said their master is worshiped by everyone, but ours is feared by all!"

The Chu family and their servants left the Lu mansion without saying good-bye. Wisdom and Lotus stood at the door and watched them storm toward the governor's house on top of Purple Gold Mountain.

36

"I LOVE THIS PLACE!" Peony said, turning around and around with her arms spread and head back, her long hair flying behind her like a shining black cape. She was barefoot and wore nothing but an unfastened short red silk robe. She and Endurance were in a large bedroom and had just risen from an undisturbed sleep.

The mansion was a fortress with many courts. Each room was elegant and huge, the ceilings extraordinarily high. The garden contained uncommon flowers and trees that spread for acres all around.

"This place should become our permanent home," Endurance said from the bed, which was three times the size of an average one. "In other houses I feel confined . . ." He stopped when he saw Peony's robe fell.

Her naked body was all muscle. Her breasts had become larger after giving birth to four children, but her waist had remained narrow. Her hips had become wider, but her buttocks stayed firm. To Endurance she was beautiful. He kicked the quilt aside, ran to her in the nude, took her in his arms, and carried her back to bed.

They pillowed with an urgency that went beyond passion. They both tried to forget the insults they had borne and the unpleasantness they experienced in the Lu house. For Endurance, the pillowing momentarily soothed away the pain of Wisdom's betrayal.

They did not leave their bed until mid-morning. And when they searched the wardrobes of the Mongol governor's family, they found the most fabulous garments they had ever seen. They kept what they liked and gave the rest to their helpers. Once they had dressed like a lord and lady, they liked what they saw in the large brass mirror. Soon after they were dressed, one of their men appeared. "An old monk named Merciful Heart has arrived from the north!"

Peony and Endurance warmly welcomed the kind old monk from Emerald Valley. At the sight of him, Peony remembered her childhood days as a jade miner's daughter. She saw once again in her memory, Merciful Heart showing her the precious jade mined out of the mountain by her father. She was sad to realize that Merciful Heart had not only aged, but also looked ill.

"I received your summons and carried the jade all the way here like a loving mother carrying her only child," the old monk said soon after he collapsed into a chair. He then unwrapped the many layers of quilt and padding from the large bundle. "I promised your father that I would keep it for you. I am very old now, and the death Buddha may come for me at any time. I am glad I am able to put the jade in your hands when I still can."

Endurance and Peony, worried by Merciful Heart's feeble condition, helped him to the best room in the mansion and immediately summoned the most famous doctor of Yin-tin City. Like an exhausted candle with only one more drop of tears to shed, Merciful heart held Peony's hand and uttered one more sentence, "Please tell me that the things I heard about you and your husband are untrue . . ."

Before Peony could answer, Merciful Heart died.

"The mayor of Yin-tin and his lady are at the door," a servant announced while Peony and Endurance were still mourning Merciful Heart.

"I've come to apologize, Endurance," Wisdom said, bowing deeply. "My guests were rude to you. I'm sorry."

"And I've come to apologize for the ladies," Lotus bowed with the help of a young maid. "Please forgive them."

Peony took Lotus's arm and waved the maid away. "I guess my husband and I are supposed to apologize for our sons. But you know how children are. Well, I'll tell them never go near your breakable daughter again." Peony couldn't resist adding, "But I really don't mind if they beat up all the other children who called us names."

Lotus bowed in appreciation to Peony's arrogant apology. She remained bowing for some time, because she needed to hide the tears in her eyes. Peach Blossom had a swollen nose and a black eye this morning.

After tea and sweets were served, Endurance pointed at Wisdom. "I just want you to know that your helping my opponents and refusing to help me hurt me more than the whip of Tin-check Wan. His whip left marks on my skin, but your betrayal will always be a scar in my heart." He looked from Wisdom to Lotus. "However, I will never forget how the two of you saved my life fifteen years ago. I guess our friendship will last as long as the moon, and I'll accept the wound you placed on my heart as the moon's dark spots." He then took his dagger out of its sheath and showed it to the Lu couple. "It's been my lucky charm. I carry it at all times."

"This is the chain and pendant I gave you?"

Wisdom shivered as he imagined blood splashing over his carefully created artwork.

"It's a beautiful dagger," Lotus said politely, looking away from the fearful weapon, so totally unlike her husband's beautiful creation.

Endurance said, "Wisdom, I want to show you something."

The peasant couple led the Lus to another room, where a shaft of green jade was placed on a piece of red silk on a teak table. Peony stopped by the jade and put her hand on it. The radiance of the gem reflected in her eyes, and her eyes sparkled as she looked at the mayor. "Wisdom, my husband said you are an excellent sculptor, and I'm sure you can carve whatever you desire. We want you to carve us a jade lotus. Make the flower big and the stem long. I'll never forget the many lotus ponds at the outskirts of Yin-tin, and I like the name Lotus Land." She looked at her husband. "Tell them that we have wanted an icon for a long time. And share with them our future plans."

Endurance said proudly, "Peony and I have conquered five provinces and killed five kings. I am really the king of all five provinces, and Peony my queen. We thought of Peony's jade before we came to Yin-tin. We knew even then that as we conquer more provinces and add more territories to our rule, we'll need a title." He looked at Peony.

She said, "The Chu Fighters can be called the Jade Lotus Warriors. My husband and I will become the king and queen of Jade Lotus. We will bring your sculpture with us wherever we go, exhibiting it in the largest temple of every village we conquer. We'll convince people that by following Endurance Chu, one can reach the Lotus Land on earth. We'll soon have not only the south, but the entire China as our faithful followers."

Endurance looked at Wisdom, "Carve the jade lotus for us. Support us by using your rare talent."

Wisdom eyed the jade thoughtfully. It was the largest and best piece of jade he had ever seen. He would be delighted to turn it into a beautiful lotus. But then he looked at Endurance and Peony. After seeing his necklace changed into a dagger, could he be sure that his artwork wouldn't become another tool in their bloodthirsty campaigns?

Lotus suddenly stood up. Holding onto the furniture to keep her balance, she stepped forward to face Endurance and Peony. "Please, the two of you." Her voice was trembling and low, but firm and clear. "Do not use my husband. He is an artist. His art is not to be used for political reasons. If people followed the jade lotus for wrong purposes, my husband will never forgive himself."

Lotus's words were like a gong sounded against a dreamer's ear. Wisdom woke up. He cringed as he edged away from the jade. "My wife is right. I cannot sculpt the jade for you," he said firmly.

Endurance's fingers dug into his palms and his knuckles turned white. He shouted, "Wisdom Lu! How can you turn down a request that will cost you nothing? Are you still my friend?"

"I have been your friend for the past fifteen years. I will always be your friend in this world and the world after," Wisdom answered.

Still angry, Endurance and Peony led the Lu couple back to the grand room. They sat and drank tea in stony silence. At length Wisdom sighed deeply. He had wished that he could avoid asking Endurance a difficult question, but now he knew that there was no escape. He closed his eyes momentarily, then opened them and spoke in a heavy tone, "The League members and I know that the Mongol governor had a large amount of money in his vault. After your second commander left and before I came to your tent, we searched this mansion thoroughly. The vault was broken and the money gone." He gazed at Endurance and asked, "If your second commander took the money and you have it, will you please give it back to me?"

Endurance looked at his friend in disbelief. "You, a rich man, want me, a poor man, to give you the only money I have?" He shook his head and laughed. "My second commander did give the money to me and I have it, but I will never give it to you!"

Peony chimed in, "Wisdom Lu! When my husband longed to reunite with his best friend and I waited impatiently to meet the man who means so much to my husband, you were busy looking for money?"

"I'm sorry I kept you waiting," Wisdom said with true regret as he bowed to Peony, then added, "But the League needs the money for the poor. Our people are hungry. Plague and famine came on top of the war—"

Peony interrupted him, pointing at his and Lotus's fine jewelry. "Why don't you give those to the poor?"

Lotus covered her jade pin with her shaking hand and whispered, "Our Jewelry has more than monetary value. It has to stay in the family."

"Ha!" Peony bellowed as she slapped the arm of her chair. She then waved her naked fingers at the Lu couple. "Lord Fong gave me a ruby ring. It was the only jewelry I ever owned in my life. But I put it together with the Mongol governor's money. My husband and I always give all we have, including our lives, to the revolution. We don't eat our fill first, then throw a few crumbs to our fellow countrymen, and call ourselves good samaritans."

As the Lu couple blushed deeply and bowed their heads low, Endurance pointed at the clothes they had on. "You wear silk, eat delicacies, live in a mansion." He pointed at what he and Peony wore. "This is the first time we wear something that's not coarse and torn." He described the lives he and his family had led, then asked, "If you and your rich friends are willing to sacrifice a little, you could help the poor all you want."

Wisdom uttered in a voice of shame, "I know this is hard for you to understand, but our life-style cannot be changed. We are born into it. It's not only our birthright, but also our obligation to hold on to it." He bowed his head. "I would give you money instead of asking you to return the Mongol governor's money if only I could afford it."

His voice began to tremble. He was not very good at lying, and he hated to lie to his best friend. "Endurance, I have lowered the tax and rent on the people of Yin-tin. The Lu family income was greatly reduced because of it. I have a big household. Money disappears fast, like water through a colander. I . . ." Wisdom blushed deeply and could not go on.

Endurance looked at his friend closely. "You've suddenly become a poor man? It seems that yesterday you still could afford a big banquet!" He watched Wisdom's face turning from red to scarlet, and knew for sure now that Wisdom was lying. He felt an unbearable pain inside him. Wisdom's lie was a blow that wounded him more deeply than all the other things.

After the Chu couple had left the night before, Wisdom and Lotus had talked almost until dawn. Wisdom had developed second thoughts about

helping Endurance with his own money. The
reason was Endurance's attitude. It had showed
his ruthlessness and made Wisdom unwilling to
give money to a vicious man, who would make
weapons to kill with abandon. Lotus had supported her husband's decision, but disagreed
with his plan to lie about it.

Lotus cleared her throat. She looked at the
mottled faces of Endurance and Peony and knew
that they were about to explode. She must prevent the explosion, or her husband would be
hurt. She forced herself to intervene. She offered
to help Peony fill the mansion with new servants, hire tailors to make new wardrobes, and
find a suitable tutor for the boys. Peony was uninterested in any of those things, but she was
aware of Lotus's effort. Because of this she held
her temper. Endurance watched Peony restraining
herself and tried his best to control his anger as
well.

The explosion did not take place. But the
friendship between Endurance and Wisdom was
now a mended teacup with many deep cracks.
The gashes could be clearly seen and felt. With
the slightest further agitation, the cup would be
shattered into a thousand pieces.

37

Winter, 1362

"ENDURANCE AND PEONY CHU are coming!" the people of Gold Meadow shouted as they ran, then added just before bolting their doors, "May they defeat the king of Yunnan and all the Mongols!"

Gold Meadow was a small village in the western region between the Yellow and Yangtze rivers. The people were ruled both by the Chinese king of Yunnan and by the Mongols, who ruled the king.

Shivering, the villagers waited as the sound of running and tramping continued from morning to noon. Soon after that, the battle was over.

"The king's men are defeated! The king is dead! And the Mongols have been chased away!" they yelled once they ventured outside.

The peasants, waiting for their saviors, soon saw a long procession marching into town, led by two boys wearing red silk garments and fur coats, riding white horses side by side. The good-looking boys waved at the villagers, grinning mischievously. Their horses pulled a small gilt wagon carrying a four-foot-high altar.

The villagers looked into the wagon and gasped. Red silk hung from the top of the altar, half covering the most beautiful lotus that had ever bloomed on earth. "The magical White Lotus!" they whispered in awe.

"May the White Lotus bring us good fortune!"

The villagers bowed their heads and began to pray. "Please cure the sick, destroy the evil, and create joy in our lives!"

As the wagon moved past, two black stallions appeared. "Here comes the White Lotus king and queen!" the villagers shouted with great respect.

Endurance wore a black fur cape, Peony a white one. They both had on wide-rimmed fur hats and tall boots trimmed with fur. Their capes were lined with red satin. As the wind tossed their capes around, the satin glistened like red fire. Endurance waved and Peony smiled at the villagers. They both nodded slowly, like a noble king and queen entering their newly conquered domain.

"I don't hear anybody laughing at us here. Do you?" Endurance asked, continuing to wave.

"No," Peony answered, smiling broadly. "We've learned how to impress our majesty upon people. It's a lesson as important as fighting battles."

As people shouted out their faith toward the White Lotus, Endurance and Peony smiled at each other. The White Lotus had been created by accident. They had left the green jade with Wisdom, together with a note: "We'll be back to Yin-tin, and we expect to see the jade lotus carved by then. We also assume that by then you'll accept our rule, and will be willing to persuade all the southerners to follow your example." In one of the conquered villages, they had found an elephant's tusk. The ivory was pure white and smooth as silk. They had hired an artist and instructed him to create a white lotus.

Peony and Endurance were followed by soldiers, now called the White Lotus Warriors. Behind them were monks and nuns wearing white robes. They had been expelled from various temples for misconduct, and they had created a new religion and called it the White Lotus. They had

convinced people that White Lotus was the combination of Buddhism and Taoism, that their
many Buddhas had the power of all Buddhas in
heaven. In reality, though, these monks and nuns
were merciless killers. When people dared to
argue or doubt, they killed them. In order to gain
worshipers, they had carved a stone man who
had only one eye on his forehead. They had buried him in the riverbank, then waited for the
water to recede. The one-eye man had been discovered by fishermen, who had quickly called
someone to read the stone plaque that bore this
message: "Help the White Lotus Warriors and
you shall reach Nirvana." The discovery had
soon spread throughout the area, then the entire
country.

There was only one rich landlord in poverty-
stricken Gold Meadow, and he rushed to the
street, bowing at Endurance and Peony as he followed them. "My king and queen, please honor
my humble home with your presence. I've prepared food and wine, and some gifts that might
please your eye."

Endurance threw his fur cape back and nodded his consent. Peony peered from under the
wide brim of her fur hat and smiled at the
landlord.

"Please allow me to lead the way," the man
said, overwhelmed by the honor. He rattled on,
"We've been praying to the great Buddha that
you and your White Lotus Warriors will come
here soon. We have only a small Buddhist temple, but will spruce it up right away so that the
people can have a chance to view the sacred
White Lotus."

Endurance and Peony were shown to the best
room in the landlord's home. After bathing
themselves, they found two silk garments on
their bed; the landlord and his lady would be

blessed by Buddha if the White Lotus king and queen would wear these robes.

A feast was attended only by men, with the exception of the White Lotus queen. After the meal the landlord brought in his wife and the youngest of his concubines to his honorable guests.

"I am an unfortunate man, my king and queen," he said. He and his two women kneeled at Endurance and Peony's feet. "I have a wife and four concubines, but no son. Now my wife and this concubine of mine are both pregnant. I heard that in another village you laid your hands on the swollen belly of a woman, and she soon gave birth to a healthy boy. Please help me as well!"

Endurance and Peony placed their hands on first the wife and then the concubine. "You will have two sons," Peony said, and Endurance nodded.

The landlord and his women kowtowed to the White Lotus king and queen. "I must thank you," the landlord said. "I would be willing to trade half of my fortune for a son!"

"We never take money from anyone," Endurance said, shaking his head uncompromisingly. "Buddha's charity box is in the temple, next to the White Lotus."

As the rebel couple slept in the landlord's house, the ivory lotus was mounted on the highest pedestal in the Buddhist temple. Nearby, the charity box was large and made of iron, and every time someone dropped a copper coin into it, it made a clinking sound. To the ears of the givers, the sound was a positive answer from the powerful Buddha.

"Thank you for granting my humble wish," they chanted and walked away happily, often after parting with the last coins they owned.

Several White Lotus Warriors guarded the

altar that housed the White Lotus, each holding
a pair of scissors in his hand. With a silver coin
a person could purchase a small piece of the red
silk hanging from the altar, which showed signs
of smoke made by candles and incense.

"I'll burn the silk and mix the ashes in a cup
of tea," an old woman said. "My son will drink
it, and then blood will stop pouring out of his
lung."

Throughout the night the temple remained
crowded. The charity box became full and the
clinking sounds turned dull. The monks and
nuns who lived in the temple looked at it envi-
ously. They did not dare to say anything when
they watched the White Lotus Warriors carrying
the box away at dawn.

Endurance and Peony were having breakfast
with the landlord when the warriors arrived
with the box. From the way the men carried it,
they knew it was heavy and full. Their faces
were expressionless, but their hearts filled with
joy. They could continue to feed their followers
well, and someday they would be able to make
their Fire Bags and Firing Dragons.

Snow was falling heavily as the White Lotus
Warriors moved away from the village. Glancing
back at the thin faces and bony frames on the
street, Endurance and Peony exchanged a look
of guilt.

"Don't feel bad. We have no choice," he said,
comforting his wife. "No one would give us anything if we had not invented this hoax."

"Don't you feel bad either. We are not the first
to play this trick, and won't be the last," Peony
consoled her husband. "There will always be religion, and perhaps all religions are created for
personal gain."

They kicked their horses and rushed forward;
they had many more towns to conquer. Behind

them galloped the White Lotus princes, White Lotus Warriors, and White Lotus monks and nuns.

Summer, 1364

The cicadas chanted endlessly. The Lu mansion was a picture of serenity under the flourishing weeping willows.

The front door opened, and eight sedan carriers came out. They prepared two sedans, then waited in the shade.

A thirteen-year-old girl appeared at the door, wearing a pink garment and leaning against a maid. "Mama, don't worry. Jasmine will take good care of me," Peach Blossom said, looking over her shoulder as she moved toward one of the sedans.

Lotus came to the door, supported by her maid, and waved at the girl. She called softly. "Give my regards to Jasmine and Ah Chin. Tell them the next time the entire family will visit them."

Lady Peach Blossom entered one sedan, her maid the other. Lady Lotus waited until both had disappeared at the direction of the Dais of Rain Flowers, then left the door and headed for the patriarch's court.

At age thirty-eight, Wisdom Lu looked like an old man from the back, bending his thin frame over a workbench. In the past year he had not spent much time with his family. He had ignored eating and sleeping, and had been doing nothing but working on the jade day and night.

Lotus put a hand on her husband's shoulder, and Wisdom turned. His eyes brightened at the sight of her, and he smiled. Enthusiasm illuminated his face; it was the face of an artist eternally young at heart.

"Look at this," he said, pointing at the unfinished carving. Lotus was surprised and pleased. He had never shown his work to her before, always draping something over the jade when she visited the studio.

Out of the large piece of precious jade had been chiseled a well-shaped man in his scholar's robe. His face was beginning to appear, and it looked like Wisdom, wearing a gentle smile.

"Endurance will be very surprised to see that I did not carve him the jade lotus but the jade lovers," Wisdom said, holding his chisel knife. "I am creating a jade lord and a jade lady just as I've always dreamed."

He had carved a pair of wood statues long ago as a study, and they were based on a drawing of Wisdom and Lotus. "I miss my carving teacher," he said as he looked at his earlier work. "If he hadn't died, he could have helped me finish the jade lovers in time."

"In time for what?" Lotus asked, frowning. She knew that Endurance and Peony would be furious when they discovered that Wisdom had used their precious jade to carve something wholly different from what they had ordered.

"In time for Endurance to return," Wisdom answered, then started to work again. "I have the feeling that he will come back to Yin-tin soon. And I want to surprise him with the jade lovers." He continued without looking at his beloved wife. "With one look at the jade lovers, Endurance will be touched by the kindness and compassion that shall appear in their eyes." he said dreamily. "Endurance and Peony will become as kind and compassionate as my jade lovers someday. I really believe they will."

Winter, 1366

The north wind wailed over the frozen water in Hui-tung Canal. In the city of Tsinan, at the foot of a high mountain, many tents were gathered, flapping in the slicing gale. The felt tapestry over the largest tent was lifted, and six people came out.

"Let's go for a walk," Endurance said. A fur robe was wrapped around his massive body, and his boots were lined with fur.

"How about along the canal?" Peony asked, leading the way. She was also wrapped in fur. Over the past four years, the White Lotus had brought them enough money to start making Fire Bags and Firing Dragons. Fine lines appeared at the corners of her eyes as she turned to the boys and laughed. "Let's have a race! Whoever touches that old pine first is the winner!"

Power, already very tall at age twelve, began to run as soon as he heard his mother's last word. Dominance was a year younger but the same height as his older brother. He was determined to beat Power in everything, and he ran with an intent look. Bravery and Vigorous, still boys, soon forgot the race and began sliding down a nearby slope. Endurance and Peony stopped for their younger sons, leaving only Power and Dominance in the race.

"I win!" Power yelled from far away, standing beside an old pine.

"I win! I touched the tree before you!" Dominance yelled.

The boys called each other names and began to fight over who had actually won. Fighting was a part of their daily lives, and it never bothered their parents. For a long while Endurance and Peony watched their older sons spar and the younger sons play.

Then they turned to look at the many torn lanterns in the frozen canal. Hui-tung Canal was connected to Yellow River, and when lanterns filled the river, they overflowed into the canal.

"Peony," Endurance said, softly, continuing to stare at the mangled lanterns.

Peony saw sorrow on her husband's face and read the cause of it in his eyes. "You are not responsible for the lanterns," she said, taking his hand.

"Two hundred and fifty thousand soldiers have died in the past year." Endurance sighed. "And the deaths among civilians are even greater than that. How can I not feel responsible?"

Peony pulled her husband away from the canal. "Count your victories instead of the casualties," she said.

The White Lotus Warriors had advanced north from Yunnan, through the already conquered provinces of Szechwan and Shensi, and entered Kansu. In short order, Endurance had killed the King of Kansu and added the province to his sway. They had then followed the Yellow River for the final campaign up the Hui-tung Canal.

Peony continued as they walked toward the older boys, "You have conquered all of China except Da-du. All the killing was necessary. Any of the other rebel leaders would have killed you if you had not attacked them first. You can call yourself the king of all provinces now, and this is exactly what the other kings were warring among themselves for."

Endurance knew that Peony was telling the truth and was comforted somewhat. He and she stopped and looked at the far horizon. The Hui-tung Canal was many miles long. Da-du was at the end of the canal, protected by three layers of city walls.

Many battles would be fought before they

could reach the end of Hui-tung, because the Mongols had placed their best forces alongside the canal to keep all rebel forces from reaching their capital. The assault on Da-du would be the most difficult battle, and it was impossible to predict a Chinese victory.

Endurance sighed. "Let us pray that by the time we reach the end of the canal, the Firing Dragons will be made. We will need them to destroy the city walls."

Peony suddenly turned to face her husband and put her arms around his waist. She buried her face against his chest and said in a trembling voice, "I am afraid, Endurance. For the first time, I am afraid that we may lose and the Mongols will take their revenge on us."

Endurance paused for a long time, then answered with a sigh, "Peony, I, too, am afraid."

38

IN THE WINTER of 1367, the White Lotus Warriors reached the outskirts of Da-du.

Throughout the night, snow fell softly and the men advanced carefully through the woods bordering the Mongol's capital city on all sides. The first group cleared dead trees to make pathways, the second group pushed the Firing Dragons forward, and the third carried Fire Bags and Dragon Eggs. During the past year Peony had helped the armorers to improve the design of the former two, she had created Dragon Eggs by melting iron and then shaping it into balls.

The first ring of the city walls was eight miles on a side, and each wall contained two gates with solid iron doors. Behind these eight gates various guards were alerted by strange sounds, and they climbed their ladders to look around.

In the early morning hours the snow stopped, and heavy clouds shrouded a crystal moon. The guards continued to hear the breaking of tree branches but could not detect any movement. Most assumed it was wild animals foraging for food. When a few of them caught a glimpse of something flashing white, they thought it was the tail of a running deer. They descended their ladders and continued to doze.

Peony's cape was lined with white fur. She walked among the soldiers to be sure the Firing Dragons were set up correctly. Endurance's horse

had a white nose. It did not neigh, but carried its
master quietly at the head of his calvary corps.

Behind them was the White Lotus general
leading a large army of foot soldiers, each carrying either a broadsword or a long spear, several
Fire Bags or a Flaming Snake.

When night neared its end, Peony climbed a
tall pine. She looked toward the east until a
touch of gray finally appeared at the far horizon.
A faint glow of pink emerged hesitantly. The
shape of a red sphere eventually surfaced like a
shy girl unwilling to face the world.

"Ready . . ." Peony called from the treetop.

The Firing Dragons, with their muzzles turned
on the city walls, were fed quickly: first the explosives, then the Dragon Eggs. Behind each can-
non stood a soldier with a lighted torch and
several men guarding a wagon loaded with fresh
balls.

"Fire!" Peony shouted.

The Firing Dragons roared in an earth-
shattering sound as the explosives blasted the
Dragon Eggs out of their iron throats. The eggs
sailed out of the woods and smashed a series of
gaping holes along the walls.

The Mongol soldiers behind the gates saw
their solid walls crumble and the metal doors
fall. The residents were awakened and astounded
by the thundering noise of falling masonry. The
acid smell of explosives filled their nostrils. Dark
smoke lingered in the air.

"Advance!" Endurance bellowed. Spurring his
horse, he then bent over its mane and charged
out of the woods.

Following him, the horsemen and their mounts
leapt through gaps in the demolished walls, and
the men began to slash whoever stood in their
way. In the dawning light they could not see if
the victims were Mongols, Chinese, or color-eyed

people, but even if they had, it would not have
mattered.

"Charge!" the White Lotus general ordered his
men, who advanced quickly through the dust left
by the horses' hoofs.

The foot soldiers sprinted forward, dashed
into the outer city of Da-du, waving their spears
and broadswords, casting their Fire Bags. "Kill!
Kill!" they shouted as they slaughtered everyone
in sight.

As calvary and infantry wreaked havoc, the
artillery brigade loaded their Firing Dragons
again and aimed them at the second ring of the
city walls.

There were eight brightly colored fortresses on
these, four on the corners where the walls met,
the others in the middle of each wall. The Mongol generals, officers, and their families lived in
these fortresses together with their soldiers and
slaves.

The Dragon Eggs smashed the walls, turned
the fortresses to rubble. Women screamed as
they gathered their children and looked for
places to hide. Men separated into two groups,
one collecting their bows and arrows, the other
their Killing Hands to face their attackers. The
Chinese slaves looked up at the morning sky,
thanking the great Buddha for freeing them.

Endurance's sword decapitated everyone within
reach, and his horse trampled Chinese as well as
Mongols. The other men on horseback followed
Endurance's example. In the melee the Chinese
slaves were killed while still thanking the great
Buddha.

The raging assault took the Mongols by surprise. It had taken the Chinese a year to fight
their way to Da-du from the southern end of the
Hui-tung Canal. Mighty Sword had massed his
best soldiers along the canal as it led closer to

Da-du. For the past month the White Lotus Warriors had hardly made any advance. Indeed, only a few days before, the supreme general had told his men within the Da-du walls that the Chinese would never reach the capital city.

The Mongols had not expected the last miles of the canal to be taken over night. The Chinese had attacked from three directions in the dark. With finely honed technique, they had soundlessly exterminated every Mongol soldier guarding the last section of the canal before any warning could reach Da-du.

The Mongols posted in Da-du were high-ranking courtiers and auxiliary troops who were not battle-tested. These were soft city folks bearing no resemblance to their nomad ancestors who had conquered China. Living as masters to the Chinese for too long, they had developed feelings of superiority: the Chinese were easy to kick around. They would pay for this mistaken belief with their lives.

When the eight fortresses were taken and the second ring secured, Peony ordered her men to direct the Firing Dragons at the last tier of the city walls, embracing the Mongol palace.

The Great Khan Eastwind and his Queen Sunflower were awakened by the thunderous clamor. They saw the walls shaking and felt their bed vibrating. The huge candelabra swung from the ceiling and bits of plaster fell.

"Earthquake?" Eastwind uttered as he jumped out of bed, grabbed his robe, then ran toward his treasure room. He stopped after only a few steps.

He and Sunflower could hear the Chinese shouting in a distance, "Kill! Kill! Kill!"

Shadow Tamu ran from his bed to the window, opened it, and saw smoke rising from within the city walls. His thin face drained of blood. His claw-like fingers trembled as he packed his gold coins and other valuables. He wished that his shaking legs would move as fast as he ordered them to, but his feeble limbs moved in the palest imitation of his commands.

Mighty Sword opened his eyes, bolted upright between the two young beauties in his bed, and listened to the commotion. Drawing on his armor, he pulled up his boots and put on his pointed metal hat. As he glanced into the brass mirror, he saw a faint scar on his forehead. Like the scar on his left arm, it was the work of Peony Chu. He clenched his teeth. Today he vowed, he would kill the Chu couple.

He buckled his wide belt around his waist, felt his sword in its proper place. He then grabbed his Killing Hand. His temples were gray and his dark face lined. But alertness sparkled in his black eyes, and determination tightened his lips into a firm line to give his handsome face the terrorizing appearance of Buddha of death.

The White Lotus Warriors stormed into the palace garden like a tidal wave engulfing a village. The shock troops of White Lotus monks and nuns jumped over the low walls that separated the royal princes' courts, and the others created a punishing fire of Fire Bags and Flaming Snakes that killed princes, princesses, and their children by the dozens.

Behind them, Endurance and Peony mounted marble steps that led to a solid copper door thirty feet high. Instead of entering the Mongol palace by stepping over the collapsed walls, they preferred its formal entrance. The Mongols who had guarded the many watchtowers had been slain, and the White Lotus Warriors unbolted the doors for the White Lotus king and queen.

Endurance and Peony walked over the headless bodies of the Mongol guards. After only a few steps they encountered a fully armed, powerful man and recognized him as Mighty Sword.

At thirty-nine, Endurance looked like a lion with a graying mane. When his eyes met those of Mighty Sword, the angry lion roared, "It's been twenty-two years since we first met in Prosper Mountain!"

Mighty Sword grinned. "I'm surprised that a peasant like you can even count."

With their eyes locked, they drew their swords. Their faces were distorted with hatred and their hearts filled with burning memories.

Out of their many encounters, the most unforgettable had been their first, when a young Mongol general saw a poor Chinese boy staring at him from a street corner and decided to destroy both the boy and the child who was his friend.

"My family and friends are waiting for you in the world of the dead! I'll send you to them so they can torture you there!" Endurance declared.

"I've let you live far too long on borrowed time! You'll never see today's sunset!" Mighty Sword hissed.

They raised their swords.

•

The great khan's residence was located far from the royal courts of the other princes and princesses. Listening to Sunflower's suggestions, Eastwind gathered almost a hundred loyal guards. Some had been fighting in the other courts, and they reported, "The rebels have killed all your relatives and are coming this way!"

Eastwind nodded grimly. He and Sunflower each picked up a Killing Hand, then ran from

the palace under the protection of their guards.
They had only minutes to hide themselves.

Shadow Tamu's palace was next to the great
khan's, and he left his court holding a leather
bag in each hand, filled with gold coins and precious stones. He toted them across the garden,
resting now and then, finally reaching the
platform.
He dragged the bags up the stairs, laid them
down to wipe his brow, then quickly got down
on his knees and reached for the Buddha's left
foot. Suddenly he heard sounds coming from behind him. Turning, he saw the great khan and
his queen approaching.

Despite the icy weather, Endurance and Mighty
Sword were soaked in perspiration. The snow
around them was spotted with blood, for both
men had been wounded several times, neither
paid any attention to their injuries, though.
The sun had disappeared and the wind began
to moan. Dark clouds, piled high, kept roiling in
the turmoil overhead. Bystanders could not tell
what cloud formation would appear in the next
moment, nor could they predict which of the two
warriors would remain alive when the duel
reached its end.

"It's you," Shadow Tamu said to Eastwind in
his usual slighting tone. "You can forget sharing
my escape route . . ." he gasped.
Eastwind and Sunflower walked toward
Shadow Tamu, aimed their Killing Hands at the
adviser who had advised many khans in the past
decades.
Shadow Tamu glanced at the Killing Hands
and the large number of guards. Fear appeared
in the old adviser's eyes, and his pale face be-

came chalk white. He tried to laugh. "If you dared to pull that trigger, you'll be tracked down by my brother and tortured slowly!" he uttered, using the threat that had never failed him before.

Mighty Sword was growing tired. Sweat streamed down his face, dripped on his breastplate. He had already lost his metal hat during the fight. He was still capable of defending himself, but no longer able to attack. He was ready to order his guard to help him when he heard an explosion to his rear.

He felt a painful tug in his heart, then heard, either with his ears or his soul, his brother's dying cry, "Mighty Sword! My brother! Where are you?"

The cry echoed through the garden as Shadow Tamu's body fell forward. His feet kicked the bags, and his hand landed on the Buddha's big toe. The two leather bags rolled down the steps, opening as they went. Gold coins and precious stones scattered over the ground that surrounded the platform.

One of the blood-splashed boards began to slide aside. An entrance appeared on the platform. Eastwind and Sunflower ran through the opening and descended the narrow steps. They were followed by their long procession of guards.

Reaching the secret room, Eastwind twisted the gold candlestick on the bedside table. The entry was concealed, and the secret passage was out of sight.

Endurance was so immersed in the duel to the death that he blocked out everything else. His opponent, on the other hand, was losing his concentration, as if hearing something. Suddenly realizing this, Endurance lunged forward. His broadsword swung in a downward arc, catching Mighty Sword's blade on the upward swing and knocking the blade from his hand.

Endurance cast aside his own sword and pulled out his dagger. Seizing Mighty Sword with his free hand, he pulled the Mongol forward and buried the dagger up to its hilt in his heart.

Mighty Sword did not fall immediately. He stood staring at Endurance as blood gushed out of his wound.

In his eyes, Endurance's face kept changing: a peasant boy, a mailman, a rebel leader, and then a peasant boy again.

"Killed by a peasant boy . . . ?" Mighty Sword murmured as he stumbled forward.

Endurance used his right hand to pull his dagger out of Mighty Sword, wiped it on his left sleeve. He kissed the jade centerpiece on the cross guard, then put the dagger back into its sheath.

The powerful Mongol fell at Endurance's feet. He kicked the unmoving body to make sure he was dead, then ordered his men, "Cut off his head and display it on a high pole!"

All around them, the remaining Mongols were surrendering. Peony took Endurance in her arms and began to tend his wounds. They then looked up the pole where Mighty Sword's head was being exhibited.

The supreme general's eyes were wide open, his lips pulled back into a frozen smile that revealed his white teeth.

"Baba and Mama, your death is avenged!" Peony whispered to the gray wintry sky.

"My family and my friends, you can smile in the world of the dead now," Endurance cried, directing his voice to the heavy clouds that kept changing shape in the powerful north wind.

In Endurance's eyes, one of the clouds was shaped exactly like the face of a thirteen-year-old boy named Longevity Ma.

The Great Khan Eastwind and Queen Sunflower furtively emerged from the Lamaist temple. They and their followers took the horses prepared by the monks, and galloped north toward the Great Wall.

Hours later, just before entering the Gobi Desert, Eastwind and Sunflower halted their horses. They turned and looked back toward the south.

"Please don't be sad about leaving all your inventions and collections in China," Sunflower said to her husband.

"Why should I be sad?" Eastwind answered his queen. "The knowledge of my inventions stays in my mind, and the memories of my collections live in my heart. Besides, you and I will have many children, and one of our descendants will conquer China once again!"

Endurance and Peony decided to position themselves in Da-du until next spring. They set their soldiers free to roam the city streets, making it clear that as conquerers, they had the right to everything.

Endurance and Peony then proceeded to survey the Mongol palace. The crumbled walls had to be rebuilt. The damaged buildings needed to be repaired. The entire palace had to be stripped of all Mongol influence.

Bricklayers and carpenters were set to work day and night, and one night a few weeks later when Endurance and Peony walked into one of the salons, they did not notice that there were three carpenters still working on the high beams.

"I can't believe this!" Endurance looked around and roared. "You and I, two peasants, are now the White Lotus king and queen, owners of a palace!" Looking up, he spotted the three carpenters. He knew they had heard him. He ordered them down.

Two of the three followed the order immediately. The third one paid no attention to Endurance, but continued to polish the beam.

"How dare you not obey me?" Endurance shouted at the man. "I said come down! Now!"

The man kept ignoring Endurance, and Peony laughed. "Can't you see that he is deaf?"

Endurance did not carry a sword, but he took his dagger out of its sheath. When the two carpenters realized what fate waited for them, they kneeled and begged.

"Please spare us. We have families to feed. We will never repeat what we've heard—" They were killed before they could beg any further.

During the past year, while fighting his way up the Hui-tung Canal, Endurance's heart had hardened a great deal more. With a heart as stony as the frozen earth, he no longer counted the number of soldiers and civilians that died on his account. He now wiped the carpenters' blood off his dagger with his robe, then looked up at the beams once again.

The man up there had never stopped working. He didn't seem to have seen anything.

"Are you sure he is deaf?" Endurance asked Peony.

"Of course," she answered. "Unless he is a superb actor."

When the couple were gone and the bodies of the two carpenters dragged away, the survivor came down from the high beams. He sneaked out of the palace, left Da-du, and headed for the high mountains, to search for the monks hiding in temples embraced by ancient forests and enveloped by low clouds.

When the apple blossoms bloomed along the Hui-tung Canal, Endurance, Peony, and their four sons were ready to leave Da-du.

"I worked on the building of it," Endurance said, pointing at the canal. He remembered his heavy hoe, his bleeding hands, his growling stomach, his aching back, and the whips in the hands of the Mongol foremen. "And now we shall sail in state on it!"

The largest dragon boat built by the Great Khan Eastwind was lowered to the canal. The Chu family lounged in the boat, while their soldiers marched on the shore. Long ropes were tied to the boat, pulled by coolies who were dragged from the villages along the canal and forced into labor.

When the Chu family wanted the boat to go faster, the White Lotus general ordered his soldiers to raise their whips on the coolies. Though the Chu family ate or slept their fill, the coolies were never fed or allowed to rest. At the border of their village, they were replaced by those who lived in the next village. Only the strong and fortunate lasted long enough to survive their ordeal.

Besides the coolies, other villagers stood on the waterfront and watched the dragon boat float by.

"Look at the White Lotus queen's big feet!" one woman said, unable to repress her amazement. "She had the nerve to dangle them over the side for everyone to see!"

Her voice traveled to the dragon boat, where Endurance signaled his general with a menacing chop. The woman was killed instantly.

"Is it true that the White Lotus king is the son of a lowly peasant?" a man asked curiously.

The spring breeze carried his question to the ears of Endurance. He signaled his general once again, and the curious man's blood splashed the waters of the canal.

39

Summer, 1638

"IT'S HUMILIATING to be treated like this! This is worse than the last time!" Endurance bellowed, trembling with anger as he rode through the streets of Yin-tin.

"How dare they ignore us completely!" Peony yelled, riding beside her husband.

"Not even one person greets us on the street!" Power bellowed furiously from his horse. "Don't they want to see their heroes?"

"All the doors to their homes are closed. And even the merchants are not glad to see us. Look at the hatred in their eyes!" Dominance cried, pointing all around. "The people of Yin-tin need to be taught a lesson. Maybe we can set the town on fire!"

Bravery and Vigorous, nine and eight, were not offended by the lack of welcome, but were bored by having to ride through the deserted streets.

Their reception in Yin-tin hurt Peony and Endurance so much that when the Lotus Warriors, also angered by the cold reception, decided to raid the town, neither of them tried to curb them.

The store owners tried to smile at the raiding soldiers, but it was too late. The warriors took the things they wished to possess, demanded

free meals from all restaurant owners, and killed
those who dared to show resentment.

"We need places to sleep! We have slept in
tents long enough!" they shouted, then burst
into homes and demanded to be treated like honored guests.

Behind the laymen soldiers were the White
Lotus monks and nuns. They did not stop any-
where, but went directly to the Purple Gold
Mountain. Many of them had been expelled from
the two temples there, and were now ready to
revenge. They were disappointed to find both
temples deserted, "So the old monks and nuns
have run away! Well, it's time that we take over
the places and declare new laws," they said. The
first law proclaimed was: each family in Yin-tin
must bring a certain percentage of their income
to these temples at every full moon.

Wisdom Lu watched his servants bolt all the
doors, then walked toward the inner court.
While working on his jade sculptures, Wisdom
had eaten or slept so little that he now weighed
less than a hundred pounds.

Reaching the inner court, he gathered his families and told them of his decision. His grown
sons objected, his young daughter cried. Lotus
did not say anything, only looked at her husband
with her lovely but tearful eyes.

Sending the children away, Wisdom took Lotus
in his arms. His eyes lingered on her beautiful
face. He kissed her almond eyes and her eyebrows shaped like willow leaves. His lips caught
her little mouth painted red only in the middle
to resemble a cherry. He then lowered his gaze to
her two-and-a-half-inch feet, the most attractive
feature of a southern gentlewoman.

In the aging woman, Wisdom saw only his
youthful bride. He still remembered the first

time they had melted the clouds and created
rain. "We have wasted a lot of time. Tradition
has deprived us of much joy in life," he
whispered.

When he undid her sash, she did not push his
hands away. This was not the proper time, and
neither Confucius nor Buddha would be pleased.
But how could they make up the lost time? Besides, she must help her husband release all
the tension, fear, and worry. She leaned against
him as he helped her to their bed. She held onto
him tightly as he pillowed with her. She circled
her legs and arms around her husband with more
than passion—she was terrified of losing him.

"Bring him here!" Endurance said to the servant through clenched teeth. He and Peony were
seated in the gazebo, having dinner.

Wisdom trudged toward Endurance and Peony,
carrying a heavy bundle. He bowed with diffi-
culty holding the parcel. "It's good to see you
again," he said simply, then placed the package
on the gazebo table. "I have a gift for both of
you."

From underneath the silk wrappings, two statues appeared. The jade man was dressed like a
noble lord, the jade woman a lady.

"How dare you waste my father's precious
jade!" Peony screamed, staring at the statues.

"Did we not make it clear enough that we
wanted a jade lotus?" Endurance yelled.

Wisdom bowed once again. "The jade lord and
jade lady should please you much more than a
flower." He then waited for the royal couple to
take a second look.

The two studied the statues carefully. The
lord and lady resembled Wisdom and Lotus, and
the likeness went far beyond their features. Both
statues had a dreamy look on their faces. Besides

that, honesty, sincerity, peacefulness, kindness, and compassion also appeared in every carved line. Moonlight embraced the statues softly, brightening the lord and lady's eyes. The statues seemed to be alive, ready to open their mouths to speak.

"For your information, they do not please us at all!" Peony said coldly.

"Why did you carve them for us?" Endurance asked suspiciously.

Wisdom explained calmly, "I carved them for you as a role model." He paused, then added, "Please imitate them. If you can become as kind and compassionate as they are, then you will be accepted by everyone."

Sullenly, Endurance and Peony walked around the table, peering at the statues from every angle. The more they studied the jade lord and lady, the more angered they were.

"You want me to imitate the jade lady? Then why did you give her bound feet?" Peony compared her own large feet with the statue's tiny ones.

"You think I can imitate the jade lord? I'd die in the clothes he has on!" The statue's robe concealed his entire body, while Endurance's garment was parted very low at all times to reveal his hairy chest. "That high collar alone would choke me to death!"

Wisdom waited for the two's furious voices to stop reverberating through the quiet garden. A nightingale sang from a deep forest. Frogs exchanged love songs in a pond. Cicadas chanted from the moonlit trees. "Listen," Wisdom said, "the jade lovers are talking. They are telling you that the war is over, that it's time for you to lay down your weapons and make China a beautiful and peaceful nation."

Endurance cocked his head to one side, eyed

Wisdom distrustfully. "The jade lovers did not say anything! You put words into their mouths! You're speaking for yourself!"

Peony pointed at the jade statues, "They look exactly like you and your wife. I think you and Lotus want to rule China yourselves, and wish to use the jade lovers as your icon."

"Rule China yourselves!" Endurance repeated Peony's words. It made sense. Yin-tin was the largest city in the south, and the southern Chinese were wiser than the northerners. Since Wisdom controlled Yin-tin, the steps in his rise to head of Kiangsu, and then the ruler of all provinces, and eventually the emperor of China, were not all that daunting.

Wisdom shook his head. "I have no intention of ruling. I only want to retire and perhaps advise you from a distance—"

Endurance did not let him finish. "So you want to be a Chinese Shadow Tamu! You want Peony and me to be puppets and you the puppeteer. That's why the jade statues and all this nonsense!"

Wisdom met his friend's eyes unwaveringly, then took in Peony as well. He spoke slowly but clearly, "My friends, you are wrong. I have no desire to either rule China or be a puppeteer. But please try to change yourselves into a kind pair like the jade lovers. Otherwise I will make sure that people in China will never accept you as their ruler!"

"We will not let you do that!" Peony yelled.

"We will destroy you before you can destroy us!" Endurance cried, advancing on Wisdom.

The room had a small window barred with iron rods. Its thick wooden door was locked from outside. The bed was low and the hard boards covered only by a damp straw mat. There was

no pillow. The walls and low ceiling were made
of stone and thick with mildew, because this
room was located in the northern corner of the
mansion, where sunshine was blocked away by
the surrounding weeping willows. The Mongol
governor had used this room to keep his prisoners, and now Endurance found this room an
ideal jail cell.

Wisdom paced the dirt floor. Walking parallel
to his bed, he could take six steps from wall to
wall. He had been pacing since he had been
thrown into this room by Endurance's men.

"I'll give you three days to think it over," Endurance had said uncompromisingly. "And if
you ever want to go back to your family again,
you had better agree to make a public speech to
the people of Yin-tin."

Wisdom had not told him that such a speech
was not needed. The poor scholars and rich
elites were already willing to bow to the new
ruler's yoke. The peasants were not sophisti-
cated enough to pretend, but they would also
bow at the point of a sword.

Wisdom stopped at the barred window. Peering through the willow, he saw the waning moon.
He listened carefully and heard the nightingale.
He knew that below in the foothills, his entire
family was awake and waiting for his return.

"I'm sorry," he whispered. "It's a matter of
principle. With or without my speech, Endurance will rule just the same. But if I became
his advocate and then the people suffered
under his rule, I would never be able to live
with myself."

Leaving the window, he went to sit on the bed.
Out of his topknot he pulled all the jade hairpins, and his long queue fell free. He took the
end of the queue and began to undo the braiding,
separating the several yards of silk threads inter-

twined with his hair. He wound the long thread around one of his hairpins, then put them together with the two handkerchiefs in his pocket—one red, the other white.

Wisdom lay on his bed with his arms folded under his head, staring at the barred window. The nightingale stopped singing when the moon disappeared and the dark sky turned gray.

"Lotus, you must know by now that I'm no longer free to come home," he whispered to the dawning sky, wishing for the morning breeze to bring his voice to his wife. His heart ached at the images of his family. He closed his eyes and felt hot tears on his face. He turned away from the window and waited for the day to begin. He soon heard the servants stirring. A while later a man unlocked the door and brought him a tray.

Wisdom searched the tray anxiously until he saw the chopsticks. He did not touch the food, but took the chopsticks and began to work immediately.

At the door, Endurance frowned at the summer heat that filled the tiny room. His eyes widened at the kite held in Wisdom's hands. It was made with a white handkerchief, two chopsticks, and the many yards of silk thread from Wisdom's queue.

"You scholars are weird! Making a kite at a time like this!" Endurance murmured, shaking his head. "Have you made up your mind?" he asked.

Wisdom answered slowly, "No." He looked at the white kite. It was impossible to lie and meet his friend's eyes. "That's why I made the kite. It is a habit of mine—I can think better when flying a kite."

Endurance shrugged as he granted Wisdom's wish. "I'll go with you."

They walked in the garden, stopped beside a large pond. Wisdom tossed his kite into the breeze and began to unwind the thread quickly. The wind's invisible hands held the kite and lifted it high. By the time Wisdom stopped unwinding the thread, the white kite was soaring above the garden walls and dancing noticeably over the Purple Gold Mountain.

"The kite is white!" Lotus said, and her knees buckled. Ardent supported her on one side, Earnest on the other.

"Baba!" Peach Blossom cried. "I prayed all night for you to fly the red kite and tell us things will be fine! Please, Baba! Take the white kite down and tell us we don't have to run!"

Her older brothers looked up at the white kite once again, then quickly dried their tears. Ardent helped Lotus leave the garden and said bravely, "Mama, we must obey Baba's order. We need to move fast."

Earnest supported Peach Blossom and urged the young girl forward, "You are a young woman, Sister. Please don't act like a baby. Baba is a brave man. Let's make him proud of us."

They went from the garden to the matriarch's court, closed the doors, and had a long talk with Lady Lu and Lady Lin, who were both in their sixties. After tears were shed and discussions made, the six of them started to pack.

They did not trust any servant. The people of Yin-tin might not like Endurance, but everyone could use the reward for their capture. The family did not pack any fine garments, for silk and satin would be out of place for their new life. Besides gold and silver coins, they only took what could be sold easily—mostly precious stones that did not bear the identity of their owners. The only useless things packed by Lotus were a jade comb, a few hand-carved jade rings, a drawing, and a pair of wood statues. She could not part from them, because each item represented a period of the happiness she and Wisdom had shared.

When night took the mansion into its dark bosom, the six of them sneaked out of the back door, walked as far as the four ladies' bound feet could carry them.

The ladies waited until the young men halted six sedan chairs for hire. "To the Dais of Rain Flowers," Ardent said to the carriers.

In the Lu mansion, a woman in her mid-fifties had observed her masters and mistresses carefully with her keen eyes. She knew they had escaped and why. Her name was Sesame. She had been sold to the Lu house as a child slave, and had become Wisdom's concubine when he reached fourteen. She had known no other man since. She loved him all her life, although he only used her when Lotus was kept from him by tradition. She had no hatred or jealousy for Lotus. She loved the Lu children as if they were her own, even though they treated her as one of the servants.

Sesame was sad that the masters and mistresses did not trust her enough to share their secret with her. But her sorrow did not affect her loyalty.

She went to Lotus's room, put on Lotus's clothes, and sat on Lotus's chair, then turned the chair to face the wall. If any servant should have anything to report to Lady Lu, they would find only that the lady was not in a mood to talk, not that the real Lady Lotus Lu was gone.

"Wisdom, my lord, this is the least I can do for you," Sesame whispered as she stared at the wall. She sobbed quietly when she saw on the empty wall the image of Wisdom, growing from a baby to a child, then a young lord to a middle-aged governor.

The Lu family headed for the south of Yin-tin and arrived at a farm near the Dais of Rain Flowers. The aged owners of the farm was Ah Chin and Jasmine, living with their grown children.

The Lu and Chin families talked throughout the night. When morning came, a wagon left the farmhouse, driven by young Chin and headed for the South Gate.

The White Lotus warriors had taken over the guard posts at the gate, but had not yet learned to inspect the travelers with sharp eyes. They saw a young farmer driving a wagon, and the passengers were six peasants, four women and two men. They waved the wagon on.

Ah Chin and Jasmine waited nervously from morning to night. When a farmer arrived at sunset and told them that their son and the Lu family had crossed the border of Kiangsu Province and continued on to the province of Kiangsi, they breathed with relief.

Hurriedly the couple left their farm and climbed up the Dais of Rain Flowers in the setting sun. Ah Chin had been sick and became exhausted after the climb. Finally he rested on the colorful stones that gave the dais its name, and watched his wife taking out of a bag a large red kite.

Standing on top of the dais, Jasmine sent the kite high in the sky. It rose above all the trees, and could be seen clearly by people on the mountain.

Wisdom asked for Endurance's permission to

walk in the garden. The emperor not only granted the permission, but also walked with him.

"This is your third night here, and the last night of your stay in my home as a guest," Endurance said in a hoarse voice. "I need an answer from you in the morning."

After a pause he repeated his question: would Wisdom declare his loyalty in a public address and urge the Kiangsu people to follow his example?

Wisdom didn't seem to have heard the repeated question. He walked to the edge of the garden and looked at the city down below. He squinted his eyes toward the southwest, searching the tall trees that surrounded the Dais of Rain Flowers.

Then he saw a kite flying above all trees, as red as the setting sun.

Wisdom smiled for the first time that day. "Have a good life, my sons and daughter," he mouthed without making a sound. "Have a good life, my Lotus. We'll be together again in another world . . ." His lips trembled.

Endurance was saying, ". . . And if your answer is still no, then I'll have to execute you publicly. Since you are their favorite mayor, your death will affect them greatly. I prefer to rule with the people's approval, but you're forcing me into ruling them by fear."

Turning away from the red kite, Wisdom faced Endurance with a peaceful expression. He put his hands on the arms of his old friend, then looked up at the big man. "Endurance, you know as well as I that you are only trying to frighten me into saying yes. You don't have the heart to humiliate me with a public execution."

The former peasant eyed Wisdom a moment longer and screamed, "You stubborn fool!" He spread his arms and freed himself from Wisdom's grasp. "Did you just say no for the last time?"

Wisdom nodded calmly. "Yes, my friend. My final answer is no. I will never make that public address to the people. As a matter of fact, if you allow me to live, I'll do two things: help people resist your rule, and be your conscience and remind you how ferocious a ruler you are."

Endurance put his large hands on Wisdom's shoulders and shook the little man violently. "You idiot! You may not value your own life, but what about the lives of your family? I can kill all of them, you know!"

Wisdom shook his head. "No, you cannot. I knew you might use them to threaten me, so I sent them away. They are out of the province now, and you'll never find out where they are."

Endurance screamed once again and shoved Wisdom away. The frail scholar landed hard on the gravel, skinning his elbows and palms. He watched Endurance walking away furiously, calling his guards to put the prisoner back in the cell.

Wisdom stood up without the guards' help. Just before they escorted him to his prison room, he looked at the Dais of Rain Flowers once again.

The sun had disappeared and the sky had turned gray. Darkness was approaching quickly. But a small dot of red was soaring freely like an eternal flame.

A three-quarter moon brightened the night sky, illuminating the silent garden. Seeping through the willow leaves, silver beams entered the barred window and enabled the prisoner to see the door opening.

From the soundless, slow way it opened, Wisdom realized that the visitor did not wish to

wake him. He was lying on his back, using his
folded arms as a pillow, and now he remained
in that position as if sound asleep.

Wisdom's eyes had adjusted to the darkness,
and he could see better than his visitor. But he
kept his eyes half-shut, maintaining his rhythmical breathing.

Endurance closed the door carefully. He paused
to wait until he could see better in the semidark-
ness. Wisdom's face was pale in the moonlight,
and his small frame looked like a child's.

"My friend," Endurance uttered in a barely
audible voice as he advanced toward the bed.
"My very dear friend!"

Wisdom's even breathing stopped, and Endurance halted immediately. He couldn't do this
if Wisdom should wake up and look him in the
eye.

All of a sudden Endurance was sixteen again.
He was fighting a tiger. The tiger looked at him
in the eye. It made his stomach turn to kill the
king of all beasts. He had told himself with painful regret that when two warriors fought, one
must die.

Wisdom's breathing returned to normal, and
Endurance edged forward again. When he reached
the bed, he leaned toward Wisdom and thought
carefully once again.

He had not realized how much of a fighter
Wisdom was, until Wisdom had said no to him
for the last time. He was not frightened by Wisdom's threat of inciting the people against him.
They were against him anyway. But he could not
allow Wisdom to be his conscience. He had
fought for everything he ever had, and he would
never change.

"I'm so sorry, my friend." The whispered
words barely escaped Endurance's throat.

Wisdom caught the words. They touched his

heart. Would it be very wrong to lie for one's friend? People lied all the time. He could make the speech, then run away from Yin-tin and join his family. How he would love to take his Lotus in his arms and hug his children!

But the temptation lasted only a fleeting moment. He could lie to everyone except Endurance. He must be Endurance's guide as long as he lived.

Wisdom used all his willpower to remain motionless as he heard Endurance pull the dagger out of its sheath. He peeked through his eyelashes and saw the gold chain glittering on the handle. Moonlight shone on the cross guard, brightening the jade centerpiece. The two grasping hands glistened clearly: one hand was much larger than the other.

Endurance raised the dagger high.

Wisdom waited.

"My best friend . . . !" Endurance whispered in agony, then brought the dagger down.

At the time the dagger plunged into Wisdom's heart, he opened his eyes wide. As the two men looked at each other, Endurance knew instantly that Wisdom had been awake all the while, but had pretended to be asleep to make the killing easier for him.

Endurance sank to his knees, shattered by remorse. For a hopeful moment, he looked at the dagger, thinking to take it back. The entire blade was buried in Wisdom's body, though. The gold chain and the jade pendant radiated on the handle and reflected the moon. It was too late now. If he withdrew the dagger, Wisdom would only die faster.

"Why did you let me do this? Why? Why? Why?" Endurance screamed.

Wisdom opened his mouth, struggled to speak. "Don't regret . . . I understand . . ."

When the guards heard the cries and entered the cell, they saw the prisoner dead, and the White Lotus king kneeling beside the body, crying and pounding his chest in despair.

Epilogue

Autumn, 1368

IN YIN-TIN CITY, when the moon was full, Endurance Chu was crowned the emperor of China and Peony his empress.

They called their empire the Ming Dynasty. Ming was a word written by combining the symbols of sun and moon, and it meant blazing.

"China's dark days are over," the emperor said.

"From now on, we are a nation with blazing power," the empress added.

The coronation was a grand event attended by ambassadors from many foreign countries. The world was in awe of a man who had risen from peasantry, defeated his many opponents, and overpowered the descendants of Genghis Kahn.

Gifts arrived from around the world. Among the gold and precious gems stood lovely young girls in various costumes, selected from China and other countries such as Japan, Korea, India, and Thailand.

The emperor glanced at the young beauties. Some of them flinched, the others shivered. All of them bowed their heads in fear. Greatly annoyed by their attitude, the emperor looked away. Instead he went to his empress and took her hand.

"What will you do with these beautiful young things?" she asked.

Endurance shrugged. "Keep them in a faraway

corner of the palace, the same way we stowed those other unwanted gifts in that storage room."

The enormous storage room in the palace had shelves from floor to ceiling on all four walls. Various objects, from solid gold swords to emerald teacups, were ranked side by side. On one of the highest shelves was a pair of jade statues. A jade lady leaned against her jade lord. They both smiled dreamily, wearing the looks of love, understanding, forgiveness, and eternal peace. When the moon filtered through the window and shone on them, their eyes glowed as if they had a long story to tell the world.

The moon that night also shone on a manmade pond in the palace garden. With the crowning celebration over and the guests gone, the emperor and empress walked hand-in-hand. They stopped at the azaleas newly planted around the pond.

"Many years ago, when I was looking for you, I saw a village house with azaleas blooming beside its thatch door. I wanted to plant azaleas for you ever since then," he said, then squatted beside the water.

"Now I finally have my azaleas. Thank you, Endurance," she said, squatting beside him.

The emperor waved his hand and a guard appeared carrying a white paper lantern. Endurance lighted the lantern himself, then placed it on the pond with trembling hands.

Peony saw the sorrow glistening in her husband's eyes and she sighed. The beautiful dagger was buried in Wisdom's coffin, resting in peace, but the everlasting betrayal of their friendship would always live in his heart.

The empress pulled the emperor up, then guided him out of the garden.

The autumn wind blew the lone lantern to the other side of the pond, then it glided out of a narrow opening under the palace wall. The lantern bobbed through a winding canal, drifting from east Yin-tin to the west and eventually sailed into the River Yangtze. It became but one among thousands of others in the timeless river of lanterns.

There's an epidemic with 27 million victims. And no visible symptoms.

It's an epidemic of people who can't read.

Believe it or not, 27 million Americans are functionally illiterate, about one adult in five.

The solution to this problem is you... when you join the fight against illiteracy. So call the Coalition for Literacy at toll-free **1-800-228-8813** and volunteer.

Volunteer Against Illiteracy. The only degree you need is a degree of caring.